The Courts of Garrowville

A Novel by

Ken Siegel

The Courts of Garrowville
Copyright ©2015 Ken Siegel

ISBN 978-15069-0000-1 PRINT
ISBN 978-15069-0001-8 EBOOK

LCCN 2015948753

September 2015

Published and Distributed by
First Edition Design Publishing, Inc.
P.O. Box 20217, Sarasota, FL 34276-3217
www.firsteditiondesignpublishing.com

Prologue

It was referred to as "The Murder." You should note that it was not referred to as "a murder," or simply "murder," but rather it was known as "The Murder." That is what happens when a small town with zero homicides in over 100 years of existence, and practically no other publicly known criminal activity, suddenly has a murder. It tends to be big news. In a close-knit small town like Garrowville, located in western Pennsylvania, everyone knows everyone else and the local news predominantly consists of bake sales and church outings. Therefore, it is easy to understand how a murder can dominate the local chatter.

But this was no ordinary murder. The victim, Jennifer Stohler, was a beloved member of the community who couldn't possibly have had any enemies. She was a school teacher who was adored by her students, their parents, and her colleagues. She was a leader in the town's church, and was the one who often organized the community's charitable events. She lived her whole life in Garrowville and had been the captain of Garrowville High School's cheerleading squad, as well as the prom queen.

Jennifer was beautiful, smart, and funny. She was the only child of a single mom, who tragically died of cancer at the young age of 44, when Jennifer was only 20. After losing her mother, many of the town's residents looked after Jennifer as if she were their own daughter or sister. But she had no real family other than me and my parents. I was her husband.

My name is Michael Stohler and I had, until a few years ago, lived in Garrowville. I was born and raised there and can trace my family roots in the town all the way back to my great-grandfather, Otto Stohler. Otto settled in Garrowville and founded the highly successful steel manufacturing plant named Stohler Steel during the Industrial Revolution of the late 1800's. Stohler Steel had been a profitable family business for four generations. The plant employed many of Garrowville's residents and was a substantial part of the town's economy for a long time, until "The Murder."

I attended all the public schools in Garrowville and I starred on the Garrowville High School's football and basketball teams. Other than my four years at Ohio State University, I had, until recently, lived my whole life in Garrowville. Immediately after college, I returned home to continue the family tradition of working at the plant. Each day when I arrived for work, it was a source of great pride for me to see my family's name in large, gold letters above the grand front entrance of a magnificently successful steel plant that was presided over by several generations of Stohlers.

After ten years, I took over the company when my father, George Stohler, retired. I was very happy and proud to be running my family's business and living in such a great town where I was surrounded by life-long friends.

Most of all, I was happy and proud to be married to Jennifer. She was 5'6", had long blonde hair, and blue eyes. She was thin, athletic, and shapely. Not only was she the prettiest woman in any room she was in, she was also the most popular.

Starting with my days as the school jock, I was popular as well. With my dark hair and my tall (6'3"), large, and muscular build, I was well-liked by women throughout my life. But I only had eyes for Jennifer.

We were high school sweethearts, the prom king and queen, the sports star and the cheerleader. We were your prototypical all-American couple. We went to Ohio State together because we couldn't stand to be apart for four years. We were married shortly after graduation when we were both just twenty-two years old. We had our whole lives ahead of us and neither one of us at that time could imagine living our life without the other.

However, as is typical of many marriages, we would have our rough patches. The economy plummeted in recent years, causing severe strain on both my company's and our personal wealth. Financial distress is one of the most common causes of arguments within a household and we were no different. At the time of "The Murder" in 2009, we had been married for twelve years and we were having both marital and financial difficulties. I was sleeping every night on our living room couch or at my parents' house a few miles away.

However, my feelings for Jennifer never waned. I loved her more than anything in the world and I always thought we would work things out. We were meant to be together and I knew there can be no better person in the world with whom to spend my life. Unfortunately, "The Murder" would not allow that to be my fate. "The Murder" took away my soul mate.

It also took away my home, my hometown, my company, my friends, and most of my financial resources. I lost a lot more than my beloved wife. Though still alive, I essentially lost my own life as well. I lost it all because of a horrific crime that I did not commit.

But, as my story will illustrate, the general public does not await the receipt of all facts and information before reaching their collective conclusions. Gossip, suspicions, and innuendos will result in society's rush to judgment. The court of public opinion does not operate under the rules of evidence required in the criminal court system. Yet the court of public opinion can be equally as powerful in destroying lives. It certainly destroyed mine.

I often wondered how such injustice can occur in the United States of America, especially for someone like me who was surrounded by so many friends and long-time acquaintances in a town where my family went back generations. Certainly I would have a public support system made up of people who knew me well and knew I was incapable of such a heinous crime.

But I was wrong. The court of public opinion rules quickly and harshly and there is no recovery from the force of an immediate conviction among the public in which you live, even if you are innocent of the crime for which you are accused.

Maybe you are skeptical as to the powers of the court of public opinion. Or maybe you are skeptical of how such an injustice can occur in our civilized society. Or maybe you are simply curious as to what truly happened to my wonderful wife. If so, I encourage you to read the following story, which will detail the shocking events that unfolded in the previously quiet and peaceful town of Garrowville, Pennsylvania.

Chapter 1

Jennifer Stohler was awakened out of a deep sleep when she heard the screen door opening just beneath her second story bedroom window. Her room was just above the front door and overlooked the front yard as well as the whole cul-de-sac at the end of which was the Stohler residence. There were only five homes on the cul-de-sac, theirs being the middle one, and the only one still occupied. Once upon a time, the Stohlers had neighbors and a vibrant piece of paradise on their scenic block. But the economy hit hard and the four surrounding homes were foreclosed.

Jennifer opened her eyes just enough to see her digital clock illuminated on her nightstand. It was 2:35 a.m., which meant that she needed to get back to sleep. She had to be up early for what was to be an exciting day at the school where she taught. Just as she was drifting back to sleep, she heard keys jiggling in the front door's keyhole. It must be Michael, she thought, but why was he getting home so late?

There had recently been some tension in their marriage, resulting in Michael often choosing to sleep at his parents' house a few miles away. The tension also resulted in an increase in Michael's drinking, which when times were tough, was his escape. His favorite pub, O'Leary's, was just a couple of blocks away, so, occasionally, if he was too drunk to drive, he would walk back to the house and sleep on the couch downstairs in the living room.

But it was Thursday night, and on weeknights, the pub closed at 1 a.m. Even if Michael had stayed there until closing, it was still late for him to be getting home. Maybe he was more drunk than usual and it was a slow stagger back to the house. He seemed to be having some trouble with the key, so perhaps that was the answer.

Eventually the front door opened and Jennifer started drifting back to sleep. Michael would just collapse onto the downstairs couch and would likely be sound asleep when she would leave for work in a few hours.

A few moments later, in a half-asleep state, Jennifer thought she heard a faint noise on the steps. She listened carefully and was pretty sure she heard someone quietly ascending the stairs. Why would Michael come upstairs? He had toiletries in the downstairs bathroom and several changes of clothes in a closet next to the front door. It was arranged that way so that he would not have to come upstairs to get anything if he decided to come home for the night.

The footsteps also did not seem like the sounds of a large intoxicated male who was too drunk to drive a few miles to his parents' home. No, this sounded like someone slowly and quietly coming up the steps, carefully attempting not to make any noise. Well, whatever Michael's reason may be for coming upstairs, he's apparently trying to be careful not to awaken her. After all, it was the middle of the night, and he knew his wife would have to wake up early for work.

While Jennifer pondered these matters, she was now wide awake and clearly heard the sounds of the step climber reaching the top of the steps. There were only two other rooms on this level of the house, a bathroom and a baby's room. There was no baby, but Michael and Jennifer had set up a room for a baby they had been expecting a couple of years ago. However, Jennifer had a miscarriage and neither of them had the heart to convert the room back into a guest room. They had very much wanted a baby for a long time so when Jennifer was finally pregnant, they purchased everything imaginable for their unborn child and set up a baby's dream bedroom just across the hall.

To get to Jennifer's, and until recently, Michael's bedroom, you would make a left turn at the top of the steps. The bathroom was straight ahead. The vacant baby's room was to the right, which was also the direction in which the footsteps headed.

Why would Michael go toward the empty baby's room? There was no bed to crash onto in there. There was just an unused crib and a lot of toys and dolls. The door to the baby's room creaked open, prompting Jennifer to sit up in bed and turn on the lamp on her nightstand. What was Michael doing in the baby's room?

She got up out of bed and started toward her bedroom door. As she reached for the doorknob she heard footsteps now coming toward her. She opened her bedroom door and saw an approaching male figure in the darkness. She let out a loud, piercing scream when she realized that it was a man in a ski mask who was certainly not Michael. And, whoever the intruder was, he had a gun.

Chapter 2

All of the first graders of Garrowville Elementary School were lined up near the school buses early on Friday morning, December 11, 2009. It was the day they have been long awaiting and there was a lot of excitement in the air. Today was the day they would be going on a class trip to the aquarium.

They had been learning about fish and other sea mammals in school and now they would get a chance to see them up close. There were two first grade classes in the school, each with 25 students, and today was one of the few days of the school year in which all 50 first graders were in attendance and were on-time.

The trip was the idea of Mrs. Jennifer Stohler, the teacher for one of the first grade classes. She believed that it would be a fun and educational day for the children, and a break from their normal routine in school. She also believed that in the difficult economic times that have recently hit the area, it was less likely that these kids would be able to experience such outings with their families.

It was tough economic times for the school as well and the idea was a difficult sell to Principal Ronald Walker. Principal Walker actually loved the idea but was concerned about the school's finances and about asking parents for money toward the event. But Jennifer had persisted, working with him to find some room in the budget so that they can reduce how much money to ask for from the kids' parents.

Jennifer even went one step further. If any child's parents could not afford to pay their share for the class outing, she would contribute the money from her own pocket. There would be no child left behind on this fun-filled learning experience. Jennifer Stohler ended up contributing several hundred dollars to make sure this event happened for everyone.

The time for the trip had finally arrived. It was 8 a.m. and the kids were excited and ready to go. But there was one problem. There was no sign of the popular teacher.

"Have you seen Jennifer?" Principal Walker asked Carol Joyner, the school's other first grade teacher.

"No. I've called both her cell phone and home phone. There was no answer on either one. I left a message on both lines. What should we do?"

"I'll ask my secretary to call her husband. We have his contact information on file."

Principal Walker was soon informed that the husband's cell phone went straight to voicemail and that he was not at work, nor expected there until 9 a.m.

He told Mrs. Joyner, "I don't know where she is and we can't reach her husband. She hasn't missed a day of work in years and certainly wouldn't miss today. She was the organizer of this whole event."

"Something may be wrong. Should we have someone stop by her house?" asked Mrs. Joyner.

"I think we should call the police to have them check on her. If there is something wrong it would be better for a police officer to be there first. I'll call Chief Lumpkin right now."

Principal Walker dialed his long-time friend and former classmate Chief Carl Lumpkin to express his concerns about Jennifer. "She has worked here for more than ten years and has never been late. She hasn't shown up yet this morning on a day we have a class trip she had organized. She didn't call in and no one has seen or heard from her. I want to make sure there is nothing wrong. Can you have someone stop by her house to check on her?"

Carl Lumpkin was approaching fifty years old and had done very little in recent years to maintain his level of physical fitness. He clearly has not been too concerned with the possibility of one day needing to chase a fleeing suspect on foot. He was a big guy, overweight, and balding. He looked like your prototypical police chief sitting behind a desk, chomping on a donut while barking out orders to subordinates. In nearly ten years as the town's chief of police he's had no serious crime to worry about. Therefore, he wasn't going to start panicking about Jennifer Stohler.

"Sure. No problem" he responded, "Let's not worry yet. She may have just overslept. That can happen to anyone. Maybe it was a late night for her. I hear that she is separated from her husband, so maybe she was out partying more than usual. Maybe she went home with a guy. Anything is possible. But we'll check it out. I'll send Radford right now. I'll call you back with any news."

They hung up and Chief Lumpkin instructed Officer Dan Radford to stop by the Stohler residence to check on Jennifer. He knew that Radford would be more than happy to oblige. Radford had grown up with both Stohlers and always had a crush on Jennifer. So Radford would be pleased to be presented with an excuse to chat with her. But what Chief Lumpkin didn't know, as he relayed his orders to Officer Radford, was that there wouldn't be an opportunity for Radford, or anyone, to chat with Jennifer Stohler ever again. Chief Lumpkin also didn't know yet that his small police department was about to embark on their biggest, most highly publicized case ever.

Chapter 3

As Officer Dan Radford headed toward the Stohler house, he thought to himself how he had known Jennifer Stohler since kindergarten. He also thought about the crush he has had on Jennifer that extended back nearly as far. It was a long time, unfulfilled crush. They had been classmates throughout grade school, so, she knew who he was, but his feelings toward her were clearly never reciprocated.

Officer Radford had also gone to school with Michael Stohler, but his feelings toward him were vastly different. Michael had been the star quarterback of their high school's football team while Dan rode the bench. Michael's family had money; Dan's did not. Michael went to the big time university at Ohio State; Dan went to community college. Michael ran the largest company in town; Dan was low person on the totem pole in the small Garrowville police department. Michael was tall, muscular, and good looking. Dan was average height, pudgy, and balding. But worst of all, Michael dated and married Dan's dream girl. Dan Radford was still single and had dated very little.

Call it envy, jealousy, spite, whatever you want, but the bottom line was that Dan Radford didn't like Michael Stohler. He realized that Michael was a nice guy and he couldn't think of anything malicious that Michael had directly done to him over the years. But when you are envious of someone you tend to have negative feelings toward that person.

Radford arrived at the Stohler residence and saw Jennifer's car parked on the driveway. He also noted that a light was on in the upstairs room above the front door. He pulled up in front of the house and walked toward the front steps. As he approached, he noticed that the front door was partially open.

He rang the doorbell and waited a few moments. No one came to the door. He rang again, but there still no response. He poked his head inside and called out "Jennifer? Michael? Anyone home?" No response. It was time to take a look around.

He started with the downstairs level, searching each room while periodically calling out to anyone who may be home. He found nothing out of the ordinary. He then started up the stairs to check on the upper level of the house. As he reached the top of the steps, he saw that the door to his left was partially open and the light was on in that room. He called out again to anyone who may be in there. Getting no answer, he approached the bedroom door.

What he saw next was unlike anything that he had encountered in more than ten years with the Garrowville police force. An occasional drunk driver who became belligerent was the closest Garrowville police officers had gotten to any violence. Other common offenses around the town consisted of some mischievous teenagers spray painting the side of a building, or making too much noise on a residential street on a Saturday night. None of these previous experiences compared to what Officer Radford now saw in front of him.

Lying dead in a pool of dried blood on the floor of her bedroom with a single bullet through the middle of her forehead, was Jennifer Stohler, Dan Radford's dream girl.

Chapter 4

The other three members of the town's police department quickly arrived at the Stohler house after Officer Radford called in his gruesome finding. They secured the scene while searching in and around the house to try to figure out how this senseless crime occurred. They were also awaiting the arrival of the county's crime scene investigation unit. The Garrowville police department didn't have, nor have they ever needed, such a unit.

After looking around and not finding much, the officers reconvened by the front door to compare observations. "Ok, what do we know so far?" asked Chief Lumpkin.

Radford spoke first. "The victim was shot one time in the forehead. The weapon has not been found, therefore, suicide is out. It would be impossible for someone to shoot themselves in the head and for the gun to not be in the immediate vicinity. Based on the victim's body temperature, the crime could not have been too long ago. It was probably sometime in the middle of the night."

"We should be able to obtain an estimated time of death from the medical examiner" added Lumpkin.

Radford went on to report that he noticed that the victim's jewelry box on top of her dresser was open and that there was some jewelry in plain sight. He also noted that she was not wearing her wedding ring nor did it appear to be on the dresser. He didn't add the fact that he had looked for that for more reasons than just his investigative instincts.

Officer Roy Hodges informed everyone that he found no signs of a forced entry anywhere around the house, nor did he see any open or unlocked windows. Radford then mentioned that he had found the front door open upon his arrival.

"That is probably a result of the perp leaving in a hurry through the front door after the crime" replied Lumpkin. "The fact that there is no forced entry means one of two things: that Jennifer knew the killer and let him in, or the killer had the key."

"Who besides her husband may have a key to the house?" asked John Riley, the fourth officer present at the scene.

"Let's think about this for a minute" said Lumpkin. "When a woman is killed in her own home, who is the most common offender? Obviously, the answer is the husband. I don't know the exact percentage, but whatever the percentage is, you can add to it for the facts that they were having marital problems and there was no forced entry. I'd say that increases the odds through the roof. Even if it wasn't him, if the perp had a key, the husband may have given it to him. The odds are pretty good that the husband is involved somehow. The open jewelry box and missing wedding ring could just be his way of making it look like a robbery gone wrong."

"How do you know they were having marital problems?" asked Riley.

"Everyone knows it. You can't sneeze in this town without everyone knowing it. He's been sleeping at his folks' house and going out to O'Leary's without his wife. I also just saw him pull into an auto shop last night with another woman. We need to talk to him as soon as possible."

At that moment the county's crime scene investigation unit drove up to the house. The officers looked out front and saw them coming. They also noticed that some people were starting to mill around outside. They knew the block was vacant, other than the Stohlers, so these people had to have walked over from at least a block away, maybe more. It was not a common occurrence to anyone in these parts to see police activity near their home, so the presence of several police vehicles sparked their interest.

"Great, just what we need right now, gawkers and nosy neighbors getting in everyone's way" complained Hodges.

Chief Lumpkin looked out at the growing crowd and said, "Don't worry about it. We'll need to interview the neighbors anyway to find out if anyone saw or heard anything. Riley, you can start questioning some of the nosy bodies outside. Radford, you know the husband best. Go to his office and inform him of the news. Watch his reaction then bring him back here. I'd like to speak with him. Hodges, you and I will continue working the scene and assisting with the CSI."

It was 9 a.m. and Officer Radford was on his way to Stohler Steel as the bearer of the grimmest news one can deliver.

Chapter 5

As instructed, Officer Riley headed out into the growing crowd in front of the house in search of anybody who may have seen or heard anything useful. The closest anyone in the crowd would reside would be around a long corner, therefore, the likelihood of someone seeing or hearing anything relating to the crime was not great. But you never know. Someone might have heard a gunshot, which would help the police hone in on a precise time of death.

Riley made his way through a crowd of people eager to speak with him. No one had heard a gunshot, nor did anyone have any information specific to the murder. But that didn't stop them from relaying their extensive thoughts to the officer.

Many people reported to him that the Stohlers were having marital problems. One person said she saw them arguing in a restaurant last month. Three different people conveyed that Jennifer had been contemplating divorce, and one person said that she had already gone as far as actually filing for divorce. Another person said that her husband had recently sold Michael Stohler a life insurance policy on his wife. Yet another person told Riley that he saw Michael in a car with another woman just last night. Several people informed the officer that Michael had laid them or their spouse off from his company and that he had done the same to others as well. Finally, several people thought it was important to tell Officer Riley that they wouldn't be surprised if Michael had been seeing other women. It was fairly clear what the preliminary consensus was among the citizens of Garrowville. It didn't take long for people to make up their minds, Riley thought.

If Riley had been a writer of a gossip column for the local newspaper, he would have a great deal of juicy information. Unfortunately though, as an investigating officer on a homicide case, he didn't have any concrete evidence. However, all of this information did serve to reinforce the fact that Michael Stohler was their primary, and in fact their only, suspect at this time.

Just then, a news van screeched onto the street while swerving to avoid bystanders. A reporter and cameraman jumped out of the van and before Riley knew what hit him, a microphone was shoved right in front of his face.

"What do you know so far about the murder? Do you have any suspects yet?" shouted an eager reporter who Riley immediately recognized as being Chelsea Forgeous from one of the Pittsburgh stations. She was well known in western Pennsylvania as an aggressive and attractive on-scene reporter who was often referred to as "Gorgeous Forgeous." She was tall, had long straight black hair, and had mesmerizing green eyes that when glaring at you seemed to make you tell her whatever she wants to hear. It was said that she can smell a story a mile away and can squeeze information out of a rock. She knew she was good and that she was popular, therefore she had aspirations to make it big someday on the national level. Riley thought it was odd to see her in Garrowville as there had previously never been anything of interest in their small town for a television reporter from a major city.

Riley gave a quick "no comment" and worked his way back to the house. He could hear Forgeous shouting follow-up questions at him, but he kept walking away from her. He was sorry not to be able to speak with the famous reporter, but he knew that he didn't have a lot of information and that the police force hadn't yet discussed what they would and would not be informing the public. But he figured that Forgeous would have no problem finding plenty of people out there who were more than happy to spill their guts to her. The last thing he heard as he walked back into the house was shouts from several people telling the reporter that the killer had to be the husband.

Meanwhile, back in the house, Chief Lumpkin was hovering around the CSI unit, impatiently awaiting any light they can shed on the crime. On a couple of occasions he had to be asked to give them room to do their work. Finally, a senior member of the CSI unit named Ben Alford walked over to Lumpkin to give him an update.

Alford informed Lumpkin that the killer was likely standing very close to the victim while she stood in the doorway of her bedroom. She was shot with a .22 caliber handgun and died instantly. There were no obvious signs of a struggle or a pursuit, so the theory is that she was shot immediately upon being confronted by the killer.

Alford stated that they were taking fingerprints all around the house but that he was not optimistic that any will come back as being from someone besides the victim or her husband, as it was possible that the killer may have worn gloves. He added, "If we do find fingerprints of the husband it may simply have resulted from the fact that he does live in the house and may have nothing to do with the homicide."

Alford reported that his preliminary estimate as to the time of death is between 2 a.m. and 4 a.m. and that he would inform Lumpkin if they get any additional information.

Officer Riley then pulled Lumpkin aside and updated him on the feedback from the crowd outside the house. "We better be careful when the husband arrives here. The mob outside may hang him from a tree."

At that moment Officer Hodges came over to speak with Lumpkin and Riley. Hodges had been looking around the house for anything useful and came back holding Jennifer's daily planner. He specifically pointed to an entry from two days earlier in which Jennifer had an appointment with someone named David Bergman.

"You won't believe who David Bergman is" teased Hodges.

Chief Lumpkin and Riley both simultaneously asked "Who is he?"

"I called the number in Jennifer's appointment book and found out that he's a divorce attorney. Her appointment was at 5 p.m. this past Wednesday and she also had another appointment scheduled for a week from now."

"So, Jennifer was seriously considering divorce," said Lumpkin, "and two days after her appointment with a divorce attorney she winds up dead. That's another arrow pointing directly at the husband. Radford should be back soon with him. We'll protect him from the mob outside long enough for me to ask him all of the interesting questions I have for him."

Chapter 6

You've been given some information thus far that doesn't sound so great for me. So, I thought that now would be a good time to take a break, and to give you some facts from my side of the story. I'll give you my perspective throughout the story as it unfolds.

We'll start on Thursday, December 10, 2009, the last full day of my wife's life. That day had been an ordinary day at work for me. By 'ordinary' I mean slow. Business had been steeply declining in the preceding years due to the downtrodden economy that had affected all of the United States, but even more so in our blue collar, industrial part of the country.

At first, when business for Stohler Steel started declining, I reduced my own pay to make up some of the difference, without affecting the salary or benefits of any of my loyal employees. I didn't want to do that to my hard working staff when I knew that any cuts in their pay would hurt them more than it would hurt me.

Unfortunately, business continued to decline and I had to reduce my pay some more. As the downward trend continued further, I had to implement pay cuts for all employees. I explained that I had cut my own pay by substantially more than I was asking from others, and that the pay cuts for everyone was the "lesser of two evils" as opposed to my having to let some people go. At least everyone would still have jobs. Of course no one was happy with this development, but I think that they understood. I hoped they were thankful that I hadn't laid anyone off when the decline in business certainly would have justified a reduction in workforce.

I continued to reduce my own pay so that layoffs would be a last resort. After a couple of years my take home pay was only a quarter of what it had previously been. During the time in which I was earning less and less money, I had several conversations with Jennifer about the need for us to reduce our personal spending. Although Jennifer was a fabulous teacher, unfortunately, as is typical for her profession, her earnings were not substantial.

We had both been accustomed to spending in accordance with my higher earning level, and it is not easy to make the necessary adjustments when times get tougher. Additionally, Jennifer was always giving a lot of money to various charities, as well as toward many school and church events she organized. I loved her generosity and her genuine concern for less fortunate people. It was wonderful traits such as these that made me fall in love with her in the first place.

But as we were struggling, I had to explain to her that we couldn't afford to give as much as we had been in prior years.

Those conversations turned into arguments and as our financial situation got worse, so did those disagreements. Jennifer couldn't bring herself to reduce her spending, whether it was for the various good causes in which she was involved, or for personal luxuries that had been a normal part of our lives not too long ago.

The economy had hit the real estate market very hard causing foreclosures all around our area. Thankfully, we had not reached that level of despair, but we were upside-down on our mortgage, so borrowing money from the equity in our house was not an option. Nor was borrowing money from my company. Stohler Steel was losing money at an alarming rate. A family business that had been run successfully by three generations of Stohlers before me was now in grave danger.

Eventually, I had no choice but to start reducing my workforce. I had far more people than was needed for the diminishing workload and the company couldn't afford to keep paying all of them. I gave all laid off employees a very generous severance package, exceeding what I really could afford, and I promised that if business picked back up, they'd be my first calls to come back to work if they still needed jobs. I was genuinely apologetic and felt horrible about the layoffs. These were people and families I knew my whole life in the community. But there really wasn't any choice in the matter, and I had delayed the inevitable much longer than most business owners would have in my position.

My administrative staff had also been recently reduced from four down to one. One receptionist had left a few months earlier on her own initiative, but I was forced to eventually lay off two others. There simply wasn't enough work for three administrative assistants and I couldn't afford to keep them all any longer.

The one I had chosen to keep was Brenda Challey, a twenty-five year-old single mother of a four year-old boy. The boy's father was not in the picture and Brenda had only one parent, her mother, who was very ill at the time and living with Brenda, giving her another dependent. I couldn't bring myself to let Brenda go, knowing that she'd be ruined if she lost her job while the other two administrative assistants both had working husbands. Additionally, the others had more experience, thus would likely have a better chance to find another job.

On a personal note, I was also sympathetic toward Brenda's situation in life because it reminded me of my wife's stories about growing up as an only child of a single mom who had worked so hard to keep up with both her work and home responsibilities. I could see how hard Brenda worked, knowing how important the job was for her, and how she was always juggling her work and personal responsibilities to make sure both her son and her mother were taken care of at all times.

Maybe it wasn't entirely the best business decision to keep the less experienced person, but I made the decision to keep Brenda with the best and most considerate thoughts in mind.

Late in the workday of Thursday, December 10th, Brenda came to me and asked if I could give her a lift to the auto repair shop nearby to pick up her car, which had broken down on her way home from work the night before. A friend of hers had driven her to work that morning, but that friend, and a few others in the office that day, all were unavailable to drive her after work, and her mother was too ill to drive.

I had no plans other than to go to O'Leary's later that night to watch the Steelers on Thursday Night Football, so I said 'yes.' It was the first time Brenda had ever asked me for anything, and I figured that it was the least I could do for all of Brenda's hard work for me.

We left the office just after 5 p.m. and I drove her fifteen minutes away to get her car. We didn't talk very much during the car ride other than a few items on the "to do" list for work the next day. I didn't want to pry with any personal questions about her situation at home, nor did I want to start talking about any of my own issues. Therefore, other than work, I really didn't know what to talk about with her.

After we arrived at the auto shop, I waited in my car in the shop's parking lot for a few minutes to verify that her car was ready. I wanted to make sure that she wouldn't be stranded there if her car wasn't available yet. It was in fact ready, and as she drove off she gave me a nice wave and smile while mouthing a "thank you" toward me.

I then drove to my parents' house. As expected, my parents were not home because they had dinner plans with friends that night. There was a note from my mom telling me that I can heat up some meat loaf in the refrigerator for dinner. I decided to pass on it because I was planning to have dinner at the pub while watching the game.

I changed, relaxed for a little while, then left for O'Leary's. I arrived there shortly before 8 p.m., and saved a table for my friends, Jimmy Papadakis and Donald Starr, both of whom would be meeting me there shortly. The three of us went back a long time as friends. We had gone through grade school together and had been teammates on our high school football team.

Jimmy was my go-to wide receiver; the short, speedy type with great hands. Today he is the owner and manager of the town's most popular eatery, Jimmy's Diner, on Main Street. Ron was my center; a big burly guy who was as soft and kind as a teddy bear. Today he is a dentist with an office right by Jimmy's Diner in the center of the town. The three of us often met at O'Leary's for Steeler games and various other big sporting events. That night, we ate dinner, drank, and watched the Steelers lose an ugly game to the hated Browns.

I actually only had one beer early in the game, then switched over to soft drinks because I didn't want to have to stagger over to my own house. Jennifer and I had been fighting a lot lately and my showing up drunk in the middle of the night wouldn't help matters. I had been talking with her almost every day trying to patch things up, so I didn't want to risk hurting those efforts if I were to arrive home drunk and wake her up. At halftime, I tried to call her on my cell phone just to say hello, but I noticed that my phone was off because the battery had died, so I made a mental note to make sure to call her the next day.

Because I had stayed sober, I drove back to my parents' house after the game. I arrived there just after midnight and was surprised to see my father still awake. He was sitting in the kitchen drinking a beer and he invited me to join him. I grabbed a beer and sat down next to him at the kitchen table. We chatted about the business, my marriage, and the lousy Steeler game. These were all depressing subjects that led me to drink more than I had intended. One beer turned into two, then three, maybe more. I was getting fairly intoxicated. At least I wasn't driving anymore that night and would be going to bed right after we were done.

At about 2 a.m., I was tired and drunk and decided that I had to go to sleep as I would need to wake up for work in a few hours. I went to my room, quickly threw my clothes off, and collapsed into bed. In my exhausted and intoxicated state, I had forgotten several routine matters such as setting my alarm, charging my phone, and brushing my teeth.

As you may have predicted, I overslept in the morning, waking up at 8:45 a.m., which is the time I am usually arriving at work. I quickly showered, got dressed, grabbed my keys, phone, and other essentials and raced off to work. I arrived in the office in record time, but I was still roughly 20 minutes late. It was about 9:20 a.m. on Friday when I walked into Stohler Steel. I was out of breath and I looked somewhat tired and disheveled.

You could imagine my surprise when I saw that Officer Dan Radford was waiting for me in my office.

Chapter 7

As I walked past the reception area just in front of my office, I could see Officer Dan Radford sitting in a chair in front of my desk. Brenda greeted me by saying, "Good morning Michael. Thanks again for the lift last night. Officer Radford is waiting for you in your office. Is everything ok?"

"Good morning Brenda. I am not sure why he is here. No problem about last night. Anytime you need anything, please feel free to ask me."

Radford heard us approaching, stood up and turned around to face me as I entered the office. "Hi Michael" he said without a lot of enthusiasm.

I thanked Brenda and closed the door to my office. I wanted to get some privacy because I did not know why a police officer had come to visit me. "Hi Dan. How's it going? What brings you in here this morning?"

Dan Radford and I had grown up together and been classmates in school for many years. He had also played on some of the school's teams with me but was never one of the better players. I wouldn't say that he and I were close friends at any point in time, but we've known each other forever. Yet this was the first time I had ever seen him at the plant.

"You seem pretty close to your secretary." he said, "Are you on a first name basis with all of your employees?"

"We've always had a casual, laid-back atmosphere at the plant. It is a family business and most employees know me and everyone else from the community, so we are all on a first-name basis." I soon realized that this inquiry was not going to be his last somewhat odd comment.

Dan then said, "You're late. Your secretary told me you usually get in before 9 a.m."

Another strange comment, but I let it go and simply said, "Yes. That's true. I had a late night and overslept this morning. I'm sorry to have kept you waiting."

"You look tired. What was going on last night?" asked Dan.

"Not much. I watched the Steeler game at O'Leary's with Papadakis and Starr."

"Did you go back home after the game, or to your parents' house?"

I thought to myself that it was yet another strange question from someone with whom I wasn't really very close. I had the feeling that Radford was either hesitant to tell me something and/or was trying to get some type of information from me. I decided to get straight to the point.

"What can I do for you Dan?"

He hesitated a bit, then said that I should sit down. Now I was starting to get nervous. I didn't sit down. Instead I said rather anxiously, "What's going on Dan? Out with it."

"There's no easy way to say this. I'm very sorry to say that Jennifer was murdered last night."

I was too shocked to coherently respond. I don't remember exactly what I said or did immediately thereafter. At some point I fell down into my chair, put my head into my hands, and started crying uncontrollably. How could this have happened? It wasn't possible! Who would ever want to kill Jennifer?

Officer Radford simply stood there watching me for a few minutes. I'm not sure if he didn't know what to say or wanted to watch my reaction. It was probably a combination of the two. Eventually, he repeated that he was sorry and he asked if I wanted him to take me over to the house.

I agreed and he led me out of my office, through the reception area and out the door. Fortunately, Brenda wasn't at her desk when we emerged, nor was anyone else around. I was in no condition to start trying to explain what was going on. Besides, I really didn't know anything myself, so I was relieved that we made it out to his police car without seeing anyone.

He opened the front passenger side of his car for me to get in. He then drove to the house. I couldn't stop crying and I couldn't believe or accept what I had just been told. I was in denial and I had the irrational belief that when we got back to the house everything would be ok, as if it were all somehow a big mistake.

But everything would not be ok, and though I did not yet realize it, my nightmare had only just begun.

Chapter 8

I don't recall many of the specifics regarding the ride back to my house. I was basically in a daze and had not yet come to grips with the news Radford had just delivered to me. Neither of us spoke during the short drive until we turned onto my street. I remember us both then being surprised by the scene as we approached the house. I couldn't understand what was going on. Why was everyone mulling around in front of my house? I asked Radford, "What's going on?" I was still in denial.

He didn't directly answer my non-sensible question. He just said that there were more people here than there had been when he left to get me. So apparently, the wild scene in front of my house was growing.

I saw several news vans on the block and did not immediately understand why they were there. I only remember clinging to the belief that I would run into the house, see Jennifer, and prove to everyone that all this commotion was somehow a big misunderstanding.

Radford parked as close to the house as he could get and before he had even come to a complete stop, I got out of the car. I was in a hurry to get to Jennifer but I had to fight my way through several reporters and their microphones. They shouted questions at me, but I wasn't paying attention. I just shoved my way through the crowd, trying to get to the house.

I made it into the house and starting shouting Jennifer's name. Two police officers came up to me and tried to calm me down. I recognized one of them as Chief Lumpkin. I don't remember exactly what he said to me but it seemed his primary concern was not to express sympathy, but rather to get me to stop shouting and to listen to him. Eventually, he told me that they needed for me to identify the body and that it was upstairs.

Lumpkin instructed another officer, named Hodges, whom I didn't know personally, to bring me upstairs. I followed him up the stairs and toward our bedroom. It was then that I saw a body covered up with a sheet, lying on the floor by our dresser. A woman wearing a CSI jacket approached me and said, "I'm very sorry Mr. Stohler. I know this will be very difficult for you. But we need for you to officially identify the deceased for us. Are you able to do that at this time?"

I don't think I responded verbally, but I must have nodded my head, because she then led me toward the shape under the sheet. She asked if I was ready, then she slowly removed the sheet from the top to reveal the face underneath.

It was Jennifer. My wife. The love of my life. I was shocked and I started hysterically crying. I repeatedly and desperately cried out her name. I reached toward her as if I could somehow revive her, but the CSI technician stopped me. She sympathetically said how sorry she was for my loss. But she said that she needed for me not to touch anything so that they can continue analyzing the scene in its present condition.

The CSI technician, whose name I do not know, was the only person I had encountered in the house who had seemed warm and sympathetic toward me. She gently led me out of the room and back to the waiting Officer Hodges who then led me downstairs and sat me down in the kitchen. He instructed me to wait there for Chief Lumpkin who needed to speak with me. I sat there and cried for a while as I waited for the Chief.

Chapter 9

As soon as Officer Hodges had taken Michael Stohler upstairs for the formality of identifying the victim, Dan Radford made a beeline to Chief Lumpkin to report on his interactions with Stohler.

"So what was his reaction when you told him the news?" asked Lumpkin.

"He cried, but it was probably for show. I also have several interesting observations to tell you."

"What is it?"

"Well, for starters, he seemed pretty chummy with the secretary. Secondly, he was late. The secretary told me he's always in before 9 a.m., but he was late this morning."

"Did you ask him why he was late?"

"Yes. He said that he had a late night and had overslept. I asked him what he was doing last night and he said he watched the Steeler game at O'Leary's. Knowing that the game was over long before the murder, I asked him where he had gone afterwards, but he wouldn't answer that. He then just asked me why I was there. At that point I gave him the news and that basically ended the 'Q&A'."

"Yeah. I wonder why he wouldn't want to answer that question!" Lumpkin sarcastically replied.

Lumpkin then asked, "Did he say who he was at O'Leary's with?"

"Yes. Papadakis and Starr. I know both of them. I'll talk with them today" Radford answered.

"Ok. Also, go to the bar and talk to Brian O'Leary, the owner. Find out who worked there last night and question them also. See if they noted anything interesting about Stohler's demeanor, who else he may have interacted with, and when he left. Get names of other patrons there last night, interview them as well. I want to know what Stohler's frame of mind was, how much he drank, when he left, and anything else that may be interesting."

"You got it boss. One other thing about this morning; I noticed that Stohler looked tired and a bit messy. He looked like he had just rolled out of bed and raced into the office. He was even a little out of breath when he came in" Radford added.

"Well, you'd look that way too if you had the eventful evening he had last night." Lumpkin joked. He then asked, "Did he say anything to you during the car ride over here from his office?"

"No. He was just crying the whole time. Pouring on the theatrics if you ask me."

"Ok. Get to work on the O'Leary's front. The bar is closed now, so go to the owner's house and wake him up. We need to talk to him ASAP. I need to talk to Stohler now. I have a lot of questions for him."

Chapter 10

I was still sitting at my kitchen table when Chief Lumpkin approached me. I wasn't particularly close or friendly with the Chief, but I've known him for a long time. I was expecting that he was coming over to try to comfort me, but I was wrong.

He said, "Michael, I need to talk to you. As you can imagine, we have a lot of questions about what happened here. Would you mind coming with me to the station so that we can talk about this?"

"Does it have to be right now?" I asked, "I'm not really in the frame of mind at this time to think rationally about this."

"Yes. We need to do this now. Time is of the essence. We have a murderer on the loose out there. That is, assuming it is not you."

"What the hell is that supposed to mean? Why would you say 'assuming it is not you'?"

"I just mean that right now everyone is a suspect until they can be eliminated as one" explained Lumpkin. "Also, we need to catch whoever did this as soon as possible to protect the public and to be able to give your wife the justice she deserves."

Even in my somewhat dazed frame of mind, I did understand where Lumpkin was coming from. I knew that the police needed to have an open mind to all possibilities and that included me as a suspect. I also knew that the police had an obligation to the public to catch the killer as soon as possible. But I still thought it was a strange and insensitive comment for him to make just minutes after I saw my wife lying dead in our bedroom. Nevertheless I responded, "Ok. I understand. Of course I'll help you in any way I can."

With that, he motioned for me to follow him. He led me out the front door and back into the mayhem outside the house.

I tuned out the shouts from my neighbors and the questions from reporters as Lumpkin led me toward his car. Oddly, as anxious as I had been just a little while ago to get into the house, I was now equally as anxious to get away from it.

A strange thing happened as we reached the passenger side of Lumpkin's vehicle. I was walking on Lumpkin's left side as we approached the car and he had his arm on mine, leading me through the crowd. I then leaned toward my right to get into the front passenger seat but Lumpkin shifted left, opened the rear door for me and guided me into the back seat. It was clear that he wanted me there and I wasn't sure why. I had just ridden to the house sitting in the front seat with Radford.

Lumpkin closed the door and slowly walked around the front of the car to the driver's side. As I waited for him, cameras were fixated on me from both sides. I also took a quick glance at the crowd surrounding the car and couldn't help but get the uneasy feeling that the stares toward me were not quite the sympathetic types toward someone who had just lost his wife.

I told myself that I was just being paranoid. I had recognized some of the faces in the crowd as our neighbors and friends and I thought that of course they too were saddened by what happened, and were probably scared about a killer on the loose. I tried to convince myself that I was silly for being so paranoid after only a quick glance into a crowd of people during such an extraordinary time and when I clearly wasn't thinking straight. Still, I couldn't shake the feeling that something was off in the reactions toward me among the police and the crowd outside the house.

Lumpkin finally got into the car and carefully eased us away from the house. As we slowly departed, the television cameramen followed us on foot for as long as they could keep up and keep their cameras on me. It was then that an alarming thought hit me. My parents!

I had to call them immediately so that they could hear this devastating news from me, rather than on television or from a friend on the phone. I reached for my cell phone and saw that it was dead. I then realized that I had forgotten to charge it last night, and in my haste to get into work this morning after oversleeping, never noticed that it was still uncharged.

"Excuse me Chief. Can I use the phone in the car?" I asked Lumpkin.

"No. Only police officers can use it and only for official police business."

"I need to call my parents to tell them what happened. What about your personal cell phone? Can I borrow it?"

"No. We'll be at the station in a few minutes. You can make your call then."

I couldn't believe it. I wasn't a criminal in handcuffs having just been arrested and transported to booking. Yet, that was how I was starting to feel. I was a civilian who had voluntarily agreed to go to the station to try to assist the police with their investigation and he wouldn't let me use his phone. That uneasy feeling I was developing was starting to grow.

We reached the station and Lumpkin pointed to a phone I could use. I dialed my parents' house, but it was too late. They had already seen the news and had left their house. They initially came to my house, but they arrived just a couple of minutes after Lumpkin and I had left. One of the neighbors told them where we had gone and they arrived at the station a few minutes after we did.

My father was first to run into the station shouting my name. He saw me standing just a few feet away and embraced me. We both were already crying when my mother came in a few seconds later and joined the embrace.

"Does anyone know what happened?" my father asked me after our tear-fest slowly subsided.

"I don't know. I agreed to come here and speak with Chief Lumpkin to see if there is anything I can tell them to help them figure this out. But I really don't know anything. I just can't believe this happened and I don't understand why it happened."

That led to more hugging and crying. Chief Lumpkin started to grow impatient and stepped toward us. He asked me if I can come into the other room with him so that we can "get a move on this" as he put it.

I told my parents that I would just be a few minutes. They said they'd wait for me. But apparently my estimate of a few minutes was quite naïve. I figured it would have to be quick because I didn't know anything. How long could it take for me to tell them that I had no knowledge as to what happened?

I should have noticed a clue to my fate when the name of the other room that we entered was the "Interrogation Room." My uneasiness about my initial interactions with the police on this terrible morning would soon be confirmed.

Chapter 11

Chief Lumpkin didn't waste any time getting to the point. "Why don't we start with you telling me where you were last night?" he asked.

"I was at O'Leary's watching the Steeler game." I responded.

"Were you with anyone?"

"Yes. I was with Jimmy Papadakis and Donald Starr. We met there just before kickoff and stayed for the whole game."

"Anyone else?"

"Not specifically with me, but there were a lot of people at the bar last night. It is usually pretty crowded there when the Steelers play."

"What about your girlfriend? Wasn't she with you?"

"What? What are you talking about? I am married. I don't have a girlfriend" I answered. Where did that come from? That was an odd question. I kept those thoughts to myself.

Lumpkin then pressed on. "The game was over before midnight. What did you do then?"

"After the game ended, we all left."

"Where did you go?"

"I went to my parents' house. I arrived there around midnight."

"Then what?"

"Well, my father was still awake when I got there. We talked for a while and drank some beers. Then I went to sleep."

"What time was that?"

"I don't know exactly. Probably sometime around 2 a.m."

"Did anyone see you after 2 a.m.?"

"No. As I said, I went to sleep."

"Alone?"

"Yes. I said I was at my parents' house, so I wasn't with my wife, and I don't know why you seem to think I have a girlfriend, but I don't. So, yes, I was alone when I went to sleep."

"Just so that I understand, you are saying that there is no one who can vouch for your whereabouts after 2 a.m. Is that correct?"

"Yes. I suppose that is correct. But where else would you expect me to be at 2 a.m. on a work night other than asleep?" I asked.

Lumpkin didn't answer. Instead, he continued firing away with his questions.

"Why did you drive back to your parents' house in the first place? Isn't your house closer?"

"Yes. But Jennifer and I had been having some problems lately and we decided to give each other a little space as we worked things out. So, I've been staying at my parents' house most nights for the past few weeks."

"What kind of problems?" Lumpkin inquired.

"That is somewhat personal, don't you think?" I replied.

"There is no such thing as personal in a murder investigation. Any information could potentially be useful and we can't have you or anyone else withholding information from us. So, I'll ask you again. What kind of problems were you and Jennifer having?"

"Ok. I get it and I am here to help you guys as best I can. We've been arguing a lot lately. Mostly about money. Times are tough and the general theme of most of our disagreements was that we needed to cut back on spending. She was having some trouble with that. It sounds worse than it is. We were talking on the phone most nights and working things out. We would have gotten back together soon."

"I assume that you still have keys to the house?" Lumpkin asked.

"Yes. Of course I do. I still live there. I've just been staying with my parents temporarily while we work through our issues" I replied.

"When was the last time you spoke to your wife?

"Wednesday night."

"What time?"

"Around 8 p.m."

"Did she ever mention the idea of divorce to you?"

"No! Absolutely not! As I said, we were working things out. Neither of us had ever mentioned divorce and I know that I had never even considered it. I assume that Jennifer hadn't either."

"So, you are saying that in that conversation on Wednesday night, or any other time, she never mentioned divorce?"

"No. She definitely did not."

It should be noted that at this point in time, I did not know that Jennifer had just recently gone to see a divorce attorney. It was a shock to me when I learned that later on. But, as I also learned later on, Lumpkin already knew about that appointment at the time of this interrogation. It probably didn't help my credibility with him, but I was truly being honest with him.

Lumpkin then asked, "So, you were having money problems?"

"Yes. As I am sure you know, the economy has been lousy lately. Also, as you already know, my company has been struggling greatly. That is why I had to lay off a lot of people, including your wife. I still feel horrible about that and for all the people I had to let go, but I had no choice. Of course I also had to cut my own pay a great deal, which is why I needed to convince Jennifer to reduce spending."

"Do you have a life insurance policy on your wife?"

"Yes."

"How much?"

"$250,000."

"Wow! Why so much?"

"It is really not that much when you think about it. She was 33 years old when I took out the policy. Life insurance is intended to compensate for lost earning potential for someone's life. She theoretically could have been working for another 30+ years. $250,000 is not a lot of money to replace 30 years of lost earnings."

"She was just a school teacher!" Lumpkin emphatically stated.

"As I had said, I cut my own pay significantly. So, her earnings had become a significantly greater percentage of our combined income. Also, my company isn't doing well, and our house has declined in value. We are upside down in our mortgage, so there is no money to be taken from our home's equity. Our 401(k) plans had also declined and suddenly didn't seem as reliable as a savings mechanism. So, I was advised to take out a life insurance policy for each of us."

"Who advised you to do that?"

"Our financial advisor."

"Must be nice to have a financial advisor" Lumpkin chided.

I didn't respond to that. What was there to say? Obviously, he had a negative attitude toward me and he wasn't professional enough to hide it. He didn't like me because I had let his wife go a few months ago, and it was becoming apparent that I was his number one suspect right now. I also started thinking about my parents waiting outside. I had assured them that I wouldn't be long, and this was taking longer than I had anticipated. They were probably getting worried.

So I said, "How about if you ask me some questions about other possibilities regarding what happened? You seem to be honed in on only me as a suspect."

"Don't tell me how to do my job! Just answer my questions!" Lumpkin angrily snapped back at me. Then he said, "Ok. Who do you think may have done this?"

"I don't know. I can't believe this happened. No one could possibly have wanted her dead" I answered.

"Well, that was helpful" Lumpkin sarcastically said. "Now, back to you. Who was the woman I saw you with yesterday?"

"That's it. I'm done. My parents are waiting for me. I came here to help you, but you are not thinking openly about this. If you have any questions for me about any new developments or other suspects, you can call me. If not, then leave me and my family alone so that we can grieve for my wife. I am leaving now."

I stood up and started toward the door. Lumpkin rose also and temporarily blocked my path. He then pointed very close to my face and warned, "We'll be watching you Stohler. This is not over yet."

He slowly stepped aside and I left the room. He was certainly right about one thing. This was definitely not over yet. My troubles were just beginning.

Chapter 12

Just as the Stohlers left the police station, the other three officers in the Garrowville police department returned from the crime scene. As they entered the station, Chief Lumpkin informed them that he had just finished speaking with Michael Stohler and that he needed to fill them in. Lumpkin suggested that the four of them gather in his office to discuss the case.

As they sat around Lumpkin's desk, he started the meeting by saying, "Ok, let me first go over the key points from my interview with Stohler. Then we'll go over everything we know about the case, and discuss where we go from here."

Officer Radford then chimed in, "Chief, I saw the Stohlers getting into the father's car outside the station when I arrived and I overheard Michael cursing your name. I thought that was interesting. You must have struck a nerve when speaking with him."

"There are a lot of interesting things about Michael" Lumpkin responded. "First, he has no alibi for the estimated time frame of the murder. He claims that he went to sleep around 2 a.m. He also was at O'Leary's earlier in the night, and despite being at the bar, he admitted to drinking more after getting back to his parents' house. So, he was likely intoxicated around the time of the murder.

"He admitted that he was having marital problems with the victim, which apparently were bad enough to make him sleep at his parents' house for the past few weeks. He also said that he still has keys to his own house, which of course is relevant as there was no sign of forced entry at the murder scene. I assume that no such evidence emerged after I left the scene?"

"No Chief" responded Hodges. "We checked and re-checked every door and window and found nothing."

Radford added, "Which means that she either let the killer in, or the killer had the key. Either way, she knew the killer."

Lumpkin continued with his summary, "Stohler told me that he was having money problems, which was the primary cause of his marital problems. I then asked him if he had a life insurance policy on his wife. He said that he did. You won't believe how much. $250,000! Do you believe that?"

After a collective chorus of "Wows," Radford asked, "Isn't she a school teacher? How much do school teachers make these days?"

"Not much" responded Riley. My wife is a teacher at the same school. I assure you that she does not make a lot of money."

Hodges then added, "So, he's having marital and money problems. We know she went to see a divorce lawyer. If she proceeds with the divorce, then he has to incur legal expenses during the divorce process and alimony payments indefinitely thereafter. But, on the other hand, if she is dead, he collects life insurance money."

"Exactly" Lumpkin empathetically agreed. "And we also know that she met with the divorce lawyer at 5 p.m. on Wednesday. I asked Stohler when he last spoke with his wife and he said around 8 p.m. on Wednesday. It was just three hours later. I asked him if she had mentioned divorce in that conversation or any other time, and he adamantly said 'no.' But my instincts tell me that he was lying about that."

Lumpkin went on, "I think he was also lying about not having a girlfriend. I asked him about having a girlfriend and he denied it. I know I saw him with another woman just yesterday. When I asked again later on about his girlfriend, he refused to answer and said he was done talking with me. It was obvious that the question upset him. It's probably what struck the nerve, as you noted before, Radford."

"Probably" answered Radford, who was eager to agree with his chief and also eager to pin this crime on Michael Stohler.

"He was even acting strangely before our discussion" added Lumpkin. "In the ride to the station, he kept asking me to use my phone to call his parents. He didn't want to wait to get to the station to call his parents."

"He knew he was in trouble and he figured Daddy would save him" mocked Radford.

"Radford, what happened with owner of O'Leary's?"

"He confirmed that Stohler was there and that he was with Papadakis and Starr. He didn't have much to say about Stohler's demeanor or who else he may have interacted with. He didn't think Stohler drank much but couldn't be sure. The bar was busy last night due to the fact that the Steelers were playing. He gave me the names of all employees who worked the evening shift and some names of patrons he specifically remembered being there. I'll follow up with all the names on the list."

"Ok. Good work Radford" Lumpkin replied. "Make sure to speak with everyone on that list."

Lumpkin then moved to a portable chalkboard standing on the side of the office. "Let's list on the left side all facts that we know about the crime itself." He then wrote the following list on the board:

Case facts:

- Victim was shot once in forehead from close range.
- The weapon was a .22 caliber handgun.

- The weapon is not at the scene, thus eliminating suicide as a possibility.
- Estimated time of death is between 2 a.m. and 4 a.m.
- No signs of forced entry. Victim likely knew the killer.
- Front door was found open. Likely where the killer fled the scene.
- Jewelry box was open on the dresser, possibly to make it look like a robbery.
- Victim's wedding ring is missing.

Upon writing the last two points, Riley asked, "How do we know definitively that it wasn't simply a random burglary gone bad?"

"Why would the burglar have to kill her? And how did he get in without forcing his way in?" Lumpkin angrily retorted.

"Sorry Chief. I'm just brainstorming here. I'm just trying to think of all possibilities."

"Let's stay focused and not get sidetracked by unlikely scenarios. Now, on the right side of the board, let's list what we know about our suspect." Lumpkin then proceeded to list the following:

Suspect facts:

- Married to victim.
- Having marital problems – sleeping at parents.
- Denies the fact that victim was considering divorce.
- Last spoke to victim just after she had a meeting with a divorce lawyer.
- Has money problems.
- Has a life insurance policy on victim.
- Has no alibi at time of crime.
- Likely was intoxicated at time of crime.
- Was late to work the next morning (very unusual).
- Has a key to house.
- Probably has a girlfriend but denies it.

After completing his list, Lumpkin said, "Based on all of this information, here is my theory: She informs him on Wednesday night in their phone conversation that she met with the divorce attorney. That angers and upsets him because according to him, they are going to work things out. He has no intentions of divorcing her, and won't stand for her initiating divorce proceedings against him. He drinks a lot the next night and his intoxication fuels his anger. So, after his father goes to sleep, he drives back to his own house, uses his key to let himself in, kills her, then throws some jewelry around to make it look like a robbery. He also takes the wedding ring for the same reason as well as to possibly sell it and/or collect insurance on it. He leaves the front door open when exiting to make it look like a burglar fleeing the scene because if he closes the door and locks up with his key after the murder, it would be obvious who had last been there. How does that sound?"

"Sounds about right, Chief" Radford chimed in.

"Anyone have any alternate ideas?" Riley asked.

"No. There are no alternate ideas" shouted Lumpkin. "I even asked Stohler if he knew who else may have committed this crime and he had no answer. Let's face it, the victim was loved by everyone. Who would want her dead? There is only one person with motive. And that person had opportunity too as he had access to get into the house in the middle of the night."

"Ok, Chief. So, what's the next step?" asked Hodges.

"Well, first I want to make sure you all understand that this case is going to be very high profile. It is the type of case that makes or breaks careers. You've already seen the media coverage and the mob scene of onlookers at the Stohler house, so you can imagine how this is going to be the biggest news in this town in generations. The people are going to demand that the killer be caught and justice be served. Our townspeople are going to be scared until they are secure in knowing that the killer is off the streets. So we need to act quickly on this.

"I don't know about you guys," Lumpkin continued, "but I am tired of this thankless, no-action, dead-end position. I want to move up to bigger and better places and onto bigger and better challenges. Nothing ever happens here, so now that something actually has happened, we need to be all over it. If you guys are ambitious and want to make something of yourselves in law enforcement, we need to nail this case. Otherwise, we'll just be viewed as bumbling idiots who can't solve a simple murder with an obvious culprit. Does everyone understand what I am saying here?"

The others nodded in unison and simply replied, "Yes Chief."

Lumpkin continued, "Now that we understand what is at stake, let's talk about our next moves. We need to get more evidence against Stohler and we need to maintain continuous surveillance on him. The surveillance is for three reasons. Number one, to make sure he doesn't try to flee. Number two, to make sure he doesn't try to discard any evidence before we can get a warrant and secure it. And number three, to make sure that he doesn't try to kill anyone else."

Hodges countered, "I don't think he will kill anyone else. He doesn't have motive regarding anyone else as he had with…"

Lumpkin cut him off and angrily retorted, "Let's not make assumptions! We are responsible for the safety of the people, so we can't afford to make any assumptions and be wrong!"

Lumpkin then went on to say, "So, as I was saying, we'll set up shifts between the four of us to always have someone on him. If we need coverage assistance we can put in a request for help from one of the neighboring police departments, but I'd rather keep this internal as much as possible. Hodges, you'll watch him for the remainder of the day. He likely went back to his parents' house. He left here with them in his parents' car.

"Riley, you go back to the scene and continue interviewing neighbors and anyone who may have seen or heard anything or knows something useful. Radford, you continue following up with the list of names from O'Leary's. Also, you know Stohler best, so you can try to talk to him again. He probably won't speak with me, but maybe he'll speak with you. Try to think of anything we don't know or haven't asked him yet. Then get a few hours of sleep so that you can take the night surveillance shift tonight. Coordinate with Hodges where to relieve him later on. I'll work on getting cell phone records to try to hone in on his whereabouts at specific times last night."

Finally, Lumpkin asked, "Does anyone have any questions?"

There were no questions.

"Ok then. Let's get to work."

Everyone rose with excitement and headed out the door to start their assigned tasks. The four person police department of Garrowville had never had a homicide case. But they had one now. They knew who did it and they weren't going to let him get away with it.

Chapter 13

After I ended what seemed to be more like an interrogation by Chief Lumpkin, rather than a discussion, I joined my parents in the front of the station, and we headed toward their car. My car was still parked at work. I was upset with Lumpkin for what appeared to be his preconceived notion of my guilt. Whatever happened to "innocent until proven guilty?" Or at least, how about our town's police chief being open minded instead of jumping to one conclusion to the apparent exclusion of all other possibilities?

These were the points I was muttering to my parents as we walked toward the car and crossed paths with Dan Radford. I think he overheard me, but I didn't care. I knew that the police would be under a great deal of pressure to solve this murder, but investigating just one angle of the case didn't seem to be the best approach. Especially when I knew that the one angle they were taking was the wrong one.

I started thinking about how inexperienced Chief Lumpkin and his staff must be when it came to homicide investigations. There haven't been any around these parts that I could remember. Are they really the most qualified people in law enforcement to deal with this case? Hopefully, they'll get help from outside sources, such as neighboring police forces or perhaps at the federal level. I wanted to find out who did this more than anyone else and I wanted very badly for my wife to get the justice that she deserved.

I got into the back seat of my parents' car and we took off. My father drove and my mom was in the front passenger seat. I was glad to have them here with me as I went through this nightmare. By now they would normally be down in Florida for the winter. They were your typical retiree "snow-birds," spending the warm weather months up here, and the winters in Boca Raton, Florida, where they had a condo. They usually left just after Thanksgiving, but my mother hadn't been feeling well lately so they were waiting until she felt better before making the drive south.

My father is 68 years old and has been retired full-time for the past three years. Prior to that, he gradually eased into retirement for a few years as he transitioned the responsibility of running the family business to me. He is in great shape, thin, and exercises regularly. He is 6'4", so it is apparent that I inherited my height genes from him as my mom is just 5'4". Hopefully, I inherited his hair genes as well, as he still has a full set of hair; gray hair, but a full complement of it.

My mother, Marilyn, is 65 years old and had worked part-time at the company while Dad was working there full-time. As he transitioned toward retirement, so did my mom. She had long and straight blond hair, which of course is now gray, but that doesn't take away from her good looks. Both of my parents have always been athletic and kept in great shape, which encouraged me to do the same. I get my athletic genes from both of them.

"Do you want to get your car at the plant?" my father asked.

"No" I answered. "Not right now. We can get it over the weekend. I don't feel up to seeing or talking to anyone from work at this time. Let's just go back to your place."

"What specifically was Lumpkin asking you?" my mother inquired.

"He seems pretty convinced that it was me who did this. How can anyone even think that? He asked me questions about where I was last night, what kind of problems Jennifer and I have been having, the life insurance policy I have on her, and he asked some strange questions about me having a girlfriend. I have no idea where that was coming from."

"A girlfriend?" my father asked incredulously. "Why would he think that?"

"I don't know. I'd had enough when repeated the inquiry. That was when I walked out."

"I think that we should consider getting you a lawyer" my father suggested. "If the police are going to be investigating you as a possible suspect, I think it is wise to have someone to protect your legal rights during the process."

"I didn't do this" I responded, "so the police can't possibly have any actual evidence that I did. Therefore, I can't see this going much further than Lumpkin's hasty assumptions. I think that if I went running to a lawyer just a few hours after my wife was murdered, people will interpret that incorrectly. They'll think that I did it and am hiding behind legal counsel."

"I know you didn't do this" my father said, "but you can't worry about what people think. You have to make sure that your rights are protected during this process, especially if the police seem determined to pin this on you."

"Let's just give it a little more time and see how this plays out. Hopefully, the police will soon realize I didn't do it and they'll uncover some evidence as to who really did commit the crime. I went to the police station this morning to try to help them. I want them to catch the killer more than anyone. I didn't expect to be interrogated like a suspect. I just wanted to help them."

"Well, I wouldn't wait too long" my father responded. "I know just the person we can call whenever you decide to do so. Ben Orensen, my old college friend, has a son, Jeff, who is a very successful criminal defense attorney. He went to the University of Pennsylvania law school and has a practice now in downtown Pittsburgh. You may remember that case that was in the news last year regarding the killing in the train station in Pittsburgh. He was the defense lawyer in that case and the defendant was acquitted. A few months later, the police caught the real killer when he struck again. It was on all the news stations and Jeff was on television all the time when it was going on. He should be our first choice if you decide to go that route."

"Ok. Thanks. I'll let you know. Let's hold off for a little bit and see what happens. I don't feel like talking to anyone right now anyway. I just want to stay at your place for a few days and grieve."

My mother then mentioned that we would have to start making funeral arrangements. My father said that he would take care of it and that I shouldn't worry about a thing. Like I said, it was good to have them around. I couldn't imagine dealing with all of this without them.

After arriving back at their house, I went into my room and closed the door. I just wanted to be left alone to cry. My father started making phone calls about the funeral and my mother sat in the living room and turned on the television. Every major station was covering the murder.

On one station she saw the popular reporter she always admired, Chelsea Forgeous, reporting from in front of the police station. She was interviewing Chief Lumpkin, which prompted my mom to yell for both my father and I to come into the room. We gathered around the television and watched the interview.

"I'm here with Carl Lumpkin, Garrowville's Chief of Police for the last ten years and with more than twenty years on the town's police force" Forgeous informed the television audience. "Chief Lumpkin is in charge of the investigation into the murder of Jennifer Stohler. Chief, what can you tell us about the investigation so far?"

"Well, I just want to assure the people of Garrowville that we will be working around the clock to make sure we catch the killer as soon as possible and get him off the street. Just like everyone else, we are appalled by this horrible crime, and we won't rest until the murderer is behind bars."

"Do you have any leads or suspects thus far?" Forgeous asked.

"We have someone who I would call a 'person of interest' at this point."

"Who would that be?" Forgeous pressed.

"Whenever a wife is murdered in her own home, the husband is naturally a 'person of interest' in the case until such time in which he can be crossed off as a possible suspect. We haven't reached that point in time yet." Lumpkin answered.

"We know that you brought the husband, Michael Stohler, to the police station for questioning. Did you learn anything useful from that conversation?"

As I listened to this last question, I realized that the wording of the question was misleading to anyone watching this interview. It was misleading because the phrase 'brought the husband, Michael Stohler, to the police station for questioning' had a certain implication to it that made it sound worse than reality. Lumpkin had simply requested that I come to the station, and I agreed because I wanted to help with the investigation. I wasn't 'brought' anywhere against my will as the phrasing of the question seemed to imply.

Lumpkin answered, "I can't go into specifics yet regarding the interrogation, but again, I assure the public that we will make an arrest as soon as humanly possible."

Lumpkin was referring to our chat this morning as an "interrogation" and was already talking about an arrest. Could this get any worse? The answer is 'yes.'

Forgeous then asked, "Are there any other persons of interest?"

Lumpkin replied, "No. There are not."

Now the world knows that not only am I a 'person of interest' but that I was the only one labeled as such.

"Thank you Chief Lumpkin." Forgeous gratefully said.

Chelsea Forgeous then turned to the camera and assured the viewers that she was on the case and that she will update everyone as soon as there are any developments.

The anchor took over from there, rehashing the facts of the case for what was probably the hundredth time that day. He showed video of several of Jennifer's first grade students, all of whom were crying, and their parents, who were also crying. He talked about the various charities that Jennifer has organized in the community. Then, he described in specific detail the gruesome way in which she had died, emphasizing that the murder had occurred in her own bedroom.

Next, the station cut to video from earlier in the day in front of the house. Suddenly I was watching myself sitting in the back seat of Lumpkin's police car. I was sitting in the rear right seat and it was just after I had gotten into the car. Lumpkin seemed to have lingered for a few extra seconds on the passenger side of the vehicle and faced the camera. It actually appeared as if he was posing for the camera. It seemed like he was showing the world how he had already apprehended a suspect. Now I understood why he wanted me in the back seat.

It occurred to all three of us in the room that if what we were watching was representative of the coverage the case had been receiving all day, then it wouldn't be just the police who would suspect that I was the killer. It would also be the whole community.

Chapter 14

As expected, the murder was the talk of the town throughout the day. Anywhere one went it was the topic of conversation. The hotbed of news and gossip in the area was usually the Center Street Salon in downtown Garrowville, and today was no exception. Employees and customers talked about nothing else.

One of the salon's regulars happened to be Diane Lumpkin; wife of Chief Lumpkin, and one of the administrative employees who had been let go from Stohler Steel earlier in the year.

"He was probably having an affair with that bimbo he kept on instead of me" she said loud enough for everyone in the small salon to hear. "He always seemed overly friendly with her. If he wasn't having an affair with her, why then would he keep her instead of me? I had more experience and I had been with the company longer."

"You're probably right" agreed Carla Lucinda, the salon's owner.

"Why keep the middle-aged, married woman when he can keep the young, single, eye candy instead?" added Diane for no apparent reason other than to further hammer home her point.

Soon other patrons and employees chimed in.

"He's laid off half the town in the past few years;" said Sally Troutwig, "including people with kids and mortgages. Some people have had their homes foreclosed because they've lost their job with that company of his."

"Meanwhile, he still has his company and his home" added Judy Logan, another patron in the salon. "Heaven forbid he should cut his own pay instead of firing other people."

"Also, his parents are loaded. They even have a second home in Florida. He could afford to take home less pay." added Diane.

"I heard he's been staying with his parents because Jennifer kicked him out of his house" stated Barbie Jenson, one of the salon's hair stylists, who was working on Judy's hair during the gossip free-for-all.

"That proves he was having an affair" Carla proclaimed. "If they were just arguing, he'd probably be sleeping on the couch. Why leave the house altogether if he wasn't kicked out?"

"I saw him driving yesterday with another woman. He was in the car next to me at a red light" said Tara Saunders, the salon's cashier.

"Was she blonde?" asked Diane.

"Yes."

"Then it was probably the bimbo I was talking about from work, Brenda Challey."

"I heard someone say that he had a $1 million dollar life insurance policy on his wife" added Carol Jennings, a customer who had just walked in during the conversation.

"More motive for him to kill her" said Diane. "He gets the money and is free to be with the bimbo."

On and on it went. But not just at the Center Street Salon. The patrons of Jimmy's Diner, located just around the corner from the salon, were having similar conversations. Evan Longwell, a regular at the diner, was sitting at the counter when he said, "We all knew Jennifer well. She was great. Who would ever want to hurt her? No one would have any motive other than Michael, who stands to collect a lot in life insurance. So there you have the only possible motive. It had to be Michael who killed her."

Patrick Rollins, the cashier, and Jimmy's right-hand man in running the day-to-day operations of the eatery added, "And there was no forced entry, so if it wasn't Michael, how did the killer get in?"

Andy Forman, another regular customer, then held up his hands to get the other diners' attention and confidently proclaimed, "Listen, it's a very simple, common sense case. The evidence all points to the same answer. No one else had motive. No one else had opportunity. We all know Michael did this. The police know Michael did this. I'm sure they'll be making the arrest very soon. They can't have a known murderer roaming around town for very long."

Everyone within earshot nodded their heads in agreement. The court of public opinion had already rendered its verdict.

Chapter 15

Even at O'Leary's, my 'home turf,' the sentiments were the same. O'Leary's was also the next site from where our favorite member of the media, "Gorgeous Forgeous" checked in. Once again, my mom called us in to hear her report.

"This is Chelsea Forgeous, live from O'Leary's, where Michael Stohler is a regular customer, and where he hung out on the last night of his wife's life. I'm here with Brian O'Leary, owner of the pub.

"Mr. O'Leary, you stated that Michael Stohler was at your bar last night. How would you describe his demeanor during the evening?"

"He seemed somewhat down and quiet. He was here with a couple of friends, but he didn't really speak much."

"Has he been to your bar often?"

"Yes. In fact he's been here a lot lately and he's been drinking more than usual. He also confided in me that's he's been having problems at home, so I think that this pub and alcohol was his escape."

"And what time did he leave here last night?" asked Forgeous.

"I'm not sure exactly but I'd say sometime around midnight" answered O'Leary.

"Thank you Mr. O'Leary."

Chelsea Forgeous then turned toward the camera and added that preliminary reports from the crime scene investigators are that the estimated time of the murder was between 2 a.m. and 4 a.m. She didn't specifically say it, but the implication clearly was that my presence at the bar last night was not an alibi for the murder.

I turned the television off and vowed to myself not to turn it back on for a while.

About an hour later, the doorbell rang. My mother answered it and called out to me that Officer Radford was here to see me. This couldn't be good.

"Hi Michael. I need to ask you a few questions" Radford said as I approached.

"This really isn't a good time Dan, as I'm sure you can understand. Why don't you call me in a few days."

"This will only take a few minutes. It is important for the investigation."

"Ok," I reluctantly agreed, "but make it quick." I was hopeful that if I can give the police some guidance, maybe they will get on the right track, so I still wanted to help despite the disaster earlier with Lumpkin. Maybe it will be different with Radford.

We sat down on the couch in the living room. My parents left the room to give us some privacy, but I suspected that they weren't far away. They were probably in the next room, listening intently to every word.

Radford started with a quick, not so heartfelt condolence for my loss, then asked his first question.

"Do you know of anyone who may have had a reason to want Jennifer dead?" he asked.

"Lumpkin asked me that earlier. The answer is 'no.' She couldn't possibly have any enemies." I answered.

"What then could a possible motive be for someone else besides you to kill her?"

Here we go again with the "besides you" talk from the police.

"I don't know. Why does there have to be a motive? Maybe it was simply a random robbery. I have no idea."

"Did you see anything missing when you were at the house this morning?" Radford asked.

"I wasn't looking. I was in shock after just learning that my wife had been murdered and having just seen her body. I wasn't in a frame of mind to search for missing items."

Radford then said, "There was some jewelry on the dresser near her body. Any idea if any jewelry was missing?"

"Again, I wasn't looking" I impatiently answered. "I don't know."

"Do you know if she had been wearing her wedding ring lately?"

"I assume so. She was married. Why wouldn't she have been wearing it?"

"Well, you two have been having some problems lately. You've been staying here rather than at home."

"Yes. But we were still married and working things out so I assume she was still wearing the ring."

"When we discovered her body, there was no ring on her finger" Radford stated.

"Well it makes sense. She was killed in the middle of the night so she wouldn't have had it on. She didn't sleep with it on."

"We didn't find it anywhere in the house." Radford said.

"Well then, it appears we have a missing item." I said with even less patience than before.

"Will you be willing to come with me to the house to see what else, if anything, may be missing?"

"Not today. I'm not going anywhere today. Call me tomorrow and maybe I'll go then, if I'm feeling up to it. Is there anything else?" I asked in a tone that made it clear that I was done with this discussion.

"That's it for now. If you think of anything that may be useful, please call me or anyone in the department. Here's a card with my cell phone number. Call me anytime with any information you can think of that may help. I'll call you tomorrow."

He then got up to leave. I didn't bother to walk him to the door. I figured he'd find the way. I was glad that he was leaving. I just wanted to be left alone to grieve for my wife. But, apparently someone else had other ideas.

Shortly after Radford left there was another unwelcome visitor at my parents' front door. This time my father answered the door and was greeted by Chelsea Forgeous and a cameraman, whose camera was live and focused directly on my dad. Forgeous was seemingly everywhere today.

"Mr. Stohler, do you have anything to…" Forgeous started to say.

"No! Leave us alone. We've suffered a terrible loss and we just want to be left alone to grieve in private. Now get off my property!" my father emphatically demanded as he slammed the door shut.

I didn't see it for myself because as I had said, I vowed not to watch any more television for a while. But, according to my mother, who was still monitoring the coverage of the case, the video of Officer Radford coming into the house for "questioning" as it was called on air, and then the video of my father snarling angrily at the pretty and popular reporter dominated the evening news. It couldn't have helped my cause.

Chapter 16

Television was not the only mode of reporting to slant and sensationalize the crime. After a long, mostly sleepless night, I was greeted very early on Saturday morning by my mother handing me the local newspaper. The front page headline of the Garrowville Gazette read, "Wife Murdered In Own Home." Of course I had expected the murder to be front page news. However, it seemed to me that use of the word 'wife' to describe the victim implied that the husband was responsible for the crime. Maybe I was being paranoid, but my experiences from the day before justifiably led me to such paranoia.

The story that ensued essentially followed the same template as we had seen in the television coverage. It stated that the husband had been brought in for 'questioning' and it quoted Chief Lumpkin as saying that he had a 'person of interest' and that there were no other 'persons of interest.' There was even a photo of me sitting dejectedly in the back seat of his police car. I couldn't help but think that anyone reading this story would be led to believe that the husband killed his wife. I tossed the paper aside and vowed to add newspapers to my list of things to avoid for the time being. I was starting to run low on ways to keep up with the outside world.

It was very early on Saturday morning and my mom was already awake, so I thought it would be a good time for us to retrieve my car from the company's parking lot without seeing anybody. We drove over to the Stohler Steel parking lot and pulled up alongside the right side of my car. I got out from the front passenger seat of my mother's car and walked around the back of both vehicles to the driver's side of my car and was shocked by what I saw.

Spray-painted in big black bold letters across the left side of my car was the word, 'KILLER.' I couldn't believe it. It must have happened during the night because I couldn't imagine someone vandalizing my car in this manner in broad daylight without being seen. But who would do this?

I wished that I had video surveillance in the lot, but I did not. Truthfully, until now, I had never even thought of installing video cameras in the lot or anywhere else on the company's property. It was a very low crime area and we've never had any problems. But apparently that wasn't the case anymore.

I certainly wasn't going to drive back in a car that screamed the word 'KILLER' on its side. But I didn't want to leave the car out in the open lot in that condition either. Our office building had an underground parking garage. With our smaller workforce, it was now rarely used, so I moved the car in there. I parked in an end spot with the driver's side close up against the wall so that the graffiti wouldn't be seen by anyone who happened to go down there. I'll deal with the removal of the graffiti later on. It wasn't my biggest issue right now.

I got back into my mother's car and we returned to my parents' house. I spent the morning sulking around the house while my father finalized the funeral arrangements. The funeral was scheduled for Tuesday morning. A few of my parents' friends visited during the morning to offer their condolences. None of my friends stopped by and just a few left messages for me on my cell phone. I don't think any of my friends wanted to be seen visiting me. Calling me was a safer option, though only a few did.

Around midday Officer Radford returned to see me and said that he wanted to take me over to my house to assess what other items, if any, may be missing. I told him that unless there was a huge void where the big screen television was, I wasn't likely to notice anything missing. But I went anyway. If we could determine that there was a robbery, then maybe the police would shift their focus in that direction and away from me.

After arriving at my house, we started with a tour of the downstairs. We didn't expect to find anything down there, but for the sake of thoroughness, we figured we should check the whole house. I couldn't tell if anything was missing. All the televisions and other major appliances were still in place, so unless someone took something very small, everything seemed to be in order.

I took my time examining the downstairs because I was dreading going upstairs and into the bedroom. But inevitably, we made our way up there. I cringed as we entered the bedroom and saw blood stains on the carpet. Of course Jennifer's body had long since been removed but there were still a lot of indications of what had transpired. I froze for a moment staring at the blood. It hurt so much to think how all that blood had come from my wonderful wife. Who could have done this? I still couldn't believe that this had happened.

Radford then snapped me back into focus and told me to start looking around.

"Look specifically at the jewelry in the box, on the counter, and anywhere else around the room where she may have kept valuables" he said.

I looked around but the truth of matter was that other than the wedding ring, Jennifer had purchased most of her own jewelry. I never really knew much about jewelry and wasn't very observant as to what she was wearing. All I knew was that she had a lot of jewelry.

"I don't see her wedding ring anywhere," I answered "otherwise, I can't tell if any other jewelry is missing. She had a lot of jewelry."

"Are there any other items missing? Any money? Other valuables? Do you have a safe or any other place where you kept valuables?"

"No. We never needed a safe around these parts. And other than Jennifer's jewelry, there weren't a lot of valuables around the house. There could have been some loose cash sitting around, but it wouldn't have been much."

"Ok. Let's look around the rest of this level, then we'll go" Radford said.

The rest of the search wasn't fruitful. The only item that I could tell was missing was the wedding ring, which was quite valuable. There could have been other missing jewelry, but I didn't know. Nevertheless, my theory of a robbery seemed to me to be the most likely scenario and I mentioned this to Radford. I told him that if someone were to rob the house, Jennifer's wedding ring would be the most appealing item to a thief, based on value and portability.

The police, however, apparently still had a different theory.

Chapter 17

After Officer Radford returned Michael to his parents' home, he went back to the police station to touch base with Chief Lumpkin. Lumpkin had asked Radford and Riley to report back to him with an update so that they can compare notes. Officer Hodges was assigned to keep tabs on Michael so he wasn't included in the meeting.

When the three of them were all seated in the Chief's office, Lumpkin commenced the meeting.

"Radford, you start. What do you have?"

"I went to see Michael at his parents' house yesterday and today. Both times he did not seem very happy to see me or talk to me. Yesterday he was short with me and basically just wanted me out the door. It is obvious that he is not keen on helping us out."

"Shocking" quipped Lumpkin. "How many murderers are excited to talk to the police?" he asked rhetorically.

Radford continued, "I asked him if he knew of anyone who may have had motive to kill Jennifer."

"I asked him that yesterday. He had no answer then. Did he have one now?" Lumpkin asked.

"No. He didn't have any specific suspects in mind," answered Radford, "but he seemed anxious to tell me that it could have been a random robbery. It was as if he was worried that we wouldn't think of that. He even went as far as to ask me why there has to be a motive. He was really trying to sell his random robbery theory."

"See what I was saying" said Lumpkin. "He threw some jewelry around and took the wedding ring. Then tries to convince us it was a robbery. It's all coming together."

"He didn't want to go visit the house yesterday, but he agreed to go today when I returned" said Radford. "When we were there, he identified the fact that his wife's wedding ring was missing. He even said that the missing ring was evidence of a robbery. Otherwise, he didn't provide any other useful information. It was all about how this was a robbery."

"Ok. Thanks Radford. I am working on getting his cell phone records. Maybe we should also get a search warrant for his parents' house, his office, and his car to see if we can find the murder weapon and/or the missing wedding ring. We know what happened but we need more evidence to be able to make an arrest. Riley what do you have?"

Riley had been interviewing neighbors and Michael's work associates. "Unfortunately, none of the neighbors saw or heard anything out of the ordinary. I did get more of the same song and dance about the Stohlers and their marital issues. It seems that everyone knew this couple was having problems. Almost everyone I interviewed told me stories of Jennifer revealing her marital woes to them."

"What about at his work?" asked Lumpkin.

"No one really had much to say at his office. I think they are fearful of losing their jobs. If someone speaks to us and Michael is subsequently arrested, they fear that the company may collapse. Or if someone gives us information detrimental to him but he ultimately is not arrested, they fear they may be the next one laid off as a result. Either way, no one wants to say anything detrimental about their boss. And they certainly didn't have anything to add in his favor."

"My wife repeatedly reminded me last night about how he had kept that young, cute secretary instead of her. Did you speak with her?" asked Lumpkin.

"Yes. Her name is Brenda Challey. She confirmed that she was with him after work last night but claims that it was only to give her a lift to the auto shop. I asked if Michael makes a habit of giving lifts to employees after hours and she said that she didn't know. She claimed that it was the first time he had given her a lift."

"Yeah sure" Radford said sarcastically. "I saw those two interacting the next morning. As I mentioned yesterday, they seemed very chummy."

"Thanks Riley. Keep looking for possible witnesses or anyone who may know something useful" said Lumpkin who then went on to say, "Ok. My theory is that Michael took the wedding ring for three reasons. The first reason, as we've noted, is to mislead us into believing that the murder was a random robbery. The second reason is to hock it. Remember, he's admitted to having significant financial problems and now that Jennifer is gone, she won't need the ring anymore. So, he's going to try to sell it. Maybe he already has. Holding onto the ring would not be wise for him because he doesn't want to get caught with it. Radford, check out any places locally that buys jewelry. Start with the high end places and work your way down to the pawn shops."

"Sure Chief. Your comments also remind me that Michael was making a point to me earlier that the ring is very valuable. He said it in the context of that it would be a likely target for a thief" said Radford.

"I'm sure it is" said Lumpkin. "He's always had a lot of money so he probably bought her a big-time ring. And now that he doesn't have as much money readily available, the ring and the life insurance policy he has on his wife will make up for his recent financial shortfalls. Some people just can't handle not having a lot of money."

Lumpkin continued, "The third reason he took the wedding ring may be to collect insurance after he reports it as stolen. This would be consistent with his financial motives in the case. I want to find out if he had coverage on the ring. I suspect that he would."

Just then the phone rang in Lumpkin's office. He answered it and grinned from cheek to cheek as he listened. He hung up and proudly announced to his staff, "We've obtained Michael's cell phone records. We can also use his cell phone information and the towers the phone emits to for the purpose of determining when and where he was at precise points in time. Score one for the good guys!"

Chapter 18

Chief Lumpkin spent most of the rest of his weekend examining Michael's cell phone records in the days and weeks leading up to the murder, as well as during the brief time that has elapsed since the murder. He had two objectives in mind. First, he wanted to determine if there were any phone calls out of the ordinary that may somehow be linked to the crime. An example may be if he had hired someone to commit the crime, Chief Lumpkin was hoping that there would be phone calls to and from that person. The second objective was to track Michael's movements during the night of the crime. Based on the location of the nearest cell phone tower at any point in time in which a cell phone is on, a user's approximate location can be determined. Chief Lumpkin knew that the closest tower to Michael and Jennifer's home was not the same tower as the one closest to Michael's parents' house. So, depending on which tower his phone was emitting signals to at the time of the murder, Lumpkin hoped to punch a big gaping hole in his prime suspect's supposed alibi.

Unfortunately for Lumpkin, he struck out on both objectives. After carefully tracking all the phone numbers for which calls were made and received in the weeks and months leading up to and just after the crime, he noted nothing unusual. Essentially all calls were either to or from Michael's wife, his parents, and various work related calls. On the evening in question, he made one phone call to Jimmy Papadakis about an hour before meeting him at O'Leary's, presumably to confirm their plans to meet at the pub.

Lumpkin was not deterred by this minor "speed bump." He was hoping for an easy and obvious connection between the cell phone records and the crime, but it wasn't meant to be. However, by no means does this fact serve to exonerate Michael. He knew that Michael is a smart guy which means that Michael wouldn't be dumb enough to make incriminating phone calls from his own cell.

The cell phone records did lead to an interesting discovery though relating to his second objective. While Lumpkin was working on tracking Michael's whereabouts on the night of the murder, he lost all tracing of his location a little after 8 p.m. on Thursday night. Lumpkin was able to determine that Michael had been at work until roughly 5 p.m., then was likely at his parents' house shortly thereafter. A little while later, Michael had made it to O'Leary's. All of these steps in the chronology of the evening were consistent with his story to that point in time. But suddenly the trail went cold. The phone must have been turned off at O'Leary's and not turned back on until well into the next day. But why?

The only logical explanation was that once again Michael was intelligent and didn't want the police to be able to disprove his story for the rest of the night by tracking his movements through his cell phone records. This murder was obviously premeditated and here was another example of that fact. Lumpkin went back several weeks to see if there were any other gaps in the tracking of his phone and didn't see any. It was quite a coincidence that his phone was always on except for the time frame during which his wife turned up dead!

Lumpkin wanted to question Michael about this fact but knew that asking him to come to the station would be met with resistance. He also knew that Radford had stopped by the parents' home twice already, so a third visit also would not be warmly received. Instead, he tried another approach; one that would maybe catch Michael a bit off guard. He called Michael on his cell. It was late on Sunday night, but Lumpkin didn't care. If Michael was tired, all the better; maybe he'll slip up. He dialed the number and after a couple of rings, Michael nervously answered, "Hello?"

"Hi Michael. This is Chief Lumpkin. Quick question for you. Why was your cell phone turned off on Thursday night, into Friday morning?"

Michael was surprised by the question. In all the chaos of the past few days, Michael hadn't immediately remembered how his phone's juice had run out that night and he had forgotten to charge it during the night due to his state of intoxication and fatigue. Upon thinking back for a few seconds, he remembered that had happened. But how did the Chief know about that?

"My phone died sometime during the night, then when I got back to my parents' house, I forgot to charge it. I didn't get a chance to charge it until the next day" answered Michael.

"Is that so?" Lumpkin said skeptically, "do you forget to charge your phone often?"

"No. I am usually pretty good about keeping it charged. It's just that I drank more when I got back from the pub. Then, being drunk and tired, I fell asleep without remembering to charge it."

"Just so I understand this, you always keep your phone charged, but on the night your wife happened to be murdered, you coincidentally forgot. Do I have that right?"

"I'm hanging up now. I answered your question. As I said at the station, when you are ready to talk to me about other possible scenarios as to what happened to my wife, then I'll talk to you again. I shouldn't have answered the phone. I was hoping you had other news. Good night." Michael then disconnected the call.

On Monday, Lumpkin requested and received a search warrant for Michael's car, his office, and his parents' house. He had laid out all of his circumstantial evidence in his affidavit to the court in order to establish probable cause to justify the searches.

Lumpkin gathered his officers together at 12 p.m. at the station, and assigned each one to concurrently search each site; Radford to the parents' house, Hodges to the office, and Riley to the car, which based on surveillance throughout the weekend, the police knew was parked in the garage under Michael's office building. Lumpkin wanted the searches to take place at the same time so that they would have the advantage of surprise at each location and that nothing can be moved from an area still to be searched to one that already had been searched.

Lumpkin instructed each to show up at his assigned location at 2 p.m. Obviously they were looking for anything relating to the crime, but specifically, to be on the lookout for a murder weapon, any signs of bloody clothes, and the missing wedding ring.

Radford then mentioned that he had spent part of the day on Sunday and most of Monday morning visiting jewelry stores and pawn shops, showing Michael's picture. He added that other than several people saying that they recognized Michael's picture from television or the newspaper, no one had reported seeing him at their store.

"That must mean that he still has the ring;" answered Lumpkin, "which is all the more reason for the urgency of these searches. If we can find the ring in his possession it would give us the evidence we need to make an arrest. Even better, let's find the murder weapon. We need to make an arrest as soon as possible. Think of how bad we'll look if everyone knows he killed his wife and we can't piece together the evidence to get him."

Lumpkin's trusty followers filed out of the station and on their way to hopefully find their "smoking gun."

Chapter 19

The first part of Monday had been quiet and uneventful for me. I spent the morning moping around my parents' house and not doing anything productive, while my father continued making arrangements for the funeral scheduled for the next day. I didn't feel up to assisting on that front, nor did I feel up to checking messages or emails at work. I knew I would have to soon, but I wasn't ready yet. Nothing at work seemed important at this time. It is strange how that works. Before my wife was murdered, I spent almost all of my waking hours stressed about the company and how to keep it afloat. Now that she is gone, I don't seem to care as much about work anymore. I can only think about how I wished I had spent more time with her and less time at the office.

I knew that I would eventually go back to work and I would still do my best to make the plant successful. It had been my family's legacy and a secure place of employment for so many of the town's residents over the years. So of course, I would do everything I could to turn it back around. But now wasn't the time. Now was the time for me to think only about my wife. And that was what I was doing when there was a sharp pounding on the front door at 2 p.m.

I was lying on the couch in the living room right by the front door when my mother answered it. I overheard the conversation that ensued.

"Hello Dan. What can I do for you?" my mother asked.

It was Radford again. His third visit in four days. I was sure he wasn't here to express any condolences or to apologize for how the police had treated me.

"Good afternoon Mrs. Stohler" Radford replied. "I have a warrant here to search the premises."

I jumped off the couch, ran up to the front door and yelled at Radford. "What are you talking about Radford? What would you be searching for here? Nothing happened here. You should be searching my house. That's where my wife was murdered. Leave my parents alone."

My father heard the commotion and asked what was going on.

"I'm sorry to intrude Mr. and Mrs. Stohler. I have orders from the Chief to conduct a search of the premises. Here is a copy of the warrant. Now, please step aside and let me get started so that I can be out of your way as soon as possible."

"I'm calling Lumpkin right now" I angrily retorted.

"That's fine. But I need to get started."

My father then turned to me and said, "You call the Chief. I'll watch him while he searches the house. If he even so much as scratches something, we'll sue the department."

I called the police department and got Lumpkin on the phone right away. Even though he said otherwise, I don't think he was surprised to hear from me.

"Look who suddenly wants to talk to me" Lumpkin chided. "You weren't so anxious to talk to me when I called you last night."

"What is up with this bogus search warrant Lumpkin? What can you possibly expect to find here? You are wasting your time. Keep this up and you'll never solve this crime." I angrily replied. It was probably not a good idea to speak back to the chief of police like that, but I was at the end of my patience with his one-angle investigation.

"I'm just covering all bases, Stohler. Isn't that what you wanted?"

I was about to reply when I heard the call waiting beep. I looked at the phone and recognized that the call was coming from the office. Who from the office would be calling me on my parents' home phone? I knew I had better take it, so I hung up on Lumpkin, which was again probably an unwise move, but I didn't care.

I then answered the call from work. It was Brenda.

"Michael. There are two police officers here with search warrants. They want to search the office and your car. What should I do?"

"It's alright Brenda" I tried to calmly reply. "Just get a copy of the warrant and make sure it clearly says where they are to search. Then have someone watch them as they search. If they have a warrant, there isn't much we can do to stop them. They won't find anything anyway. It is a waste of time. I just don't want them disrupting our business for too long. Let them get in and out as soon as possible."

"Ok. Thanks Michael. I hope you are alright. Sorry to bother you."

"That's fine. You did the right thing by calling me. Please let me know when they are done and what they took."

We said good-bye and hung up. I was livid. I decided it was the last straw and that it was time for me to talk to a lawyer. My father's suggestion for a lawyer seemed like a good one, but I was concerned about costs. Big-time lawyers don't work cheap.

I found my father in the guest room where I was staying. He was watching Radford go through my sock and underwear drawer. I felt a combination of anger at what was going on and humor in the lunacy of it. What was he going to find in my boxers?

Radford then asked, "Where is the dirty laundry?"

"I always had my suspicions about you Radford." I replied. "Thirty-four years-old, single, no girlfriends. I guess I now know why. You want my dirty underwear? It is in the hamper in the bathroom. Have fun."

Radford glared angrily at me, but didn't reply. He just headed toward the bathroom where he started going through our dirty clothes. He even took a few items.

"Souvenirs?" I asked.

"You'd better hope we don't find any blood or gunshot residue on any of these" Radford snapped back. "If you had even so much as a bloody hangnail that dripped onto these clothes, I'll spin it to be an injury you sustained during the crime."

"Well it's good to know that the police are taking an objective approach to this investigation. Very comforting to the public" I sarcastically replied.

Radford spent the next hour going through the house on his wild-goose chase for phantom evidence. I didn't bother him anymore because doing so was pointless and I just wanted him to get done and get out. He seemed to randomly bag a few items to take with him, with no apparent logic as to what he did or didn't take. When he was done, he provided us with an inventory of what he took and said that if they were clean, we'd get everything back.

After he left, I called Brenda back to see what was going on at the office. She was following Officer Hodges around the office as he collected various files. I told her to make sure to get an inventory of everything he took. Brenda told me that they had to take possession of my car for "processing." I assumed that meant that they would be looking for blood, weapons, etc. I wasn't worried. They wouldn't find anything. But I was very annoyed.

After talking to Brenda, I told my father that it was time that we contacted the lawyer he suggested. It was already late in the day on Monday, and the funeral was the next day, so we made an appointment for Wednesday. Wednesday couldn't come soon enough.

Chapter 20

It was Tuesday morning, December 15, 2009, the day of my wife's funeral; an event that I never fathomed could possibly come so soon. It is always sad when anyone close to you dies, but so much more tragic when it is someone so young.

The skies were fittingly overcast and gray on this depressing day, with intermittent rain. If we had children, I would have told them that the rain was God's tears. I remembered my parents telling me that when I was eight years old and we were going to the same church for my grandfather's funeral. I believed it at the time, and while I don't really believe that today, it did seem appropriate that such a gloomy event should take place on a gloomy day.

The funeral was called for 10:30 a.m. I arrived at the church with my parents well in advance for the final preparations and to speak with the pastor. Pastor Frank Solomon had been with the Garrowville Church for over 40 years and had officiated my parents' wedding as well as my wedding with Jennifer.

After expressing his condolences and going over some of the details of the funeral, he asked who would be delivering the eulogy. I answered that of course I would be doing so.

"Michael," he calmly responded in his very soothing voice, "do you think that it is best under the current circumstances that you should be the person to speak to the audience today?"

"What do you mean? Why wouldn't I speak on my wife's behalf at her funeral?" I replied incredulously. I hadn't even thought of any other viable alternative.

"Well, as you know, we are expecting a large crowd in the church today. Most of the town will be here. And while I won't ever tell a grieving spouse what to do or not do, I would respectfully advise that you consider if it is best, based on the open questions as to your wife's death, for you to be addressing that crowd. I would be happy to give her eulogy on your behalf."

"I appreciate your concern Pastor. But my wife had no other family. I am exactly the person who should give the eulogy. You are welcome to speak as well, but I am going to give the eulogy. And although I don't really care what the crowd thinks, how would it look if the grieving husband didn't speak at his wife's funeral?"

"Ok. Michael. It is your decision of course. I will also say a few words on your wife's behalf."

One of the other decisions that had been made regarding the funeral details was that we went with a closed casket. The coroner had done a great job in cleaning Jennifer up, but it is still difficult to make her look her best after being shot in the head. Furthermore, I didn't want everyone's final image of my wonderful wife to be lying dead in a casket. I'd prefer that people's final thoughts and images of Jennifer be of the active, vibrant, loving, and caring person she had always been. It is better for that to be the image in all of our heads during the funeral and forever after, rather than of seeing her in the casket. The pastor may not have agreed with my eulogy decision, but he agreed with the closed casket decision.

People started filing in around 10 a.m., figuring they'd need to be early to get a seat. Pastor Solomon was right about the big crowd. Almost everyone in Garrowville was present. Whenever someone young dies, the attendance at a funeral is generally larger. Add to that the facts that Jennifer was so popular, lived her whole life in the town, and had died in tragic circumstances that had been getting around-the-clock media attention, and the funeral became more than just a funeral; it became an "event" not to be missed.

The church had set up a lot of extra chairs, even opening up the side wall to expand into an adjoining room, but it still was not enough. The overflow crowd was standing room only with rows of standees against all walls around the church. As people entered, some of them approached my parents to express their sympathies. No one directly approached me. A few of my friends nodded discreetly toward me from afar, but it seemed that everyone was conscious not to be seen by the whole town conferring with the presumed murderer.

Pastor Solomon commenced the service a few minutes late to be sure that everyone had arrived. He then conducted the service, leading the church in the usual funeral prayers, after which he spoke briefly and eloquently on Jennifer's behalf. He then turned to me and spoke about how long Jennifer and I had been married, how long we had known each other prior to that, and how my parents and I were Jennifer's only family. He was basically doing his best spin to justify my deliverance of the eulogy.

It was a gallant effort, but it was fruitless. As I rose and approached the podium, you could hear the whispers and gasps throughout the crowd. I didn't care. I was there to pay my respects to my wife and to speak as best I could on her behalf.

I spoke about how we knew each other since we were kids, how close we became so early on in our lives and how we always knew that we were meant for each other. I spoke about how we were so inseparable that we couldn't bear to go to different colleges. I spoke about our wonderful wedding in this very same church and how we had envisioned spending the rest of our lives and growing old together. I also spoke about all the charities and events Jennifer had organized; how she cared so much for others, and was always looking for ways to improve the lives of everyone else. I spoke about how devoted she was as a teacher and to her students; all of whom adored her. I told the audience how she always knew that she wanted to be a teacher because it was the best profession to genuinely make a tangible difference in people's lives and to society as a whole.

I couldn't have spoken more highly and more lovingly about my wife. It was the best and the most heartfelt speech I had ever delivered in my life. But it likely fell on deaf ears.

Throughout the eulogy, I noticed that some people got up and left the room. Others either tuned me out and/or glared at me with contempt. I couldn't help but think that if my speech had been in any other setting, I likely would have been booed, heckled, or worse. Fortunately, people had the sense not to act out in such a manner at a funeral, but it was clear that my eulogy had been poorly received by a biased audience that had already made up its mind about what happened to my wife. There was nothing more that I could say that would have made the people of Garrowville think differently.

After the service, the same scene unfolded as had occurred when everyone had entered the church. Many attendees briefly approached my parents to express their sorrow and did their best to avoid me. Other attendees simply left right afterwards in order to not have to converse with any of the Stohlers.

The funeral was a big media event. News cameras were not allowed inside the church, but all the major media outlets were camped outside. News vans and reporters were lined up and down the street and all cameras were filming as the whole town filed out of the church after the service.

Of course the omnipresent Chelsea Forgeous was on the scene interviewing, on live television, anyone she could corral in front of the church.

"I'm in front of the Church of Garrowville as the crowd from the Jennifer Stohler funeral service lets out" reported Forgeous. "Here comes Chief Carl Lumpkin and his wife. Chief, how is the investigation into Jennifer Stohler's murder proceeding?"

"We are making significant progress and we anticipate making an arrest soon" answered Lumpkin.

"Does that mean that you have learned anything new related to the crime?"

"I can't get into specifics at this time, but rest assured that the police are working around the clock to close this case."

At that point, Mrs. Lumpkin leaned in and added the following, "Even if my husband can't say anything, we all know who killed her. And I think it was horribly distasteful that the monster who murdered Jennifer gave her eulogy today. I can't believe that we were made to sit there and listen to him talk about the person he had just killed."

Others who spoke with Forgeous expressed similar sentiments. Chelsea Forgeous had a line of disgusted citizens begging to convey their thoughts to her. Needless to say, those interviews were played over and over again on the news throughout the remainder of the day. The most disturbing comment however was that Lumpkin mentioned making an arrest soon, and as far as I knew, he was only investigating me.

Chapter 21

Our appointment with Jeff Orensen, Attorney at Law, was scheduled at 11 a.m. on Wednesday, in his downtown Pittsburgh office. Orensen was a highly successful defense attorney and at the relatively young age of forty-two, was already one of the most powerful partners at Zimmerman and Brand LLP, the largest law firm in western Pennsylvania. Jeff Orensen also had received a lot of press in recent years for his successful defense in several high profile cases. He was young, good-looking, well-known, and very media savvy; the ideal person to help me reverse the avalanche of negative publicity and sentiment toward me.

My biggest concern was the potential expense that would undoubtedly result from hiring such a renowned attorney. Well-known, high-powered lawyers will typically have enormous billing rates, and if my case were to drag on, and/or go to trial, I couldn't begin to fathom what the cost of my defense would be, or how I would pay for it. I expressed these concerns to my father during our drive to the meeting.

"Dad, if he takes our case, how am I going to afford this expense? His billing rate will probably be several hundred dollars per hour and there is no telling for how long this case can go on."

"Don't worry about that right now" my father replied. "This meeting is free. He told me on the phone that he doesn't charge for an initial consultation. We can discuss his fees in this meeting if we decide to go forward with him. Hopefully we can work something out with him. It is possible that he will give us a discount. I go back a long way with his father."

I was still concerned. "If I were to get arrested and tried, this could go on for months, even years. How can I pay for my defense over such an extended period of time, even at a discounted rate?"

"If need be, your mother and I will help out. We can always take equity out of our home, which is fully paid for, or we can sell the condo in Florida. But let's cross that bridge when we get there. Let's just worry about today's meeting right now."

"I don't want you to have to sell your retirement home. That is crazy."

"If you were on trial, the rest of your life and freedom would be at stake. That would trump everything else. But again, let's not worry about that yet. You haven't been arrested, let alone tried, and the police can't possibly have any evidence against you anyway. They just have their preconceived, biased theories."

My father's efforts to reassure me were appreciated, but unfortunately, were unsuccessful. I couldn't shake the feeling that this situation was not going to end well. When the Garrowville police department appears to be hell bent on nailing me, it seemed to me that my actual innocence may just be an inconvenient and unimportant speed-bump along the way toward achieving their objective. Alleviating the public pressure to make an arrest, and looking good in the media by doing so expediently, are seemingly far more important goals for them than actually arresting the right person. Those were my thoughts at the time. Was I being paranoid? Perhaps. But I would say that I had good reason for such paranoia based on events so far.

We arrived at the office of Zimmerman and Brand LLP, which was located on the 15th floor of one of the tallest downtown buildings. We then waited in the lobby after a pretty receptionist informed Mr. Orensen's administrative assistant of our arrival. The décor of the office did little to alleviate my cost related fears. The place was huge and was magnificent. It practically screamed out that you had just entered a place of power, prestige, and wealth.

After a few minutes, we were told that Mr. Orensen would see us and we were escorted to his office, which naturally was a large, extravagant, corner unit with a view of the city skyline through ceiling to floor windows on two sides of the room.

Jeff Orensen rose to greet us, warmly smiling as he shook hands with each of us. He then turned toward my father and said, "I understand that you went to school with my dad."

"Yes. Ben and I were very good friends and were fraternity brothers. I can tell you some great stories. Those were fun times. How is your father doing?"

"He is great. He recently retired and is living on the west coast of Florida."

"That's great. Please say hello to him and to Deborah for me."

"Sure. Why don't you both sit down and we'll get started. Can I get either of you a drink?"

We both declined the drinks and my father got down to business.

"Mr. Orensen. I contacted you to discuss the possibility of having you represent my son. As you have probably heard in the news, my son's wife was murdered last week and although no charges have been filed, it is very apparent that the police are vigorously investigating Michael to the extent that they are not seriously looking into any other possibilities. We are concerned that their "tunnel vision" approach to this matter, along with mounting public pressure on them to close the case, will lead them to arrest Michael fairly soon. Therefore, we want to talk with you today about the specifics of the case and how you may be able to assist us."

"Ok. First, I am very sorry about your loss. Please accept my condolences. Second, please call me Jeff. May I call you by your first names as well?"

We both nodded our heads.

"Next, as Michael would be my client, before we can proceed with discussing the case, I need for him to agree to have you remain in the room. Everything I discuss with a client is privileged, therefore, I just need to make sure it is agreeable to Michael that you be here."

I told him it was fine and that there is nothing we would be discussing that my father doesn't already know. However, I then added, "Before we dive into the matter at hand, can we get an idea of what your fees would be should you take this case?"

"Yes. As you know, today's consultation is free and confidential, whether I take the case or not. Even if I don't take the case, or if you decide not to use me, I may be able to advise you today and recommend someone else. If I do take the case, my standard rate is $400 an hour, but I'll reduce that to $300 per hour because George goes way back with my father. I would require a $5,000 retainer up front. Also, there are other miscellaneous expenses, such as paralegal, administrative, and investigative expenses that may be incurred during the process in addition to my hourly rate. Finally, should the case proceed to trial, I'll require an additional retainer as there will be a lot more of a time commitment for me and my associates."

"I'm not sure that we could afford you if this case were to extend for a period of time, especially if it goes to trial." I responded.

My father then scolded me by saying, "I told you not to worry about that yet. Let's talk to Jeff and decide afterwards."

"Yes. George is right. Michael, why don't we discuss the case thus far and maybe I can advise you as to a proper course of action. You can decide afterwards if you want to retain me. Either way, our meeting today is at no cost, and is confidential, so it can't hurt you to talk with me."

I agreed and I proceeded to lay out for him everything that has happened thus far. I omitted no details. I told him about the marital problems Jennifer and I had been having prior to her death. I told him about the various police interrogations that had taken place and my perception as to their single-minded approach to the investigation. I also told him about my negative encounters with the public at large, which I attributed in large part due to circumstantial evidence pointing toward me as the culprit and sensationalist media coverage of the case.

Most of all, I repeatedly told him that I was innocent and I spelled out for him my every move throughout the evening of Jennifer's death. After I recounted all of these details, I took a deep breath and said, "That pretty much sums it up. What are your thoughts?"

"I think that you came to the right place. I have a lot of experience defending homicide cases, should this one come to that, and I have extensive experience dealing with the media and the police."

"What would be your first course of action?" my father asked.

"Should you hire me, we would immediately inform the police that I will be serving as your representative and that you are no longer to be questioned in any way, shape, or form outside of my presence. I would advise you to say nothing to the police or the media without me present or without my consent. There would be no more road trips with the police to the murder scene, the station, or anywhere else for that matter. As for the media, we would set up a press conference as soon as possible. I would address the media as a representative of the family, saying that the family is grief stricken, is in mourning, and that you have and will cooperate fully with the police as there is no one more anxious to find out what happened to his wife than Michael. I would add that we have great confidence that the police will conduct a thorough investigation into the matter, and will thoroughly look into any and all possible suspects. I would conclude by stating that while we understand and appreciate everyone's heartfelt sorrow and anger as to this senseless crime, we ask that people allow the police to conduct their investigation and wait for all information to come forward about this case before jumping to any conclusions. I would politely suggest to the townspeople that we are all "innocent until proven guilty."

My father practically jumped forward with his hand extended saying "You're hired" while barely restraining his jubilance.

"Dad, don't we need to discuss the matter of the cost involved in this decision?"

"Don't worry about that. Your life is at stake here. We are not sparing any expense in this matter."

"But Dad..."

Jeff Orensen stood up and said, "Why don't I leave you alone for a few minutes to discuss this? I'll be in the conference room next door. When you are ready, you can ask me to come back in." Orensen then exited the room and closed the door behind him.

"But Dad," I continued, "how am I going to pay for this? $300 an hour will add up to a fortune very quickly."

My father wasn't listening. He whipped out his checkbook and started making out the check for the $5,000 retainer. As he was writing he said, "The police can't have any evidence, so this case won't go on much further. Sooner or later, they will get a lead on the real killer and forget about you. In the meantime, everything he said about what he can do for us at this point in time makes sense. It's about time that we have an advocate in this mess. Everyone is against us."

"But..."

"No buts. It's settled. I'm bringing him back in the room. Even if this goes on longer than I expect, there is no expense that is too great to protect your life. Think of it this way, if we aren't willing to spend what is necessary to defend you and you are wrongfully convicted of this crime, what would you think as you sit in your jail cell about the decision we made today that was based solely on saving money?"

He then got up, walked to the door and brought Orensen back into the room.

"Here is your retainer check. We want you to start right away" my father told him.

"You've made the right decision" Orensen replied. "Let's get to work."

Chapter 22

My attorney's first order of business was to call Chief Lumpkin to inform him that I would no longer be communicating with the police without the presence of legal counsel. After Jeff Orensen hung up the phone, he reiterated to me very clearly that I was not to answer any questions and/or go anywhere voluntarily with the police without him being present. Furthermore, I was instructed that should I be arrested, I must not say a word to anyone other than to request my attorney.

Orensen's next order of business was to set up a press conference for later that day. As a result of his office having numerous media contacts, as well as the media's substantial interest in my case, getting a turnout for a press conference on such short notice was not a problem.

We decided that the best location for the press conference would be in front of my parents' home. This way, it may come across to viewers as a more personal plea for privacy from a grieving family who has had to endure tremendous scrutiny from the press. Conversely, if we were to hold the press conference at my attorney's downtown office, it may appear as if I am running away to hide from the gruesome truth. Also, a press conference in his office would look too corporate. Instead, we believed that a more personal approach was warranted in the circumstances.

We also decided that Orensen would introduce himself as a spokesperson for the family rather than as our attorney at this point in time. The reason was that I hadn't been formally charged with any crime as of yet; therefore, there was no need to use the term 'attorney' and give the wrong connotation to a general public who may adhere to a flawed notion that the retention of legal counsel implied guilt.

The press conference was called for 4 p.m. and started precisely at that time. Every major media outlet was represented among the many reporters present. There had to be over 100 reporters crowded together on my parents' front lawn, driveway, and extending out onto the street for more than a house length in both directions.

We had strategically determined beforehand that Jeff Orensen would do all the talking. He would give a brief prepared statement after which the press conference would end. Neither he, nor anyone else, would answer any questions.

Orensen stepped up to the podium that his staff had set up on the front steps of my parents' house, and with many cameras and microphones aimed at him, he delivered the following statement:

"Good afternoon. Thank you for coming out on short notice. My name is Jeff Orensen. I am a friend of the Stohler family and I have agreed to act as a spokesperson for the family during this incredibly trying ordeal.

"As you know, a truly horrible, tragic, and senseless murder of a wonderful and beautiful young woman has occurred. As everyone in this community is heartsick about this tragedy, you can imagine how difficult this is for the family. Therefore, the family politely and respectfully requests for the media and for the community as a whole to allow them the time and space to grieve their loss in peace and in privacy.

"The family has utmost faith in Garrowville's police department to conduct their investigation thoroughly so that the person or persons responsible for this heinous crime can be brought to justice. We know that the police will leave no stones unturned in their dogged and determined search to uncover the truth. We are confident that Chief Carl Lumpkin and his veteran staff of investigators will explore all angles and all possible explanations and suspects to assure that the culprit or culprits are taken off the streets as soon as possible.

"The family is as anxious as everyone else to make sure that the case is solved and that Jennifer gets the justice she deserves. As such, the family has been very cooperative with the investigation, and has responded to every request made of them thus far. Going forward, with my assistance, the family will continue to work with the investigators in any way possible.

"Finally, we ask that the media and the public as a whole allow the police to do their work, and that everyone await the accumulation of all information and evidence before jumping to any conclusions. We also respectfully ask that the media and the residents of Garrowville remember that in our country we are all innocent until proven guilty beyond any reasonable doubt in a court of law.

"Thank you for your time this afternoon."

At that point, Jeff Orensen stepped away from the podium and gently ushered me and my parents back toward the house. As we stepped back, I heard many questions simultaneously being shouted at us. Orensen turned back just for a moment to state that no questions would be fielded at this time and to again thank everyone for their attendance. He then turned away from the crowd again and this time more emphatically led us back into the house.

The press loitered around outside for a little while longer until the two members of Lumpkin's staff present at the press conference started instructing the remaining attendees to depart. Every local news station had broadcast Orensen's statement live and each one now had reporters and legal pundits analyzing this latest development. I was fairly certain that such analysis would be going on throughout Garrowville that night.

Chapter 23

One of the many places around town where the press conference was the dominant topic of conversation was at Jimmy's Diner.

"Why would he need a 'spokesperson' if he didn't do anything?" said patron Mark Stanton. "If he is innocent, all he'd need to say is 'I'm innocent.' He wouldn't need to conduct an elaborate press conference for that!"

"Spokesperson is just a deceptive way of saying 'lawyer' without admitting to having hired a lawyer" added Chris Timmons, another customer.

"Only guilty people need lawyers" proclaimed Marcia Bennett to a chorus of agreement from others around her. "Lawyers are hired to get people off when they committed a crime. If you don't commit a crime, you don't need a lawyer."

Elsewhere around town, similar sentiments were being expressed. Naturally, who else would you expect to televise public reactions, than our town's favorite on-scene reporter, Chelsea Forgeous? She made her way around the area to gauge the reactions of the locals and air the highlights, such as the following interview, on the evening news.

"I'm Chelsea Forgeous reporting live in Town Square in downtown Garrowville where it seems that the talk of the town is about today's press conference. With me is Garrowville resident James Libman. Mr. Libman, what was your reaction to today's press conference?"

"I'm disgusted by it. How dare he hide behind the protection of a 'spokesperson' who had the nerve to say that they want the culprit or culprits to be apprehended? You know what that reminded me of? It reminded me of O.J. Simpson saying that he was searching for the real killer or killers. Well, Mr. Spokesperson, the culprit was standing right behind you. The search should be very easy!"

"You seem convinced that Michael Stohler is guilty. What makes you so certain?" asked Forgeous.

"Common sense makes me certain. He had motive and they were having problems. He has a life insurance policy on her and he has keys to the house. There was no forced entry. And besides, who else would have motive to kill her? There's no one else. You don't have to be a rocket scientist to figure out what happened here! It is simple common sense! Everyone knows Michael is a murderer!"

"What did you think when Michael Stohler's spokesperson reminded us of the notion of "innocent until proven guilty" in our country?"

"I thought that it is he who needs to be reminded of a few things in this country. For example, in this country, we are all entitled to our opinion and to freely express our opinion. It is my strong opinion that Michael Stohler is a murderer and it is my right to say so! So I am doing just that! Michael's a murderer! He deserves the death penalty for what he did!"

With that, the crowd that had gathered behind James Libman roared with approval. Before long, as Forgeous was signing off, the crowd was repeatedly chanting "Michael's a Murderer." It didn't take much to rile up this crowd with their pre-conceived notions, and James Libman did just that. So much for our "innocent until proven guilty" campaign.

Other stations had similar reports from various parts of town. However, the most disturbing report airing that evening was an interview with Chief Lumpkin who mocked the fact that we had been cooperative thus far. In that interview Lumpkin stated that I have refused to answer certain of his questions and that we had informed him this morning that we would no longer be communicating with him.

Of course that was simply untrue. Orensen had told him that I would no longer answer any of his questions without Orensen being present. We never said that we wouldn't communicate with him at all. But it appears that Lumpkin either has selective memory or is one who doesn't like to let the facts get in the way of his desired spin to the media.

However, Lumpkin was not alone in his single-minded quest to pin this crime on me as soon as possible. There was another, even higher ranking official, with the same motive.

Chapter 24

Stanley Murdoch came from a family tradition of power, prestige, and wealth in Pennsylvania. From early in childhood, it was made clear to him by his family patriarchs that the legal profession was the way to make a name for oneself. It was the best and most rewarding avenue to money and fame.

Stanley's grandfather, Jacob Murdoch, was a powerful district attorney best known for cracking down on the mob in Philadelphia. After being credited with cleansing the city of criminal activity, he was elected mayor, serving two terms before becoming governor of Pennsylvania.

Stanley's father and Jacob's son, Nelson Murdoch was a prosecutor and district attorney in western Pennsylvania. He prosecuted and gained convictions in several high profile capital cases before becoming an influential judge. He has also written several best-selling books about his most well-known cases.

Stanley attended law school at Carnegie Melon, where he finished first in his class. Due to his academic standing and his lineage, he was in high demand among the most prestigious law firms throughout Pennsylvania. Stanley Murdoch chose one of the largest and most powerful firms in the region, Reemer Caldwell, LLP, to start his career. However, after several years working as one of many lawyers on the defense teams in several big corporate litigations, he yearned for more spotlight for himself.

Stanley Murdoch didn't want to work on corporate cases, didn't want to work as just one member of a large legal team, and didn't want to work on the defense side of the courtroom. To Stanley, the true rewards of the profession, as evidenced by his heritage, was to crack down on criminals, put them away, and reap the ensuing public recognition and prestige.

So, Stanley Murdoch crossed over to the other side of the courtroom. He worked as a prosecutor, gradually working his way up the ladder until recently becoming his county's district attorney. He had been in that position for less than one rather uneventful year. Uneventful, that was, until the murder of Jennifer Stohler.

For Stanley Murdoch, the Stohler murder was the first big ticket, high profile case to cross his desk since becoming district attorney. In fact, it was the first high profile case he's seen at any point during his time on the prosecution side of the courtroom. It was the type of case that can make or break the career of an ambitious district attorney, who sought the fame, fortune, and notoriety of his family's previous generations.

Stanley Murdoch also had political aspirations. He had his eyes on the governor's office, maybe higher. He was going to be the most successful and powerful Murdoch yet, and this was just the case to jump start that process.

This case had everything. It had a tragic victim who was loved by everyone; someone who had devoted her life to her students, her church, and various other great causes. She was the prototypical All-American girl; a cheerleader and prom queen. This case had an element of greed, as the victim had been murdered by a money hungry business owner desperate to keep his business, reputation, and legacy alive with the funds from a life insurance policy taken out in a large sum not long before the murder. This case had captured the attention of the population, making it one that can propel its heroes to new heights of fame and fortune. Quite simply, this was the case Stanley Murdoch needed to get to where he had to be in his career.

Unfortunately, this case also had a police department handling a murder investigation despite having no experience in such matters. What Stanley Murdoch didn't need, and couldn't afford, was for this gold mine of a case to be butchered by the police. It was an open and shut case. Just gather the evidence, arrest the obvious suspect, and Stanley Murdoch would personally handle the prosecution, putting away a despicable murderer before the adoring eyes of the public.

But it had already been more than a week since the murder, and other than a lot of interviews, press conferences, and other media noise, there appeared to be no tangible progress. What was going on with Lumpkin's team down in Garrowville? Why were they dragging their feet? It was time to pay Lumpkin a visit and crack the whip. Stanley Murdoch's fame and fortune was not to be needlessly delayed.

So on Monday December 21, 2009, District Attorney and aspiring governor-to-be Stanley Murdoch marched into the Garrowville police station to get an update from Chief Lumpkin and to provide the necessary instruction and motivation to expedite the investigation and eventual arrest.

"Lumpkin!" barked Murdoch, "What are you guys doing down here? It's been more than a week! What evidence have you compiled thus far? We all know who did this. How much longer before there is a public outcry railing against us for not arresting the obvious suspect?"

"Good morning Mr. Murdoch" replied Lumpkin. "We are working on it. We conducted searches of the crime scene, the suspect's parents' house, the suspect's car, and his office. We interviewed neighbors, friends of the victim, co-workers of both of them, and patrons from the bar the suspect was at the night before. We've examined cell phone records and we are awaiting the results of the CSI's examination of the crime scene. We also have the suspect on around-the-clock surveillance. We are doing everything we can do at this time."

Murdoch then requested that Lumpkin rehash to him all facts as known thus far. Lumpkin led Murdoch toward the chalkboard in the office which currently contained the following:

Case facts:
- Victim was shot once in forehead from close range.
- The weapon was a .22 caliber handgun.
- The weapon is not at the scene, thus eliminating suicide as a possibility.
- Estimated time of death is 2 a.m. to 4 a.m.
- No signs of forced entry. Victim likely knew the killer.
- Front door was found open. Likely where the killer fled the scene.
- Jewelry box was open on the dresser, possibly to make it look like a robbery.
- Victim's wedding ring is missing.

Suspect facts:
- Married to victim.
- Having marital problems – sleeping at parents.
- Denies the fact that victim was considering divorce.
- Last spoke to victim just after she had a meeting with a divorce lawyer.
- Has money problems.
- Has a life insurance policy on victim.
- Has no alibi at time of crime.
- Likely was intoxicated at time of crime.
- Was late to work the next morning (very unusual).
- Has a key to house.
- Probably has a girlfriend but denies it.

"We need more" Murdoch emphatically stated. "Individually these are each circumstantial in nature. We need physical evidence. We need to bring him in again and get a confession. Anything you have to do to get that confession! What about others who have spoken to him? If he won't confess to us, maybe he'll pour his heart out to someone else. Everyone needs to unload at some point, especially in matters of this magnitude. I want us to interview everyone he talks to. Maybe he'll get drunk one night and spill his guts to a bartender. He needs to be followed everywhere and we need to talk to anyone with whom he comes in contact."

Murdoch then came up with another idea. "We also need to set up a hotline for anyone to call who may have any information. Set up a press conference and repeatedly cite the number. Make sure all of the television and radio stations, and the newspapers have the number and that they run it. Someone out there knows something and maybe we haven't gotten to that person yet."

"We've spoken to practically everyone, Mr. Murdoch" Lumpkin protested. "This isn't a big town. We've been making the rounds everywhere."

"I don't care Lumpkin! Just do the hotline. You may even get an anonymous tip; someone who you've spoken to, who didn't want to say something in person. The hotline will give that person a way to get the information to us."

Lumpkin argued further. "The hotline will also give every nut job out there a way to send us off on wild goose chases. Do you know how many false leads and confessions come through on these types of hotlines?"

"So what! Where has the investigation gotten you so far? We need to do something different. Just do it Lumpkin. We'll get something out of the hotline." Murdoch ordered.

Murdoch then added, "As soon as you do get anything good call me immediately. We need to make an arrest and we need to do it as soon as possible! The press is going to be all over us if this drags on much longer. We can all forget any career ambitions if we screw up this case. And God help us if he kills anyone else while we sit here scratching our asses."

"Ok. We're on it Mr. Murdoch. I assure you we'll have an arrest as soon as possible. He's not going to get away with this."

"Good. I'm personally holding you to that Lumpkin. Now, go get him!" Murdoch stated as he marched out the door.

Chapter 25

After more than a week of crying, grieving, battling with the police, listening to my friends and neighbors call me a murderer, and seeing my name dragged through the mud on every media outlet in the area, it was time for me to try to return to some form of normalcy. Was I ready to return to work and face the monumental task of keeping my company afloat? Probably not. I won't ever be truly ready. Without Jennifer, my life will never be the same again, and certainly will never seem right again. But, though there were less of them, I still had employees who counted on me, as well as loyal customers who needed my product. So, with a heavy heart, and with the stress of an ongoing police investigation against me, I returned to work on Monday, December 21.

The first indication that this would not be a normal workday was the police car trailing me from my parents' house to the office. In actuality, I noted that the police had been trailing me all week. I'm not sure if they were trying and failing to be subtle about it, or if they didn't care if I saw them. Either way, everywhere I went, the police weren't far behind.

My police tail often attracted the attention of other motorists and pedestrians along the way. There was not much police activity in the area, so the presence of a police car, especially in the days immediately after a murder, was an attention grabber. As a result, I had to endure a lot of dirty looks, heckling, obscene gestures, and even a few objects thrown at my parents' car en route to work. I drove my parents' car because my car, graffiti and all, had been confiscated by the police.

Not long into my work day, I noted several protesters gathering in front of the main entrance to the office, with signs saying "Murderer" and other similarly themed comments. As they marched and shouted outside, some of my employees expressed concern for their safety. My tailing police officer, parked outside, didn't seem to be overly concerned as he let the protestors do as they pleased.

At 10 a.m., I met with several key members of my company's management team to be caught up on the past week at the office. Predictably, the news was grim. Several of our larger customers and suppliers had informed us that they intended to stop doing business with us. They didn't want to chance losing business as a result of dealing with a murderer. Some of these customers and suppliers had done business with Stohler Steel for generations. They were my friends. Their fathers were friends of my father. Their grandfathers were friends of my grandfather. But all that meant little in comparison to the public relations fear of losing business for dealing with a perceived murderer. Apparently "innocent until proven guilty" had as little impact in the business world as it did in the community. I now realized that in the corporate world decisions are usually based first on public relations, which of course, is driven by the court of public opinion. And as I've already learned the hard way, the court of public opinion has no patience for "innocent until proven guilty."

I informed my management team that I would personally call all of these long-time business partners. I believed that if I spoke with them and explained my side of the story, that our close relationships over the years would ultimately prevail and that I can convince them to continue working with us. I was wrong.

Most of them refused to take my calls. The few I did talk to explained to me rather clearly that they couldn't afford the risks associated with dealing with such a public pariah. A couple of them were sympathetic and understanding, but apologetically said there was nothing they could do; that the risk of doing business with me far outweighed the potential gains. They wished me luck while also asking me not to contact them again. In summary, in the past week I lost the majority of the previously low business level I had before losing my wife. The business could not be sustained much longer at this rate.

Although I knew I'd be better off locking myself in my office and eating lunch at my desk, I needed to get out for a little bit. The protestors outside were in front of the building, so I went out the back way. I headed to my friend Jimmy's place, Jimmy's Diner; a place I had eaten lunch hundreds of times in the past. Jimmy was a great friend and I knew that if there was anyone around town I could count on it was him. I was wrong again.

It was before noon, so I was hoping to beat the lunch crowd, eat quickly, and get out before it got busy. The diner was less than half full but the people who were eating there certainly noticed my entrance. I immediately got sneers, jeers, and insults of varying and unrepeatable types. Additionally, a few people who had been outside the diner followed me inside so that they too can let their feelings be known. A couple of patrons even stormed out, saying that they wouldn't eat there if I was eating there.

Undoubtedly noting the commotion, my buddy Jimmy came out from the kitchen and walked over to me. I knew where this was heading. It was going to be the same conversation I had just endured with long-time associates on the phone all morning. Jimmy put his arm on my back, gently leading me toward the door and said, "Look buddy. I'm really sorry about this, but I can't afford to have you coming in here. I'll lose all my customers. I hope you understand. Sorry." He then opened the door and led me out.

Another friend lost to the court of public opinion. I figured my day couldn't get any worse. Once again, I was wrong.

Chapter 26

I returned to my office and had lunch at my desk, which was what I should have done in the first place. As I was finishing, Brenda poked her head in to tell me that Chief Lumpkin was here to see me. Just what I needed. Without waiting for any further invitation, or any invitation for that matter, Lumpkin stormed in.

"Hello Chief. What a pleasant surprise" I sarcastically said before he had a chance to say anything first. "What brings you here today?"

"We need to talk Stohler. I suggest you come with me to the station."

"Am I under arrest?" I asked.

"No. Not yet anyway."

"Then I believe my lawyer has informed you that I wouldn't be accompanying you anywhere, nor would I speak with you or any of your cronies without him being present."

"So now he's your 'lawyer'! That's funny. On television he introduced himself as your spokesperson. Which is it Stohler?"

"It is not relevant Chief. Unless I'm under arrest, I'm not obligated to come with you. And I'm certainly not going to answer any questions here or anywhere without Mr. Orensen by my side."

"Only people with something to hide need a lawyer or spokesperson to protect them. Innocent people don't need to be protected by anyone. So call him. I don't care. We'll get to the bottom of this one way or the other."

I called him. Jeff Orensen advised me to tell Lumpkin that Orensen and I would meet him at the station at 3 p.m. I was not to go there with Lumpkin. Orensen didn't want to chance me speaking to him while being transported to the station. Instead Orensen would come pick me up and take me there himself. I hung up and informed Lumpkin of the game plan. He wasn't thrilled, but sensing that it would be his only way to get me to the station for questioning, he reluctantly agreed.

"You'd better show up" Lumpkin meaninglessly threatened on his way out.

Soon afterwards, Orensen arrived. "What did he say and how did you respond before calling me?" he asked.

"Nothing really. He said he wanted to take me to the station to talk and I reminded him that I wasn't doing so without you. He mocked me for that then said to call you."

"You didn't say anything else to him right?"

"No."

"Ok. Good. The good news here is that obviously the police don't have much. He wasn't here to arrest you. He was here to grasp at straws. He figures that the more he talks to you, the more he can either bully you into a confession or get you to slip up somehow. Let's head over there. Once we are there, let me speak first. Then don't answer any questions or say anything at all without me giving you the green light. I'll do so by nodding my head to you. As soon as I say that the discussion is over, we both get up and walk out without saying anything else. Got it?"

"Yes" I answered. "Thank you for coming."

We rode in silence together in Orensen's car for the quick drive to the station. Once we arrived, Orensen led the way, walking in front of me as he confidently marched inside.

"Ok Lumpkin, let's get a few things straight before we get started" Orensen stated immediately after entering. "Number one, we are here voluntarily to assist you as best we can with your investigation. We are not obligated to be here. Number two, this will be a discussion between two parties with a mutual interest in apprehending the person or persons who committed this murder. It will not be conducted as an interrogation. Number three, we can answer or not answer any question we so choose, and because this is a two-way discussion, we may even ask some questions of you. And number four, we can end the discussion and leave at any time we want. Do you understand these points Lumpkin? I hope so because your understanding and agreement are prerequisites for this discussion to happen at all."

"Yes, Mr. 'Spokesperson.'" Lumpkin snidely responded as he started to lead us toward the same interrogation room where he had previously questioned me.

"Actually there is a number five" Orensen added. "This discussion will not take place in an interrogation room where you typically question suspects. We will speak with you in your office."

I was starting to really like Jeff Orensen. I had to admit that my concern about the costs of hiring a big-time lawyer was furthest from my mind as I watched him dictate the terms of our meeting with Lumpkin. He was exactly what I needed in the circumstances. Lumpkin now knew he wouldn't be able to bully me. In fact, he had to "walk on eggshells" as he had to figure that one false step by him and Orensen would end the meeting.

Lumpkin reluctantly led the way toward his office. He entered first and quickly turned a chalkboard around. I assume he didn't want us to see what was written on it. He then motioned us to sit down in chairs in front of his desk as he went around to his seat behind it. He didn't waste any time getting started.

"Michael, who do you think may have killed your wife?"

Orensen jumped in to answer "Isn't that your job, Lumpkin? Haven't you been investigating any and all possibilities?"

"You said that this was a two-way discussion with the mutual interest to find the killer or killers" Lumpkin responded, "so I wanted to hear from Michael what his thoughts were."

Orensen lightly nodded toward me while giving me a silent look telling me to be careful.

"I really don't know Chief. I wish I had more to share with you on that front." I answered. I knew that didn't really help much, but it was the truth.

"Helpful as ever Stohler" Lumpkin chided.

"Careful Lumpkin" warned Orensen. "Do you have any other questions?"

"Yes I do. I want to hear again Michael's step-by-step timeline of his activities the night of the murder."

Orensen put his hand up to stop me from saying anything. He then said toward Lumpkin, "Technically, that is not a question. I asked you if you had any other questions and instead, you made a statement. And anyway, Michael has already informed you of all of his actions from that night. You can assume that all information previously given is still the same. Do you have any questions not previously asked that may help you shed new light on the case?"

"Where is Jennifer's wedding ring Michael?" Lumpkin asked.

I looked to Orensen. He nodded and again gave me the 'be careful' look. I don't know how he did that, but I knew exactly that is what he was saying to me without uttering a word.

"I don't know. All I know is that Radford told me it wasn't on her finger or in our house when he found her and it wasn't on her finger when we buried her."

Lumpkin lost it. "Where is it Michael? Did you sell it? Where is it?"

"That's enough Lumpkin" Orensen shouted back. "He said he doesn't know where it is. Now it is my turn to ask a question. What other possible angles have the police pursued besides Michael?"

"Don't tell me how to do my job Orensen! I don't tell you how to do yours. Why was there no forced entry at the house? Jennifer obviously knew her killer. Who else was going over there in the middle of the night?"

"You didn't answer my question Lumpkin" Orensen snapped back. "I asked you about other angles you are pursuing. You obviously don't have much evidence against Michael other than your suspicions, so I would hope that the police are keeping an open mind as to any and all possibilities. So I will ask you again, what other angles are you pursuing?"

"There are no other possible angles!" Lumpkin shouted. "Michael is the only "angle" there is! He is a murderer! You are standing here protecting a murderer! Do you understand that?"

"That's it. This discussion is over. Michael, we are out of here." Orensen rose and motioned for me to walk out with him. I happily obliged.

"Where's the ring? Why was your phone turned off that night? Why were you late to work the next day?" Lumpkin fired off questions as he followed us out the door. "Why did you need such a large life insurance policy on her? This isn't over Michael. I can't wait to slap handcuffs on you. I'm going to make sure that I am the one to do it."

He was still shouting as we got into Orensen's car and drove off. So much for the mutually helpful chat Orensen had described to Lumpkin at the outset. That didn't last long. It was unnerving to think how narrow minded this investigation was unfolding, but it was good to have Jeff Orensen in my corner.

"Michael. It's apparent that the police are not interested in any explanation that doesn't point to you as the murderer, or having set up the murder" Orensen stated as we drove back to my office. "My firm has a private investigator that we use on a case by case basis who can look into matters on our behalf. He's very good. I suggest that we use him on your case. We need to find alternative scenarios as to what may have happened to your wife so that the police and everyone else do not remain hell bent on nailing you for the crime."

"What would it cost to bring your investigator on board?" I asked.

"That would ultimately depend on how much time he'll need to uncover the truth and what expenses he would incur in doing so. I won't lie to you, it is not cheap. But he's saved several of my clients in the past and I would propose that the cost would be worth it to you if he ultimately saves you as well."

"For now, I think I'll pass. As you noted earlier, the police can't have any evidence against me, otherwise they would have arrested me by now. Nor can there be any evidence for them to get because I didn't commit this crime. Eventually they'll have to realize that and start looking in other directions."

"Ok. Your choice. But I wouldn't wait too long on this. Let me know if you change your mind."

When we arrived back at my office, I thanked him again for coming today and told him I'd keep his offer in mind regarding the investigator.

In the back of my mind I kept replaying the scene that had just unfolded at the station and Lumpkin's promise to slap handcuffs on me. Why would they arrest me? I didn't do anything! They don't have any evidence, nor could they as there can't be any evidence against an innocent person! This is the United States! These things don't happen here. Sure, they may happen in other places around the world, but not here. This is a free country. We have constitutional rights. So, what should I have to worry about?

I didn't realize yet how truly naïve I was about such matters. I would learn very soon.

Chapter 27

Chief Lumpkin stormed back into the station and threw his notepad across the room in disgust. He then swatted a few miscellaneous items off of the front counter for good measure. He realized that he didn't handle the meeting with Michael Stohler and his lawyer very well, and that he likely blew his chance to question his suspect further as the investigation progresses.

It was easy to understand why Lumpkin was getting very agitated regarding all facets of the case. For starters, it was moving too slowly. They hadn't yet been able to uncover any concrete evidence. No "smoking gun" had been unearthed. Quite simply, they knew who the killer was, but couldn't prove it. What could be more frustrating than that for anyone in law enforcement?

Meanwhile, a killer roamed free on the streets, meaning that the very public who Lumpkin was responsible to protect continued to remain at risk. He and his staff have had to field many complaints asking why Michael was out and about, free as a bird, and what the police are doing to get him off the streets. Lumpkin and his staff have also had to endure constant press coverage of the case, which most recently had started focusing on the lack of progress in the investigation and the absence of an arrest. Whenever possible, the press had been showing pictures or video of Michael Stohler around town. For example, today's midday news report showed Stohler strolling into Jimmy's Diner for lunch. What must the public think of a police chief who allows a killer to eat freely among all the business men and women at lunch time in a popular Garrowville restaurant? Lumpkin's reputation was taking a big hit.

As if the lack of progress and evidence, the civilian complaints, and the negative press coverage weren't enough aggravation, that morning Lumpkin had to endure admonishment and threats from a powerful and ambitious district attorney, who made it clear that he was getting impatient with the investigation and that he was holding Lumpkin personally responsible. In other words, Lumpkin could forget about any career advancement if he blew this case.

And finally, to top it all off, his only suspect had "lawyered up" to the point where it is virtually impossible to interrogate him. Lumpkin was confident that if he could lock himself in a room with Stohler and continuously question him, that Lumpkin would be able to get a confession. Or if not a confession, he would at least be able to catch Stohler with inconsistencies in his obviously false story. But that wasn't happening with the high powered attorney hanging around.

So, you can see why Lumpkin was irritable. He had tremendous stress on him and the only way to alleviate that stress was to make a very public arrest of

Michael Stohler as soon as possible. But first he had to get more evidence. Nothing yet had come back from the searches conducted last week, nor was there anything yet from the CSI unit's investigation of the crime scene. He had tried Stanley Murdoch's advice from this morning to interrogate Stohler further, but that didn't go so well. Murdoch did have some other ideas though, and it was time to put them into action.

So, Lumpkin made all the necessary arrangements to set up a tips hotline. He half-jokingly thought of making the phone number 1-800-MICHAEL as it was the right amount of digits, but he thought better of it. He contacted all media outlets to inform them of the hotline and he set up a press conference for later that day to publicly announce it. Hopefully very soon, the tips would be pouring in. He figured he'd get a lot of bogus tips and crank calls, but maybe there would be a few useful ones as well.

Lumpkin then got on his walkie-talkie and gave the rest of the police department specific instructions. Very loudly and animatedly, Lumpkin barked out orders that going forward there would always be least two officers tailing Stohler. Whenever Stohler came in contact with anyone, one of the officers would subsequently question that person. Lumpkin relayed his hunch (which was really Murdoch's idea but Lumpkin didn't bother giving such credit) that Michael Stohler would slip up somehow and may even confess to someone. Lumpkin added that the confession or slip likely won't happen while talking to the police, so it was imperative that they pounce on any other opportunity that presented itself.

Lumpkin told his officers that no one could keep a secret of this magnitude to himself. Stohler would need to unload his burden somehow and confess to someone. He may also need to unload a wedding ring, murder weapon, and other evidence as well. Police surveillance needed to be more intensive. No contacts go unquestioned. No actions go unwatched. The police weren't fooling around anymore. They needed evidence and they needed it now.

Chapter 28

While Monday, December 21, 2009 was a rough day, it only got tougher as the week progressed. Business was continuously declining. Public pressure caused more and more of my customers to stop doing business with us. Some of the citizens of Garrowville started a movement to boycott any company doing business with Stohler Steel, and they managed to get coverage of their movement in the Garrowville Gazette. The result was that I lost even more customers and suppliers. Almost every hour during the week, at least one customer or supplier informed me of their intention to cease working with us. The long-term standing of our relationships or the quality of our work did not matter. All that mattered was that these entities couldn't risk the public wrath for dealing with Stohler Steel.

Protests and demonstrations increased outside our building, which led to some of my employees resigning that week. They feared for their safety coming to and from work and they feared living in a community where everyone knew everyone else. Thus, everyone knew that they worked for a perceived murderer. Some of them were getting threats and they couldn't risk their own safety or that of their families.

Actually, these resignations would prove irrelevant. The simple truth was that the company couldn't be sustained much longer due to the magnitude of business lost. I only had a few remaining orders to fill and no new orders on the horizon. Even if I were able to get new orders from my dwindling list of customers, I didn't have suppliers from whom to get the required raw materials to fulfill them. I also did not have enough money left in the company to meet payroll for more than one more month.

So, on Wednesday December 23, 2009, after four generations of my family's business, spanning over 100 years, I regretfully and tearfully had to disclose to my remaining loyal employees, some of whom had worked with the company for over 20 years, that we would be shutting down the business. I told them that the closing would be effective at the end of the business day on December 31st, which gave us just enough time to complete the few remaining orders we had. I also told everyone that to thank them for all their hard work and loyalty, I'd be giving each of them one month's worth of severance, which was the maximum that I could afford. I even included the employees who had just resigned that week in these severance payments. I'd give everyone more if I could, but even that amount was only possible because I'd leave no money from the business for myself.

I don't know who the leak was, but somehow, the headlines in the Garrowville Gazette on Thursday December 24, 2009, pertained to my laying off all remaining employees. The ensuing story focused on how evil I was to do such a horrible thing on the brink of Christmas to the few people who had remained by my side. I was called the Grinch, but of course, that label was the least severe among the things I had been getting called all around town. Nevertheless, I was now known as a murderer who laid off a company full of employees during the holiday season. However low public perception had previously been, it was now worse.

For obvious reasons, I didn't venture out in public very much. I spent the week almost exclusively at my parents' house and at the office. During the few times I was outside, I observed an intensification of my police surveillance. Now I had two police cars tailing me. I'm not sure what they expected to accomplish with more of their limited resources following me around, but I couldn't help but think that with two of the four members of the Garrowville police always with me, it must be a prime opportunity for any real criminals out there to conduct their business. So much for protecting our community. Whoever the real murderer or murderers were, I assumed that they were getting a good laugh.

Chapter 29

Thursday, December 24th was also the day that Chief Lumpkin got the call he was hoping for on his newly created tips hotline. The hotline was up and running two days earlier. But during the first couple of days the police were bombarded with more than 200 useless calls.

Many of the callers cited various circumstantial reasons why Michael Stohler had to be the murderer, such as his infidelity, the life insurance policy, the impending divorce, etc. None of these "tips" revealed anything the police didn't already know. Numerous callers angrily blasted the police for having not made an arrest yet and inquired how they can let the obvious culprit be seen around the town as if nothing had happened. Some of these callers expressed concern for their safety as a murderer was on the loose and they questioned what, if anything, the police were doing about it. It was apparent from these calls that public pressure on the police was mounting and the perception thus far of how the police had been handling the case was very poor.

There were also a few crank calls, such as one creative caller who informed the police that Lee Harvey Oswald had shot Jennifer and that he had acted alone. There were even two confessions left on the hotline. The police followed up on those confessions but quickly ruled them out as they came from two inmates who had been locked up for the past few years in a state mental institution.

But finally, after enduring all of the above inane volume, came the call the police had wanted. A Garrowville resident named Morton Engfield stated that he lived a few blocks away from the crime scene and that at about 2:45 a.m. on the morning of the murder, he had witnessed a large vehicle traveling at a high speed, zoom by him as he was waiting to turn onto his driveway.

Engfield left his address and a number to reach him on the hotline. The police quickly deduced from the address that it was directly en route between the crime scene and Michael's parent's house. And of course, the timing was right. Lumpkin immediately dispatched Officer Hodges to Engfield's residence to gather more information.

"Good morning Mr. Engfield. I am Officer Hodges. Thank you for your phone call to our hotline. I would like to ask you some follow-up questions."

"Sure. No problem. Please come in."

"Thank you." Hodges responded as he entered the house. Engfield led him to the living room area and invited the officer to sit down. He then offered a drink, which Hodges politely declined. Hodges then got to work.

"Mr. Engfield. Please tell me exactly what you saw in the early morning hours of Friday, December 11th."

"I was returning home from work. I work the 6 p.m. to 2 a.m. shift at a manufacturing plant just outside of Pittsburgh. I usually get home between 2:30 and 2:40 a.m., but on that night, I was a few minutes later than usual because I had to stop for gas. So, I believe the time was right around 2:45 a.m. I was driving east on my street, Penley Lane. I made it to my house and was about to turn left onto my driveway, when I heard and saw a car coming toward me from the opposite direction, traveling at a high rate of speed. I waited for the car to pass before making my turn, and it whizzed by me. I thought to myself that the car was going too fast on a small residential street. I then turned into my driveway, came in, and went to sleep. I didn't think anything of it again, until the thought occurred to me this morning as I was reading more about the murder in the newspaper, that based on the time the murder took place and the fact that I am just a few blocks from the crime scene, that maybe the car I saw was driven by the killer fleeing the scene. So, I decided to call your hotline."

"Thank you for doing so Mr. Engfield. Can you tell me anything you noticed about the car other than the speed it was traveling?"

"Well, it was very dark out, so I couldn't really see much. But I did notice as it was coming toward me that the right headlight was out. Also, as it raced by me, I could see that it was a fairly large car. It was almost definitely a four-door vehicle."

"Did you happen to get a license plate number? Even a partial? What about make or model?"

"No. I'm sorry. It was too dark and it was going too fast."

"Did you notice anything about the driver?"

"I am pretty sure it was a male driver. I did look toward the driver as he went by. Other than that though, I didn't notice much else. Too dark."

"Did you see if there was anyone else in the car?"

"I only looked toward the driver. I wasn't really looking at any other seats inside the car, so I can't be sure as to whether or not there was anyone else in the car."

"Mr. Engfield, our officers had made the rounds throughout a several block radius of the crime scene in the days immediately after the murder. Didn't one of our police officers come to your residence previously asking if you had seen or heard anything?"

"Yes. An Officer Riley came here later that day. He asked me if I had heard a gunshot and I said that I hadn't. He did ask me if I knew anything useful about the murder, and I again told him I hadn't. I'm sorry. I hadn't put two-and-two together yet about the car I saw and the murder. Truthfully, I had simply forgotten about the car by the next day. I should have told him then."

"It's ok. Thank you for calling us today. This information is very useful."

Hodges asked Engfield a few more questions, then informed him that the prosecutor may need his testimony should there be a trial in the near future. Engfield assured the officer that he would be happy to assist any way in which he could. The police finally had a witness who had seen something useful to add to their list of evidence.

Chapter 30

The fact that it was the holiday season made my depression unbearable. It would be my first Christmas without Jennifer since we started dating in high school. Nothing is lonelier during the holidays than being without your soul mate for the first time since you met. The idea of being without her on Christmas Day was intolerable. So I did the only thing I could in the circumstances. I spent most of the holiday beside her at her grave.

On a snowy Christmas Day morning, accompanied by my rear police convoy, I drove to the cemetery. On the cold ground, I lied beside her. I told her how much I loved her and how sorry I was for all the problems and fights we had in our final times together. I was sorry that I had tried to curtail all the events and causes she cared so much about. I was sorry that our final conversations had been arguments. I was sorry that I hadn't been there at the house with her that night so that I could protect her. I was sorry that I hadn't had a chance to say goodbye and to tell her that despite all of our problems, how I felt about her. And most of all, I was sorry that it was her who was gone rather than me. I was so sorry for all of this and I kept apologizing to her over and over. I wished I could turn back the clock and undo everything that had happened.

As if to add salt to my wounds, and to make it an even worse Christmas day, I was pulled over by one of the tailing police cars on my way back to my parents' house. Apparently, the right headlight of my parents' car was out and I was issued a ticket.

Really? This is what the police needed to be focusing on right now? They don't have more important things to worry about? I just figured they were looking to harass me anyway they could. But I didn't care. The ticket was the least of my concerns these days.

As you can imagine, I was still somewhat of an emotional wreck when I returned to the office on Monday December 28. At one point, Brenda must have heard me sobbing in my office and checked in to see if I was alright. I broke down and while crying told her how I visited Jennifer at the cemetery. I also told her that I couldn't believe that everyone thought I killed Jennifer. What happened to all my friends? What happened to the only hometown I've known my whole life? I kept repeating, "Why does everyone think I killed my wife?"

Brenda comforted me as best she could. Truthfully, there was not much she could say or do to alleviate my pain. And our relationship wasn't really that close, so she probably felt a bit uneasy finding herself in a role of comforting me. I shouldn't have burdened her in that way, but I guess I had to unload a little bit.

It was very difficult to shoulder the type of pain and despair I had been carrying in the past few weeks without periodically letting out some of the negative emotions.

I thanked Brenda and told her that I was going to leave early and that I'd see her the next day. I hadn't realized yet that the next day, even though just December 29 and still two days before the closing of the business, would be my final day at work. It would also be my final day of freedom.

Chapter 31

Tuesday, December 29, 2009 was the day that Chief Carl Lumpkin had been waiting for since the murder. On that day he had finally accumulated enough evidence to get an arrest warrant for Michael Stohler and to personally make the arrest he'd been dreaming about for nearly three weeks. The breaks were finally going his way and the future looked bright once again.

It started four days earlier on Christmas Day. In accordance with Lumpkin's sage instructions, two officers, Dan Radford and John Riley, in separate cars, followed Michael Stohler as he left his parents' home in the morning. Stohler headed directly to his deceased wife's gravesite where he stayed for several hours. Radford and Riley initially just observed him lying on the ground by where Jennifer was buried.

Then, communicating from their separate cars on the police frequency, they concocted a plan. Radford pulled away to make it appear that he was leaving, but in actuality, he circled to the back of the cemetery, parked his car, and crept up near to Jennifer's grave under the cover of some brush, so that he could watch Michael more closely and perhaps eavesdrop on him in hopes he would say something incriminating.

Radford couldn't get close enough to hear every word clearly, plus the howling wind impeded his efforts, but he was certain that he made out a few key words. He very distinctly heard Michael Stohler say that he was sorry. Radford was certain that he heard Stohler apologize multiple times.

Radford crept back to his car, drove away, and reported this development back to Riley, as well as to Lumpkin. Lumpkin was ecstatic and instructed him to get some bugs from the station and return to the cemetery to try to record Michael's apologies to his wife. But when Radford returned with the bugs, Michael had already departed. No worries, with Radford's testimony, they would have another piece of evidence pointing to Michael Stohler as the killer.

As Stohler drove away from the cemetery, Officer Riley noted that the vehicle the suspect was driving had just one functioning headlight. Riley remembered the tip that had come in the day before and called Lumpkin to see if it was the same side that was out. Lumpkin informed him that the tip was that the vehicle seen speeding away from the crime scene had a right headlight out, upon which Riley told him the same was true of the car Stohler was driving right now.

"He must have been driving his parents' car the night of the murder" Lumpkin stated. "Makes sense too. He figures if anyone sees him driving to or from the crime scene they won't identify it as his car. Why didn't we notice this light out earlier?"

"I don't know Chief. I assume it is because he hasn't been out at night, so he hasn't had his headlights on when we've been tailing him. He has it on today because it is snowing."

"Well, pull him over and give him a ticket. I want to get it on the record that the car has the headlight out so it matches up with what the witness is saying. I'm going to get a search warrant now for the parents' car. I'll have you go over there later on with the warrant to search the car. In the meantime, as you are issuing the ticket, glance around inside the car to see if you notice anything interesting."

"No problem Chief" Riley answered as he turned on his siren to pull over Michael Stohler.

Lumpkin was starting to feel that luck was turning in his favor. He now had the tip, which will also match the ticket Riley was issuing, and he had a confession overheard by Radford. He was getting so close to an arrest he can feel it.

Lumpkin's luck extended to Monday, December 28 when he received a phone call from an employee of Stohler Steel who had also overheard an incriminating statement out of the mouth of Michael Stohler. The employee, Ronald Johnson, reported that he had gone to see Michael in his office. Typically, Michael's secretary Brenda Challey was at a desk just in front of Michael's office, but when Ronald approached, Brenda was not there. So, Ronald walked up to Michael's door and was about to knock when he heard Michael's sobbing voice inside saying "I killed my wife." To be certain, Lumpkin asked Johnson, "Are you 100% sure that you heard him say the exact words 'I killed my wife'?"

"Yes. There is no question that is what he said." Johnson responded.

"Did you enter the office after hearing that?"

"No. I wanted to get away before he knew that I had heard him confess."

"So, if you didn't go in, how are you sure that it was Michael who said this?" Lumpkin inquired.

"It was Michael's office and definitely Michael's voice. Plus, just as I was turning away, Brenda came out and saw me leaving. I then said that I had wanted to see Michael but his door was closed so I thought I'd come back later. I asked her if he was in there and she said 'yes' but that it wasn't a good time to meet with him right now."

Lumpkin thanked Johnson and asked him to come to the station to make an official statement. In the meantime, Lumpkin was giddy about a 2nd reported confession. Now, there can be no doubt. Anyone could argue that perhaps one person had misheard, but two confessions independent from one another? There can be no such mistake.

The final autopsy report was provided to the police later that day. There was no additional news to report as to the cause of death, which everyone already knew to be a single gunshot wound to the head. Also, there was no new development regarding the time of death, which had been correctly estimated at the scene as sometime between 2 a.m. and 4 a.m. However, that timeframe was important to Lumpkin as it was after 2 a.m., which was the latest time covered by Michael Stohler's alibi, and it fit the timing as reported by the hotline's tipster.

Although the search of the parents' vehicle didn't turn up anything useful to the investigation, Lumpkin did get some great news on another front. On Tuesday morning, December 29, Chief Lumpkin received a report from the CSI unit. Upon their analysis of the position of the body, the entrance and exit wounds caused by the path of the bullet, and the location in the bedroom where the bullet was found, they are able to ascertain, with reasonable certainty, where the killer had stood when shooting the victim. More importantly, piecing all that information together, they reported to Lumpkin that they can be reasonably sure that the killer had shot Jennifer with his left hand, most likely meaning that the shooter was a lefty. Additionally, they were able to determine that the killer was likely significantly taller than the victim, and was probably over 6 feet tall. Guess who is a lefty! You got it, Michael Stohler! Guess who is over 6 feet tall! Once again, Michael Stohler!

With all of these latest developments, Lumpkin now believed he had enough evidence to obtain an arrest warrant. He contacted District Attorney Stanley Murdoch to update him on recently gathered evidence. Murdoch agreed that they should proceed with the request for the warrant. Together they submitted the proper paperwork, including a written affidavit to the court, with all evidence they possessed to establish their probable cause. Murdoch also "flexed his muscle" a bit around the courthouse to expedite the process, citing the severity of the case and safety concerns for the public while a murderer was on the loose.

Within an hour, the court granted the arrest warrant. But despite the safety concerns previously cited to get the warrant, both Murdoch and Lumpkin took some extra time to maximize their publicity in making the arrest. Therefore, rather than go directly to Stohler Steel with the warrant and simply make the arrest, a few leaks were made to various media outlets, in which anonymous tipsters informed the press that an arrest was going down at Stohler Steel at 4 p.m. that afternoon. That would give the press adequate time to be there in force, thus assuring that everyone in Garrowville will see that Lumpkin and Murdoch had captured the killer.

The arrest was going to be a media circus and would be the highlight of Chief Lumpkin's long, and until now, not so extraordinary law enforcement career.

Chapter 32

Tuesday, December 29th started out as a predictably slow and depressing day at the office. Work was light and employees were visibly saddened by the imminent end of the company and their jobs. Throughout the morning there were protestors marching and chanting outside our front entrance. But the low morale and the demonstrations outside were to be expected. What wasn't to be expected happened later in the afternoon.

Sometime mid-afternoon, I noted the gradual appearance of news vans and camera crews outside. Upon the appearance of the first news van, I simply thought that one of the stations had decided to run a story on the protesters. No big deal. Not a day went by without some type of negative media coverage for me. But soon thereafter, more news vans, and other members of the media arrived. The press corps outside gradually accumulated to the point where it seemed the whole situation out there was getting out of control. What was going on?

Naturally, all of us inside the office building were frequently peering outside to watch the scene unfold. Shortly afterwards, several police cars arrived. I assumed that it was for crowd control as there were a lot of people outside, many of whom were not in their most sane frame of mind.

However, the police did not seem interested in the crowd. Instead, at approximately 4 p.m., several police officers, including Chief Lumpkin, approached, then entered the building. A few moments later, Lumpkin and his sidekicks were in my office.

With what I am fairly certain was a grin on his face, Chief Lumpkin loudly and very clearly stated, "Michael Stohler. You are under arrest for the murder of Jennifer Stohler."

He then asked me to turn around and place my arms behind my back. I obliged. As he had previously promised, he then personally cuffed me while reading me my Miranda rights. "You have the right to remain silent. Anything you say can and will be used against you in a court of law. You have the right to an attorney. If you cannot afford an attorney, one will be appointed for you...."

He finished reading my rights. I started tuning him out at some point midway through. I was in shock. I was trying to think of what evidence could have suddenly come up since my latest visit with Lumpkin during which time he hadn't arrested me. Why was he arresting me now when he hadn't previously? I then realized that my impending arrest must have been why there was a sudden emergence of the media outside. How did they know?

"Do you understand these rights I've recited to you Stohler?" Lumpkin asked.

"Stohler! Do you understand these rights?" Lumpkin repeated impatiently.

I snapped back to reality. "Yes" I uttered.

Lumpkin then ordered officers Radford and Riley to take me away. They each grabbed an arm and led me out on the "perp walk" through the hallways of the company that I proudly ran and my family had built. We passed by all of my precious few remaining loyal employees, each of whom had obviously stopped what they were doing to witness the arrest. It was a most embarrassing end to my run as owner and president of my family's four generation business.

At some point during the humiliating escort toward the front of the building Radford leaned into my ear and strangely sneered, "This is for Jennifer!" Well, I'm glad he cleared that up! At least they weren't charging me with anyone else's murder.

Lumpkin followed just behind, beaming with pride, as we exited the building, and into the press frenzy. Camera lights shined on me and microphones were shoved aggressively toward my face as reporters shouted questions at me. I didn't respond to any of the questions. I just kept my head down and let the officers lead me into one of their cars. Once I was secured in the back seat, we drove off. Camera flashes continued nonstop until we turned the corner and were no longer in sight.

Meanwhile, back at the front steps of Stohler Steel, the press redirected their attention to a podium being set up by District Attorney Stanley Murdoch's staff. Soon, Murdoch stood behind the podium, and with all the cameras on him, Murdoch addressed the media, speaking into the microphones of every major network.

"Good afternoon esteemed members of the press. I am very proud to inform you and the great people of Garrowville, that we have arrested Michael Stohler for the murder of his wife Jennifer Stohler. This arrest is the product of the hard-nosed and diligent investigative work of Chief Carl Lumpkin and his fine staff of officers with the Garrowville Police Department. They turned over every stone in their quest to capture Jennifer's killer and to protect the people of this fine town. The citizens of Garrowville can sleep easy tonight knowing that they have a tremendous police force protecting them and that Michael Stohler is off the streets."

Murdoch continued, "Going forward, I want to make clear to everyone that I will personally prosecute this case. Jennifer Stohler was a wonderful person and a beloved member of our community. She deserves justice for the heinous act that was done to her and I will see to it that she gets that justice. Therefore, I would like to announce that it is the intention of the District Attorney's Office to seek the death penalty in this case. Not only will doing so represent the best justice possible for Jennifer, but it will also serve as a deterrent to any potential future killers out there, who may think twice now about going forward with their malicious intentions. My office and our police force are tough on crime, and we firmly believe that is the only way to fight crime in our society. Now, I would like to turn the microphone over to Chief Lumpkin to say a few words. Chief…"

"Thank you Mr. Murdoch. As Mr. Murdoch stated, my staff worked very hard on this case and we are proud to have accumulated all the evidence necessary to make this arrest today. We look forward to presenting that evidence in court and seeing Michael Stohler put away and eventually executed for what he has done. Thank you."

The press then threw some softball questions at the gleaming pair. Murdoch and Lumpkin smiled their way through their vague responses, all of which led back to the hard work of the police force and the justice they sought for Jennifer.

The press conference reeked of a political stump speech orchestrated by Murdoch who was using this shining moment to get his name and face on television in the best possible light for himself and his lofty ambitions. Who wouldn't want to elect such a well-spoken, crime fighting gladiator like Stanley Murdoch, who has such a grand family pedigree, and who makes sure that scum like Michael Stohler is executed for his gruesome crime?

And who better to ride Stanley Murdoch's coattails up the hierarchy of life than Chief Lumpkin, who diligently cracked this case?

Chapter 33

I arrived at the police station and went through the normal booking process; fingerprints, mug shot, the works. I was then placed in a holding cell in the basement of the station. I asked if I could make a phone call, but I didn't get a response. "Aren't I entitled to a phone call?" I asked. Again, no response.

Chief Lumpkin arrived a little while later, seeming quite smug and proud of himself. He wasted no time paying me a visit. "Stohler, what brings you here?" he joked, cracking himself up.

I ignored his attempt at comedy. "I want to make a phone call. I am entitled to a phone call."

"Who are you going to call? Your daddy? Like last time? You want your daddy? Well, daddy can't save you now. But, sure, you can call him. Why not? There's nothing he can do to get you out of this mess."

Lumpkin handed a portable phone through the bars of the cell. I dialed my father's cell. He picked up immediately and said that he and mom were on their way. They had already called Jeff Orensen and were told that he was en route to the station, having seen coverage of the arrest on television. I was told that Orensen was incensed by the events that unfolded today. I was glad to hear that Orensen was coming and I was confident that he would straighten everything out for me.

I had barely passed the phone back through the bars when I heard Orensen storm in. But I was surprised to hear him first call out for Chief Lumpkin, who was sitting at a table near my cell.

"Lumpkin, where are you?" Orensen loudly demanded.

Lumpkin rose slowly and unenthusiastically answered, "What do you want?"

An angry Orensen then went into a tirade. "Why did you wait until 4 p.m. to make the arrest? You got the warrant five hours earlier! You needed time to tip the press so that you can be sure to show off in front of the cameras?"

Lumpkin started to respond, but was interrupted by Orensen who continued to lash out.

"And why not call me to tell me of the impending arrest? We could have surrendered Michael to you without all the hoopla and public humiliation. And now because you delayed so long, you left no time for an initial appearance today. But that must have part of your plan also. Actually, it was probably Murdoch's plan. You're too dumb to concoct anything requiring such thought."

"Watch it Orensen. You're talking to the Chief of Police."

"Get out of my way Lumpkin. I want to speak with my client."

"Go ahead counselor. Take your time. He's not going anywhere tonight."

"And I want privacy. Let him out of the cell and put us in the conference room. And I assume you know it is illegal for you to listen in on our privileged attorney-client conference."

Lumpkin grunted something inaudibly and while giving Orensen a dirty look, slowly meandered over to my cell, unlocked it and pointed toward the conference room down the hallway.

"I'll have an officer sitting right here" Lumpkin stated, pointing to a chair near the conference room door, "so don't get any ideas about him going anywhere."

Orensen ignored the ridiculous comment and led me into the conference room. He closed the door and immediately said, "Don't say a word. I don't trust them and I don't want to take any chances as to there being any bugs in the room. Just listen to me and nod or shake your head when I ask you something. Do you understand?"

I nodded. Orensen then proceeded.

"Your initial appearance is scheduled for 10 a.m. tomorrow. Unfortunately, that is the soonest it could be scheduled. By the time the police got around to arresting you this afternoon, conducting their little show-off press conference, getting you to the station and booked, the courts were closed for the day. I can only assume that was part of the strategy of waiting until later in the day to arrest you. They had a warrant for your arrest several hours earlier."

I frowned and shook my head. I didn't say anything though. I knew to follow my lawyer's instructions and would do so throughout the process from here on out.

Orensen continued, "Anyway, that means that you'll have to stay in custody tonight. The court appearance is tomorrow morning, so they won't bother transporting you to a correctional institution. Instead, they'll just keep you in the holding cell you're currently in for the night. Make sure not to speak to anyone, no matter what any of the cops may say to you to try to egg you on.

"They've already read you your rights, so anything you say at this point is admissible. So, don't say anything to anyone. Don't even speak with me or your parents about the case because we don't know who is listening in. Your parents will be here soon. I've asked them to bring you some toiletries, some clothes for the night, and clothes to wear to court tomorrow. When we are done, I'll have them come down to see you, but don't talk about the case."

I nodded my head to show I understood.

Orensen went on, "Let's talk about tomorrow's court appearance. It is just the first of several steps in the process. The primary reasons for this court appearance are to inform you of the charges against you, determine the matter of bail, and set a date for your preliminary hearing. You do not have to say a word during this process, nor should you say anything. Do you understand?

I nodded.

"Good. As for the issue of bail, I will try my best to get you bailed out tomorrow, but I have to be honest with you; it won't be easy. Bail can be denied in Pennsylvania for defendants in homicide cases. Many judges are not keen on bailing out defendants charged with murder for fear that they'll be forever known as the judge who let a killer back on the streets to kill more people. It is always safest for the judge to err on the side of caution when dealing with alleged murderers. So they either deny bail, or set it at an unattainable amount. But I'll do my best."

"Are you saying that I may be imprisoned while awaiting trial?" I asked despite my instructions not to speak. I was too upset about this possibility not to ask that question.

"Unfortunately, it is a very real possibility. Like I said, I'll do my best, but other than that, I can't promise anything."

We sat in silence for a few moments as I let the thought of staying in prison for however long it took until my trial, to sink in. Orensen then said, "That is all we need to talk about now. Your parents are probably here by now. I'll let them visit with you. Remember not to say anything relating to the case. Even to your parents. I'll see you tomorrow morning in court."

"Thanks Jeff."

Orensen opened the door to the conference room and signaled to an officer down the hall that we were done. Officer Riley then led me back to my holding cell, locked me in, and told me that he'll bring my parents downstairs to see me, but that they'd need to remain outside the cell.

I met with my parents who naturally were both teary-eyed. I assured them that I was alright, even though nothing could be further from the truth. I don't think they believed me. They told me that they brought me the clothes that Orensen had instructed them to but that the police had to inspect it first to make sure there was no contraband. I would get my items from the police in a little while. I figured that I shouldn't hold my breath.

They assured me that they would be there for me throughout the process and that everything would turn out alright. I wish I believed that, but I supposed they were trying to make me feel better, just as I had been doing for them. After a little while longer, Lumpkin appeared and snidely declared that, "visiting hours were over."

I was never so sorry to see my parents walking away from me. For the first time in my adult life, I was truly terrified. No matter what problems I had been dealing with in my life prior to Jennifer's death, I had always been confident that I could handle it and that all would turn out right in the long run. But now, I had no such confidence. Who knew how this would all play out? I had no control over my fate and nothing less than the rest of my life was at stake.

Chapter 34

The front page of the next day's Garrowville Gazette was devoted fully to a photo of me in handcuffs, head down, being led out the door of Stohler Steel, with a gleaming Chief Lumpkin following just behind. Lumpkin made sure I saw the front page when he came to bring me to court.

"Look Stohler. We made the front page! We're famous!" Lumpkin gloated.

I didn't give him the satisfaction of a reply.

"Let's go." Lumpkin said, getting back to business. He let me out of the cell, cuffed me, and then led me out to his vehicle. He was personally escorting me to court; no doubt so that he can be seen once again with his captured murderer in tow.

I didn't think it was possible, but when we arrived at Garrowville's courthouse, there was an even greater press presence than at my arrest the day before. Wasn't this just a quick, routine court procedure? Why all the hoopla over an initial appearance? I figured that it was going to be like this all the way through the process, and would probably even escalate as we moved on to the trial.

Lumpkin and his team took their sweet time leading me through the media mob scene. I couldn't be certain, but I was pretty sure Lumpkin was even smiling for the cameras. Once we got inside, I was put in a holding cell to await the hearing. Jeff Orensen met me there a few minutes later and briefly repeated the same instructions he had given me the night before. The most important instruction was to not say anything.

At precisely 10 a.m. we entered the courtroom. I followed Orensen to the defense table, which was located on our left side as walked toward the bench. A moment later, the Honorable Edgar Stevenson entered the court and we all rose. Stevenson was an older man, probably in his late 60s. He looked very stately and erudite. He had been a judge for more than 30 years. Orensen had informed me just before we entered the courtroom that Stevenson would be the judge and that he'd be fair. Orensen had appeared before him many times.

Stevenson sat down, and we all followed suit. The bailiff then read the case number and Stevenson took over the proceedings. After some routine preliminary details, he read the official charge against me. It was very brief. There was only one charge. Murder in the first degree.

After completing the reading and making sure it was on the record, Judge Stevenson declared, "The next order of business will be to address the matter of bail. Mr. Murdoch, does the Commonwealth wish to be heard on this matter?"

Stanley Murdoch rose and with as much flair and grandeur one can muster for a simple response to a simple question, he answered, "Yes your honor."

"You may proceed," replied Judge Stevenson.

"Thank you your honor. The Commonwealth respectfully submits that the defendant has been charged with a crime of the highest magnitude. Murder in the first degree. He faces the possibility of a death sentence in this case, which makes it all the more likely that he may attempt to flee. He also has substantial financial resources to allow him to effectuate such an escape; after which he may never been seen or heard from again. And finally, your honor, the defendant is an alleged murderer; therefore, we must consider the grave danger to the public at large should we allow a suspected killer to be freed pending trial."

I was shell-shocked. This was the first I had heard anything relating to the death penalty in my case, and needless to say, it shook me. I was no longer calm and composed as I had been just a few minutes ago. I hadn't really heard much else of what the prosecutor had said thereafter. All I could think of was his reference to a "death sentence."

Orensen probably sensed that I'd be unnerved by that, and gently touched my arm just after in a gesture to reassure me. It was a nice attempt, but to no avail. You can't imagine what it is like to hear a prosecutor refer to a death sentence for you. I hope you never have to experience that type of fear.

"Thank you Mr. Murdoch." Judge Stevenson replied. "Mr. Orensen, does the defense wish to make a statement on this matter?"

"Yes your honor" answered Orensen. He then rose and rebutted as follows, "Your honor, Michael Stohler is a life-long member of the Garrowville community with roots in our town extending back for generations. He has absolutely no prior criminal record; therefore, there is nothing preceding this charge that would indicate that he is a threat to public safety. And I would like to remind my esteemed colleague who referred to Mr. Stohler as an 'alleged murderer' that he is to be treated as 'innocent until proven guilty' which means that at this point in time, he is an innocent man who has the right to his freedom until such time that he is proven guilty beyond a reasonable doubt, should that ever happen. Finally, as for the supposed 'substantial financial resources' my colleague referenced, I assure the court that it isn't true and I remind everyone that my client has recently had to close down his business due to financial strain. He has his parents in town and they would likely have to put up substantial collateral to assure his presence at future court appearances."

Murdoch countered, "Your honor, the Commonwealth also wishes to remind the court that there would be significant safety risk to the defendant should he be freed, as the public is not too keen of him, to say the least."

"I'm fairly confident that your diligent police force would keep tabs on him, as they've been doing for the past few weeks" Orensen answered, "and that such surveillance would serve to protect both Mr. Stohler from the public and the public from Mr. Stohler. It would also alleviate any concerns of Mr. Stohler being a flight risk."

"Such surveillance requires a substantial commitment of the police's resources, your honor" argued Murdoch. "It would not be fair to ask that of a police department that is already short in numbers."

"Your honor, what would not be fair would be to incarcerate a citizen with no criminal history while it has yet to be proven that he committed this crime or any crime" Orensen countered.

Judge Stevenson pounded his gavel. "Thank you counsel. You both have made your points. I am ready to issue my ruling."

"Due primarily to safety considerations for the public as well as for the defendant, and based upon the added risk of flight for this defendant in light of the charges he faces, it is the court's ruling that there will be no bail set. The defendant is to remain in custody pending trial. Are there any other matters on which either side wishes to be heard at this time? Mr. Murdoch?"

"No your honor."

"Mr. Orensen? Anything further from you?"

"Your honor the defense requests that a preliminary hearing be scheduled to assess probable cause, and in light of the fact that Mr. Stohler will be held in custody, we request that the hearing be scheduled as soon as possible."

"Thank you Mr. Orensen. A preliminary hearing is hereby scheduled for Monday, January 11, 2010 at 9 a.m. Court is adjourned." Stevenson pounded his gavel once, got up, and left the courtroom.

I was then immediately surrounded by court security and taken back into custody. My odyssey through the penal system would now begin.

Chapter 35

Stanley Murdoch had won Round One of the case, having secured the detainment of the defendant until trial. It was now time to bask in the glory once again. There was no such thing as too much media exposure for someone looking to get his name out there for a future run for office.

Murdoch exited the courthouse and once again into the lights and cameras of the hordes of reporters who were lunging at him with their microphones while shouting questions. Murdoch smiled, waved his hands up and down in a gesture asking for the noise to come down a notch so that he can be heard. Once he had everyone's full attention, he commenced his oratory.

"The District Attorney's office is always looking out for the safety of the people as our first and foremost concern. With this point in mind we argued very strongly this morning for Michael Stohler to remain in custody. We are very pleased that Judge Stevenson agreed with us and ruled to keep this dangerous man behind bars where he belongs."

Reporter Chelsea Forgeous fought her way to the front of the mob scene and shouted a question toward the District Attorney. "Mr. Murdoch, would your office consider a plea bargain to a lesser charge and lighter sentence should Michael Stohler be willing to confess and plead guilty?"

"We would be very pleased to accept a confession from the defendant and spare the time and expense of a full-blown trial. However, confession or no confession, this office is going to recommend a sentence of death. That is the only just end to this tragic situation. We will not back down in any way in our quest to ultimately rid our community of crime."

Murdoch fielded a few more questions, and then was escorted to his vehicle. He had a lot of arrangements to make regarding Stohler's incarceration and he had some interesting ideas up his sleeve.

Once back at his desk, Murdoch started thinking about the upcoming trial. He knew that it would be a media circus. It would be western Pennsylvania's equivalent of an O.J. Simpson trial. It was just what he needed for his career; but only if he were to win.

He also knew that winning wouldn't be as easy as his public demeanor was portraying. He was up against a tough, smart, and experienced defense attorney, and he didn't have a lot of evidence to present. There was no murder weapon, no DNA, no fingerprints or any other type of physical evidence, and no eyewitnesses to the crime itself. He just had a lot of circumstantial evidence. Any experienced defense attorney would poke holes through his case and this was the one case in his life that he couldn't afford to lose. He would never live down the notoriety of letting such a highly publicized killer back on the streets. Imagine if Stohler killed again after Murdoch let him slip through his fingers? His career would be ruined.

What Murdoch needed more than anything was a confession. Any way he could get it. And he had an idea as to how to get it. He picked up the phone and dialed his long-time friend Raymond Culler. Raymond was the warden at the county correctional institution where Murdoch had arranged for Stohler to be remanded while awaiting trial.

"Hey Ray. How's it going up there?" Murdoch warmly greeted his buddy and fishing partner.

"Well, well, well. If it isn't the celebrity himself! I've been seeing quite a lot of you on television lately." Culler replied.

"Listen up Ray" Murdoch said, getting down to business. "I've got the big fish headed your way. We're sending Stohler over to you. I have a game plan as to how to handle him and I need your help."

"What can I do for you Stanley? I'll help anyway I can."

"Great. I want Stohler paired in a cell with an inmate who fits very specific criteria. Number one, his cellmate should be at the beginning of a reasonably long sentence so that he has a number of years behind bars still ahead of him. Number two, the cellmate should be fairly young, somewhere around Stohler's age, and preferably someone with a family, maybe some kids, so he'd be desperate to get out sooner to be with his family. Number three, I want someone non-violent and not too intimidating. I don't want Stohler to be afraid to approach or start talking to his cellmate. I want them to bond and for Stohler to open up to him."

Murdoch continued, "My thinking is that you would meet with the cellmate just before moving him and instruct him to befriend Stohler. Don't make any specific promises, but hint at the fact that if he hears anything that may help the prosecution, you'll see what you can do for him. I figure that if all goes well, one of two things will happen. Either Stohler will open up to this guy and confess, or even if he doesn't confess, if we pick the right cellmate, someone without any regard for the truth, or for anything but himself, he may still tell us that Stohler confessed to him. We can't knowingly use the testimony of someone who is lying, but if we don't know he's lying, we're ok. So, no bugs or anything like that. I just want it to be the cellmate's word that Stohler confessed. No way to prove otherwise."

"I got just the right guy Stanley" Culler responded. "Greg Luckman. You may remember the case. He's in for embezzlement and various other cons he ran to trick old people out of money. The truth is not a big concern for him. He's in his first year of a ten year sentence. Clean cut looking, non-violent or threatening in any way. He has a look that gets people to think they can trust him, which is exactly how he was so successful taking people's money. He's thirty-two years old and has a wife and two young kids at home. He's exactly what you're looking for."

"Sounds perfect Ray. Meet with him today to get him on board with the plan. He'll jump at the chance to help his own cause. But be careful not to make any specific promises. It would compromise his testimony. Just hint at the fact that it may be beneficial to him if he cooperates."

"Got it Stanley. No problem. I'm on it. Luckman is a pro at gaining people's trust. Everyone trusted him with their money. Stohler is going to spill his guts to him. And even if he doesn't, Luckman will tell us he did."

Chapter 36

I was immediately transported to the County jail to start my period of incarceration. How long that period would be was anyone's guess at this point in time. If all went well, it would be just a few months until I was acquitted at trial, or maybe even less time than that if law enforcement was able to figure out I wasn't the killer before then. But such scenarios seemed like wishful thinking based on events to date. I couldn't help but think that more realistically, today was day one of the rest of my life behind bars. And the rest of my life may not be so long if the prosecution got the death sentence they seem so intent on obtaining. These were the despondent thoughts going through my mind as I was escorted into the prison.

The first order of business once inside was the booking process, which could not have been more demeaning. It is meant to strip you of any ego, pride, confidence, and of course of any contraband. The stripping was not just metaphorical. It was actual. I had to stand completely naked, waiting to be examined. I'm pretty sure they made me wait longer than necessary just to increase my discomfort and humiliation.

Eventually, I was examined from head to toe and in every imaginable crevice in between. I was asked numerous medical and psychological questions, such as if I had any suicidal thoughts. I thought to myself that if I didn't yet have any such thoughts, I may form them if this examination lasted much longer.

Finally, I was given some prison garb to throw on and was led out toward my cell; my new home for an undetermined length of time. We passed by many cells en route and of course, just as you'd expect to see in a movie or on television, I was subjected to all sorts of whistles, cat calls, and various other intellectual shout outs. How was I going to survive in this place?

We made it to my cell, which was roughly the size of a walk-in closet. I was going to be living in this tiny space with another person? All the cells we had passed had two inmates, so I assumed mine would as well. But there was no one else there when we arrived. Is it possible that I would not be getting a cellmate because I technically wasn't a criminal, having not been convicted as of yet?

As if reading my mind, the prison guard said, "Your cellmate will be here soon." Then he added a little taunt, "I'm sure whoever it is, you'll get along very nicely. As you can see, we have a great group of people here." He laughed out loud, then slammed my cell door shut. It was the loudest and scariest sound I'd ever heard. Symbolically it represented the official separation of me from my life as I had previously known it. At least I had all 48 square feet of the cell to myself for the time being. What shall I do with all this space?

I started thinking of my future cellmate. What if this guy wants to do nothing else all day but beat the crap out of me? Or molest me? Or even kill me? What's going to stop him? He could be in for murder, rape, or various other frightening offenses, and unlike me, he may have actually done the crimes for which he's here. Forget about my trial, I started to think that I'm not going to live to see tomorrow.

About an hour later, I was sitting on my bed when I guard came by and informed me that I had some visitors. He opened up my cell and led me toward the visitation area. Jeff Orensen and my parents were there to see me. As soon as I saw my parents, I started crying. I couldn't help it. So much negative emotion bottled up inside me came pouring out at the sight of them. My mom cried too. She never imagined visiting her son behind bars. My father was able to hold back tears, but he was visibly shaken as well. These are not the types of dreams parents have for the future of their children while raising them.

I tried to assure them that I was doing alright and that everything would be fine, but my tears and probably everything else about my delivery compromised my efforts. It was fairly apparent that I truly believed nothing of what I was saying.

Orensen then said that we didn't have a lot of time for the visit so there were a few things we needed to discuss. "First, I'm sorry to have to bring this up Michael, but I've given your father an invoice for my first bill, for time spent representing you thus far. And please remember that when we initially met, I informed you that should this case head toward trial, I would need an additional retainer. I included that in the invoice. George has already agreed to pay the invoice, but I need to discuss it with you as you are the client. It would ultimately be your decision whether or not you wanted me to proceed with your case."

I couldn't imagine how much the invoice was for, but at this point in time, and at this particular location, it didn't seem to matter. All that mattered to me was that Orensen was probably my best, and only, hope to ever get out of this place, and how could I put a price tag on my freedom and my life? So, I nodded my head in agreement and said that I would like for Orensen to continue as my lawyer.

"Good." Orensen replied. "The next order of business is to discuss the upcoming preliminary hearing. The purpose of the hearing is to determine whether the prosecution truly has probable cause to charge you with the offense with which you are charged. It is intended to assure that citizens are not charged arbitrarily with crimes without a reasonable basis for the accusation.

"There are a couple of things you should understand about this hearing. You should understand that the burden of proof for the prosecution at this stage of the process is a lot less than at a trial. At a trial, they'll need to prove "beyond a reasonable doubt" that you are guilty and they'll need to prove it to the extent that twelve jurors unanimously believe you are guilty and have no such reasonable doubts. At the preliminary hearing, the prosecution only needs to show enough evidence to demonstrate they have probable cause to believe in your guilt. It is very uncommon that the prosecution, having made an arrest, especially a highly public one like this, wouldn't have enough evidence to at least get by this step of the process. So, unfortunately, I don't want you to get your hopes up before this hearing.

"However, this hearing can still be advantageous to us. It will give us a sneak peak at some of the prosecution's case without us having to tip our hand as to any of our future defenses or trial strategies. We don't have to say a word in this hearing if we don't want to. Typically, I pay close attention to the prosecution's evidence to start plotting trial strategy. I'll make a brief motion to the judge asking that he throw out the case due to insufficient evidence, but realistically, I don't expect that to happen. I just want you to understand what is going to take place at the hearing."

"Can't we call witnesses, or show any evidence that I am innocent?" I asked.

"We can't call our own witnesses. The hearing is only about the prosecution's evidence and whether or not it is deemed to be sufficient. Guilt or innocence is not determined at this stage; only sufficiency of evidence to proceed. We can however cross-examine their witnesses if we choose. However, I usually prefer not to do so extensively as I would rather save the key aspects of my cross-examination for the actual trial. I don't want any of their witnesses, many or all of whom likely will also testify at the trial, to have a preview of all of the questions I'll be asking them."

"Ok" I responded. "I understand and I trust your judgment. I am just anxious to get out of here as soon as possible and I was hoping that maybe that hearing would save me."

"I understand Michael. But it is not likely to happen as a result of this hearing. I need to brace you for that reality in advance. Moving on, there are a couple of additional items for us to discuss.

"The next item pertains to our use of our firm's own private investigator, as we've briefly discussed in the past. It is my recommendation that we proceed with this as soon as possible. You need to understand that at this point in time the Garrowville police are done with any open minded investigative work, if in fact they ever did any such work in the first place. In the viewpoint of the police, they've captured the killer. All work from here on out by the police and the district attorney's office will be geared toward the conviction of Michael Stohler. Period. For this reason, it will fall upon us to investigate other angles to ideally find the real killer or killers, or at least to create some reasonable doubt as to your guilt.

"We have a great investigator, with a lot of key contacts inside and outside of law enforcement. He has assisted me on many cases over the years and almost always finds useful evidence or information. He is your best hope to find out who really killed your wife."

Despite what I had previously thought, this new expense was starting to get me worried again about how we were going to afford all this. "How much would this cost" I asked, "and is it in addition to, or a part of, your billing rate?"

"It is in addition to my rate. He has a rate of $100 an hour, plus expenses, and will require a retainer of $1,000" Orensen answered.

"I don't know. This is going to be too…" I then abruptly got cut off.

"Michael!" my father scolded me. "Do you see where you are? Do you see the predicament you are in? How can we worry about cost right now? Your life is at stake! Don't you get that?"

He then turned to Orensen and said, "Yes, we will proceed with your investigator and I will add his retainer to the check I'll be giving you tomorrow. Please start as soon as possible."

Orensen turned to me to verify. I was the client. I dejectedly nodded my head in agreement. My father was right and I knew it.

"Ok. I will be back here soon with the investigator to speak with you. Last but not least, Michael, this is very important; do not talk to anyone in this prison about your case! Do you understand? No one! You never know who may be a snitch for the warden, police, district attorney, etc. Trust no one. Everyone in here will do anything to help their own cause. There is no such thing as a confidential conversation with an inmate or guard. Assume anything you say to anyone may potentially get repeated all the way back to the prosecutor. Got it?"

"Yes. I got it. I won't speak about the case to anyone. I promise."

Just then, a guard came in to break up our little powwow. I started tearing up again as I had to say goodbye to my parents. They promised they'd visit as much as possible. Orensen repeated that he'd be back soon with the investigator and then gave me a stern look while mouthing "no one" at me to remind me one last time to keep my mouth shut about the case.

I was then returned to my cell where I was surprised to see that I now had a cellmate. As the guard opened the door, a cheerful, clean-cut looking guy around my age jumped up from his bed, smiled, and warmly extended his arm to shake my hand.

"Hey roomie! Glad to meet you. My name is Greg."

I shook his hand. Was this for real? In a building full of all sorts of violent criminals, I got this friendly fellow as my cellmate? Could luck be starting to change in my favor?

"I'm Michael. Nice to meet you." I responded. This greeting reminded me of first meeting my freshman roommate in the dormitory at Ohio State. This definitely did not seem like a typical first meeting of cellmates in a correctional institution.

"Hi Michael. Listen, I know you're having a rough time. The first day behind bars is always the hardest. I understand the emotions you are going through right now. I've been there. I'll help you get through this as best I can."

"Thanks. I appreciate it."

We talked for a while after that. Greg basically told me his entire life story. Everything except what he is in for. I didn't want to pry, so I didn't ask. I also didn't want to talk about my case, as per my lawyer's instructions, so, I didn't ask about his situation. I just listened to him talk about his wife and kids, how he passes time in the prison, some of the dos and don'ts of the prison, who the nice and not so nice guards were, and which inmates to try to avoid.

Soon, I was getting tired and wanted to go to sleep, but Greg apparently wasn't done talking. He was a very chatty guy. I suppose of all the types of cellmates one could potentially get in this place, 'chatty' would be very low on the problem list. All in all, I thought how lucky I was to have Greg as my cellmate. Apparently, I was wrong.

Chapter 37

Stanley Murdoch's quest for more evidence wasn't going to stop at the manipulation of the prison's living arrangements. He knew that even if he got the cellmate's testimony of a confession, such testimony wouldn't be coming from a most reliable source. Also, even without making specific promises to the cellmate, a good defense attorney such as Jeff Orensen would make sure to expose whatever incentive there was in exchange for the testimony.

Murdoch also had that gnawing feeling in the pit of his stomach that they were missing something. Despite what he was saying publicly, he feared that Lumpkin and his team had targeted Stohler as the sole assassin from the get-go. Murdoch had no doubt that Stohler was involved in the murder, but what if he had help? For instance, what if he hired a hit man to do the job for him?

After all, Stohler had the financial resources to hire a hit man. And as far as Murdoch knew, Stohler didn't possess a gun, nor was he known to have ever handled one based upon interviews with many of his friends and associates. Furthermore, there was no physical evidence at the crime scene, which means that not only can't Murdoch prove physically that Stohler committed the murder, but it seemed a bit impractical that a criminal novice would pull off a homicide without leaving a shred of evidence.

Then there was the issue of the missing wedding ring. Where was it? It didn't turn up in any of the searches conducted by law enforcement, nor was it found anywhere at the crime scene. The murder took place in the middle of the night and Stohler was contacted by the police early the next morning. From that point on, he had almost always been in the presence of, or watched by, law enforcement personnel. When would he have had the chance to unload the ring? The more Murdoch thought about it, the more reasonable it was starting to seem that Michael hired a killer to do his dirty work.

Murdoch also thought about how great it would be if he were to uncover another murderer working in cahoots with Michael Stohler. Two for the price of one! Killing two birds with one stone, so to speak. Just think about all of the phenomenal press coverage for Stanley Murdoch when he leads an investigation that takes another killer off the streets. He would be seen as having not simply been satisfied with putting Michael Stohler away. He was always tirelessly fighting to protect the people. A real life, present day, crime fighting hero.

However, there were some flaws in the hit man theory. For instance, information from the crime scene indicated that the shooter appeared to be left handed and was several inches taller than the victim. Both of these descriptions fit Michael Stohler. But of course, it fits a lot of other people as well. Maybe the hit man was also left handed. Or maybe, being a smart, professional assassin, he intentionally shot with his left hand to align the evidence with Michael, keeping law enforcement further off the trail of an outsider.

So many questions to address. But no one was going to accuse Stanley Murdoch of not thinking of everything. It was time to delve into the hit man angle.

The first order of business was to get a warrant for Michael Stohler's bank records. A hit man had to be paid somehow and Murdoch wanted to investigate all payments Michael made in the months leading up to the murder. Of course Murdoch knew that it would be highly unlikely that the payment would be made by check. Not too many assassins accepted personal checks. So, Murdoch and his team would also be looking to see if any significant cash withdrawals or wire transfers were made.

As for the ring, Murdoch wanted all pawn shops and jewelers throughout Pennsylvania to be questioned. He would have a photo of Michael Stohler shown at each one, and would also ask about valuable diamonds brought in during the timeframe just after the murder. Maybe the hit man's payment was the ring itself, which would be why it was taken from the crime scene. In that case, showing Michael's photo won't help, but if they could identify the place where the hit man unloaded the ring, they may be able to get a description of him, or there may even be surveillance video.

Murdoch barked orders to his associates to draft the necessary paperwork for the warrant to obtain Michael's bank records, then got on the phone to instruct Lumpkin. He assigned Lumpkin and his staff to carry out the investigation of pawn shops and jewelers in search for the wedding ring transaction, and to question everyone at such places as to where else one may be able to unload a valuable piece of jewelry.

Lumpkin was clearly agitated by the extensive legwork being thrown his way on a case that had been solved. "Murdoch, why are we doing this? We've got the killer. He's behind bars as we speak. Why are you questioning now what we've always known to be the answer to this case?"

"I'm not questioning Michael's involvement. But what if he wasn't the actual shooter? Then, we'd have another killer still out on the streets. We can't afford to let assumptions and shoddy investigative work allow a killer to remain free. Also, think of the press we'd get for capturing another one. We're heroes for getting Stohler. Think of all the accolades for another killer behind bars. They'll be putting up statues of us."

"Won't the press wonder why we didn't think of a hit man before?" Lumpkin asked.

"That's easy Lumpkin. We say we had always thought of it and have been diligently investigating that angle, but that we kept it hush so that Michael's cohort wouldn't know we were after him. We didn't want him fleeing or doing something rash. If he feels comfortable, he's more likely to slip up and be found."

Murdoch continued, "I'll handle the press, Lumpkin. I know what to say to them to put us in the best possible light. You just worry about the investigation. We've got one killer. Now, let's see if we can get another one."

Chapter 38

Derrick Martin was born in 1972 and raised on the mean streets of Shelton, Ohio, which is located in the eastern part of the state, close to the Pennsylvania border. The families of Shelton were all poor and many were no longer intact for various reasons; divorce, domestic violence, victims of crimes and/or criminal offenders, etc. There were no Norman Rockwell families in Shelton. Many children in this area grew up with one or both of their parents behind bars at various points of their youth.

This fact made a young Derrick Martin a targeted boy in school, as his father, Dan Martin, was a police officer. Needless to say, police officers, and their families, were not popular figures among those living in the broken homes of Shelton. Derrick had to learn at a young age how to defend himself. He lived in a rough area and he was a target. In that situation, you either got tough or you got hurt. So as Derrick got older and entered his teen years, he got tough. He worked out, got some piercings, added a few menacing tattoos, and soon, he looked the part of a tough guy.

But Derrick was a classic example of the old adage, "don't judge a book by its cover." He was a good kid at heart and would never physically harm anyone. He was taught by his parents that violence should only be reserved for purposes of self-defense. He was one of the few kids in the area who had two parents at home, both of whom raised him and his three sisters as best they could with their limited financial resources and time. In addition to Dan's job as a police officer, he also worked part-time as a night-time security guard to add a few extra dollars to his police earnings. Derrick's mom, Linda, worked with a cleaning service, which didn't pay a lot of money, but every cent counted when Dan and Linda had four kids to feed.

Derrick idolized his father and wanted to follow in his footsteps. Dan talked to Derrick whenever he could about his job. He told his son how he was working hard to move up the ladder so that one day he could become a homicide detective. That was Dan's dream job and he wasn't far from getting there.

Tragically, he never did achieve that goal. In 1987, when Derrick was just fifteen years of age, his dear father was shot and killed in the line of duty. Dan Martin had responded to an armed robbery in progress, which upon the arrival of law enforcement on the scene, escalated into a shootout. Officer Dan Martin and all three suspects were killed in the melee.

That left Derrick as the man of the household, which was a lot of responsibility for a despondent teenage kid who had just lost his father. Even with some money provided by the police department for families of officers killed in the line of duty, plus a small life insurance policy, there wasn't nearly enough money for the Martin family, with four kids, on Linda's earnings alone.

Thus, Derrick had to start working after school to help the family make ends meet. He took a job working at a pizza place across the street from the school. Each school day, he endured the usual taunts from his classmates about his late police officer father, and he stuck up for his sisters whenever they experienced the same treatment. Then, after school, he went directly to work until 9 p.m. at which time he came home, did his homework, went to sleep, and started the process all over again the next day. It was a rough life for a kid.

So it is easy to understand how a kid in this most unfortunate situation can get disillusioned. His father had worked hard, did everything right, and look at what happened to him. Derrick was also working hard and trying to do right, but still, life was miserable and there was never enough money for the family. One day his mother told him that they were behind in their mortgage payments and they may lose their house. Where would they go if that happened? Derrick was the man in the family now and he couldn't let the situation get to that point.

So Derrick did the only thing he believed that he could in the circumstances. He stole money from the pizza place. He felt badly about it, but it was a necessity. He didn't take much at first; just a little here and there. But as he saw that he could get away with it, and that his initial thefts still weren't enough for the family, his petty larcenies started escalating. Inevitably, he was caught, and for the first of several times in his life, he was arrested.

As a fifteen year-old with no prior record and with a fallen ex-cop as a father, he was treated very gently in his first venture into the justice system. After just a stern warning from the juvenile court, he was back at home. But now he was without a job and the family's financial situation was still desperate. Additionally, word had spread around town that he had stolen money from his workplace, so no other local business owners would hire him.

What was he to do now to help his struggling family? He had no choice. He had to steal money somehow. So, his criminal activity escalated to pick pocketing and grabbing purses from women in stores, malls, etc. Nothing violent; just grab what he could and run. He succeeded for a few months before finally getting caught. He was arrested once again.

The juvenile court wasn't going to be so easy on him this time, and would likely have sent him to a juvenile correctional institution if not for several of Dan Martin's police officer friends stepping in and vouching for Derrick. Dan Martin had been a popular member of the police force and his friends had all known

Derrick since he was born. Several of them spoke up on his behalf and also spoke with Derrick directly to try to help straighten him out.

As a result, the court put Derrick on probation, ordered him to pay some restitution, and perform a few hours of community service. But no incarceration; he was free to go home once again.

Derrick temporarily made an effort to clean up his act, but threats of foreclosure from the bank didn't allow that to last very long. So Derrick went back to his petty larcenies; a few purses here, a few pick pockets there, all of which didn't add up to nearly enough. Derrick would have to step it up a bit if the family was going to keep their house. So, he did just that, graduating to holding up convenience stores.

He didn't actually have a gun or any other type of weapon, but he pretended to have one under his jacket. This game plan worked at a few stores and brought in some money for a little while. But naturally, Derrick's luck ran out and he was caught by an off-duty police officer who happened to be in another aisle of one such store as Derrick was robbing the place.

Now, having just turned seventeen years of age, having escalated to holding up stores while threatening the cashiers with what they thought was a gun, and having an ever growing rap sheet, there was no chance for Derrick Martin to avoid incarceration. He was tried as an adult and convicted. He was sentenced to five years behind bars.

The sad story of a local kid whose dad had been a police officer killed in the line of duty, being convicted for holding up a convenience store ran in the local papers. The story showed a mug shot of Derrick Martin and mentioned that it had been his third arrest in a fairly short period of time. The creative reporter pegged him, "Mug Shot" Martin.

The nickname stuck and he was called "Mug Shot" inside the prison. Soon, "Mug Shot" was shortened to simply "Mug," which essentially became his new name. Everyone in his life thereafter knew him just as "Mug," without knowing his real name. Derrick liked the nickname as it added to his tough guy persona. When you thought of someone called "Mug Shot" or "Mug" you didn't think of an accountant or a banker. You thought of someone with whom you didn't want to mess around.

Mug spent a great deal of his time behind bars working out. He bulked up to the point where he had a physique nearing that of a body builder. As a result, no one messed with him, and in fact, Mug went out of his way to protect some of the weaker inmates who had been getting beat up. That made Mug some friends and some enemies within the prison. But the guards liked him as he helped keep the peace. No one dared attack Mug, nor did they go after anyone Mug protected.

Due to good behavior, Mug was paroled after serving three years of his five year sentence. Now, at twenty years of age, he was determined once and for all to clean up his act and get his life on the right track. He started taking some GED courses to work toward the high school diploma he had missed out on while in prison. One of his father's old friends got him a job with his wife's company, working in the mailroom. So now Mug had some income. Life was starting to turn around for him.

A few months later, shortly after Mug's twenty-first birthday, he was driving with Terrence Williams, a friend from prison who had just been released. Mug had just purchased a beat-up used car, his first ever vehicle, and was proudly driving around Shelton with his buddy, who had also just recently turned twenty-one.

Williams suggested that they stop at a 7-Eleven to get a few beers to celebrate their recently obtained freedom and their reaching legal age to purchase alcohol. Mug agreed. They walked in, grabbed the drinks, and got on line to pay. The man in front of them on line paid for his purchase with a $100 bill.

As the cashier opened up the register to give change, Williams pulled out a gun and demanded the $100, plus all cash in the register. Mug was stunned, as he didn't even know Williams had a gun on him. Mug was shouting at Williams, pleading with him not to do this, but Williams wasn't listening. Williams had no money and the sight of the $100 set him off. He menacingly pointed the gun at the cashier and the customers in front and behind him on line, demanding everyone's money, watches, and any other valuables they had on them.

An employee sitting in an office in the back saw what was happening and quickly dialed 911. The police were there almost immediately, catching Mug and Williams as they exited the store. They were arrested and charged with armed robbery, along with several other related charges.

Mug was now in serious trouble. He was facing a long sentence for these charges. But, what made these charges unique as compared to Mug's prior offenses, was that in this particular matter he was actually innocent. He was just in the wrong place at the wrong time with the wrong person.

But who was going to believe that? Mug had a track record of similar offenses. He was clearly present at the scene. There were witnesses and surveillance footage. He was hanging out with someone else just sprung from prison also for similar offenses. Mug was screwed and his life hung in the balance.

Mug couldn't afford an attorney, so a public defender was appointed to him by the court. But Mug got lucky. He didn't just get any run-of-the-mill public defender. He got a young, up-and-coming superstar attorney who was just starting his career. He got an attorney with energy, enthusiasm, and intelligence. He got an attorney who genuinely believed in Mug and was willing to do whatever was necessary to give him the best possible defense. He got Jeff Orensen.

The year was 1993, and Orensen was fresh out of law school. He was paying his dues as a public defender to get trial experience. This would be Orensen's first ever trial and he was determined to win it. Orensen was brilliant in court and was able to prove, through expert lip reading testimony from the surveillance footage, that Mug was genuinely surprised by and disturbed by what had transpired. Mug was acquitted. His life was saved.

During the course of the case, Orensen and Mug had bonded. Mug admired Orensen's investigative instincts and he confided in Orensen how he had always wanted to follow his late father's dreams of becoming an investigator, but that unfortunately, with his record, he'd never get a job.

Orensen found that he liked his first client and that despite the prior rap sheet, Orensen could see that Mug was a decent person who had been dealt a rotten hand in life. He also recognized that Mug had something that many people do not. He had contacts on both sides of the law enforcement fence. Mug had contacts within law enforcement through his father's old friends. He also had contacts on the other side of the law from the neighborhood in which he grew up and from people he'd protected behind bars. Mug also seemed to have street smarts, an important pre-requisite for a successful investigator. So Orensen had an interesting idea.

Orensen offered Mug to be his personal investigator on future cases. He couldn't promise much yet in the way of payment. But Orensen told Mug that soon Orensen would be hired by one of the larger law firms in town and he'd have much bigger cases, those with clients who can pay a lot of money at which time, he'd be able to charge clients for Mug's investigations on their behalf.

Mug jumped at the opportunity. It would be his best chance to do the type of work he always wanted to do, and hopefully also help innocent people avoid getting erroneously convicted, which had almost happened to him. A partnership had been born.

Since then, Mug has assisted Orensen on many cases. In that time, he had made numerous contacts all throughout law enforcement and all throughout the underworld. Mug was tough, had street smarts, and seemingly knew everyone and everything. He also worked his butt off for anyone who Orensen believed may be wrongly accused of a crime. Orensen had saved his life and Mug never wanted to let him down on a case. Mug was the perfect person to get to the bottom of what had happened in the Stohler case. Upon being informed by Orensen that he'd be used in the Stohler case and that Orensen believed in Stohler's innocence, he couldn't wait to get started.

Chapter 39

The next few days were the worst of my life. I spent most of my time sitting in my cell, which at least kept me safe from the general prison population. The most depressing moment was at the stroke of midnight on New Year's Eve, after which I could hear fireworks on the outside. I thought back to many happy New Year's Eves with Jennifer, the many trips we took together, and the many parties we had thrown or attended. Now I was behind bars and Jennifer was gone. I couldn't help but think how each January 1st always represented the fresh start of a new calendar year, with all the hopes and dreams for what that year and beyond may bring. What laid ahead for me in 2010 and thereafter? The depressing answer to that question was most likely nothing more than rotting away in prison.

One of the few things that made my current predicament somewhat bearable was my cellmate. Greg was great. He had essentially told me his whole life story, and he seemed genuinely interested in mine. He also stayed near me outside the cell when we went to eat or for our recreation time in the yard. He made sure that I didn't have any trouble with any other inmates. I couldn't have asked for a better cellmate.

Greg finally spoke about the criminal activity that had landed him behind bars. He had a lot of financial troubles and had to find creative ways to get money. He said that he was a good guy but that money troubles had forced his hand. He felt badly about what he had done, but didn't see any alternatives. He said that a lot of guys in this place had similar stories in that life's circumstances forced their hand into actions they would never have committed otherwise. It didn't make them bad people he said; just unfortunate ones.

Greg asked me on multiple occasions about my case and was very interested in what had happened. Remembering the advice of my counsel, I didn't want to speak with him about it. I felt bad because he had divulged so much of his life to me, but I needed to follow Orensen's instructions. So I simply told Greg that it was too painful for me to talk about at this time. I left it at that.

On Monday, January 4, 2010, Orensen returned to prison to meet with me. He brought his investigator with him. At least I hoped it was his investigator. It looked like it could be a guy Orensen had randomly plucked out of one of the other cells in here.

"Michael. How are you holding up in here?" Orensen said as he greeted me in the visitation room.

"I need to get out of here" I answered with desperation in my voice. "I won't survive long in this place. The only positive thing is that I seem to have lucked out on the cellmate front."

"I hope you haven't been talking to him about your case" Orensen said.

"No, though he seems very interested in my case. I haven't said anything to him about it." I replied.

"Listen to me man" said Orensen's yet-to-be-introduced companion. "Don't talk about your case to your cellmate no matter how nice he may be. In fact, don't talk to anyone in here about your case. You never know who the snitch may be. And trust me, there are snitches here. Everyone is looking for a way to sweeten their own deal and it doesn't matter at whose expense. Talk to no one! It's rule # 1 behind bars. You got that?"

I nodded my head. This guy seemed to know about life behind bars. Who was this guy who looked scarier than most of the inmates in here? I looked at Orensen. My look silently conveyed that question to him.

Orensen then made the introduction. "Michael, this is Mug. He is my chief investigator and he's here to start working on your case."

"Nice to meet you Michael" Mug said. He then confidently added, "I am going to find out what happened to your wife and get you out of this place. You have my word."

Orensen added, "Mug is the best in the business. We are lucky to have him on our side. He is going to ask you a lot of questions to help him get started with his investigation. Answer all of his questions as honestly and as completely as you can. You can trust him Michael. He'll be working his butt off for you and he'll need as much information as you can give him."

"Is your name really Mug?" I asked.

He smiled. "It's what I'm known as by everyone on the streets. I've gone by Mug for years. Are you ready to get started?"

"Yes. Thank you for your help. Let's do this." I answered enthusiastically.

I couldn't help but think how nice it is going to be to finally answer questions geared toward finding the truth, as opposed to simply trying to pin a murder on me.

Chapter 40

"The way I see this," Mug started off, "is that there are four possible scenarios here. In no particular order, they are: number one, your wife was targeted to be killed for some reason; number two, you were targeted to be killed but that unfortunately for the killer and for your wife, she was the one present, not you; number three, this was a targeted robbery of your house that escalated beyond what was intended; and number four, it was a random robbery that escalated beyond what was intended. We are going to explore all four scenarios."

Mug went on, "We'll start with the first one; that your wife was targeted for murder. Who do you think may have had any incentive to harm your wife?"

I shook my head. "No one. She was loved by everyone. She was an angel."

"Come on Michael, I need you to think deeper than that. What had changed in hers or both of your lives in recent years? Any behavioral changes? Any issues at work? Any marital troubles? Any affairs?"

"Hey!" I answered defensively. "There were no affairs."

Orensen stepped in, "Michael. Mug needs to ask all questions; even the tough ones. Don't take any of the questions personally. He's trying to help."

"Ok. I'm sorry." I replied.

"It's ok Michael" Mug said, soothing me a bit. "You have to understand that "love triangles" are fairly common and that many of them end badly. It doesn't even have to be as extensive as an affair. It isn't far-fetched to think that some guy may have had a crush on her and when she turned him down, he snapped. One of those "if I can't have her, no one can" nut cases. So, I wouldn't be doing my job if I didn't explore that possibility. We need to consider all possibilities."

He continued, "Also, remember that there was no forced entry. It is possible that she knew her killer and may have even let him in. So, with that in mind, think about it Michael, was she spending any more time than usual with anyone? Did she mention any new people she had recently met at work or elsewhere? Was she working later or different hours at work? Was she doing anything differently that you can think of?"

I put aside my defensiveness and truly gave it some thought. But honestly couldn't think of anything. "No. I can't think of any new names that she had mentioned or anything different as to her schedule or activities. She was active at the school and church, and otherwise, didn't do much else."

"Tell me about what else was going on in your lives leading up to the murder."

I told him about our financial troubles, money related arguments, and that I had been sleeping at my parents' house or on the downstairs couch. Our marriage hadn't been great in recent months.

"Did she cut back on any contributions to any causes that she had been generous with previously?" Mug asked.

"No. That was part of the problem. She wasn't cutting back. That was often what we fought about."

"Who might she have confided in as to her side of your marital problems or anything else? Can you give me a list of names of her closest friends?" He slid over a notepad, motioning for me to write names on the pad.

I gave him a list of six names of girlfriends that to the best of my knowledge, would have been her closest confidants, if in fact she actually did confide in anyone.

"Ok. Thanks Michael. I am going to interview these people." Mug said. "Let's talk about you as a target now."

Mug continued, "I know that you've had to shut down your business, and that over the course of time, you've laid off a lot of people. Was there anyone you can think of who took the news unusually hard? Any threats?"

"Obviously most people were upset. Many of them had worked very hard for a long time. None of them were wealthy in that they could get by for long without a job. So, naturally they took the news hard. But most understood that there was nothing I could do and most understood that I had been as fair as possible with them through to the end. No one went so far as to threaten me."

"I'm going to need a list of all employees who you laid off in the past few years. We need to look into each and every one of them as persons with a possible motive. Especially those who were hit the hardest financially. Do you know of anyone who lost their homes, and/or went bankrupt after being laid off?"

I told him that there were many foreclosures in Garrowville in recent years, including homes previously owned by former employees of Stohler Steel. I added that I knew all these people personally and couldn't imagine any of them being a murderer. And even if someone had it in for me, why kill Jennifer?

"Like I said before, someone could have been after you, and unfortunately found your wife instead. She may have seen the intruder and could have identified him or her; thus leaving the culprit no choice but to silence her. It's only a possibility, but again, we need to look into everything. Where can I get a list of all former employees of your company?"

"You can get it from my father. He would have all the records."

Mug then slid me the pad once again. "Write down all names of former employees who you can think of who had lost their homes after losing their jobs. We are going to look at these people more closely."

I wrote down as many names as I could think of. Sadly, it was a fairly common occurrence in Garrowville in recent years, so my list was fairly long.

"Do you know if any of these people owned a gun or had access to a gun? Do any of them have experience handling guns?" Mug asked.

"None that I know of." I answered. "But it wasn't a common subject of conversation for me with anyone."

"The list of people who were laid off, especially those who lost their homes will also serve as a suspect list for the next possible scenario; the one in which this was a targeted robbery. Someone who lost so much and blames you for his or her woes, and wanted to steal back some of what was lost. But there was no forced entry. It's possible the intruder rang the doorbell, then planned to rob you at gunpoint, but that seems unlikely. If the motive was a revenge robbery, the burglar wouldn't want to chance being recognized by sight or voice. So, the question then becomes, 'who may have had a key'?"

"The only ones who had the key besides Jennifer and I were my parents." I responded.

"What about anyone who previously had a key? Have you changed your locks in recent years? I know that the other homes on your block are now vacant, but did any of your former neighbors once have a spare key to your house?"

"I don't know. Jennifer would have handled that as she was home more than I and was more social with the neighbors."

He slid the pad over to me again. "Please list on the pad the names of all people you can remember who had previously lived on your block."

I did as instructed.

"Your wife's wedding ring was the only known item to have been taken. Is there anyone you had confided in as to the value of the ring, or any other information about the ring?"

"No. I barely knew anything about it myself. I don't know much about rings and I had a lot of help in selecting it."

"What was the size and shape? Do you remember?"

"I think it was around 2 carats. Square shaped."

Orensen stepped in, "Probably a princess cut" he said to Mug. Clearly neither Mug nor I were diamond experts.

Mug asked, "Who might she have shown off her ring to? Maybe a girlfriend whose husband was around and overheard?"

"She's probably shown all her friends over the course of time, but none that she would have specifically shown off to lately. We were married for 12 years, so it wasn't as if the ring was a new development. Also, people were having financial troubles. Jennifer wasn't the type to flaunt a valuable piece of jewelry at people who were struggling."

"It could have been someone who simply noticed it on her finger. Can you recall anyone ever commenting to you about your wife's ring, or your wife mentioning that someone had complimented her on it?"

"No. I don't recall that." I answered.

Mug then said, "Ok. Finally, as for the random burglary scenario; that one is a bit harder to investigate. But I'll look into robberies in surrounding areas and see if there are any similarities in M.O.'s. The lack of a forced entry makes this one the least likely of the four, but I'll lean on some of my law enforcement contacts to look into other break-ins in western Pennsylvania."

A guard then came in and told us that visiting time was over. Mug told me that he would get right to work on this information and thanked me for my time. Do you believe that? Him thanking me? He was the one who was trying to save my life. And I had nothing but time on my hands right now. Could there be a better way to spend that time than helping in an investigation upon which the rest of my life depends? Could a guy named "Mug" figure out who killed my wife? I can only pray that he could. He may be my only hope.

Chapter 41

The next morning, Mug decided to start with Jennifer's closest girlfriends. There were six of them as per Michael's list. The objective would be to find out what each one knew about Jennifer's life in her last few months. It was also possible that these people, and/or their spouses could be suspects; especially the three people on the list who Mug knew had their homes foreclosed. Two of those people had spouses who were laid off from their jobs at Stohler Steel. Certainly there could be motive for these people to lash back at Michael and Jennifer.

The first visit was with Sarah Glenn. Sarah and her husband Bill had lived two houses away from the Stohlers until Bill was laid off by Michael. Their home was foreclosed and now they lived in a one bedroom apartment on the other side of town. Life had clearly taken a downturn for them.

"Good morning Mrs. Glenn. I'm sorry to disturb you this morning but if you can spare a few minutes, I'd just like to speak with you about Jennifer Stohler. I'm an investigator and…" Mug was cut off.

"An investigator for who? Michael? Everyone already knows he killed her. He's in jail where he belongs. What else is there to investigate? It's a waste of time. They should execute him already and get it over with."

"I understand how you feel ma'am. Can you tell me why you are certain Michael killed her?" Mug politely responded.

"It's obvious. They were having marital problems. She wanted a divorce. Why get divorced and pay alimony when he could kill her and collect life insurance money? And he was cheating on her. If she's gone, he could carry on with his girlfriend."

"Did Jennifer tell you that Michael was cheating?" Mug asked.

"No. But everyone knew. Jennifer must have known also."

"Do you know if Jennifer had any new friends or spent more time with anyone new in the past year?"

"Are you asking if Jennifer was also having an affair? How dare you! Show some respect for the deceased! She absolutely was not doing any such thing!"

"I'm sorry ma'am. Let me clarify. I'm not saying that she was having an affair. I just want to know if perhaps she made any new friends, especially in light of having issues at home. Maybe just a co-worker with whom she confided. Or, someone who liked her and hung around her even if she didn't reciprocate the feelings? Do you know of anything along those lines?"

"No I don't!" Sarah emphatically responded. "And stop wasting my time with this nonsense. The case is closed. Michael killed her and I hope he is executed for what he did. An eye for an eye!"

With that, Sarah Glenn slammed the door on Mug. The conversation was clearly over.

Mug spent the remainder of the day visiting with four of the remaining five people on the list. Though not necessarily as adamant as Mrs. Glenn, the other four friends had similar viewpoints. The only person on this list that Mug couldn't speak with was Christine Dennison. Christine and her husband Willie had lived next door to the Stohlers, but about six months earlier, their home was foreclosed and they left the area. Mug made a note to look into where they moved so that he could contact them.

In the meantime, Mug summarized what he did learn from his five discussions today. In general, the consensus was: Michael and Jennifer had marital problems, Jennifer wasn't happy and wanted a divorce, Michael must have been having an affair, Jennifer wasn't having an affair and no one knew of any new friends in her life. None of the conversations shed any light as to who else may have had any motive to kill Jennifer. And of course, all five of the interviewees stated that Michael was the killer, though none of them had any specific evidence to offer as support for their unwavering viewpoint on the matter.

He had also asked several of them if they owned guns or knew anyone in the Stohlers' circle of friends who did. He got no useful information. But no worries. He would find out who the gun owners were through his various law enforcement contacts.

After one day of pounding the pavement, Mug was starting to realize that he had an uphill battle on this case. This one wasn't going to be easy.

Chapter 42

The defense team wasn't the only side carrying out the hunt for evidence. Under the orders of Stanley Murdoch, Chief Lumpkin and his team were visiting every pawn shop and jeweler in the county. At each one, they showed a photo of Michael Stohler, and at each one they got the same response. Stohler was recognized as the guy who had been arrested for murder, but had not been seen on the premises. Nor had any valuable wedding rings or expensive diamonds been bartered lately. The search for the missing wedding ring was going nowhere.

Lumpkin reported back to Murdoch that they weren't getting anywhere with this "wild goose chase" as Lumpkin put it. "Obviously Michael has it stashed somewhere. He didn't have a chance yet to unload the ring. We were all over him right from the start. We need to be searching everywhere he's been since the murder."

Murdoch told Lumpkin to search anywhere and everywhere. Murdoch was gradually losing patience with the lack of progress in the case. The ring needed to be found, along with the murder weapon for that matter. If he stashed the ring somewhere, the gun may be hidden there as well. Maybe even some bloodied clothing. Think of the treasure trove of evidence that was just waiting to be found.

The ring hunt wasn't the only dead end for Murdoch. He had received Michael Stohler's bank records and he didn't find any large and/or unusual transactions that stuck out to him. In fact the only observation Murdoch had upon examination of the bank records was that Michael seemed to have less money than Murdoch had thought.

He wasn't sure what exactly that observation meant. On one hand, it made it less likely that Michael would be able to simply pay a large sum of cash to a hit man. However, on the other hand, it lent more credibility to their theory that the wedding ring itself may have been the payment. If an outside hit man was used, the ring may have been unloaded outside the immediate area. They would have to expand the search beyond the county's borders. More legwork would be needed. Murdoch contacted various police precincts in the surrounding areas and requested that every jeweler and pawn shop in each of their jurisdictions be paid a visit.

The paucity of Michael's financial resources did also serve to increase the motive angle for the case against him. Murdoch made a note to himself that the financial difficulties of the Stohlers would need to play a key part in the prosecution's arguments throughout the case. Michael had every imaginable financial motive to want Jennifer dead. Jurors need motive to be comfortable with returning a guilty verdict. Murdoch would make sure he pounded home the financial motive that clearly existed in this case.

Murdoch was also getting impatient with the lack of progress at the prison. Warden Culler had not yet reported back anything on the confession front. Murdoch called his buddy to press the matter.

"Culler. Murdoch here. What's doing with Stohler's cellmate? Have you gotten anything from him yet?"

"Hello Stanley. I checked with him earlier today. Nothing yet. But it has only been a few days. These things take time. He has to build a friendship with Stohler to gain his trust. Stohler isn't just going to blurt out a confession to anyone. He can't be that dumb."

"Did you make it clear to the cellmate that his situation would be improved if he cooperated?" Murdoch asked.

"Yes. Not directly. But I think he got the point."

"Make sure he got the point. We're desperate here. Remind him about his young kids at home. Ask him if he wants to get back to them as soon as possible."

"Of course Stanley. I'll speak with him today. We'll get what we need. Don't worry about it."

Murdoch thanked the warden and hung up. Despite the reassurances from the warden, he was still worried. His worries also pertained to a new development in which he has learned that Mug was on the case for the defense. He knew of Mug. Everyone did. Mug was a fierce investigator who had won many cases for Orensen in the past. Murdoch had tried to recruit Mug to be a homicide detective for the "right side of the law" as Murdoch had told him. But Mug had no interest. He wouldn't leave Orensen's side. Now the two of them were teaming up to threaten all of Murdoch's dreams. He couldn't let that happen. He needed that damn confession whether there really was one or not.

Chapter 43

We all rose as the Honorable Edgar Stevenson entered the courtroom, then on command, sat back down as he did. It was Monday, January 11, 2010 and it was time for my preliminary hearing. The usual media circus had greeted us as we entered the courtroom. There were even some reporters outside the prison simply to get footage of me being transported to my court appearance.

Despite my attorney's forewarning not to get my hopes up regarding this phase of the process, my hopes were up nonetheless. The past week and a half behind bars had been brutal; the worst days of my life. Therefore, any glimmer of hope that this hearing afforded me was most welcome. Even just getting out of the prison to attend the hearing was a welcome reprieve.

After some initial instructions, Judge Stevenson started the proceedings.

"Mr. Murdoch, your opening statement."

"Thank you your honor. The Commonwealth has probable cause to believe that Michael Stohler deliberately caused the death of his spouse Jennifer Stohler. We will demonstrate that the defendant had motive and opportunity to commit this crime. Additionally, this was not an act that was committed in the heat of the moment or in a fit of anger. The Commonwealth will demonstrate that this malicious act was premeditated by the defendant. For this reason, we believe that a charge of murder in the first degree is warranted in this case and we will provide evidence sufficient to support that charge."

"Thank you Mr. Murdoch. Mr. Orensen, do you wish to make an opening statement at this time?"

"No your honor. "

"Mr. Murdoch. You may call your first witness."

"Thank you your honor. The Commonwealth calls Garrowville's Chief of Police Carl Lumpkin to the stand."

Chief Lumpkin lumbered his way through the courtroom, climbed up into the witness chair and was sworn in by the bailiff.

Murdoch started Lumpkin off with a few questions to establish that Lumpkin had been in law enforcement for many years, having worked his way up to the Chief of Police. Then Murdoch dove into the matter at hand.

"Chief Lumpkin. Tell us how you first learned of the murder of Mrs. Stohler."

"On the morning of Friday, December 11th, 2009, I was informed by the principal at the school where Mrs. Stohler worked that she had failed to show up, which was very unusual for her. It was particularly troubling in that there was to be a special class trip on that day for which she had been the primary organizer. This fact raised our level of concern about her well-being." Lumpkin replied.

"What did you do next?"

"I directed Officer Dan Radford to check up on her at her residence. Radford found her body and phoned it in."

"How did you make a determination that this was a homicide as opposed to suicide?"

"Mrs. Stohler had been shot one time through the middle of her forehead at point blank range. There was no gun present at the crime scene, thus ruling out any possibility that she had killed herself."

Murdoch then asked, "What evidence at the crime scene led you to believe that the defendant was your prime suspect?"

"The first indicator was the fact that there was no sign of any forced entry, which means that the killer either had a key to the house or was let in by the victim. Either way, it was apparent that the victim knew the assailant. The crime took place in the middle of the night. It was not likely that the victim was letting too many people in at that time."

"What else led you to believe the assailant was the defendant?"

"We started interviewing numerous friends and neighbors. All of them reported how the Stohlers were having marital problems. Some of them informed us that the victim had been contemplating divorce. So, here we have a wife who is found dead in her own bedroom. In such cases, the husband is the culprit more often than not. Add on that there was no forced entry and the couple is having marital problems and it raises the odds significantly." Lumpkin confidently stated.

"But certainly, the police didn't simply rely on these general statistics. What else did you learn from the crime scene?"

"The CSI unit initially estimated that the time of death was between 2 a.m. and 4 a.m. Autopsy results corroborated that finding later on. The CSI unit also later established, based on the location of bullet fragments, blood splattering, and the victim's body position, where the shooter was positioned. They were able to determine that the shooter was most likely left-handed and significantly taller than the victim. Both of those attributes fit the defendant."

"Did you find anything else at the crime scene?"

"Yes. We found an appointment book belonging to the victim. We noted that she had just met with David Bergman, a divorce attorney, two days earlier. This supported the feedback we had been getting from numerous sources about the couple's problems."

"Did you have an opportunity to ask the defendant about his relationship with his wife?"

"Yes. The defendant painted a much rosier picture. While he acknowledged that they had been having some issues, he claimed they were working things out."

"Did you ask him about the possibility of divorce?"

"Yes. The defendant vehemently denied that either one of them had ever entertained any ideas of getting a divorce. It was then we realized that we couldn't believe everything that the defendant said to us."

I was listening in shock to all of this. I hadn't known that Jennifer had met a divorce attorney just a couple of days before she was killed. She never mentioned it to me. I scribbled a quick note to Orensen to tell him that I didn't know about the divorce attorney. He glanced briefly at the note, then focused back on the testimony at hand. He didn't seem too concerned about the divorce attorney issue at this time.

Murdoch continued with his direct examination of Chief Lumpkin. "Going back to the time of death, which was determined as having taken place between 2 a.m. and 4 a.m., was there any further significance of that timeframe?"

"Yes. We subsequently asked the defendant to give us a timeline as to his whereabouts throughout the night in question. He had no alibi during the time in which the murder occurred. He had specific details about his whereabouts and activities during earlier hours, but no alibi for the time of the murder."

Murdoch pressed the matter further. "Did you try to obtain any other evidence that would hone in on the defendant's whereabouts during the time of the murder?"

"Yes. We obtained a warrant for his cell phone records. We noted that his cell phone was turned off during the timeframe of the murder, thus making its location impossible to track at that time. We noted that there were no other significant periods of time in the records in which his phone was turned off. It was only off during the time of the murder." Lumpkin then sarcastically added, "Quite a coincidence!"

"Any other significance regarding the estimated time of death?" Murdoch asked.

"Yes. We received a tip from a homeowner who lives a few blocks from the crime scene that he observed a vehicle traveling at a high rate of speed down his street at approximately 2:45 a.m. that same morning. The vehicle was traveling in the direction away from the crime scene. Additionally, this particular street would be a part of the quickest route between the crime scene and the defendant's parents' residence, where the defendant slept that night."

"Did you question this tipster further and if so, what more did you learn?"

"We did follow-up with him and learned that the vehicle's right headlight was out. This fact was also true of the defendant's parents' car. Additionally, our tipster described the speeding car as a large four-door, which again is true of the defendant's parents' car."

"Any other useful information from the crime scene?" Murdoch asked.

"We noticed that the victim was missing her wedding ring. It wasn't on her finger, nor was it anywhere to be found in the house. There was other jewelry all around her bedroom dresser, but no wedding ring."

"What did that seem to indicate to you, Chief?"

"It seemed to indicate that the ring was taken to make the murder look like a burglary gone wrong. The scene looked staged to appear as if the burglar was caught in the act of the crime, shot the potential witness, and fled as soon as he could, without taking time to grab anything else. It seems too coincidental that if it were a random burglar, caught in the act, that he just so happened to snare the one piece of jewelry that was the most valuable before fleeing in a panic. And oh by the way, how did this random burglar get into the house? The victim let him in at two in the morning? Come on!"

Murdoch chuckled a bit, then asked, "As you started looking more closely at the defendant as a viable suspect, what else did you learn?"

"We learned that he had a hefty life insurance policy on the victim and that it was taken out not too long ago. This fact, coupled with a downward economy and the defendant's struggling business, makes it pretty easy to see how Michael Stohler would have incentive to want his wife dead. Their marriage wasn't going to last anyway. Why pay alimony when instead he could collect life insurance money? Motive is as clear as day in this case."

"Any other evidence pointing to the defendant?"

"We have two instances, independent from each other, in which the defendant was overheard confessing to the crime."

"Thank you Chief Lumpkin. No further questions your honor."

Judge Stevenson then turned to the defense table. "Mr. Orensen. Any cross-examination?"

"Yes your honor." Orensen rose, then asked, "Chief Lumpkin. I listened to your testimony and I didn't hear any references to a single shred of physical evidence directly linking the crime to Mr. Stohler. Did you find any such evidence?"

"As I testified, we know that the shooter was left-handed and…"

Orensen stopped him. "Chief. I am asking about specific physical evidence directly linking the crime to Mr. Stohler. For example, did you find Mr. Stohler's fingerprints at the scene?"

"No."

"Any footprints?"

"No."

"Any DNA?"

"No."

"Any blood stained clothing of Mr. Stohler found at the scene or anywhere else?"

"No."

"Any murder weapon?"

"No."

"Chief Lumpkin. Is it true that you searched more than just the crime scene? For instance, didn't you also search Mr. Stohler's office, vehicle, his parents' residence, and his parents' vehicle?"

"Yes. That is correct."

"Did you find any physical evidence, such as those I previously listed, in any of those searches?"

"No."

"Were there any eyewitnesses to the crime?"

"As I previously stated, we have a witness who saw a vehicle speeding..."

Orensen cut him off. "Chief Lumpkin. I am referring to any witnesses to the actual crime. Do you have anyone who specifically saw the crime being committed?"

"It took place in the middle of the night in the victim's bedroom! Who's going to be there to witness it?" Lumpkin defiantly answered.

"I assume that is a 'no' answer, Chief. There were no witnesses to the crime?"

"No."

"Isn't it true Chief that in all the times you spoke with Mr. Stohler during your investigation, that he always vehemently denied any involvement in the crime? Is that correct?"

"So what? Many guilty people say they didn't do it!" Lumpkin angrily retorted.

Orensen looked to Judge Stevenson, "Your Honor, please ask the witness to answer the questions directly."

The judge instructed Lumpkin to do so.

Lumpkin then said, "Yes that is correct. He didn't confess. So what?"

"Regarding the supposed confessions that were overheard, did you overhear them directly?"

"No."

"So you can't be sure as to the exact context of the confessions, is that correct?"

"I don't know what you mean. I was given reports from two separate people stating they heard him confess. That is what I testified."

"Is it possible that they misheard? Or heard something out of context?"

"No. Not when it's two separate instances of it."

"How would you know that if you weren't there?"

"They are reliable sources."

"Who are these reliable sources?" Orensen asked.

Murdoch shot up, "Objection your honor. The witness is not required to divulge that information at this time."

Orensen rebutted, "Your honor. We are here to establish whether or not there exists enough evidence for this case to proceed to trial. If the witness is not required to provide specifics as requested, then how are we to know that this information is legitimate?"

Stevenson pounded his gavel. "Mr. Orensen. You know that hearsay evidence is permissible in a preliminary hearing. If the prosecution wishes to present this evidence in trial they will then have to bring in the specific sources to testify and of course you will be given the names in advance as part of the discovery process. Please note that Chief Lumpkin was sworn in before his testimony so I'll remind him that any testimony given in this courtroom that is later found to be false will subject him to possible perjury charges. As for the objection; it is sustained. The witness does not have to answer that question at this time. Mr. Orensen, do you have any further questions for this witness?"

"No further questions your honor." Orensen walked back to the defense table.

Judge Stevenson then asked, "Mr. Murdoch, do you have any other witnesses to call."

"No your honor."

Orensen then stated, "Your honor. Based on the fact that there is no physical evidence and no eyewitness testimony, and based on the fact that the Commonwealth's case consists solely of circumstantial evidence and hearsay, I move that the charges in this case be dropped, until such time as the Commonwealth has more sufficient direct evidence, should that ever occur."

Judge Stevenson contemplated the motion for a moment then addressed the court. "The evidence as presented in this preliminary phase is sufficient to warrant continuing the case toward trial. The defendant will be held to answer the charge against him and will continue to be held in custody. Are there any other motions?"

Orensen answered, "Your honor. Due to the intense coverage of this case in the local media we believe that the potential jury pool in this jurisdiction has been tainted. As such, we would like to file a motion for a change in venue."

Stevenson answered, "We will conduct a hearing one week from today to address this motion and any other pre-trial motions. We will also set the timeframe for the trial at that time. In the meantime, I am implementing a gag order for both sides. No conversing with the media regarding the case. Court is adjourned."

Stevenson pounded his gavel, rose, and left the courtroom. I was then handed over to the bailiff and taken back into custody. There was no longer any hope of getting out before the trial.

Chapter 44

Back behind bars, I was greeted by my talkative cellmate who was apparently very curious as to everything that took place in court. I responded by vaguely saying it was just a routine, preliminary hearing. In the past few days Greg had gradually become more and more interested in my case. Now it was to the point where it was the primary topic of discussion, almost to the exclusion of anything else. It was also a somewhat one-sided conversation as I continued to adhere to the advice of both Orensen and his sidekick, Mug, both of whom vehemently cautioned me not to discuss the case with anyone.

My parents visited me daily, which was the highlight of each day. I always tried to put on a happy face for them, as best I could in the circumstances, so as to not worry them any more than was necessary. We talked mostly about how they were doing and about progress in the case. They reported to me that Orensen and Mug were hard at work investigating on my behalf and preparing for the trial.

I inquired about the costs that must be mounting now that the billing was two-fold. We had Orensen's billing rate and now we also had the time and expenses associated with his personal investigator. My father gave me the usual speech that I had now heard numerous times. That speech could essentially be summed up as "don't worry about it."

I didn't press the matter too much. What was I going to do? Pull them off the case at this stage? They were my only hope. The cost was a trivial concern compared to the fact that the rest of my life hung in the balance; a life that may not be very long if I were to be convicted.

I often inquired with my parents as to the media coverage of the case and what exactly was being reported. My parents seemed to be vague and evasive with their answers, primarily saying that they try to steer clear of the media. Even without their specifically saying so, it was apparent that the press coverage of the case was no different than I had grown accustomed to prior to my incarceration. Why should it be any different?

I've found that nothing is more mundane and pointless than the day-to-day life of an inmate. Every day is exactly the same as the day before and the day after. Wake-up time, meal times, recreation time, and bedtime are the same every single day. I've been here for two weeks and I'm already losing my mind with the monotony. How could I live like this for the rest of my life?

The only reprieves from the monotony were my court appearances and the visits from either my parents or my legal team. Even visiting hours are at the same time each day. However, three days after my preliminary hearing, I got a very pleasant surprise visit from my former administrative assistant, Brenda Challey.

"Hello Michael. I hope you don't mind my coming here. I just wanted to say hello and see how you are holding up."

"Hi Brenda. Of course I don't mind. It is nice to see you. Thank you for coming." I answered.

She asked me some questions about what it is like in here and how I'm handling it. I painted a rosy picture, similar to how I would put on a happy face for my parents. Then I said, "Brenda, I'm glad you're here. I've wanted to tell you that I am really sorry about having to close the plant. I know how much you and your family needed the job and I stayed open as long as I could. But I feel really badly about it."

Brenda responded, "Actually, I had come here because I wanted to thank you. I know how hard everything had been for the business and I know you had to let a lot of people go over the course of time that you didn't want to. But you kept me on to the end and I'll always be appreciative of that. Thank you for that Michael."

I felt like crying. As someone who felt like the world hated me and as someone being portrayed publicly as a monster unworthy of life, you can't imagine what it felt like to hear those kind words. Such kindness was few and far between these days for me.

We talked for a little while longer before the announcement that visiting hours had ended. I thanked her again for coming and I wished her and her family the best of luck. She wished me luck as well and promised to keep in touch.

I was then escorted back to my cell where I was in for another surprise. Upon returning to my cell, I learned that my cellmate was gone. A guard told me that Luckman had been transferred to another prison and that he wasn't coming back.

Chapter 45

Of course District Attorney Stanley Murdoch was pleased with the outcome of the preliminary hearing, but he was disappointed that he couldn't bask in the glory of his victory with the media immediately afterwards. The court had essentially muzzled him for the time being. But he told himself that when all was said and done, and Michael Stohler was on death row, there would be plenty of opportunity for him to toot his own horn.

In the meantime, it was back to work on the case. He had shown in the preliminary hearing that they had enough evidence to proceed to trial, but Murdoch knew that the required standard of proof was much higher for an actual conviction at trial. As such, Murdoch knew that there was much work to be done to achieve the magnitude of evidence that would assure the conviction.

His first order of business after the preliminary hearing was to chat with Chief Lumpkin to get an update on the search for the missing ring. But Lumpkin had little to report.

"Well don't give up on it" Murdoch ordered. "Expand the search wider. He may not have hocked it locally. Let's find out exactly what the ring looked like; size, shape, etc. so that we can get an estimated value. Also, ask some of Jennifer's friends if they know where Michael originally purchased the ring. He may have gone back there to sell it."

"We've also started looking into if Stohler had insurance on the ring." Lumpkin added. "If so, he may have made a claim to collect on it, or had planned to do so before being arrested for the murder. That could add to his motive. He kills her, takes the ring, secretly sells it, and doubles the windfall with an insurance claim on the ring. All the while, getting life insurance money and not paying alimony. Quite a financial bonanza for him."

"Good thinking. Let's get on it. Talk to Michael's friends, work associates, anyone we know who's conversed with him; see if he's mentioned the value of the ring, where he had purchased it, if he has insurance on it. Someone out there must know something."

"Ok. We're on it." Lumpkin responded. They then hung up so each one could continue on their quest for more evidence against Michael Stohler.

Immediately after he was done with Lumpkin, Murdoch received some great news. It came in the form of a phone call from Warden Culler.

"Stanley! Culler here. Great news for you. Your boy Stohler confessed and Luckman sung like a canary."

Murdoch could barely control his enthusiasm. He pumped his fist in the air and gave the thumbs up to several associates who were watching him as he made a spectacle of himself by doing a mini dance by his desk. He then composed himself enough to ask, "What exactly did he say?"

"Well, I was informed that Luckman requested to see me, so I had a guard take him to me while Stohler was out of the cell meeting with a visitor. This way Stohler wouldn't know where Luckman went or why. Luckman simply told me that Stohler said several times that he killed his wife. I asked if he was sure and Luckman said it was clear as day."

Culler added, "I asked Luckman what led to the confession and why he thought Stohler confessed. Luckman said that they'd bonded over the past week or so; talking about their lives, families, and their crimes. They basically confided in each other about everything. Luckman said he won Stohler's trust in the same way he had gotten many other people to trust him over the years. Be the kind, sympathetic, caring guy that everyone wants to be able to trust, especially during hard times. Luckman says it works every time. He's a pro at this. It's why we picked him as the cellmate in the first place."

"This is fantastic news Culler. Great job as usual. Orensen, the defense attorney, was attacking Lumpkin on the stand about how the confessions we had thus far had just been overheard. None were directed specifically toward our witnesses, so Orensen was trying to paint a picture that they could have been out of context. But there can be no mistake on this one. The confession was made directly to him. Not overheard from afar."

Culler then added, "Confessions. Plural. No chance of mishearing or misinterpreting something over and over during the course of a few days. Luckman says he's mentioned murdering his wife several times. It's like Stohler felt better getting it off his chest, while saying it to someone who he figures won't hurt him. He knows not to say it to the police, but who can be further from the police than a convict in prison with him?

"So what did you do with the cellmate after he came to you with this development?" Murdoch asked.

"We've transported him to another institution. He's been rewarded for his cooperation by going to a lower security prison closer to his family. I've also alluded to the fact that his testimony on the Commonwealth's behalf in the upcoming trial will be considered as soon as he is first due for parole. I was careful not to make any specific promises, but he gets the point. He will cooperate with us."

Culler went on, "We also figured that we should immediately remove him from Stohler to avoid the off-chance that he really does start bonding with

Stohler and has a change of heart. Also, it is for Luckman's protection to remove him from a dangerous person against whom he'll be testifying."

"Again, great job Culler. Please forward me the information where Luckman is now being held. I'll need to prep him for his future testimony in court."

"Is there someone else you had in mind for Stohler's next cellmate?" Culler asked.

"No. Actually, it may be best not to give him another cellmate. It may seem strange that Stohler confessed to one cellmate, but not another. Or if we start getting a multitude of confessions, that would seem suspicious also. It would look like prisoners were coming out of the woodworks to get better deals for themselves. The story is he had one cellmate, with whom he bonded and to whom he confessed. Period. No need to push the matter further."

"Ok. Got it." Culler responded.

After some more pleasantries, the two buddies said goodbye and hung up. Murdoch was proud of himself. He had concocted the scheme to pair Stohler with a certain type of cellmate who would elicit a confession. Look at how seamlessly that plan was executed! Murdoch was a genius. It's just a shame that he couldn't tell the press about it. It will all come out later though. It will go into the book Murdoch decided he was going to write about the case after all was said and done. What a book that would be! A best seller! Who wouldn't buy a book about a heroic district attorney and his brilliant investigative instincts and courtroom talents which successfully put a cold-blooded murderer on death row in the most highly publicized case in state history? He was going to make a fortune. Murdoch smiled to himself as he whispered his thanks to Michael Stohler for committing a murder that will propel Murdoch to levels of fame and fortune far surpassing even his own high aspirations.

Chapter 46

After getting essentially nowhere in his interviews of Jennifer Stohler's closest friends, Mug decided to expand his questioning to Jennifer's workplace. He made an appointment to meet with Principal Ronald Walker, who, in addition to being Jennifer's boss, had also been a friend and mentor.

"Good afternoon Principal Walker. Thank you for taking some time to meet with me." Mug warmly stated as he entered the principal's office. The two shook hands as Walker invited Mug to have a seat. "As I mentioned on the phone, I am investigating Jennifer Stohler's murder."

"I'm glad to assist in any way I can" Walker responded. He then added, "It is such a horrible tragedy. I still can't believe that Jennifer is gone."

Mug solemnly shook his head, then asked, "Principal Walker, you knew Jennifer very well. Did she speak to you at all about her husband and any problems that she was having at home?"

"You can call me Ron. She didn't speak much about it. She was always very professional and didn't let anything going on personally affect her at work. She did briefly mention to me in the lunch room that she and Michael were going through a little rough patch, but she didn't give any specifics, and I didn't push the matter. I didn't want to pry into her personal life. I just offered that she could always come to talk to me anytime she wanted. She never did. At least not about that."

"What did she come to speak to you about?"

"Mostly school related matters; particularly the class trip she had been organizing just before she was killed. She did also talk a little bit about Mr. Durkin."

"Who is Mr. Durkin?" Mug asked.

"Robert Durkin is a new second grade teacher who started with our school this year. He moved here this past summer from Texas. He is single and he seemed to have taken a bit of a liking to Jennifer. Jennifer had befriended him at the start of the school year to make him feel comfortable in his new surroundings. She showed him the ropes around the school. Jennifer always did that with newcomers. Made them feel like a part of the family, so to speak, as soon as they start with us. It was one of the many things that made her so special."

"What did Jennifer say to you about Mr. Durkin?"

"She was concerned that he wasn't really fitting in socially with the staff. She sensed that he was somewhat of a shy, loner type and that he may have a crush on her. He always seemed to hang around her in the break room and wherever possible around the school. I think he also went with her to one of her church functions."

"Do you know if anything went on between them?"

"If you mean, did Jennifer have an affair with him, I would highly doubt it. Jennifer was just a friendly, warm, outgoing person who made everyone feel comfortable with her and like her. You know how it is; some guys may interpret that as specific interest in them as opposed to it just being someone's general kindness applied to all. Durkin's single and may have had a crush. Jennifer befriended him from a professional standpoint and that was almost certainly all there was to it."

"Ron. Who do you think killed Jennifer?" Mug asked.

"I don't know. Everyone seems convinced that her husband killed her. I suppose that is possible. Anything is possible. I'm a little troubled that everyone jumped to a conclusion about her husband so quickly before waiting to see where further evidence may lead. I've met Michael on several occasions. He seemed like a nice guy. But you never know. Looks can be deceiving." Walker then smiled and added, "You probably know a little bit about looks being deceiving."

Mug smiled, then followed up with, "What about Durkin? Do you think he could have done this?"

"Like I said, anything is possible. But, my gut feeling is no. He's just a quiet, shy teacher. A little socially off, but a nice guy. We had done a thorough background check prior to hiring him. We have to do that of course before trusting someone to be in daily contact with many young children. His record is perfectly clean. We've had no problems with him. He's a very good teacher. The kids like him."

"What does Durkin look like? Do you have a photo of him?"

"He's a big guy, roughly six foot, maybe six-one, probably at or near three hundred pounds, balding, no facial hair. Here's a photograph of him taken a couple of months ago."

Mug studied the photo. Walker's description was accurate. Durkin was tall; maybe even a little taller than Walker's estimate, definitely a big guy.

"Do you happen to know if Durkin is left-handed?" Mug asked.

"No. I'm sorry. I don't know."

Mug asked a few more questions, without getting any further useful information. He then stood up and thanked Walker for his time. Mug gave him a card and asked him to call if he could think of any other useful information.

After leaving, Mug sat in his car and wrote some notes to summarize what he had just learned. He previously had a hunch that the key to this mystery could lie in some type of love triangle, or something similar; like a guy with a crush who got rejected. It was just a hunch, but it was certainly viable. And this guy fit the bill. Loner, shy, single, new in town, not many friends, took a liking to the victim, the feelings weren't reciprocated, etc. It was exactly the type of scenario Mug had seen dozens of times in the past. Despite Walker's gut feeling that Durkin couldn't do this, Mug knew better. Every time you see a report on television of a criminal being apprehended, there are interviews of friends and neighbors in which they say, "he was such a nice guy" or "he was such a quiet guy" or "I can't believe he would do this" or "I never saw this in him." It happens all the time.

He knew that he will have to speak with Durkin. But first he wanted to dig up some more information. Mug had his first suspect and he didn't want to spook him prematurely. It was time to gather more intelligence on Durkin. Walker had mentioned that Durkin accompanied Jennifer to a church function. The next step will be to have a chat with Pastor Solomon.

Chapter 47

Mug met with Pastor Frank Solomon the next day in the Garrowville Church. "What can I do to help you Mr… I'm sorry. What did you say your name was again?" Pastor Solomon asked.

"Mug. You can just call me Mug. Thank you for meeting with me today."

"Is Mug your real name?"

"It might as well be. It's what everyone calls me."

"How did you get that name?"

"It is a very long story. Let's just say that it goes way back to a different life."

Pastor Solomon sensed not to push the matter further. "What can I do to help you sir." He didn't seem comfortable using the name 'Mug.'

"I am investigating the murder of Jennifer Stohler. I know she was very active in your church. I wanted to know what insights you may have."

"What do you mean by 'insights'? I don't really know anything as to what happened other than that she was killed. Such a horrible tragedy."

"Do you think it was her husband who killed her?" Mug asked.

"I've known the Stohler family for many years. I officiated at George and Marilyn's wedding. They're Michael's parents. That's how long I've known the family. I also married Michael and Jennifer. They were a great couple. And great people. It's very hard for me to fathom that Michael could have done this to her. He adored her."

"Did Jennifer confide in you as to anything or anyone troubling her?"

"No. She was always very upbeat. If anything was troubling her, you couldn't tell. I learned afterwards about the marital problems they were having. But I never could tell anything in my interactions with Jennifer and she never mentioned anything to me."

"Did she have any new friends; any new members of the church or new participants in any church activities?"

"None that I knew of."

"What was the most recent church activity that Jennifer participated in?"

"You mean other than attending each Sunday?"

"Yes."

"We had a guest lecturer one weeknight a few weeks before her death. Jennifer had arranged it and had invited some people outside our usual members to attend. She wanted a good turnout because I think she had promised the speaker a certain number in attendance. Several of her work associates at the school attended."

"Do you know if someone named Robert Durkin was there?"

"I don't remember the name, but I do remember a male teacher sitting next to her during the lecture. I hadn't seen him before. That could be him. Wait a minute, I just remembered that we had a sign-in sheet for the event. Let me get it."

Mug waited patiently for a few minutes as Pastor Solomon retrieved the sign-in sheet. He returned with a clipboard with a white sheet on it.

"Here it is. Yes, there is a Robert Durkin signed in. Here is his signature."

Mug looked at the list. Durkin's name was the 2nd one on the list. Just under Jennifer's. They were the first two arrivals. It's very possible that they arrived together. Michael Stohler's name didn't appear on the list.

"Pastor. Would you be able to make a photocopy of this list for me?"

Pastor Solomon nodded, left for a few moments to make the copy and returned. He handed the photocopy to Mug.

"Thank you Pastor. Do you remember anything unusual about Mr. Durkin? Anything about his interactions with Jennifer?"

"No. Nothing that I can recall other than that they seemed to be friends from work."

Mug asked some more questions, but Pastor Solomon didn't really have much else to report. He thanked the Pastor and departed. He then called Orensen to update him on the emergence of a possible lead. They briefly discussed strategy as to how to follow-up on this lead without "pulling a Lumpkin" and going all in on just one possible explanation. All angles would have to be explored, including but not limited to, this one. There was still a lot of work to do. Orensen instructed Mug to meet him after the court hearing on Monday.

Chapter 48

Monday, January 18, 2010, was a morning that one who is incarcerated would refer to as a good day because there would be a break from the dreadful monotonous prison life routine. This morning I was due back in court for the hearing Judge Stevenson called for to rule on pre-trial motions.

I was greeted by Orensen at the defense table and he briefly filled me in on what was going to transpire.

"Good morning Michael. This will be just a routine hearing to settle some pre-trial matters and to schedule the start date of the trial. The most important items for us will be a change in venue and to get a trial date as soon as possible. I don't foresee any issues getting what we want in these matters."

"How far out could my trial date potentially be set?" I asked.

"It depends. It can vary based on a number of factors; such as availability of the court, lawyers' schedules, allowing adequate time for the discovery process, etc. But in this case, with you being held without bail, it will more likely be pushed forward as much as possible. We also don't want to give the prosecution any unnecessary time to accumulate evidence, real or otherwise."

Just then, the court was called to order and Judge Stevenson entered the room. We all rose and sat back down on command and the proceedings commenced.

"The primary motion to address this morning was filed by the defense in which they have moved for a change in venue for the trial." Stevenson announced. "Mr. Orensen, would you care to speak on this matter?"

"Yes your honor." Orensen rose and approached the podium. "Your honor, this case has received a tremendous amount of media coverage. Television and radio stations, newspapers, and numerous internet sites have all been extensively covering the case. More alarming is the fact that the coverage has been overwhelmingly negative for Mr. Stohler. Garrowville is not a particularly large community. Everyone seems to know and talk to everyone else. And there has been no topic of discussion in recent weeks that has been more prevalent than this case. Quite simply, the potential jury pool in this area has been tainted beyond repair. It is not practical for us to believe that we could find twelve impartial jurors whose objectivity has not been affected by the barrage of negative press Mr. Stohler has been receiving. Therefore, we move that the trial should be relocated to a venue as far from this jurisdiction as possible; preferably one in a different media market. Thank you your honor."

"Mr. Murdoch. Would you like to respond to this motion?"

Murdoch knew that he wasn't likely going to win this battle. The change in venue was probably going to be approved in light of the local coverage and interest in the case. So he wasn't inclined to put up a big fight, only to lose. His ego wouldn't stand for it. But he did want to put up a light fight, maybe to at least keep the case as close to the area as possible. Also, he figured that if he was ruled against on this matter, maybe he'd get a little more leeway on the next matter to be discussed, which pertained to the timing of the trial.

"Yes your honor. Many murder cases get press coverage and we can't realistically expect that anywhere else we go that no one would have heard of this case. The key to a fair jury is in proper questioning of potential jurors during the voir dire process; a process that would take place in any jurisdiction. Just like the defense, we also want a fair, impartial jury for the trial. But we believe that can be achieved almost anywhere with proper vetting of potential jurors before the trial."

Stevenson thanked the lawyers, then stated that he was ready to issue his ruling on the matter. "I am inclined to side with the defense on this matter. It is apparent even just from the hordes of media outside the courtroom this morning that this case has received substantial local attention. Additionally, as Mr. Orensen pointed out, this community is not very large, therefore, the victim was known to almost everyone locally. It would be very difficult to find twelve unbiased jurors in this area. I hereby rule that a new venue will be found for this trial. The specific venue will be determined in the next few days depending on scheduling and court availabilities in surrounding counties."

Orensen shot up and said, "Your honor. Thank you for ruling in favor of the change in venue; however, we believe that moving to a neighboring county may not fully address the issue as it would still be within the same media market. We believe that further away from this county would give us a better chance at an objective jury pool."

"Thank you Mr. Orensen. The exact venue has not yet been decided. The court will consider your concerns. The venue will depend greatly on the timing of the trial and court availability. Therefore, let's get to the next order of business. Mr. Orensen, does the defendant wish to waive his right to a speedy trial?"

Orensen was faced with a strategic decision here. On one hand, the defense could waive the right to a speedy trial, allowing for greater flexibility in courtroom availabilities state-wide. On the other hand, there was no guarantee even with more scheduling flexibility, that Stevenson would move the case much further away. In the meantime, the added time would give the prosecution more opportunity to accumulate evidence and would require that Michael remain behind bars for longer as he awaited trial. All in all, it was better to get to trial sooner rather than later. Never give the prosecution additional time to prepare its case. The prosecution had the burden of proof and right now they didn't have a lot of evidence, so a speedy trial made the most sense.

"No your honor. The defendant does not wish to waive his right to a speedy trial; especially in light of the fact that he is incarcerated while awaiting trial."

"Very well. A trial date no later than ninety days from now will be set by the court to which this case will be moved. That court will also schedule the defendant's arraignment. Both the prosecution and defense will be notified this week as to the location and exact date of the arraignment. The discovery period will be scheduled to begin exactly 60 days prior to the start of the trial. Are there any other matters to be addressed by either side?"

Neither side had any further business, so court was adjourned. I was headed back to prison, but at least I now knew that my trial would be no later than three months away. As I was transported back to prison, I wondered where my cellmate had gone, why he was transferred, and most importantly, who would be my next cellmate? Whether or not I survived the next three months may depend very much on that last question.

Chapter 49

Mug arrived at Jeff Orensen's office an hour after Orensen returned from the morning's court hearing. Mug filled Orensen in on all the specifics of his investigation thus far.

"I didn't get much out of Jennifer's close friends. Most are convinced that Michael did it and didn't have much desire to entertain any other thoughts or to speak with me. I didn't get to one former neighbor yet. The Dennisons. They moved out of the area. I'll need to track them down."

Mug continued, "As I told you on the phone, a possible suspect came up when I spoke to the principal at Jennifer's school and the pastor at her church. A guy named Durkin. Robert Durkin. A bit of a loner type; new guy in town; took a liking to Jennifer. He probably liked her a lot more than she liked him. It fits an all-too-common scenario: strange guy has crush, the feelings aren't reciprocated, strange guy gets violent."

Orensen responded, "CSI has the shooter as significantly taller than the victim and probably left-handed. Do you know if that fits Durkin?"

"The height fits. Durkin is tall. I don't know yet if he is left-handed."

"Ok. Let's go over the game plan from here." Orensen said. "First, you should know that a trial date is going to be set this week, and it will be within the next three months. So we have to move on this."

"Three months! That is not a lot of time. We've barely scratched the surface here. All I have right now is a hunch about one guy. Nothing else. Why so soon?"

"Well, Stohler is sitting in jail for one thing. He wants out as soon as possible and I don't blame him for that. Also, right now the prosecution has no physical evidence. Their case is all smoke and mirrors. The sooner we get them to trial the less likely they'll have enough evidence for a conviction. I don't want them having more time to build a case. I don't trust Lumpkin and I don't trust Murdoch. They'll both do whatever they have to in order to build a case, even if it means bending the rules a bit."

Orensen went on, "With that in mind, a few pieces of evidence were alluded to in the preliminary hearing that I want you to follow up on."

"Ok. What is it?"

"First, Lumpkin mentioned that he received two separate instances of supposedly overheard confessions. I am skeptical of it. Either they were heard out of context or else completely fabricated. Please see if you find out more about these confessions. Second, Jennifer apparently paid a visit to a divorce attorney two days before she was killed. The attorney's name is David Bergman. Please interview him to find out anything you can about her frame of mind, what her specific plans were going forward, and, if he knows if Michael knew about the meeting. Third, Michael had a life insurance policy on Jennifer. Please get all details on it and speak with the agent who sold it to him."

"Got it boss." Mug obediently answered.

"Now, regarding other angles to pursue," Orensen continued, "We need to obtain a list of all registered gun owners in Pennsylvania. And see if you can find out what kind of gun was used in the crime. We'll get that information in discovery, but I don't want to wait for it if we don't have to. Murdoch will take his sweet time getting information to us. We'll need to be proactive whenever possible.

"You'll need to interview everyone who Michael laid off from his company in the past few years. Cross-reference that list with gun owners and foreclosed homeowners. Anyone on more than one of these lists goes toward the top of the suspect list.

"Finally, I want to track down the missing wedding ring. If we can find the jeweler, pawn shop owner, or anyone in the black market who purchased this ring we may be able to get a solid lead on the seller of it, who may also be the killer. At minimum, maybe we can get someone to testify that it wasn't Michael who sold the ring.

"Any questions, Mug? And remember, time is of the essence here."

"Yes sir. I'm on it. I also will look into other robberies in the area. It could be just a random burglary gone bad."

"Mug, listen to me. I can't be 100% certain here, but I have a good hunch that Michael Stohler is innocent. It's just a gut feeling from my dealings with him and his family, and also from the lack of solid evidence against him. This whole thing reeks of a rush to judgment by a small, inexperienced police department in a small town with little crime, and a prosecutor for whom there is no turning back without significant public humiliation. I know Murdoch well. His eyes are always on the next prize in life and he doesn't care who he has to ruin to get there. He's probably whispering in Lumpkin's ear about everything that will come to the two of them from this case if they win. They'll play dirty if they have to in order to get their conviction and the fame they anticipate resulting from that conviction. It's up to us to make sure that an innocent man is not wrongly convicted and possibly executed for this crime."

Chapter 50

Mug realized that Orensen knew the right buttons to press with him and that the pep talk he had just received was effective. They had been working together for a long time. Mug was sensitive to the possibility of a wrongly accused person being convicted of a crime and how it felt to be that person. After all, Mug had once been in that position, and if not for the legal heroics of Jeff Orensen, his life would have been ruined. For that reason, Mug would do anything for Orensen and if Orensen believed a defendant may be innocent, then Mug believed it as well. Orensen once was the only person to believe in Mug's innocence and he was right then. Orensen had a keen eye in such matters.

Mug understood that he hadn't always been in the role of the sympathetic wrongly accused innocent man. He knew that he was guilty of the earlier offenses for which he was charged, but he also knew that inside he was a good person and he had always felt badly about the crimes he did commit.

One such offense in particular had haunted him for many years thereafter. When he was fifteen years old and still going by his given name, Derrick, he had been committing random pick pockets and purse snatchings whenever opportunities presented themselves. One day, he was in the food court of the local mall and saw a young mother distracted by a baby and two young children. She had left her purse on the table and had her back to it as she was reprimanding one child, while tying the shoes of another. There was no easier time to snatch a purse. So he did. Then he ran.

The young mom had turned around just in time to see him as he ran off with her purse and she started yelling out for help. Of course no one did anything. No one intervenes in these situations. He could vaguely hear her screams and the cries of one of the children as he escaped through a back exit door to the mall that he was familiar with from previous purse snatchings and from hanging out in general. Soon Derrick was back at home with the woman's purse.

He went through the contents of the purse, and took out all the money he could find. It wasn't much; about $60. But every dollar mattered to the Martin family. He then looked for any other valuables in the purse. That was when he discovered the item that would haunt him forever. He found a photograph of the woman with her husband. On the back of the photograph she had written a date. It was six months earlier. She also wrote that the photo was taken the night before the husband had died in a car accident. She had been carrying that picture around as a keepsake; their last happy evening together. Derrick had just stolen the purse of a recently widowed mother of three children and with the purse, he had also taken an item of much greater sentimental value than any money he had been after in the first place.

Derrick was in a horrible moral bind. He needed the money he had taken to support his struggling family. He couldn't confess to the crime because with his prior offense, he may be sent away this time and his family needed him. So he did what would be expected of an immature fifteen year-old kid in this predicament. He kept the $60, removed the photograph from the purse, hid the photograph, then discarded everything else.

He didn't want to be caught with any evidence of his offense, but he vowed to one day return the photograph to this woman. So he also made sure to remember her name, which he had obtained from several items in the purse. He never forgot her name. It was Susan Caldwell. He also made sure to remember her address.

Ten years later, Mug had been working for Jeff Orensen for a few years, and for the first time in his life, was earning decent money. He was proud of how he had finally turned his life around and was doing meaningful work. He was helping to protect innocent people from getting wrongly convicted and making sure that the real criminals were being apprehended. He was providing for his family and helping to pay the college tuitions of his younger siblings. He felt like a good person for the first time in his life, except for one matter still gnawing at him; the matter of Susan Caldwell.

He envisioned that she had to endure the life his own mother had been dealt; tragically losing a husband and struggling to raise children by herself. He didn't know where she was, if she had remarried, or even if she was still alive, but he was an investigator now, so he would find out.

The investigation was easy. She was still at the same address, was not remarried, and continued to go by the name Susan Caldwell. Derrick, now known as "Mug," purchased the nicest bouquet of flowers he could find, wrote a heartfelt note of apology, which he put in an envelope attached to the flowers. In the envelope he also put $5,000, which he said was for the $60 he had stolen, plus interest, plus a "little extra for the emotional scars I had caused." Also in the envelope alongside the cash, was the photograph that he had taken from her.

Mug contemplated just leaving the package on her front porch at night for Susan to find the next morning. But, he decided that was the cowardly way out. He needed to face his fears and meet head-on the issue at hand; just as he had always done throughout his life. So, he walked right up to the front door, rang the doorbell, and was greeted by a teenage boy, roughly fourteen or fifteen years old. He was probably one of the young boys he had seen at the mall ten years earlier.

"I'm looking for Ms. Susan Caldwell. Is she at home?"

"Yes. Who are you?" the kid asked.

"I'm an old acquaintance of hers" was the best answer Mug could think of in the circumstances.

"Mom…." the kid screamed as he looked back into the house "someone's at the door for you."

A moment later, the same woman from the mall ten years ago, looking just a little bit older, came to the front door. She had a puzzled, 'who are you?' look on her face.

"May I help you sir?" she asked.

"Are you Susan Caldwell?"

"Yes. Do I know you?"

"Well, not exactly ma'am. You see… This is hard for me to say. About ten years ago, I was an immature teenage kid, and I took something that belonged to you. It was at the food court of the Shelton Mall…"

A sudden look of horror covered Susan Caldwell's face. She instinctively took a step backwards and put her hand on the front door; at the ready to slam it shut.

"Ma'am, please. I am very sorry for what I did." Mug said as he held up the flowers. "As I said, I was young and immature. I always remembered what I did because I've felt very badly about it. Please take the flowers and please also look inside the envelope."

Susan tentatively reached forward to take the flowers. She called for her son to come to the door to take them and put them in water as she removed the envelope. Susan opened the envelope, saw the money and a second later, saw the picture. She started crying immediately.

Mug said, "I'm so sorry for having taken this photograph from you. I imagine it must have great sentimental value to you."

Susan nodded as she cried. Then she said, "Thank you so much for bringing this back to me. I've always thought about this photograph and I never expected to see it again. But I can't take this money from you. You didn't take that much from me."

"Please read my letter of apology. It says in part that the money is for more than just financial reimbursement. It is also for the emotional trauma I caused for you that day and ever since." Mug then added with a smile, "And I assure you it is not money stolen from someone else. That dark part of my life is long behind me."

She nodded, thanked him and invited him in for coffee. They talked for over an hour about their lives and the odd turns life had taken for both of them over the years that had brought them to this moment in time.

Mug and Susan have remained friends since that day. Mug attended each of her children's high school and college graduations and even helped one of her kids get a job with the Shelton police department. It was a friendship that developed from the strangest of circumstances. But then again, Mug had never been one who went the conventional route in anything in his life.

But Mug was always a good person at heart. Someone who went the extra mile for anyone or anything he believed in. Now, in the present day, he believed fully in Jeff Orensen and in Michael Stohler. He knew he had a monumental task ahead of him and very little time to get it done. But no one could ever deter Mug from doing what needed to be done, which in this case was to find out what truly happened to Jennifer Stohler; and apparently he had only three months, maybe less to do it.

Chapter 51

Both sides were informed that my arraignment, as well as all subsequent steps of the justice process would be carried out in the courts of nearby Mercer County. My arraignment was scheduled for Monday, January 25, 2010 at 9 a.m.

Orensen visited me the day before to prepare me for the arraignment. "Let's talk about tomorrow's arraignment" he said. "The first order of business is for the court to formally read the charges against you. In this case, it is just one charge; murder in the first degree. You will be asked by the judge if you understand the charge. Then you will be asked how you plead to the charge. Do not say anything in court except to specifically answer those two questions. I assume you'll be pleading 'not guilty.'"

"Yes."

"Only say those two words when asked what you plead. Do not start giving any explanations, defenses, etc. This is not the time or place for that, and we don't want to tip our hand as to anything we are going to use as a defense later on. Do you understand?

"Yes."

Orensen then spent a few minutes updating me on the progress of our side's investigation before stating that he needed to get back to work to prepare for the arraignment.

The next morning, I was transported to the Mercer County Courthouse, a trip that took approximately thirty minutes. The relatively short duration of the trip reminded me of Orensen's argument during the previous hearing after requesting the change in venue due to the tainted jury pool in Garrowville. Could the jury pool really be much less tainted just a half an hour away and within the same media market? I suppose we will find out later on at the trial. There will be no jury for today's proceedings. We will just be before the judge this morning.

The Mercer County judge assigned to the case was the Honorable William Connerly. He was a tall man, roughly six foot three, slim, graying hair, probably around forty-five to fifty years old. Orensen told me that he had never tried any cases before Judge Connerly, but that some of his colleagues had, and the scouting report was that he is very fair.

At precisely 9 a.m., with the courtroom packed, as has been the norm for all of my hearings, we rose as Judge Connerly was announced by the bailiff. After Connerly sat down, the bailiff requested us to do the same. The bailiff then read the case number and Connerly took over the proceedings. After some routine preliminary details, he read the official charge against me. Murder in the first degree.

"Mr. Stohler. Do you understand the charge against you?"

Orensen rose and gently nudged me to do the same. "Yes your honor." I responded.

"And how do you plead to this charge?"

"Not guilty."

A brief murmur circulated through the crowd inside the courtroom. What plea did they expect? Connerly pounded his gavel to restore order, then instructed that my 'not guilty' plea was to be accepted and so entered in the record.

Connerly then asked both counselors if there were any other matters for which they wanted to be heard before he announced the scheduling of the trial. Neither attorney had anything to present, so Connerly proceeded.

"The trial is hereby scheduled to commence at 9 a.m. on Monday, April 5, 2010 in this courtroom. Discovery must be completed by both sides no later than February 5, 2010. Court is adjourned."

Connerly pounded his gavel once for effect, rose, and left the courtroom. My trial date was set and was a little more than two months away. While I was excited to have the trial sooner rather than later, I hoped that was enough time for Orensen and Mug to find out what really happened to Jennifer so that they can prove that I was innocent. I wasn't so confident they could do so in such a short time frame.

Chapter 52

Time was short for Murdoch, Lumpkin, and the prosecution side of the trial as well. Discovery was just a couple of weeks away and embarrassingly, Murdoch didn't have much else to add to the evidence, above what he had Lumpkin testify to in court during the preliminary hearing. Normally, Murdoch would show just enough evidence in the preliminary hearing to assure a ruling that there is sufficient probable cause to proceed to trial, while holding back other evidence so as to not "tip his hand" fully to the defense before absolutely necessary. In this case, he had to tip most of his hand to get that ruling as there was a paucity of concrete evidence.

Since that hearing, he did get the jailhouse confession. But that will be testified to by a cellmate with a criminal record a mile long, comprised of various types of fraudulent activities. Not exactly an ideal witness. Murdoch needed more and there wasn't a lot of time.

Lumpkin was getting antsy as well. He had Murdoch breathing down his neck every day asking for updates and demanding more and more evidence. Murdoch kept reminding Lumpkin that nothing less than the rest of their careers rode on the outcome of this case. Murdoch wanted something, anything, and it didn't seem to matter what it was or how it was obtained, just as long as it pointed to Stohler being guilty. That was the only bottom line that mattered here. Murdoch made it crystal clear that it was up to Lumpkin to make sure Murdoch had enough evidence for the conviction.

As is normally the case in any chain of command, the crap flows downhill. So, as Lumpkin's life was made miserable by the demands of Murdoch from above, he then did the same to his subordinates, pressing them frequently as to what they were doing and asking why it was taking so long to dig up dirt on Stohler.

Under constant duress from Lumpkin, Officer John Riley had been making the rounds of various jewelers and pawn shops. First he concentrated his efforts in Garrowville, then expanded to surrounding areas, with no luck. Each day he reported his lack of progress to an increasingly frustrated Chief Lumpkin.

Riley then interrogated those within Michael's previous circle of friends. Maybe one of them knew something about where Michael may have gone with the ring. Through several of these contacts, Riley learned that Michael had originally purchased the ring from a college friend, a guy named Neal Brennan, who now had a jewelry shop in the Diamond District in Manhattan. Riley contacted Brennan who informed Riley that he had visited the Stohlers about six months before the murder. During that visit, Michael had asked him questions about his business, and more to the point, asked if he purchased diamonds from consumers or if he just sold to them. Additionally, according to Brennan, Michael requested that Brennan appraise Jennifer's wedding ring for insurance purposes. Michael had said that his insurance policy on the ring was about to expire and that the insurance company was requiring an updated appraisal. Brennan had appraised the ring at approximately $15,000.

Riley asked if Michael had subsequently sold the ring to him, and Brennan said 'no'. However, Riley knew that it would be unlikely that Michael would have sold the ring to his friend, shortly after killing his wife. More likely, he had simply used his friend to get an idea of what he could get for the ring after the murder.

Riley investigated the alleged insurance policy Michael Stohler had on his wife's ring and found that there was in fact a policy in place, and that was renewed in July 2009 for coverage of $15,000. So that part of Michael Stohler's representations to Brennan had checked out. However, an appraisal of that magnitude just five months before the murder adds to the motive theory for the case. Also, the fact that the appraised/insured item was the only one taken from the scene was a bit too coincidental.

Riley informed Lumpkin of the latest developments and these theories, and Lumpkin informed Murdoch. "Add yet another piece of circumstantial evidence" sneered Murdoch, who was clearly still unsatisfied. The more evidence, the better; but they'd better find something that more directly ties Michael Stohler to the crime, or else they are going to be in trouble. Where was the famous $15,000 ring? Where was the murder weapon? These were just some of the questions that would need to be answered; and fast.

Chapter 53

Mug pulled some strings within his law enforcement contacts and obtained a list of registered gun owners in Pennsylvania. He then obtained from George Stohler, access to the employee listings of Stohler Steel from the past five years, from which he was able to ascertain which names were removed from year-to-year. He then verified with Michael Stohler who on the list was let go vs. who left voluntarily. Mug intended to speak with every person who was terminated from the plant, but he would start with those whose name was on both the involuntary termination list and the gun ownership list.

There were four people who appeared on both of these lists. They were: Paul Corkin, Eddie Fields, Rachel Harmon, and Thomas Stoltz. Mug met with each of them and didn't get a lot of useful information. In general, each one wasn't happy that they were let go, but they understood that the business was hurting. They each seemed to think that Michael was a fair and honest boss and they realized that he had kept them on as long as possible. None of these people had their homes foreclosed as a result of their job loss, either because they had a spouse who was still working and/or they found other jobs, albeit at a lower pay, soon after leaving Stohler Steel. Mug's general gut feeling was that these weren't his prime suspects, but, he was not one to prematurely write off any possibilities.

He did get one piece of useful information from Eddie Fields. Fields informed Mug that his next door neighbor Ronald Johnson had told him that Johnson overheard Stohler confess to the murder in his office a couple of weeks after the crime. So Mug had solved one minor mystery. One of the previously unnamed confession informants had been identified.

Mug phoned Orensen with the news and it was agreed that Mug would interview Johnson immediately. "Let's put a scare into Murdoch that we are right on his track, doing the very investigative work that he and Lumpkin should have been doing from the get go."

Mug first made a brief visit to Michael in prison to get some information on Johnson. He learned from Michael that Johnson had worked for him for about ten years, was a top performer, and as a result was kept on board to the bitter end, surviving numerous cuts along the way.

This was not good news to Mug. It meant that Johnson shouldn't be one to harbor ill will toward Michael. He had hoped that Johnson would have motive to concoct a false confession against Michael, but from Michael's version of events, there didn't seem to be any such apparent motive.

Mug knew Johnson lived next door to Fields, who he had just recently interviewed, so finding Johnson was not difficult. He arrived at Johnson's residence that night and knocked on the door.

"Mr. Johnson. May I speak with you briefly regarding the Stohler case?" Mug asked warmly and politely.

"I've been instructed by the police not to speak with anyone about the case." Johnson answered through his closed front door.

"I understand sir, but I know you realize that Michael Stohler had treated you very well over the years. He kept you employed as long as possible and longer than most other people, so I would imagine that you would be willing to give me just a few minutes on his behalf."

Mug's little guilt trip was successful and Johnson opened the front door. "Come in quickly before anyone sees you here."

Once inside Mug thanked him and got right to the point, "I won't take up much of your time. I just want to know the circumstances in which you heard Michael confess to the crime."

"It's simple really. I had approached his office door, which was closed, and I heard him inside his office saying that he killed his wife."

"You said the door was closed?"

"Yes."

"Is there any chance you may have misheard?"

"No."

"How long did you stand outside the door listening?"

"Just a few seconds. I was afraid. I didn't want him to come out and see me eavesdropping. Especially in light of what he'd know I just heard."

"So, you walked up to the door, listened through a closed door for just a few seconds, heard him say 'I killed my wife,' then scurried away? Is that correct?"

"Yes."

"How did you know it was Michael Stohler in there?"

"The secretary came out and saw me walking away. I said I was looking for Michael and I asked her if he was in there. She said 'yes' but that it wasn't a good time to see him right now. So, I know it was him in there."

"What is the secretary's name?"

"Brenda Challey."

"Ok. Thank you very much for your time Mr. Johnson."

Mug left and made a bee-line to the Challey residence. He had her address from the employee records he had obtained from Michael's father. He wanted to get there before it got too late to speak with her that night. He was making progress and didn't want to lose the momentum.

"Ms. Challey. May I speak with you for a few minutes about Michael Stohler?" Mug asked after Brenda Challey answered his knocks on the door.

"Yes of course. How can I help?"

This was a good sign. Someone not yet instructed by the police not to speak about the case. It probably meant she was not going to be on the prosecution's witness list.

"Ms. Challey. A former employee of Stohler Steel had informed the Garrowville police that he overheard Michael Stohler in his office confess to the murder of his wife. Have you ever heard Michael confess to the crime?"

"No. Absolutely not. I never heard him confess, and as his secretary I was around him often, both before and after the murder."

Mug was getting excited, but kept his poker face on. "That's odd because the person reporting this confession claimed that he had overheard Michael talking in his office when he confessed, then stated that you walked out of Michael's office and saw him there. That would mean that you were in Michael's office during the confession."

"Like I said, Michael never confessed. I also know how devastated he was about his wife's death. He was very hurt that so many of his close friends and neighbors thought he had killed Jennifer. He kept asking 'Why does everyone think I killed my wife?'"

"Did he say that to you at any time while in his office?" Mug asked.

"Yes. Actually, quite often."

"After any of those times, did you see Ronald Johnson outside Michael's office?"

"Yes. In fact there was one time Michael was very distressed and I went in there to talk with him. He kept saying those same words asking why everyone thinks he killed his wife. When I left his office, Mr. Johnson was walking away. He can come to see Michael and I told him it wasn't a good time. Is he the one saying he heard Michael confess?"

"Yes." Mug answered. "But clearly he didn't hear what he thinks he heard. Would you be willing to testify in court as to this fact pattern?"

"Yes. Certainly. Anything I can do to help. It is scary to think how easy it is for people to hear things out of context and jump to conclusions as a result."

"Thank you Ms. Challey. One final question. Has the police or anyone else before me questioned you yet about this supposed confession?"

"No. No one."

"Thank you again. Attorney Jeff Orensen will be in contact with you about your testimony. Have a great evening."

Mug left and phoned Orensen immediately on his personal cell. This was news that couldn't wait until the next morning.

"You won't believe this" Mug excitedly proclaimed. He then filled Orensen in on his interviews this evening.

"Great work Mug. We'll definitely use Challey in court. It just goes to show how shoddy the police investigative work has been in this case. They got Johnson to say he heard a confession and they never followed up with the person to whom Stohler had allegedly confessed. They were just elated to get a report that contained a confession. Period. Why risk ruining a perfectly good confession tale with any explanation to the contrary?"

Chapter 54

Orensen and Mug both realized that nothing that Lumpkin and Murdoch presented in court during the preliminary hearing could be taken at face value. Everything had to be followed up on as any piece of evidence could have been skewed toward the prosecution's favor. So, Mug's next order of business was to talk with David Bergman, the divorce attorney with whom Jennifer Stohler had met just two days prior to her death.

"Mr. Bergman, I'd like to speak with you about the Stohler case." Mug requested on the phone the next morning.

"I cannot divulge anything regarding correspondences with my clients." Bergman curtly retorted.

"But Mr. Bergman, does attorney-client privilege extend beyond the death of the client?" Mug asked.

"It is not relevant. My policy is that I still do not divulge anything unless under a court subpoena to do so. Additionally, I've been instructed by the police not to speak with anyone about the case. So I am afraid I cannot help you. I'm sorry." Bergman then hung up.

Well, that was a dud, Mug thought, though he did indirectly confirm that Jennifer had in fact met with Bergman, as he had referred to her as a client.

From Michael, Mug got the information about the life insurance policy and the sales person from whom Michael had purchased the policy. In a brief interview with John Rollins, Mug confirmed that Michael did in fact have a policy, taken out about one year prior to Jennifer's death, in an amount of $250,000, which Michael had stated he was doing under the advice of a financial advisor. Per Mr. Rollins, $250,000 wasn't an excessively large policy and in fact, he had tried to sell Michael a larger policy, but Michael declined. Rollins stated that the insurance company was withholding payment on the policy pending the outcome of the case. Mug informed Rollins that they may call him to testify in the upcoming trial. In reality, Mug figured it was unlikely they'd call Rollins to the stand because he knew that the insurance company had a financial interest in Michael's guilt so that they wouldn't have to pay him.

Mug next interviewed Michael's financial advisor, Charlie Keppel.

"Mr. Keppel. Did you advise Michael Stohler to take out a life insurance policy on his wife?" Mug asked.

"Yes. But I certainly didn't advise him to kill her." Keppel nervously joked.

"No sir. I'm sure you didn't. Can you please tell me if it was you or Michael who had initially brought up the topic of obtaining a life insurance policy? In other words, did Michael come to you to ask if a life insurance policy would be prudent, or did you proactively advise him to do so?"

"Michael had been coming to me for financial advice for quite a few years. Even more so in the last couple of years as his home value had declined, the stock market was tanking, and his company was losing money. I advised him to do a lot of different things, one of which was the life insurance policy on his wife. He already had one on himself but not for Jennifer."

"Why would you advise taking on an additional expense when he was struggling financially?" Mug asked.

"Because he was cutting out a lot of other expenses, and, with him reducing his own pay, and there being less to rely on in terms of their home value and the business, his wife's earning potential was now a greater percentage of the family's financial well-being than it had been previously. Therefore, it was worth insuring her. A policy on a young, healthy, non-smoking woman was not going to be very expensive."

Mug replied, "He took out a policy in the amount of $250,000. Did you advise him to take a policy that high?"

"In actuality, I suggested $500,000. I thought $250,000 was too low. It is meant to replace a lifetime's worth of earning potential. Jennifer was in her early 30's. She could have worked for another 30 years, maybe more. Even $500,000 would not be sufficient to replace her earnings for that long. Michael was the one who opted for less."

"Mr. Keppel. You joked before about having not advised Michael to kill his wife. Do you think he killed her, especially considering that he opted for a lower policy on her?"

"No. I'm sorry about the bad joke. I was just a bit nervous. I don't think he killed her. I've known Michael and his family for a long time. He loved her. He was also resistant to do the policy. It was my idea and he usually listened to my advice. I had helped him a lot financially over the years and he respected my opinion. He never would have done a policy at all if I hadn't advised it. And I definitely do not think he killed her."

"Thank you for your time, Mr. Keppel."

Mug informed Keppel that he may be called upon to testify, then Mug left. He was starting to feel a little bit better about the overall public perception in this case. He knew that publicly and loudly the overwhelming majority of the population seemed convinced of Michael's guilt. But these people were the ones on the outside looking in. These were the people who weren't really in the 'know' but rather were simply jumping to conclusions based on circumstantial evidence and negative media reports. It seemed that people who truly knew

Michael and were involved in various facets of the case, weren't as convinced of his guilt. It was a good sign for the defense, and it was good motivation for Mug to keep plowing along in his investigation.

Chapter 55

Days and weeks were ever so slowly, but surely, passing by for me during my dreadful prison life. Strangely, I haven't been given a new cellmate. Everyone else in this place had a cellmate except for me. The only reason I could think of was that I hadn't officially been convicted of anything yet. But why then did I have a cellmate in the first place? It seemed very odd.

But not having a cellmate was one complaint I definitely was not going to file. There weren't many desirable cellmates in this place. I had gotten lucky with my first one. I imagined that my luck would not be likely to repeat itself the next time. Where did Greg go anyway? I've asked a few of the guards, but none of them would tell me anything. They were too busy taunting me about how the lethal injection works.

I continued getting visits each day from my parents, which of course was always a welcome reprieve from my daily doldrums. Additionally, Orensen's investigator Mug was coming in often to get information from me. On one hand, I was happy that someone was investigating on my behalf. But on the other hand, cost concerns kept popping into my head each time he came to see me. I couldn't imagine, nor did I want to think of, the number of hours he was putting in, multiplied by his billing rate. Added on top of Orensen's astronomical rate, I didn't know how we were paying for this.

Most times I tried to bring up the subject with my parents, they simply cut me off and wouldn't discuss it. However, one day it was just my mom who came to visit and I pushed the matter further. I figured I may be able to get more information about the amount we were being charged and how we were paying for it without my father around. She was a little reluctant at first, but with some prodding, I got her to tell me that they were selling their condo in Florida.

"That's where your father is today. He flew down this morning to iron out the details."

I protested, but obviously to no avail.

"It's alright" my mother said, trying to soothe me. "We don't really need it anyway. We're only down there a few months a year, and up here is truly our home anyway. We can always go down there for a vacation every now and then."

"How did you find a buyer so quickly?" I asked.

"Well, we took less than market value to get it sold quicker. We may have been able to sell it for more if we held out for a while, but it was more important to have the money now than to hold out for a few extra bucks. Your life is at stake and that is what is most important."

"Why don't we sell my house?" I asked. "Wouldn't that make more sense than you having to sell your retirement home?"

"Michael. No one is going to buy your house any time soon. There was a murder that took place in there. People steer clear of such homes. Also, your house has been getting vandalized. People are spray-painting horrible things on it. It is in no condition to be sold right now, and it would be difficult to ever sell it for anywhere near market value. And besides, you were underwater on your mortgage even before all this happened. It is likely going to be foreclosed."

With everything going on, I had forgotten that I was underwater on the mortgage. So selling it, even in normal times, wouldn't have put any cash in our pockets. It was obvious that we were in desperate financial straits. I realized that my parents were doing the right thing, but I felt terrible about it.

"I'm so sorry Mom" I said, as I fought back tears. I tried to tell myself that this wasn't my fault because I didn't kill my wife, but naturally, I felt at fault anyway. My parents were selling off their retirement home at below market to finance my legal defense. And we were still a couple of months away from the trial. How much more would have to be sacrificed financially to see this process to the end? And would it be to any avail when all was said and done?

We talked for a little while longer, but my head wasn't in it any longer. I kept thinking to myself how I was ruining my parents financially after having already run the family business to its demise. As a family we no longer had any money coming in from the business, we no longer had my parents' Florida home, my home was going to be foreclosed, and we had continuously mounting legal expenses. How were we going to survive?

Chapter 56

February 5, 2010 was the deadline for the exchange of information between the prosecution and defense teams as part of the required discovery process. Naturally, Murdoch stalled as long as possible, waiting until very late into the evening, but finally, in compliance with the court mandate, he provided Orensen with the required information. Orensen was not surprised to see that there wasn't much there above and beyond what had been testified to in the preliminary hearing. Either there wasn't much else, which would be the preferred scenario, or Murdoch was still holding back information. Just in case it was the latter, Orensen filed a motion to the court demanding the release of all information. Naturally, Murdoch's response was that he had already done so. Time will tell if that were the case.

In the meantime, Orensen did learn a few tidbits of information from the evidence exchange. He learned the names of those who alleged that Stohler had confessed. The list already confirmed what Orensen and Mug already knew; that one of the sources was Ronald Johnson.

However, there were a few surprises on this front. For starters, a third source emerged. Lumpkin had referred to only two sources in the preliminary hearing. One of the other sources was Officer Dan Radford. Orensen wasn't surprised about that; it was probably one of Lumpkin's slimy concoctions. Radford would say anything his boss instructed him to say.

The third name on the list was shocking to Orensen; Greg Luckman, Stohler's cellmate in prison. He was fairly certain that Stohler wouldn't say anything incriminating in prison. He had been repeatedly warned by Orensen and Mug. It was most likely another witness testifying as per the instructions of the prosecution. It was easy to see that this guy had probably been offered some type of deal to elicit a confession. Failing to get one, he invented it to still get the deal. Orensen was licking his chops for that cross-examination in court.

But first, he'd need to do his homework and talk to Michael Stohler. He needed to confirm his theory that Stohler hadn't really said anything, just in case he had done so and Luckman had a wire on him.

It was time to pay Michael Stohler a visit and ask him some very important questions.

Chapter 57

The next day, Orensen stopped by the prison to speak with me. After some preliminary chatter and an update on the case, Orensen got to the point. "Michael, we received the prosecution's initial delivery of evidence as part of the discovery process, and one of their possible witnesses is Greg Luckman, your former cellmate."

"Luckman? Where did he go? He hasn't been around in a while."

"I don't know where he is, but he may testify that you confessed to the murder to him. They probably transferred him away from you once he snitched. They'd want to protect him from you now that he is a witness for them."

I was stunned. I thought Luckman was my friend. Apparently he had been a "plant" to get a confession from me. I thought back to how often he had brought up the subject of my case and all the questions he asked and it was all starting to make sense. He played the 'I'm your only friend in here' and 'you can trust me' cards to try to get me to open up to him. He even told me all about his life, whether or not it was true is anyone's guess, in order to get me to confide in him. When I didn't comply, he made up the confession. I adamantly told Orensen I hadn't confessed and I conveyed my theory to him.

"I agree. They probably handpicked him as your cellmate and offered him a deal. Don't worry about it. I'll rip his testimony to shreds in cross-examination. He will not make a credible witness" Orensen said.

Orensen then changed the subject. "There is another matter I'd like to talk with you about."

"What is it?" I asked.

"As you heard in the last hearing, a witness claimed to have seen a car with a right headlight out, speeding away from the crime scene around the time of the murder. He also described the car as a large 4-door vehicle, and he stated that he saw a male driver. The police have on record that they issued you a ticket a couple of weeks later for a missing right headlight while you were driving your parents' car."

"Well this one is easy to explain." I responded. "First, I never drove my parents' car until my car was confiscated. So, I wasn't driving it at any time during the night of the murder. Second, the light on my parents' car went out sometime in the two week period in between the murder and when they gave me the ticket."

"Is there a way we can prove that?" Orensen asked.

"Not specifically. But I know it to be the case. After returning to work more than a week after the murder, I was driving my parents' car and I would pull into the parking garage underneath the building each morning so as to not park outside in public. Each time I pulled in, I would turn on the headlights. The first few days, they both worked fine. I noticed later in the week that one of them went out. I told my parents about it and they said they'd take care of it. That was a day or so before I got the ticket. They hadn't had a chance yet to get it fixed."

"Would anyone else at your office have seen you pull into the garage or drive in the garage during the days in which both lights were still functioning?"

"Probably not. I was the only one who bothered parking down there. With so few employees, everyone simply parked outside right by the front door."

"Ok. We'll simply argue reasonable doubt based on the lapse of time before the ticket. It was plenty of time for us to make a sensible argument that the light on your parents' car could have simply gone out any time after the murder before you got the ticket."

Orensen stayed for a little while longer then excused himself to get back to work on the case. On his way back to his office, he contacted Mug and instructed him to find out whatever he could about Luckman. Orensen also informed Mug that per the documentation obtained in discovery the gun used in the murder was a .22 caliber handgun. He instructed Mug to look into registered owners of that particular weapon statewide and to cross-reference that list against all of the other lists they were accumulating, such as laid off employees and foreclosed homeowners.

Finally, Orensen instructed Mug to speak with Durkin, their number one suspect at this time.

"Yes boss." Mug responded. "Also, I have an idea about Durkin. After I speak with him, I'll ask him to sign a document saying that he'll agree to testify in court if we need him. I think he'll sign because if he didn't kill her he'll truly be happy to help out anyway he could, and if he did kill her, he'll be anxious to come across to us as willing to assist. I'll pay attention to which hand he signs with to see if he is left-handed. Then, just in case he is smart enough to sign with his opposite hand to throw us off, I'll compare the signature to the church sign-in sheet. If he changes hands, the signatures would differ."

"Great plan Mug. Go get him."

Chapter 58

Mug waited outside the Garrowville Elementary School for Robert Durkin to leave at the end of the school day, then followed him back to his residence. Durkin lived by himself in a town house just a few minutes away from the school. Mug watched him pull into the driveway and exit his car, at which time Mug parked in front of the house and approached Durkin.

"Robert Durkin?" Mug asked, even though he knew who it was.

"Yes. Can I help you?"

Mug wanted to tread carefully here at first. He figured his best strategy was to approach in a friendly manner looking for help with the investigation. "I'm an investigator working the Jennifer Stohler murder. I know you were a colleague of Mrs. Stohler at the school. I was hoping that you can assist me with some information."

"Yes. Of course. Anything I can do to help. It's so horrible what happened to her. Please come in."

"Thank you." Mug answered as he followed Durkin into the sparsely furnished and somewhat untidy home. The walls featured various sports paraphernalia, including a life-size Emmitt Smith fathead which took up most of one side of the main room. Clearly this was the home of a single man.

"Are you a Cowboys fan?" Mug asked just to make small talk and loosen Durkin up a bit.

"Yes. A big one. Live and die with them. I'm from the Dallas area. I just moved here last year."

"What brought you to this area?"

"Change of scenery mostly; a fresh start. I applied for teaching positions in a lot of areas and got a pretty good offer here. So, here I am."

"Do you have any family, friends back in Dallas?"

"No one I minded leaving behind." Durkin answered.

Mug didn't have a good vibe about this guy. Something just felt a little off. It didn't necessarily mean he was a murderer, but Mug's radar was up. It was time to get down to business.

"So, Robert," Mug intentionally used his first name; a subtle indicator that they were closer now having chatted a bit, and that Durkin could confide in him; "who do you think killed Jennifer?"

"It seems pretty apparent that her husband killed her. It's all over the news. Everyone thinks he did it."

"Yes. That may be true. But I am wondering who you think killed her. You knew her. What do you think?"

"I think the husband killed her."

"Why?"

"They were having marital problems. Isn't it usually the husband in cases like that?"

"Sometimes." Mug answered. "Did Jennifer ever confide in you as to her marital problems?"

"No. Not really. We didn't talk much about her married life."

"So, did you know she was having problems at home before she was killed, or did you just find out about them afterwards?"

"Well, let's just say I can tell she wasn't happy."

"How could you tell? I've spoken to some other people at the school about her and they all seem to agree that Jennifer didn't let her personal issues affect her professionally."

"Well, that is true, but I knew. Jennifer and I were close. We spent a lot of time together."

"Really?" Mug feigned a bit of surprise in his response. "Just inside the school, or outside as well?" Mug asked.

"Both. We worked together so I saw her a lot during school hours, but we also hung out a lot outside of school."

"Doing what?"

"Oh, I don't know. Lots of things."

"Was there anything more going on between you and Jennifer?"

"Well, you know. It wouldn't be right for me to say, specifically. I don't want to tarnish her reputation. What happened to her was horrible and it wouldn't be right for her memory to be tainted in any way."

Mug couldn't believe the garbage he was hearing from this guy. He was lying through his teeth directly to Mug's face. Any amateur investigator would be able to tell and Mug was no amateur. But, embellishing the status of one's relationship does not make one a murderer. Mug still had work to do here.

"Did Jennifer's husband Michael know about you and your relationship with his wife?"

"I think so. It may be part of the reason he killed her."

"What makes you think he knew?"

"Well, I only met him one time. It was at a school function. Jennifer introduced us. He didn't seem to like me."

"What makes you say that?"

"He just sorted of nodded briefly at me and then excused himself. He wasn't interested in talking with me or getting to know me at all."

"Are you dating anyone right now? Or have you recently? I mean besides Jennifer?"

"Well, not right now. I'm still trying to get over Jennifer. I've had a lot of girlfriends before her though."

Mug noted that most people would say the question was none of his business. But this guy was happy to talk about, or more accurately, lie about his dating life.

"Let me ask you this," Mug said, "who else do you think could have possibly committed this murder?"

"No one really. It had to be Michael. Everyone else loved Jennifer. Pretty ironic don't you think? Everyone loved her except her husband."

"Have you ever been in their home?"

"No."

"So where did you and Jennifer carry on your affair?"

"Mostly here in my place."

Mug wanted to puke. But he carried on with the questioning.

"Did Jennifer ever mention if Michael owned a gun?"

"No. She didn't say so, but I guess he must have. We know that now."

"Do you know of anyone around here who owns a gun?"

"No. I don't really talk to many people around here, and the few with whom I do talk, the subject of guns doesn't really come up much."

"Do you own a gun?" Mug asked.

"No. I've never touched a gun in my life. Why are you asking me this?"

Mug needed to be careful. He didn't want to lose this guy before getting him to sign the document saying he'd testify if needed. So he answered, "I'm just trying to find out how Michael may have obtained the gun he used to kill his wife. He didn't own a gun and none was found in his house. I'm thinking that he may have stolen it from someone he knew."

"Probably. But not from here. I don't own a gun. Never have."

"Ok. Thank you very much for your time and help. I know you cared about Jennifer so I know that you want to make sure that she gets the justice she deserves. So, I assume that you'd be willing to testify as to what you know if needed during the trial."

"Yes. Definitely. Anything I can do to help." Durkin enthusiastically answered.

"Great. I have a form here for you to sign. It just says that you are willing to testify to assist with the case if needed."

Of course Mug knew that such a form was not necessary. If anyone wanted Durkin to testify they could just subpoena him. But he was banking on Durkin not knowing this. And he wanted to see with which hand Durkin signs the form. Mug was careful not to scare Durkin during the questioning so he didn't think Durkin would have reason to try to sign with his opposite hand, but he'd compare the signatures afterwards just in case.

"No problem." Durkin responded as he reached for the form and the pen Mug provided. Mug watched closely as Durkin signed the form. Durkin signed with his right hand.

Chapter 59

Mug thanked Durkin, departed, and briskly walked back to his car. He was anxious to compare the signature just obtained with the copy of the one from the church sign-in list. He got back into his car, compared to the signatures, and noted that they were clearly a match. Durkin was right-handed. There was no question about it. So what did that mean?

It meant one of three things. One possibility was that the CSI finding that the shooter was left-handed was incorrect. The CSI finding was not a 100% scientific fact. After all, there could have been an unusual turn in the shooter's or victim's body position during the crime, or some other undetected variable in the crime scene. But truthfully, Mug knew that it was far more likely than not, that if the CSI team said the shooter was left-handed, they would be correct. They don't make random guesses about such things. To do so would be to send the investigation down the wrong path, and possibly to an improper conviction of an innocent person. So the CSI team would be very careful with the information they do and don't include in their findings.

Another possibility was that Durkin, though right-handed, shot Jennifer with his left hand. That scenario seemed unlikely as well. Most people would hold and shoot a gun with their stronger hand. And the shot that killed Jennifer was too precise; one shot right in the middle of her forehead. Someone shooting with an opposite hand would be less likely to be that accurate. Mug's gut feeling was that the opposite hand theory was not the correct answer.

The final possibility was that Durkin didn't do it. Unfortunately, this scenario seemed to be the most likely. Mug wasn't going to rule Durkin out entirely, but clearly this development meant that Mug had to keep searching. He was back to square one.

He phoned Orensen with the news. "He was looking and sounding like a prime suspect until he signed the form." Mug dejectedly said. Orensen simply gave him the "keep at it" pep talk and the two agreed that Mug should continue exploring all other angles.

Mug had previously interviewed former employees of Stohler Steel who had been let go and were registered gun owners. He still had to speak with the remaining names on the list; those who weren't registered gun owners. It didn't mean that these people didn't actually have guns, or that they didn't have access to them. It just meant that they weren't legally registered as gun owners.

Mug spent the next few days tracking down as many former employees as he could and speaking with each one. The interviews revealed very little. Obviously, no one came out and admitted to anything and of course Mug hadn't been expecting that. But Mug had hoped that he would get a vibe if someone seemed to be a possible suspect. For instance, anyone harboring ill will toward Michael, anyone with a background in which they handled firearms, such as being in the army or law enforcement, or even someone who had knowledge of another person who may have done it. But no one had much to offer to help Mug and the investigation. Most of them believed Michael was the killer and made sure to mention it to Mug. There were still a few names left on the list; those who weren't readily available or traceable as some had moved away. Mug would eventually have to speak with them as well to be as thorough as he could be, but for now, he needed to focus his attention elsewhere.

Through his contacts in law enforcement, as well as on-line media research, Mug looked into other break-ins and crimes in Garrowville and surrounding areas. The thought process was that perhaps Jennifer's murder had simply been a random crime committed by a stranger; one of a string of the culprit's criminal activity.

But crime was very low in Garrowville, and though slightly higher in nearby areas, no other recent crimes in neighboring communities seemed to be a good match for the Stohler crime. The M.O.'s just didn't align properly. There had been a string of home burglaries a few towns over shortly after Jennifer's murder, but the police had caught the burglar. It was a seventeen year-old kid named Lewis Portman. There was no violence involved in any of Portman's break-ins and the kid had no prior criminal record. They all took place during the day when no one was at home, so clearly this was a burglar who was not looking for confrontation with a homeowner. Also, it seemed unlikely to Mug that whoever had killed Jennifer would commit other home break-ins so soon afterwards in areas so close. It was more likely that if a random burglar's break-in escalated unexpectedly to murder, that person would want to lay low as much as possible and/or get far away from the crime scene.

Reading about Portman hit a soft spot for Mug. He saw himself in that kid and remembered back to his own troubled youth in which he was forced to commit petty crimes due to life's unfortunate circumstances. He hoped that this kid would be able to turn his life around the way Mug had, and that the justice system would allow him the opportunity to do so.

But he couldn't worry about that right now. He was hitting dead end after dead end in his quest to find Jennifer's killer and his time was getting shorter.

Chapter 60

Time was also getting short on the prosecution side as well. It was just a little more than a month away from the trial and no additional progress had been made in the quest for more evidence. Murdoch continuously worried that they didn't have enough and he was making Lumpkin's life miserable with his constant reminders of that fact.

But in the early morning hours of March 1st, 2010, some unusual and unexpected news was received by Lumpkin at the station. A man walking his dog in the park just a couple of miles away from the Stohler house called the police to report that he noticed some drug paraphernalia on the grounds in the park near the restrooms.

Chief Lumpkin and Officer Radford immediately responded to the call. It was the first of its type in the area in a long time. Upon arriving they did a quick survey of the scene and noted a few miscellaneous drug related items.

"Probably some rowdy kids partying and getting high at night when the park is deserted." Radford speculated, after which he added, "I don't think this is much to worry about Chief. Whenever I'm on night shift, I'll just cruise around here to see if I can catch them in the act. If I do, I'll scare them off with a warning. If I catch them again, I'll arrest them."

"Good plan Radford. I'm putting you on this one. You be on the lookout for them. You're on the night shift now anyway, so it makes sense."

They bagged the evidence for possible future use, though neither of them anticipated that much would come out of this matter. There were bigger issues to tackle, namely, the Stohler investigation. Lumpkin reported the news about the findings in the park to Murdoch who promptly scolded Lumpkin about wasting his time on nonsense when time was running out on the Stohler case.

"Stay focused Lumpkin. Garrowville has gone generations without any major crime. There's nothing to worry about in that town except for convicting Stohler." Murdoch emphatically declared. "I'm not interested in anything over there except evidence in the Stohler case."

After telling Lumpkin to get back to work on Stohler, Murdoch did the same. While Lumpkin was handling the investigative duties, Murdoch had been busy prepping his witnesses for their testimony in the upcoming trial. He had a long list of witnesses to call. He knew that when dealt with a case that is short on physical evidence a good strategy is to present an overabundance of any other type of testimony. If short on quality, make sure to have plenty of quantity. He figured that if he presented enough circumstantial evidence, it would in aggregate be enough to win the case.

He also presented a witness list to Orensen in the discovery process that was substantially greater in number than what Murdoch actually intended to call on during the trial. He included many names of laid off former employees of Stohler Steel on the list, as well as many of Jennifer's friends. He knew that he wasn't going to call all these people to testify, but if he gave Orensen a long enough potential witness list, Orensen wouldn't have enough time to look into and prepare for everyone and simultaneously prepare for his own case. The way Murdoch looked at it, his ruse was justified. Orensen was the one who asked for the speedy trial. He should be more careful as to what he requests.

Again Murdoch started thinking about his own legal brilliance and how it was a shame that he couldn't speak directly to the press to impart on them his gift for prosecuting the dregs of society. The court had the nerve to place a gag order that was raining on Murdoch's public parade of glory. But Murdoch wasn't one to be easily muzzled. He knew all the tricks of the trade. A strategic leak here and there, from an "unnamed source" to the right reporters would get any message he wanted out in the public forum and would keep Murdoch on the front pages. The press was always scratching and clawing for any tidbit of new information on which they could get their hands. The latest scoop in the Stohler case was the present day crown jewel of journalism and Murdoch was only too happy to cooperate.

Chapter 61

The extensive press coverage of the case was noted within the prison as well. There was one small television mounted high up on the wall of the area that doubled as the mess hall and the recreation room. The television was always set to one of the major networks, all of whom had no shortage of updates about the case. Each night during the dinner hour, the inmates hooted, hollered, and made various other degrading noises whenever their favorite reporter, Chelsea Forgeous came on air with the latest developments.

As a result, I was somewhat of a celebrity in the place. Believe me, if there is one place you do not want to be a celebrity, it is within the confines of a penal institution. My fame led to many strange and intimidating interactions with large men of varying degrees of sanity. I had received numerous physical and verbal threats from fellow inmates. It was ironic that some of them had, while threatening me, expressed their disgust at what they believed I had done to my wife. Apparently these pillars of society disapproved of my alleged actions.

It was also ironic that the very people who were prosecuting and incarcerating me, were the ones to eventually order my isolation from the general prison population to protect me. They didn't want anything to happen to me before they had their chance to try, convict, and execute me. So, my situation was that I was being protected by the very people who were trying to kill me. They just wanted to do so in a much longer drawn-out process and in a more public format.

My isolation didn't affect the barrage of hate mail that poured in for me. As is the case in any prison, all mail is examined to make sure there is no contraband, weapons, explosives, or anything else against the plethora of the institution's rules. So my mail came to me already opened, and more than likely, had been read by the staff prior to reaching me. They seemed to take great pleasure when giving me the particularly nasty ones.

The general theme of my mail could be summed up as "I hope you rot in hell for what you did." There seemed to also be a lot of people who believed in the "an eye for an eye" theory. Many letter writers expressed that sentiment in various graphic and violent ways. I did also get a few supportive letters, but they were quite infrequent.

One evening, Chelsea Forgeous did her evening news report live from right in front of the prison. That led to many of the inmates scurrying to the windows, banging on the glass, and yelling out toward her. No one ever accused the prison population of being a mature group of adults.

The other result of that evening's report was that it informed the population of where I was being held. Everyone had known that I was in prison, but it hadn't been public knowledge exactly where I was incarcerated. Starting the very next day, there were demonstrators outside the prison; people with signs and chants calling for me to be executed immediately and calling me all sorts of derogatory names. The number of demonstrators gradually grew over the course of the next couple of weeks and soon the demonstrations were being covered on the evening news.

The noise and commotion outside the prison started to cause similar noise and commotion inside the prison, as the chants from outside were being repeated on the inside. This development led the prison's administration to fear uprisings and violence, thus they contacted law enforcement to put an end to the outside demonstrations. But the demonstrators were not to be deterred. Their "Michael Stohler Must Die" message was too important to be silenced. So a march down Main Street in Garrowville was organized for the following weekend. It got a larger turnout than the town's annual 4th of July parade, and of course, the march was fully covered by all media outlets.

Watching the news footage of the 'anti-Michael' parade reminded me of the O.J. Simpson demonstrators years ago. I remembered back to the footage of many protestors with signs saying "Free O.J." or "O.J. is innocent." I remembered how I used to laugh at these protestors and how I would yell at the television, "How could you be so sure O.J. is innocent? Were you there? Did you witness the crime? Did you commit the crime yourself? If the answer is 'no' to all these questions, then how do you truly know he is innocent?"

Of course I now came to realize as I went through my own predicament, that I hadn't responded any better than the demonstrators. I had immediately concluded that O.J. must be guilty as quickly as the demonstrators had assumed his innocence, and I had no more inside knowledge than they possessed. I also now realized that my immediate assumption of O.J.'s guilt was exactly what I was currently wishing the general public wouldn't have done to me in my case.

Prison affords one all the time in the world to reflect upon such matters. Upon my own personal reflections, I've come to the realization that the best course of action for all of us in these cases is to simply refrain from jumping to any conclusions about the guilt or innocence of others until all information and evidence is gathered. It's too easy for the court of public opinion to ruin lives unjustly with premature assumptions. Clearly I am a great example of this point.

Chapter 62

With the trial creeping closer, the pressure was mounting on Mug to get some answers and to get them fast. He had spent the past couple of weeks interviewing as many friends and acquaintances of Jennifer and Michael that he could find. He also spent time making the rounds to numerous jewelers and pawn shop owners looking for anyone who had recently purchased, or had been offered to purchase a wedding ring, or at least a diamond of similar size, shape and value as Jennifer's wedding ring. He was having no success.

There was still another approach to be taken on the missing wedding ring front, and with the trial just a couple of weeks away, it was time to dig deeper. It was time to dive back into the less conventional or "underground" crowd with whom he had once been a member. One of the many attributes that made Mug a great investigator was that he had numerous sources both inside and outside of the law. He needed to tap into some of those shadier contacts; the ones with the street smarts; the ones who knew where the deals that don't get advertised in the yellow pages went down.

Mug had made a lot of friends from his days shuffling in and out of the penal system, many of whom hadn't turned around their lives to the extent Mug had achieved. He made the rounds catching up with many of them, seeking any information of interest he could get. After a few dead-ends, he stumbled across something very interesting in his chat with a former cellmate who went by the street name, "Rome."

Rome had many connections on the streets all over western Pennsylvania. That is what one builds when living a life of crime. Much like a business person accumulates a rolodex full of contacts during the course of a career, he had built up quite a "book of business" of his own. In fact, his self-appointed street name was based on the criminal empire he had put together. You know the saying, "Rome wasn't built in a day."

So for Mug, who went way back with Rome, this was a great contact to maintain. He knew that Rome was a reliable source. Tips Mug had gotten from him in prior cases usually panned out. Rome was also one of the guys Mug had protected in prison way back when, so Rome wouldn't steer Mug in the wrong direction. Rome also knew that Mug wasn't going to turn him in. It would be foolish to do so. He'd be losing Rome as a source, and he wouldn't be trusted on the streets by anyone else. Basically, if he snitched on Rome, Mug would lose his "street cred."

Mug started out by asking if Rome had knowledge of any fencing of high valued jewelry in the area lately. Mug knew that Rome moved various stolen goods such as jewelry, electronics, weapons, and who knew what else?

They may be friends, but apparently in Rome's world even friends still had to pay for information.

"What's it worth to you Mug?" Rome asked.

"Depends on what you've got. You know something useful, I'll pay you."

"I know about some interesting deals going down over at that park in Garrowville. $100 bucks and I'll start talking."

Mug peeled off a $100 bill and handed it to him.

"I've got some of my boys working drug deals in Garrowville Park. Sometimes they're paid in cash, sometimes in other forms of currency."

"What other currency? Jewelry?"

Rome stuck out his hand in the universal gesture for more money. Mug obliged.

"They've got a client they meet there once a month. The guy's got a serious drug addiction. Shows up same time every month with enough cash or other items, such as jewelry or weapons, to feed his addiction for the month. Then he comes back the next month for more of the same. Every month. Same Bat Time. Same Bat Channel. And you'll never believe who he is."

"Who is he?" Mug asked overanxiously.

"Come on, man. You know better than that. I need more money for more information." Apparently there was not going to be a 'long-time friend' discount here. Mug handed over another hundred. He'd have to add these funds to his ever growing expense reimbursement report to be charged to Michael Stohler.

Rome pocketed the cash and said, "It's a cop in Garrowville. Goes by the alias, "Rogue." Pretty creative huh? A wayward cop calling himself 'Rogue'! He's got himself quite an addiction. Must cost him a fortune over the course of time. And how much could he be making as a cop over there in that rinky-dink town? Which is why he sometimes has to pay in other ways. He'll give us anything to get his fix. Great customer."

"Which cop is it? Do you know his name? Or at least what he looks like?"

Rome laughed and said, "Of course I do brother. You think I'm just going to blurt it out? How would I make a living out here if I operated like that? One more payment, and this time make it two bills, and you get your name and the next appointment."

Mug gave him another two hundred.

"His real name is Radford. Dan Radford. He's there on the morning of the first of every month at 2 a.m. Like clockwork. The deal goes down near the back of the park, off the main trail, right by the hut with the restrooms, water fountains, and a sign on it with the park's rules and regulations, which by the way, does not include any prohibitions against police officers fencing contraband for drugs."

Chapter 63

The first of April was still a few days away, so Mug had a little time to digest this shocking development and plot his next moves. The first move would be to discuss strategy with Orensen. He called Orensen and said he needed to see him urgently. The two met an hour later in Orensen's office.

"Unreal!" Orensen proclaimed after Mug filled him in on the tip he'd received from his unnamed source. Orensen knew that Mug had numerous contacts, but it was best for Orensen not to know too much of the specifics. Need to know basis was the best approach in such matters.

"Are you sure that this information is legit?" Orensen asked.

"It's from one of my best sources. This source has always been very reliable." Mug replied.

"Ok. So where do we go from here and how does this information tie into the Stohler case, if it even does at all?" Orensen asked.

"Well, here's what we know so far: We know that Radford is a drug addict. He pays a ton to maintain his addiction. Probably more than he can afford, which means that sometimes he has to pay in other ways, such as with jewelry. We also know that Radford was the first officer on the scene of the crime at the Stohler residence. The only item known to be missing from the scene was a very expensive ring; one that could buy a lot of drugs, which would explain why the ring hasn't turned up at any jewelers or pawn shops."

Mug went on, "So, based on these facts, I'd say it is a pretty high likelihood that Radford stole the ring and sold it. The big question is whether he took the ring when he discovered Jennifer's body, or was he the one to have killed her in the first place?"

Orensen thought about this for a moment, then answered, "When he discovered the body, he was the only one there. They didn't initially send a whole team over there to check on her because no one knew yet that there had been a murder. So, if he took the ring at the time he found the body, he would have had time to take more than just one piece of jewelry before calling in his discovery. Why take just one item? Therefore, it may make more sense that he killed her in a robbery attempt that escalated beyond his initial intentions, then had to flee as quickly as possible."

Mug nodded his head, "Makes sense. Do you know Radford? Does he fit CSI's physical description of the shooter?"

"I don't know him." Orensen said. "He's never testified before in any case in which I've been involved. But I've seen him a couple of times. He's about average height. Maybe 5'9" or 5'10". Which is a little shorter than CSI's estimate, but he's taller than Jennifer, which was the primary point of CSI's assessment based on the trajectory of the bullet. Exactly how much taller the shooter was than Jennifer is guesswork. I don't know if he is left-handed."

The two sat in silence for a few minutes as they each independently contemplated the next moves.

Orensen then broke the silence by saying, "Radford was also one of Lumpkin's sources claiming to have overheard Michael confess. That claim is sounding more and more like it is bogus."

Mug replied, "I need to talk to Michael about a few things to tie up some loose ends in my investigation so far. I'll ask him about Radford also. See what he knows about the guy. I have a few ideas as to what I could do about Radford."

"What did you have in mind?" Orensen inquired.

"It's best that you don't know." Mug said smiling as he got up to leave.

Chapter 64

It was Tuesday, March 30, 2010, less than a week away from the start of my trial. Of course I was very excited for the trial and was counting the days, even the hours, to it. But I also had a tremendous amount of fear about the trial in that it represented my one great hope to get out of here and salvage my life. Should the trial go badly, any remaining hope would be gone.

I was lying on the cot in my cell contemplating these very thoughts when a guard arrived to inform me that I had a visitor. Not visitors, but visitor, singular. So, it must not be my parents, who usually came together.

"Who is it?" I asked the guard as he opened my cell door.

"I don't know. Some scary dude who looks more like he should be on the inside than the outside. He's probably some vigilante who wants to avenge your wife's murder. We forgot to frisk him when he came in. Oh well. Mistakes happen." The guard answered as he laughed heartily.

Quite the comedian I thought to myself as I walked toward the visiting area. This was the life and these were the types of people I had to look forward to spending the rest of my days with should I lose the trial.

It wasn't a crazed vigilante waiting for me. It was Mug.

"Good morning Michael" Mug warmly greeted me, rising as I entered the room. It felt good to be treated like a human being once in a while.

"Hi Mug. How is your investigation going?"

"That's what I'm here about. I need some information from you."

"Ok. Anything I can do to help." I answered.

"First, do you know of a guy named Robert Durkin?"

I thought about it for a few minutes. The name sounded vaguely familiar, but I couldn't place it. "No. I don't think so. It sounds vaguely familiar, but I can't remember where I'd have heard it before. Who is he?"

"He's a teacher at the school where your wife taught. Does that ring a bell?"

I thought some more, then responded, "No. I still don't remember him."

"Did your wife mention any new teachers at the school at the start of this school year? Anyone she had befriended or expressed any thoughts about?"

"No. Not that I can recall. She was usually the "meet and greet" type with new teachers at the school or new members at the church. That was her personality; make everyone feel welcome. Was Durkin new this year?"

"Yes. And he took a liking to your wife. I'm looking into him as a possible suspect, so, anything you can recall would help greatly."

"I'm sorry, I just don't remember him. We've probably never met. What else makes him a suspect other than liking my wife?"

"Just a hunch right now. He said he met you one time. But it was a brief encounter at some school function. He's a tall guy, heavy, and balding. He fits on the height and has some of the strange personality traits that fits one of our possible scenarios for how the crime may have played out. But, we don't have much else on him right now, which is partly why I'm here."

Mug then moved on to the next topic. "How much do you know about Officer Radford?"

"He and I go way back. I went to school with him; all the way back to elementary school." I answered.

"So you must know him well. Tell me about him."

"Well, he had always been somewhat of the shy, quiet, type. Socially awkward. He and I were never close friends, but we always knew each other. He played on the high school football team with me but he wasn't any good."

"Did Jennifer know him well?"

"Not well. Same as me. She knew him, but wasn't ever really close with him. I think he may have liked her, but if so, I'm pretty sure the feelings weren't reciprocated."

"Do you know if he ever tried to act on his feelings for Jennifer?"

"Not that I know of. He was probably too shy to make any type of move and by the time we were in high school, Jennifer and I were together so she wasn't available anymore."

"A girl not being available is not always an obstacle for some guys." Mug commented.

"True, but only for confident guys. I don't know of any interactions of that type between Radford and Jennifer, though, now that you are bringing him up, I do remember a strange comment he made to me when I was being arrested."

"What was it?" Mug asked.

"It was when he was leading me through my office building in handcuffs. I had just been arrested and he was escorting me out. He made a point to lean toward me and say, 'This is for Jennifer.' I thought it was a ridiculous comment at the time. I had interpreted it as him making it clear the crime for which I was being arrested, as if it could have been for something else. But maybe I misinterpreted it. Maybe he meant that the humiliation of the arrest in my office and being led out in handcuffs in front of my employees was his revenge for Jennifer."

"I think that's what he meant" Mug replied. "It's likely that he had feelings for her; long-term unsatisfied feelings that had frustrated him over the years. The way I see it is that it only added to his frustration that the guy who was lucky enough to be with Jennifer didn't appreciate it and worse yet, killed her so that Radford could never have her. I've seen many cases where frustrated love interests of varying fact patterns leads to violence."

"I don't know." I answered. "Like I said, I've known Radford a long time. Sure, he's a bit strange, but I couldn't envision him ever hurting anyone. He's always been a decent guy."

"Well, I always say, you never know anyone as well as you think you do. Everyone's got their secrets; their skeletons in the closet. Radford comes up because we've recently uncovered some very surprising information about him. Seems he's a drug addict. Buys the goods every month, and apparently has used jewelry at times to make his purchases. We think he's the one who may have taken your wife's wedding ring."

"Wow! How did you discover this?" I asked. I was astonished.

"Long story; and we're still verifying. The short version is that I got it from a reliable source. The big question is whether Radford also is the one who killed your wife, or if he just lucked into the ring upon discovering her body. That's why I need to know everything you know about him."

"I told you basically what I know about him. Just a strange, quiet, shy guy growing up."

"I assume he didn't date much? Is he married now?" Mug asked.

"I don't remember him dating much back in school, or ever. I'd never seen him with anyone. I don't think he's married."

"Do you happen to know if he is left-handed?"

"No, I don't remember. No wait… Actually, yes I do remember. He is left-handed. There was one football game our senior year when we had a big lead. The coach took me out as quarterback and put Dan in for the last possession of the game. I remember the coach joking afterwards that we had to be the only team in the county with two left-handed quarterbacks."

Mug consulted his notes, then asked, "Radford is one of the prosecution's witnesses claiming to have overheard you confessing to the crime. Is that true?"

"Absolutely not! I've never confessed to anyone! Anyone saying otherwise is flat out lying! Why would I confess to something I didn't do?"

Mug believed Michael. He knew that Michael had been vehemently maintaining his innocence throughout the ordeal. And clearly Radford wasn't the reliable, wholesome type of guy you'd want and expect of a police officer. Mug moved on to his final topic to cover.

"Michael, as you know, time is running short before the trial, so I need to focus my attention on the loose ends in my investigation that are the highest probability of being relevant. With that in mind, there are a few names on various lists you've provided that I haven't been able to get to yet. Specifically, if you recall, you or your father had given me lists of Jennifer's closest friends, employees who you had laid off, including those who subsequently had homes foreclosed, and people who had at one time lived on your block. There are several names on at least one of these lists who I hadn't gotten to yet. Here is a list of those names. One name is in common on each of those lists. Dennison. Willie and Christine Dennison. I know from interviews of some of Jennifer's other friends that they've left the area. A couple of people said that they think one of them has family out of town with whom they said they were going to stay. Do you know who and where that may be? And what do you remember about Willie Dennison? You had laid him off about a year ago."

"I remember the Dennisons well. They were our next door neighbors and were good friends. Jennifer and Christine were very close. Willie worked at the plant for a long time. He was a good guy, but not a great employee. I kept him on for a while longer than I should have because of our friendship, but as the company was struggling, I had no choice but to let him go. I felt bad about it and told him so. He didn't take it well. He said that he didn't know what he was going to do. Christine didn't have work either. They were barely making ends meet while he was working. Now that he wouldn't be, they would lose their home. That is what happened shortly afterwards."

"Do you know where they went?" Mug inquired.

"I'm not sure. After I let Willie go, it strained our relationship, as you'd expect. I remember that Christine has a brother in Virginia. Somewhere near D.C. They used to visit each other. We've had her brother and his wife over our house one time when they were visiting. It's possible that is the relative they went to stay with after moving away."

"Do you remember the other couple's names?"

"No, not their first names, but I know Christine's maiden name. It's Dennis. I remember that because it was a bit of a silly joke of theirs how she didn't have much of a name change when they married. She just added the 'on' to her name like her life was finally 'on' once she married Willie. So the brother's last name is Dennis and they live somewhere in Virginia not far from Washington, D.C."

"What does Willie Dennison look like?" Mug asked.

"Tall, slim, mustache, short straight black hair."

"How tall?"

"I don't know. Roughly six feet. Maybe a bit more."

"Do you know if either he or his wife is left-handed?"

"No. Sorry."

"Would either of them ever had a key to your house?"

"It's possible. Jennifer would have coordinated that. She always felt a little more secure when trusted neighbors had each other's keys in case of an emergency. So, I'd say it's a good chance they had one. But Jennifer likely would have asked for it back when they were moving away."

"Do you know for sure that she did get them back?"

"No."

"Even if they did return the key, they could have had a copy made before doing so." Mug added.

"I guess so. I wouldn't see why they would want to though."

"Just covering all bases. If one of them had any ill intentions, having a copy of the key would be helpful." Mug responded. "Remember, we need to try to think that anything is possible. We don't rule out anything until we know what happened."

I nodded. I saw his point. It was a unique suspect list. My former neighbor/employee who I had been very close to, a long-time acquaintance who I grew up with and who happened to be one of my arresting officers, and a strange teacher at Jennifer's school.

What were the odds that one of these people was the murderer? And even if so, what were the odds that Mug would figure out which one and be able to prove it in time to save me with the trial just a week away?

Chapter 65

Based on the conversation with Michael, Mug knew that he'd have to investigate the Dennison angle. Through some contacts with the Department of Motor Vehicles, he got a list of people who live in northern Virginia with the last name of Dennis. Unfortunately, the list was too long. Dennis is a fairly common last name. He'd have to dig deeper, try to get a first name to hone in on the right Dennis. He didn't have time to investigate each one of these people at this point.

On Wednesday, March 31st, he returned to the prison to visit Michael with his list of names and addresses, hoping Michael would recognize the right name or at least the right town. Perhaps the town had come up in a conversation at some point in time and mentioning it to Michael would ring a bell.

Michael went through the list and said, "I remember them saying they lived in Fairfax. Seeing the name of the town reminded me. I'm not a hundred percent certain, but it does sound familiar and I don't know anyone else who lives there. And the first names, Larry and Rachel I believe are correct. We only met them once and it was a few years ago, but it seems right."

"Ok. Thanks Michael. I've got to go now; a lot of work to do. Hang in there buddy."

Mug left. He knew he'd have to go down to Virginia to investigate further, but he couldn't go today. Tonight he had to attend the monthly rendezvous in Garrowville Park. He'd leave for Virginia tomorrow.

The next order of business was to prepare for the tonight's festivities. So Mug went to the park during the day to scout out the location. He found the restroom hut that Rome described and surveyed the area. He wanted to find a good place to hide, where obviously he wouldn't be seen, but that he could still see and hear what was going on, and wouldn't be in the path in which any of the parties would come to and leave from the meeting. He also didn't want anyone approaching from behind him. He wanted to be able to see anyone coming.

The restroom hut was located at the top of a semi-circular, slightly inclined path. Behind it was a small section of woods, and the back fence of the park. There was no entrance or exit way back there, so presumably, the logical approaches to the hut were from up either side of the semi-circular trail in front of the hut. Therefore, Mug figured that the best place to hide would be in the wooded area in the back. He tried out a few locations, and picked one that wasn't directly behind the hut. He figured that just in case someone's approach was to scale the back fence, he didn't want to be in the direct path from the fence to the hut. The front of the park had no gate or any other obstacle for entrance, so scaling the back fence wouldn't be necessary for any of the participants in the rendezvous to make it there, but Mug wasn't taking any chances. Also, he decided that he'd scale the fence as his entry strategy so as to not chance encountering anyone en route to the meeting's location.

He found a spot fitting all of the above criteria, which also had some bushes for him to hide within. He'd noted that he should wear dark green clothing to further camouflage himself. There was even a stone on the ground at the hiding spot, which will serve nicely as his seating area. It was as if someone had arranged the place for his comfort.

Later that evening, Mug arrived a few hours in advance of the meeting time to not risk anyone getting there before him and seeing or hearing his approach. He was used to stakeouts in his line of work, and this one was just another one of many he had performed. He actually liked these situations. It was one of the many things that made his line of work unique and exciting. Your typical banker or accountant didn't have such suspenseful work related duties quite like a stakeout.

Mug found his previously determined hiding spot and settled in for the wait. He sat on the stone and stayed alert to all surroundings, which for the time being, were very quiet. He was armed with a handgun just in case. Mug had never fired a gun in his life and sincerely hoped to never have to fire one. He wasn't a violent person. But in his line of work, especially in the specific situation he was operating in this evening, he needed to have the added protection.

Nothing happened until just a few minutes before 2 a.m. when Mug heard approaching footsteps up the left side path. He could also hear a couple of muffled voices, but couldn't make out any of the words. As they got closer, Mug could see that it was two people. They stopped in front of the restrooms and lit up cigarettes. Nothing else was happening so it appeared they were waiting for someone.

A few minutes later, Mug could see another figure approaching. "Here he comes" Mug overheard. He got his cell phone ready to snap some pictures as he leaned in to listen to the conversation.

"Rogue, how's it going? What will be this month?"

"The usual." Rogue answered.

Mug snapped some pictures as he watched the transaction unfold. Rogue took out a wad of bills and handed it over. Where was he getting the cash for this highly expensive addiction every month? One of the drug dealers counted the cash and nodded to his partner, who then handed a bag over to Rogue. Rogue inspected the contents of the bag, which Mug couldn't see from his vantage point. Rogue said, "Looks good. Thanks boys. See you next month." He then walked away, back in the direction from which he had arrived just a couple of minutes earlier.

Mug waited as he watched the two drug dealers light up joints. Apparently, they weren't in a hurry to leave. May it be that someone else would be coming in for another deal? Mug had no choice but to wait it out. He couldn't risk being seen or heard, and also didn't want to miss anything else that may take place.

Nothing else of interest happened though. The two druggies got high, then staggered off about an hour later down the trail away from the hut. Mug still waited a little longer to make sure they were long gone before he would emerge from his hiding spot.

Finally, as Mug started to rise off the stone on which he had been sitting for the past few hours, his arm pushed off the stone to aide him in getting up. Doing so caused the stone to roll over a bit, which revealed a dug out hole underneath it, inside which Mug could vaguely make out a shiny object. He pushed the stone to get it out of the way, bent over to take a closer look, and using the light from his cell phone, he noticed that the object that had laid underneath the stone, was a gun.

Chapter 66

Mug didn't know if the gun was related to the monthly drug deal he had just witnessed, the Stohler murder which had occurred just a couple of miles away, both, or neither, but regardless, it would need to be investigated. Using some debris he found nearby, he carefully picked up the gun, handling it in a way to not compromise any possible fingerprints that could eventually be taken from it. He put it in his coat pocket, then climbed the back fence of the park to leave in the direction in which he came, which was also the opposite way from which Rogue and his druggie friends had gone.

Mug next went to Radford's residence, which he had previously looked up on-line. No fancy investigative work and no inside connections needed this time. Finding Radford's address was as easy as a few clicks on the internet. It appeared that Garrowville police officers didn't have much to fear in terms of any criminals in their town tracking them down to their homes. Or maybe it was just those officers who played nicely with the local bad guys who had nothing to fear.

Mug waited down the block for Radford to arrive at home at the end of his night shift. His wait was only a couple of hours. It was just after 6 a.m. when he saw Radford pull up on his driveway. Mug quietly got out of his car, put on a ski mask, and stealthily scurried over to Radford just as Radford was approaching his front door.

Mug walked right up behind him, put his gun into Radford's back and said, "Don't look back. Don't say a word. Just listen to me and listen carefully."

Radford was frozen in fear. He barely nodded and mumbled some incoherent words of understanding.

Mug went on, "I know all about your monthly drug transactions. In fact I just witnessed the one that went down tonight. Here's a nice crisp picture of you being handed the goods." Mug reached around with his phone in his other hand and quickly showed Radford the picture.

"I also know that you don't always pay in cash. Sometimes its cash, sometimes jewelry, sometimes weapons. I'm sure the D.A. would be very interested in learning more about how you obtained these various forms of currencies, don't you think?"

Radford didn't say anything.

"But Radford, or maybe I should call you Rogue…" Radford cringed upon hearing his alias but didn't say anything as Mug continued, "today is your lucky day. Why you ask? Why are you to be considered lucky at a time when you've been caught conducting illegal drug transactions and are being confronted at your own home?"

Still no response from Radford.

"I'm glad you asked." Mug sarcastically said. "I'll tell you why you're so lucky. You're lucky because I don't give a crap about your little side business. I only care about one thing. Finding out who really killed Jennifer Stohler and making sure that Michael Stohler is not wrongly convicted for the crime."

"So you see," Mug continued, "as long as it was not you who killed Jennifer, then I don't care about any of your other little infractions. Did you kill Jennifer Stohler?"

No answer from Radford.

"I asked you a question Rogue!" Mug asked with a little more emphasis as he also stuck his gun a little deeper into Radford's back.

"No. I didn't do it." Radford managed to meekly respond.

"Well, that remains to be seen." Mug said then added, "You aren't exactly the most trustworthy source right now, so consider yourself a prime suspect at this time. But in the meantime, there is one more item of business for us."

Mug didn't wait for Radford to say anything, he just continued by saying, "You won't be testifying in the trial about any garbage confession you claim to have overheard Michael Stohler make. We both know you heard no such thing. Either you heard nothing at all and are making it all up, or you heard something else and are twisting it. Either way, none of that crap is to make it into the trial. You mention anything about a confession, or anything at all that will hurt Michael's chances of an acquittal, and I'll make sure all of Rogue's wonderful illegal activities are made very public. Do we understand each other?"

Radford nodded his head emphatically to make sure his attacker saw that he got it.

Without saying another word, Mug quickly raced off around the side of the house and was gone within seconds before Radford had a chance to do anything. But Mug wasn't scared about Radford doing anything anyway. He knew that it was Radford who was now scared. He also knew that while he may not be any closer to the answer as to whether or not Radford was the killer, he at least took one tidbit of garbage evidence against Michael Stohler away from the prosecution.

Chapter 67

It was Thursday, April 1ˢᵗ, 2010, and Mug's next order of business was to investigate the gun he had found in the park. He knew that it was a Beretta .22 caliber, which was the same type of weapon used in the Stohler murder. Using the serial number stamped on the gun, Mug may be able track where it was purchased, assuming it was done so legally and registered properly. It was a big assumption to make, but it was definitely worth the investigative legwork.

So Mug got to work. He called one of his childhood buddies, who currently owned a gun shop in Ohio, and asked him to run the make, model, and serial number through his data base. A little while later, Mug got a call back with some very interesting information. He was told that the weapon was sold in a gun show in Washington, D.C., and was registered to a Larry Dennis of Fairfax, Virginia. There were no other guns registered under that name as far as Mug's friend could find.

Mug recognized the name immediately. He was the brother-in-law of Willie Dennison; Michael's former next-door neighbor. Dennis and/or the Dennisons had just jumped to the top of the suspect list. The investigation would have to move down to Virginia after some more digging up here. Mug decided he should call Orensen with the latest developments.

"Hey Boss. I just wanted to update you. I'll be heading down to Fairfax, Virginia. I've got some leads that point us down there."

"What do you have?"

"I found a gun hidden in Garrowville Park, which is close to the Stohler residence. The gun is a .22 caliber, same as the one used in the murder. I had the serial number run through a database and it spit out that the registered owner of the gun is a guy named Larry Dennis of Fairfax, Virginia."

"Who is he?" Orensen asked.

"He is the brother/brother-in-law of Christine and Willie Dennison, the Stohlers' former next-door neighbors. Willie was laid off by Michael about a year ago and as a direct result, shortly thereafter, their home was foreclosed. Willie fits CSI's height estimate of the shooter. The Dennisons' left town, and based on my conversation with Michael, it's possible that they went to shack up with his wife's brother and his wife in Fairfax, Virginia. Her brother is Larry Dennis, the registered owner of the found gun."

"How did you find the gun?"

"Let's just say that is one of those things you probably don't want to know." Mug answered.

"We need to find out if that was the gun actually used in murder" Orensen replied. "If it is, then it looks like Willie Dennison or Larry Dennis may be our killer, and that Radford simply found the ring and sold it. But first we need to find out if that was the gun used in the murder."

"Leave that to me for now. I need to get more information first. I'll be heading down to Virginia very soon."

"Ok. But we need to move quickly. The trial starts on Monday. Time is running out."

"I know. As for the trial, I have some good news for you."

"What is it?"

"You won't have to worry about Radford testifying about the bogus confession he claimed to have overheard?" Mug answered.

"Why is that?"

"Let's just say that he's reconsidered his testimony." Mug mysteriously answered.

"Another thing I'm better off not knowing?" Orensen asked, though he already knew the answer.

"Yes. And don't worry so much, Boss. I'm on it. We'll get to the bottom of this." Mug assured Orensen. If only Mug was really as confident as he came across. There were still a lot of questions to be answered and time was in fact running out.

Chapter 68

In the last days before the trial, both sides were making their final strategic preparations. Murdoch spent a lot of time determining the order of his extensive witness list, preparing each witness for the questions he'd be asking them and what may be asked in cross-examination, and writing his opening statement. He was frustrated that Lumpkin and his team of inexperienced numbskulls hadn't uncovered more evidence, but Murdoch was confident that his legal talents, and the aggregate of the circumstantial evidence they did have, would suffice. It had to. Justice must always prevail. The good guys must always win.

On Friday morning, April 2nd, Murdoch contacted Officer Dan Radford to do one final run-through of Radford's testimony and the questions Murdoch would ask him. Murdoch reminded Radford that the confession he overheard would be the key to his testimony. Murdoch then received a most unwelcome and shocking response from Radford.

"Uh, I'm sorry Mr. Murdoch, but I don't think that I could testify." Radford stated with much trepidation.

"What are you talking about Radford? Of course you're testifying. The confession is one of the keys here. I'll subpoena you if I have to."

"Well, if you subpoena me, I'll have to testify that I'm not sure of what I heard. You know, I was far away and the wind was howling. I probably misheard."

"Damn you Radford! Why are you doing this? You said previously that you heard a confession! Who got to you? Were you threatened in any way?"

"No Mr. Murdoch. I just can't be sure what I heard. I'm sorry."

"You were the first responding officer. You discovered the body. We need testimony from you on those fronts as well. I'm subpoenaing you. You will get on that stand!"

Murdoch angrily hung up the phone. The last thing he needed was for his case to start falling apart on him as he neared the finish line. He dialed Lumpkin, told him about Radford, and demanded that Lumpkin "get his ducks in a row." Murdoch ordered Lumpkin to threaten Radford with termination and possible prosecution if he didn't testify. "He said previously that he heard a confession." Murdoch yelled at Lumpkin. "Now he's saying he didn't. Either he lied then or he's lying now. Either way, it's grounds for termination and maybe more. Make sure he understands that and that he acts accordingly here. Need I remind you Lumpkin that both of our futures depend on this?" Murdoch angrily hung up on the second member of the Garrowville police department in just a few minutes time. Numbskulls, Murdoch thought to himself.

On the other side of the fence, Orensen was also busy with final preparations for his case. But his witness list wasn't quite as extensive as Murdoch's. A few character witnesses, along with Michael's father and certain other people to talk timeline, though that could be a bit tricky as Michael's timeline ended before the estimated time of the murder.

The key strategic decision for any defense attorney was whether or not to put the defendant on the stand. In this case, he was leaning toward doing so because as far as he could tell from conversations with Michael, family members, other people who knew Michael, and Orensen's background checks, Michael had no skeletons in the closet that could surface in cross-examination. Also, Michael needed to explain a lot of the circumstantial evidence that the prosecution will present; such as the life insurance, the cell phone, and various other matters. Michael spoke well and looked clean-cut and professional. He should be able to come across well to the jurors. Orensen will spend some time in the prison with Michael this weekend to prepare for his possible testimony.

Of course, Orensen also knew that if the prosecution had clearly failed to prove their case beyond a reasonable doubt after the prosecution had presented their side, it would be strategically foolish to put Michael, or even anyone on the stand. It could only hurt at that stage. They'd need to make that decision when the time came. He would explain that to Michael this weekend.

Orensen was already well-prepared for his cross-examinations. He had been given a sneak preview of most of the prosecution's case during the preliminary hearing. The only new significant item that had surfaced since then was the supposed confession reported by Michael's cellmate. That should be easy to discredit though. Consider the source, would be the message to get across to the jury on that front.

Finally, thanks to Mug, Orensen may even have an ace up his sleeve. They had Radford and his extracurricular activities. If needed, they can use him as an alternative theory as to who killed Jennifer. They may not be able to prove it, but any reasonable doubt that could be presented helps the defense. He wasn't sure yet if it would come to that, but he'd keep it in mind if needed. Let's see what Mug turns up in Virginia regarding the found gun. If all goes well, it could be exculpatory evidence, or at least, more reasonable doubt. Mug needed to move fast on that front. There's nothing more frustrating than finding the key evidence after the trial is over.

The media as always was all over the case. Legal pundits from around the nation were chiming in with their analysis of what will happen and who will and won't be called on to testify. Locally, Chelsea Forgeous was everywhere, as usual, interviewing anyone who would talk to her, which was almost everyone. The approaching trial dominated the gossip around town, as it had at the time of the murder, and for most of the time in between.

Public opinion around the town hadn't changed much in the past few months. Everyone was anxious for the trial to get started so that they could finally see justice served. The Garrowville Gazette ran a survey in the Sunday paper one week before the trial, which showed that 89% of those surveyed believed that Michael Stohler was guilty, 8% thought he was innocent, and 3% said they didn't know. Of the respondents who voted 'guilty,' nearly 75% of them believed that Michael Stohler should be given the death penalty. Many of the respondents reported that they had known Michael Stohler personally in some capacity prior to the murder. None of those people had responded 'yes' to a follow-up question asking if they had previously thought Michael Stohler to be capable of a such a violent crime. When asked the primary reason they believed Michael killed his wife, the most common responses were his greed and that he must have a mistress.

Zero percent of the respondents to this survey had any inside information or concrete evidence, yet amazingly 97% of them had formed a definitive opinion on the matter of guilt or innocence, and almost all of them voted 'guilty.' Garrowville's court of public opinion had spoken loudly and clearly.

Chapter 69

Mug visited several local locksmiths around Garrowville prior to departing for Virginia. His task was to determine if either Willie or Christine Dennison had come to them to have keys copied at any point in time. Mug knew that it was a long shot that a locksmith would know the exact nature of the keys being copied, but he had to try. After a couple of fruitless visits, the third locksmith was helpful. Charlie Workman reported that he remembered Willie Dennison and that Dennison had come to him a few times to have keys copied and various other projects. As Mug had expected, Workman couldn't recall the exact nature of the keys he copied for Willie Dennison, but he did remember that the last visit was just before the Dennisons left town. Mug couldn't be sure, but his gut feeling was that the final visit was to make a copy of the Stohler keys before giving back the originals to Jennifer.

Mug then took off for the roughly 4½ hour drive to Fairfax, Virginia. He arrived mid-afternoon on Friday, April 2nd, and quickly found the Dennis residence. It was a nice, two story home on a quiet tree-lined suburban street; far enough from the hustle and bustle of Washington D.C., but near enough to commute in and out for work, or to spend a leisurely day visiting the monuments and museums.

Mug ordinarily would watch the home for a couple of days to determine who lived there and their normal comings and goings. But time was not on his side. He didn't have the luxury for a prolonged strategic observance, but he also couldn't afford to blow the investigation with a false move.

He knew what Willie Dennison looked like from Michael's description and he obtained DMV photos of all four presumed residents of the house, so he could identify any of them he observed entering or leaving the premises. The primary suspect here was Willie Dennison, so verifying Willie's presence in this residence was his top objective. After establishing that Willie was still living here, Mug's strategy would be to act as if he was investigating the missing gun. He needed to find out if Willie Dennison would have had access to it and what the circumstances were behind how the gun disappeared.

Through a law enforcement source, Mug learned that Larry Dennis had reported his gun missing to the local police. The date of the report was December 22, 2009. Presumably, nothing came of that police report as Mug found the gun several months later and several hundred miles away.

Mug staked out the residence for a few hours during which there was no activity. He did notice a couple of lights on inside the home, but could not determine if anyone was inside as most shades were closed. Then, at approximately 6:30 p.m., Mug observed Larry Dennis pull onto the driveway, exit his car, and walk into the house. Mug surmised that Larry had probably returned home from work as he was in business attire and the timing seemed about right.

After a few more hours, Mug called it a night. He figured that it wouldn't be wise to knock on the door without knowing who else was inside the home. He wanted to first talk to either Larry and/or Rachel, without either of the Dennisons present. He'd have to wait until tomorrow.

He checked into a nearby hotel, grabbed a late dinner, then hit the sack. He'd have to wake up early the next morning to resume his stakeout. It had been a long couple of days, starting with having to pull an all-nighter the previous evening to witness the activities in the park. He had only managed to sneak in a quick nap in the morning before making the rounds of locksmiths, then driving down to Virginia. So he had no trouble falling asleep.

After what seemed like a blink of his eyes, Mug was awake again when his alarm sounded at 6 a.m. He quickly showered, dressed, and checked out and was soon back on the Dennis' block. He slowly cruised past the house and noticed two cars on the driveway, one of which had a Pennsylvania license plate; a promising sign.

He parked a few houses past the target this time to deviate from the day before in which he was parked a few houses away in the other direction. He didn't want someone to look out the window of their home and see the same unrecognized vehicle parked there. He was far enough away so that it wasn't apparent to anyone in the Dennis' house that they were being watched, yet he was close enough to see if anyone were to leave the premises.

No one left until just after 9 a.m., when two people, a man and woman, exited the home, walked down the front steps, and entered the vehicle with Pennsylvania plates. Mug was fairly certain that the woman was Christine Dennison, which probably meant that the man was her husband Willie. The male had a baseball cap on, and Mug was far away, so he couldn't make a positive identification. He hoped that they would drive off in his direction so that he can get a look at them in passing and confirm their identities. But, no such luck. They drove off in the opposite direction.

It was decision time. The most likely scenario was that the Dennisons had just left and that Larry and Rachel Dennis, the homeowners, were left alone in the house, as he had wanted. He couldn't be sure, but he didn't have time to waste. He would play the odds and knock on the door. He also didn't know how long the Dennisons would be out, so he decided that he needed to move quickly. Without further delay, Mug made his move.

Chapter 70

"Good morning. Are you Mr. Larry Dennis?" Mug asked as a man who Mug had recognized to be Larry Dennis answered the door.

"Yes. Who are you?"

"I'm a private investigator." Mug answered as he flashed his private investigator badge toward Dennis. "I work in conjunction with law enforcement and with gun manufacturers to track down lost or stolen weapons in order to try as best we can to keep them out of the wrong hands."

Mug didn't know if Dennis was buying his story, but he kept going anyway. There was no turning back now. "I understand that you had reported your registered handgun, a Beretta .22 caliber to be missing. Is that correct?"

"Yes, but that was a few months ago. Why is this suddenly coming up now?"

"I am sorry for the delay. Unfortunately, you'd be surprised how large our caseload is. There are so many missing weapons that wind up getting sold illegally and even worse, being used for criminal activity. We are very busy as I am sure you can imagine."

Dennis nodded his head in understanding. Mug sensed that he'd succeeded in convincing him. Mug pretended to look down at some notes and said, "My records indicate that you reported your gun to be missing on December 22, 2009, is that correct?"

"Yes. That's correct."

"When was the last time you had seen your gun prior to that date?" Mug asked.

Dennis thought for a moment then answered, "Thanksgiving. We were hosting Thanksgiving at our house and I showed it to a few people."

"So it disappeared sometime in the four week period between Thanksgiving and December 22nd." Mug said as he wrote the information down. He then asked, "Do you remember the names of the people to whom you showed the gun?"

"Yes. It was my sister Christine and her husband Willie Dennison, and our next door neighbors, Karl and Laura Ravine."

"Who else lives in your residence with you and would any of the other residents know where you kept the gun?"

"Well, my wife lives here of course, and also my sister. Her husband had lived here until a couple of months ago.

"Were you burglarized at any time during the period in which the gun went missing? Do you know of any other missing items from your home?"

"No. We weren't burglarized as far as we could tell. We haven't noticed anything else missing."

"Were you away from home for any extended periods of time in that four week period?"

Dennis thought about it and said, "Yes. I was on a business trip down in Miami during the week of Monday, December 7th and I stayed down there all week and through the following weekend."

"Was it just you who went on the trip?"

"At first, yes. But then my wife and my sister came down a few days later to join me in Miami for the weekend."

"What about your sister's husband?"

"No. He didn't come. Said he wanted to save money. He was unemployed and looking for work and he didn't think he should spend the money on the trip. I remember him getting into a fight with my sister about it. They were always fighting about something. He didn't want her to go on the trip, but she said she needed the getaway for a few days. Times had been rough on them the past few years."

"What day did your wife and your sister leave to join you down there?"

"I think it was on Thursday."

Mug pretended to look down at his notes. "So that would be Thursday, December 10th. Is that correct?"

"Yes. I believe so." Dennis answered.

Mug looked down at his notes again as he said, "Did Willie...that's his name, right? Willie?" Dennis nodded. Mug continued, "Did Willie know where you kept the gun?"

"Yes. I had showed him previously. He and my sister were going to be staying with us for a while so it was only right that I told them upfront when they first arrived that I had a gun in the house."

Mug then asked, "Was the gun easily accessible? Or did you keep it locked up?"

"No. I didn't have it locked up. I know I should have, but we don't have any kids in the house. It's just adults. And I wanted to have it readily accessible should it ever been needed in an emergency."

"Where did you keep it?"

"In a drawer in my bedroom, underneath some clothes so at least it wasn't immediately visible should anyone open the drawer without knowing it was there."

"Mr. Dennis. It sounds like your sister's husband is a possible candidate for having taken the gun. He was alone in your house during the time period in which the gun went missing. He knew you had the gun and he knew where it was. You know him better than I do. Do you have any suspicions that he may have taken it?"

"I don't see why he would. What would he have done with it? And even if he had taken it for some reason, he had plenty of time to return it before I came back home. I wouldn't have ever known he had taken it. So why would he take it and not return it?"

"I'm not sure Mr. Dennis. Do you know of anyone else who knew about the gun and where you kept it?"

"No; just the four of us in the house and my next-door neighbors. But the neighbors didn't know where I kept the gun."

"Do you remember Willie's frame of mind during that time period?"

"It was the same as always. He was down in the dumps. He had lost his job and they lost their home up north and had to move down here with us, which they clearly hadn't wanted to do, especially Willie. He was trying to find work so that he and his wife could move out, but he hadn't found anything good and they were basically broke. He was also depressed because he is a somewhat old-fashioned type of guy who thinks it is the man of the family who is the one who is supposed to bring in the money, and he wasn't doing that. To make matters worse in his mind, my sister started working part-time as a substitute teacher in the school district here, so now she was earning some money, and he wasn't. They were fighting a lot, which is why my sister didn't really try too hard to convince Willie to join her that weekend in Miami."

"What did Willie do for work beforehand when he lived up north?"

"He had worked for some steel manufacturer in the Pittsburgh area. The company was going under in the bad economy and he was laid off."

"Did he express any ill will toward the company or anyone in particular regarding being let go?"

"Nothing specific; just general frustration and depression about his predicament in life."

"What did he do before working for that steel company?"

"He had been in the army for a few years. That is where he met my sister. She was a nurse in the army."

"You said that your sister's husband lived here until a couple of months ago? He's no longer here?"

"No. He and my sister were always fighting and she found out that he had been cheating on her. She kicked him out. I guess you can say they are separated now. They would get a divorce but they can't afford all the legal costs associated with it. They don't even speak to each other. She's even starting seeing someone else now also."

"Where did Willie go?"

"He got an apartment somewhere in the area. He wanted to stay around here to be with his new girlfriend."

"How did he get the money for an apartment if he wasn't working?" Mug asked.

"I don't know. He may have pawned some stuff. He did that a few times during the past year when he ran out of money."

"Do you know where he goes to pawn his stuff?"

"No, but my sister would know. She went with him a couple of times before they were separated. Once he made her sell diamond earrings that our mother had given to her. She was devastated. When she got some money from teaching, she went back to the pawn shop to buy it back without telling him. He found the earrings about a week later and you can't imagine the fight that caused."

"Is your sister here right now?" Mug asked. "I'd like to speak with her."

"No. I'm sorry." Dennis responded. "You actually just missed her. She left for the weekend with her boyfriend. They'll be back on Monday."

"Can I call her on her cell phone? I really need to speak with her."

"Why the sudden urgency?" Dennis asked. "I didn't hear a word about this case for four months. Anyway, she asked that she not be disturbed on her getaway unless it was an emergency. Otherwise, she wants to be left alone."

"It is very important. Can I have her number? It will be just a quick call."

"Like I said, she doesn't want to be disturbed. And I don't understand the sudden urgency after all this time. She'll be back Monday afternoon."

Mug had a difficult decision to make. Should he confide in this guy as to why the matter was time sensitive so as to get Christine Dennison's cell phone number? Or, should he try to obtain it through his law enforcement contacts, which he may or may not be able to do? He thought for a moment and decided to play it safe for now. He didn't really know this guy. "Ok. I understand Mr. Dennis. Thank you so much for your time and all the information. I'll be back on Monday to speak with your sister. I promise that I will try as best I can to find your gun. If you think of any other useful information, please call me." Mug ripped a piece of paper off his pad and wrote down his cell phone number. "Have a great weekend." Mug added as he started to step away.

"I'm sorry. I didn't catch your name." Larry Dennis said as he was handed the piece of paper.

"You can call me Mug. Thanks again for your time."

Mug took off. He was near certain that he now knew who had killed Jennifer Stohler. The only little issue that remained was that he needed to somehow prove it; preferably before Michael Stohler was convicted for the crime.

Chapter 71

Finally the big day had arrived. It was the day I had been anxiously awaiting for several months. It was Monday, April 5, 2010, which was the first day of the trial for my life.

Technically, the actual trial likely wouldn't start today. Today was jury selection day; a process known in legal circles as 'voir dire.' Orensen had briefed me over the weekend as to what to expect from this process, as well as all facets of the trial.

I lied awake in my cell for most of the preceding night. I was too excited and too nervous to get much sleep. All I could do throughout the night was to play out in my head the many different ways the testimony could unfold. So I was already wide awake and raring to go when the guards came to escort me out.

One of the nice aspects of the trial was that I'd be able to wear civilian clothes once again. Ah, the little things that I used to take for granted! Being able to wear my own clothes made me feel like a real person again. Of course, it makes sense that defendants should be allowed to wear civilian clothes at their trial. Wearing prison garb makes one look like a criminal and could influence the perception of the jurors.

I was transported to the Mercer County Courthouse in one of a caravan of law enforcement and Department of Corrections vehicles. We were driven into a garage beneath the courthouse so as to avoid the mob scene of reporters and onlookers gathering outside.

When we got inside, I was taken to a holding cell to await further instruction. Soon, Orensen arrived, along with two other men I hadn't met. Orensen had previously informed me that he'd have a '2nd chair' and certain specialists assist him during the trial. Naturally I agreed, despite my usual cost related concerns. What else was I going to do at this stage of the process?

Orensen shook my hand and introduced me to his cohorts. "Michael, this is Rudy Wimbach and Scott Bernstein. Rudy will be my 2nd chair throughout the trial and Scott will assist us today as our jury selection expert."

As I shook their hands, I asked, "Jury selection expert?"

"Yes" Orensen responded. "Scott is a licensed psychologist who is an expert in reading body language, facial expressions, voice tone, etc. He is here today to assist us in reading these features in potential jurors as they are asked questions to enable us to pick the best jury for us.

Bernstein then chimed in, "Good morning Mr. Stohler. You'd be surprised how many cases are won and lost in the jury selection process. It could be the most important part of the trial."

I figured that this wasn't the appropriate time to inquire as to his hourly rate. I was all in now with this team. I could only pray that it will end well.

"What are we looking for in an ideal juror?" I asked in the general direction of all three of them. Orensen fielded the question.

"Well Michael, unfortunately in this case, it may be impractical for us to expect to find twelve people who haven't heard a thing about you and the murder of your wife. So, our primary objective is to try to find people who at least haven't formed an opinion that you are guilty. We want people who will be able to objectively analyze the evidence and what is missing from the evidence, and make an unbiased decision."

"How do we distinguish such people from those who may already have formed an opinion?" I asked.

Bernstein responded this time. "That is a great question. It is not easy. But I've provided Mr. Orensen with some basic questions to ask, such as 'have you read or heard anything previously about this case?' and 'have you formed an opinion about this case?' I'll then study the subtle nuisances of the respondent's body language and various other involuntary expressions and movements to determine who is being truthful and who isn't and what the likely personality of the juror may be."

I couldn't believe that the fate of the rest of my life may lie in the hands of what I perceived to be psychology's version of a quack. Naturally, I kept that opinion to myself. At least the quack was trying to help me. There are only a few people in the world right now for which that could be said.

Orensen then added, "We also have some demographic preferences. For example, we'd like to try to avoid female jurors who have been recently divorced or are having some sort of marital issues. We don't want anyone with a vendetta against men in general who may have an "all men are evil" mentality. We expect the prosecution in this case to play up your marital issues as part of their motive theory and we don't want any women in the jury box sensing that they could relate to the emotional trauma that they may perceive you caused for Jennifer. But the main focus is to make sure our selected jurors have no preconceived notions of guilt based on what they've seen and heard before today."

We were then informed that it was time to enter the courtroom. We were escorted to the defense table and awaited the arrival of Judge Connerly.

Shortly thereafter, Judge Connerly arrived and commenced the proceedings by addressing the potential jurors, thanking them for their time and their willingness to perform their civic duty. He then informed both sides that he would start the questioning of the potential jurors with some general inquiries before allowing each attorney to ask questions of their own.

Judge Connerly asked the jurors if they could speak, read, and write English fluently. He asked the same question in Spanish, just in case, a juror who should answer 'no' to the question, didn't understand the English version. He then asked some questions pertaining to the time commitment involved, stating that he couldn't be sure exactly how long the case may run, but that it could potentially be a few weeks.

Some potential jurors were excused upon expressing special circumstances in their lives that would make such a commitment problematic for them. Others tried to do the same, but to no avail. I guess their stories weren't good enough.

Judge Connerly explained to the jury pool the importance of not allowing anything that may have been seen or heard previously about this case impact a juror's objectivity. He asked if anyone already had formed any opinions one way or the other regarding the defendant's guilt or innocence in this case, and/or if any of them had personally known the defendant and/or the victim in this case. A few people raised their hands to say that they had some predetermined bias. Some of these people were the same ones who were previously denied their exit on the time commitment front. I presumed they were just pouncing on their next opportunity. Everyone who expressed any issues about their ability to be impartial was excused. Bernstein whispered to me that we were still going to delve deeper into this matter when it was our turn to question the jury candidates.

Connerly then opened the floor to the attorneys. Stanley Murdoch, the prosecutor, would go first. It immediately became very clear what attribute he was prioritizing. He wanted jurors who were pro-death penalty. Anyone who expressed that he or she was against the death penalty was dismissed for cause by Murdoch.

At a break in the proceedings, I asked Bernstein how Murdoch's tactics of getting rid of anti-death penalty jurors could be allowed. "If the jury is theoretically supposed to be a representative sample of my peers in the community, then shouldn't it be made up of people who are on both sides of that issue, just as the community at large would be?" I asked.

"Great question Michael." Bernstein said, "Unfortunately, the Supreme Court has ruled that it is within the Constitution that juries in capital cases can be what's referred to as, 'death qualified,' meaning that the jury should consist only of people who would be willing to hand down a sentence of death should the defendant be found guilty. Therefore, it allows for the elimination of potential jurors who categorically oppose the death penalty in all circumstances."

"How is it a fair jury if all of them are gung-ho for the death penalty?" I asked as my follow-up question.

Bernstein replied, "The objectivity of the jury is still of upmost importance in initially determining the defendant's guilt or innocence. The questioning of one's beliefs toward the death penalty is only to assure that the prosecution will be able to obtain a death sentence should there be a guilty verdict later on. Unfortunately, studies have shown that pro-capital punishment jurors are statistically more likely to find defendants guilty than those against the death penalty."

Great, another handicap against me, I thought to myself. I wasn't feeling very optimistic at this point in time.

The voir dire process soon resumed and Orensen was given his chance to question remaining potential jurors. He asked a lot of questions about what precisely they had seen and heard about the case, and what the context of such coverage had been in their opinion. He also asked some of the women about their marital status and he dismissed a few divorcees for cause. Throughout the process, Bernstein was studying each person's every minute mannerism very carefully. Orensen looked back at him after speaking with each one to get his "yes" or "no" vote.

The jury selection process took all day to complete. By the end of the day, the original pool of one hundred potential jurors was whittled down to our twelve jurors and two alternates, all of whom apparently were avid fans of capital punishment. The twelve jurors were comprised of seven men and five women. The two alternates consisted of one of each gender. These were the people who starting tomorrow would be responsible for determining the fate of the rest of my life.

Chapter 72

Mug spent most of his time on Sunday and Monday tracking down Willie Dennison's new address, and following him around to ascertain where he worked, if anywhere, and anything else Mug could learn about his new top suspect. He found Dennison in a garden apartment complex about five miles away from his previous residence at the Dennis home.

It didn't take long for Mug to verify the existence of a girlfriend. Willie and a shapely blonde at least ten years younger than him were together during the entire two day period. What wasn't as apparent was whether or not Willie was employed. He certainly didn't go to work either of those two days.

On Monday evening, Mug returned to the Dennis residence to speak with Willie's wife, Christine. Fortunately she was back from her two day getaway and had been prepped by Larry Dennis to expect Mug's arrival. Mug soon learned that she was very willing to "sing like a canary" against her wayward husband.

"Good evening Mrs. Dennison. My name is Mug. I hope not to take up too much of your time. I just have a few questions about your husband. Did Mr. Dennis fill you in on the nature of my investigation?"

"Yes he did. You can call me Christine. I understand that you are looking for Larry's missing gun and that you think my husband may have taken it."

"I don't know that for sure, but it is a possibility worth exploring. First, can you please tell me the circumstances under which you moved down here?" Mug asked.

"Well, it's quite sad really." Christine said. "Willie got fired from his job up in Pennsylvania. We didn't have a lot of money to begin with, and our house was underwater, so upon his losing his job, and neither of us being able to find work, we soon lost our home. Thankfully, my brother was gracious enough to take us in. So we moved down here."

"Did Willie want to move down here?"

"No. Definitely not. He is from the Pittsburgh area and lived up there his whole life. He didn't want to have to live off of others and it wasn't his side of the family. He felt very uncomfortable and embarrassed."

"Why did he lose his job up north?"

"He was laid off. The company was losing money and there were a lot of layoffs." Christine answered.

"Did Willie harbor any ill feelings to the person or persons who let him go?"

"Willie blames everyone but himself for everything that goes wrong in his life. So the answer is 'yes.' It just so happened that his boss at the plant was our next door neighbor and we were very friendly with him and his wife. Oh that poor woman. She's the one who was murdered recently. I couldn't believe it when I heard the news."

"What was Willie's reaction to the news?" Mug asked.

"I guess he was sad. I don't know. He had been so depressed in general that it would have been hard to distinguish any added sadness regarding that. He's a self-centered person anyway. All Willie really cares about is Willie, so he probably wasn't too broken up about it. What does all this have to do with the missing gun anyway?"

"I'm just trying to get an understanding of Willie's frame of mind around the time the gun went missing. Based on police reports and my conversation with Mr. Dennis on Saturday, we've honed in on a four week period from Thanksgiving to December 22, 2009 during which time the gun disappeared. Only a few people knew about the gun and where it was kept, one of which was Willie; and he happened to be left alone in the house for a few days during that same time frame."

Mug went on, "I know that you met Willie in the army, so I assume he had some experience with guns. Is that correct?"

"Yes. He loved guns and had always wanted to own one, but I wouldn't allow it. I didn't want a gun in our house. I didn't know my brother kept one here until after we had arrived, but I didn't really have any other options as to where we could go. We were broke."

"Was Willie adept at handling guns? Do you know if he had a good shot?"

"Yes. He had a great shot. He won some competitions in the army."

"Just out of curiosity, is Willie right-handed or left-handed?"

"He's left-handed. Why?"

"I was just curious. You had said he was a great shot. Some types of guns are more easily handled by righties or lefties" Mug said just to cover up his real reason for asking the question. He then quickly changed the subject.

"I'm sorry if this is personal, but it may be important to determine frame of mind. Can you tell me why you and Willie are not living together right now?"

"That's fine. Believe me, I'll tell you anything you want to know about that scumbag. He's not living here because he was and probably still is, cheating on me with a bimbo. I was willing to put up with all of his mood swings, depression, and even occasional violence toward me, all caused by his frustration as to our predicament in life. But once he started cheating, that was it. He had crossed the line. We were through. So I kicked him out."

"About when was that?" Mug asked.

"It was January 11th. I remember the date exactly because it was just three days before our anniversary."

"Do you know where he went?"

"I didn't know at first and I didn't care. Larry told me that he got an apartment nearby. That is all I know. I haven't seen or talked to him since and frankly I don't care to. I'd get a divorce if I could afford it. He'd probably say the same."

"How did he have the money to get an apartment? Didn't you say that the two of you were broke?"

"I don't know. I guess there is one of two possibilities. Either he pawned more stuff, or his bimbo girlfriend gave him money. Maybe both."

"You said 'pawned more stuff.' Had he been pawning items previously?"

"He's been pawning pretty much anything he could get his hands on. He pawned practically all of my jewelry. There's no such thing anymore as sentimental value to him. All he cares about is getting money. That is, without working."

"Where does he go to pawn these items? Is there a place around here?"

"There's a place in Southeast D.C. that he goes to. I don't know why he picked that place, but he had gone there several times while we were together. I went there a couple of times with him. I even went there once on my own to buy back some items of mine that he had pawned without asking me. Could you believe he did that?"

"Do you remember the name of the place?"

"I think it's called 'Ace Pawn Shop' or something like that."

Mug asked a few more questions, thanked Christine for her time, and gave her his cell phone number for her to call should she think of anything else that may be useful. He also asked for her number in case he had any follow-up questions. But Mug believed that he had what he needed. It was becoming pretty obvious what his new working theory was in this case.

Quite simply, Mug's theory was as follows: Willie Dennison harbored a grudge against Michael Stohler for firing him. The Dennisons lost their home, and much to Willie's chagrin, were forced to move in with Christine's brother and his wife. Willie was depressed, desperate for money, and mad at the world in general and Michael Stohler specifically. Willie came to learn that Larry Dennis had a gun in the house. Then, just a short time later, Willie happened to be left alone for a few days as the other three residents in the Dennis home were in Miami. Willie took the gun, drove up north, and broke into the Stohler house using his copy of the keys that he had made before his wife had returned their set to Jennifer.

The part of the story that was a little unclear at this point in time was Willie's exact intent. Mug theorized that Willie didn't intend to kill Jennifer. Either Willie had intended to kill Michael and found Jennifer there instead, or he simply intended to burglarize the Stohlers and was caught in the act.

Either way, Mug figured that Willie's plans went awry when Jennifer spotted him. At that point, Jennifer had to be eliminated as she would have recognized him. Then, needing to flee as quickly as possible, he only had time to grab one item, which was immediately in sight where he shot Jennifer. He didn't have time to look around for anything else.

Mug figured that if Willie's intent had initially been just burglary, and had succeeded without incident, he likely would have returned Larry's gun before Larry came back home from Miami. But after Willie shot Jennifer with that gun, he couldn't have the murder weapon in the house where he was residing. So, having lived in Garrowville previously, and being just a couple of miles from Garrowville Park, Mug figured that Willie must have been familiar with the park. It would be a quick, convenient place for Willie to go to ditch the murder weapon.

Soon thereafter, Willie pawned the ring so that he wouldn't be caught with it in his possession. Also, he would want to have the money to spend on his new girlfriend. The money came in handy a month later when he was tossed out of the Dennis household and he needed to rent an apartment.

Mug realized that there was some irony if his theory was correct. It would mean that Mug found the murder weapon which led him to Willie Dennison while staking out a crime in progress which in actuality had nothing to do with the murder he was investigating. Sometimes the best investigators needed some luck on their side to be successful.

But maybe it wasn't completely unrelated. He still didn't know whether Willie had taken the ring after killing Jennifer, or if Radford had done so upon discovering the body. The next step in the investigation would obviously be to pay a visit to the Ace Pawn Shop.

Chapter 73

Tuesday, April 6, 2010 was Day # 2 of my trial. Or was it technically the first day? Does the jury selection day count as the first day of the trial? I'm not sure, but I suppose that is just splitting hairs. Either way, we were back in court for the start of the actual trial proceedings. The jurors filed in, the bailiff called the court to order and announced the entrance of Judge Connerly. We all rose as he entered and waited for the invitation to be seated; which the bailiff provided as Connerly sat down.

After Judge Connerly welcomed everyone and rattled off some preliminary instructions and ground rules, he was ready to get started.

"Mr. Murdoch, your opening statement."

"Thank you your honor." Murdoch politely stated as he rose and walked toward the jury.

"Good morning. My name is Stanley Murdoch. I am the District Attorney and I am responsible for prosecuting this case. As I am sure you are aware, the jurors in any case are the most important part of our criminal justice system. You are the ones responsible for determining that justice is properly served. I speak for myself, my office, and the Commonwealth of Pennsylvania when I sincerely thank you for fulfilling this most vital civic duty.

"It is under the most unfortunate and tragic circumstances that we must all be here today. A young, beautiful woman in the prime of her life, was cold-heartedly murdered in her own bedroom in the middle of the night. Her name was Jennifer Stohler. She was a school teacher who was loved by all of her students and fellow teachers. She was very active in the local church and was loved by all of her fellow members of the church. She was a lifelong member of the community in which she lived and was loved by everyone in that community.

"At one point in time, she was also loved by her husband. They were high school sweethearts, went to college together, got married shortly after graduating from college, and for a while were very happily married. But unfortunately, times got tough financially on the Stohlers and it strained their marriage. Soon they were fighting often and were living separately. Shortly thereafter, Jennifer Stohler was found murdered and as you can see, her husband is the defendant charged with having committed that murder.

"This is really a quite simple case. We will present to you a lot of evidence that will make it very clear that there was no one else who had the motive and the opportunity to commit this crime. Who else would want Jennifer dead? Who else would have access to her in her home in the middle of the night?

"We'll present evidence that illustrates the financial duress the Stohlers were experiencing. We'll present evidence to show that Michael Stohler had a lucrative life insurance policy on his wife at the time of her murder. We'll present evidence to show that Jennifer was contemplating divorce, which would mean that the defendant would have to make alimony payments should the divorce take place. Why have to indefinitely make such payments when instead he could receive the proceeds of a life insurance policy? We'll present evidence from the crime scene showing that there was no forced entry and that the physical description of the murderer fits the defendant. There will be no shortage of evidence all pointing to only one logical conclusion.

"This is what I like to refer to as a 'common sense' case. Common sense makes it obvious who committed this murder. You are all intelligent people. That is why you were selected for this jury out of 100 candidates here yesterday. I am hopeful that upon hearing all the evidence, you will apply the common sense I know you each have, in deciding this case. I hope that you will apply that common sense when you ask yourself the key questions I mentioned earlier. Who else would want Jennifer dead? Who else had the motive that the defendant had? Who else had the access and opportunity to achieve that objective?

"We'll present a lot of evidence that makes it very clear to you exactly what that motive was for this murder and how it was motive that logically only one person would have had. Again, it is simple common sense. If the defendant didn't commit this crime, then who did? There are no other logical answers. Therefore, it must be the defendant. Simple common sense.

"Again I speak not only for myself, but for everyone in all of Pennsylvania when I ask you to do the right thing in this case. Follow the evidence and your common sense and give Jennifer Stohler the justice she deserves. You'll also be helping to protect everyone by taking a murderer off the streets forever. You have a responsibility of utmost importance. You will be making the society in which we all live a better and safer place if you reach the right verdict and convict Michael Stohler for the murder of his wife. Thank you."

Chapter 74

"Mr. Orensen. Would you like to make your opening statement now, or defer until later?" Judge Connerly asked.

Orensen rose and answered, "Thank you your honor. I would like to make my opening statement now."

"Very well, you may proceed Mr. Orensen."

"Good morning. My name is Jeff Orensen. I am the attorney representing the defendant in this case. I also would like to thank each and every one of you for your commitment and for fulfilling your civic duty. As Mr. Murdoch noted in his remarks, it is due to the worst imaginable circumstances that we are here today. There is no doubt that a senseless tragedy has occurred. A young beautiful woman was in fact killed in her own home and for that we all feel horribly.

"However, there is in fact doubt as to who killed her. As you know, her husband, Michael Stohler is the defendant in this case. He is being accused of committing this heinous act. What we can't allow to happen is to compound the tragedy of Jennifer's murder with another one by convicting the wrong person for this crime. Doing so would fail to give Jennifer Stohler the justice she deserves, would unjustly put an innocent person behind bars, and would allow the true killer or killers to remain free on the streets to kill again. Mr. Murdoch mentioned in his opening remarks that one of the reasons why your job here is so important is to protect our society from murderers by taking them off the streets. Well, if we convict the wrong person, we will be failing in that vital responsibility in that the true killer or killers would still remain free.

"In consideration of these critical points, I urge each and every one of you to listen objectively to the evidence as it is presented to you in this case, keeping in mind that we want to be 100% sure that we are correct if we convict someone of this crime. In order to minimize the likelihood of wrongful convictions, our criminal justice system provides that to convict a defendant you must believe in his or her guilt 'beyond all reasonable doubt.' That is an important term to keep in mind here: 'beyond all reasonable doubt.' It essentially means that you need to be as close to 100% sure as you possibly can be that a defendant is guilty in order to vote for a conviction at the end of the trial.

"The prosecution in this case will attempt to show you a lot of evidence that sounds like Michael Stohler may have committed this crime. This is what's known as 'circumstantial evidence'; meaning the circumstances surrounding such evidence makes a person appear like he or she may be guilty, but in reality, doesn't directly prove such guilt.

"As you listen to the prosecution's evidence, I want you to ask yourself, 'Does this evidence really prove that Michael Stohler killed his wife, or does it just sound like it is a possibility that he did?' I want you to also ask yourself, 'Where is the direct, concrete evidence that definitively links Michael Stohler to this crime? Where is the smoking gun? Where are the fingerprints, footprints, DNA, eyewitnesses, anything that definitively proves Michael Stohler is guilty?

"If you keep these questions in mind as you listen to the case unfold, I think you will see that there exists no such evidence. Mr. Murdoch pointed out that you are all intelligent people, which is why you were selected yesterday. He is correct about that. The defense team also selected each of you for the same reason. We want intelligent people who can see through the smoke and mirrors of the prosecution's case and recognize that there is an alarming lack of direct evidence against the defendant.

"And in the absence of such evidence, there is no way that you can come to a conclusion beyond all reasonable doubt that Michael Stohler is guilty. Please don't add to this horrible tragedy with another one by convicting the wrong person. Thank you."

Chapter 75

Stanley Murdoch didn't rise to his current position of power and prominence by accident. He was no dummy. He knew how to prosecute and win cases. He had developed his own little "blueprint" as he called it, which basically was an outline as to how the presentation of his case should unfold.

The first step in his blueprint for success was to establish that a murder had in fact taken place. This phase of the presentation typically required the responding officer to testify. Already Murdoch had a problem. His responding officer, Dan Radford, was flaking out on him just prior to the trial. To further compound the problem, Murdoch had wanted Radford to also testify to the confession he had overheard at the cemetery. However, right up to the start of the trial, Radford had declared that he wasn't going anywhere near the witness stand. He did not give any reason for his stubborn stance on the matter.

On Monday evening, which was the night before Murdoch anticipated calling Radford to the witness stand, he visited Radford in his home and blasted him. Murdoch threatened Radford with a subpoena, termination, and even charges of filing a false report.

Radford didn't appear to be fazed by the threats. Either he saw them as empty threats and/or for some reason Radford wasn't disclosing, he was more afraid of testifying than of not testifying. After an hour of Murdoch's shouting, mudslinging, and obscenity laced tirades, Radford had finally agreed to testify as to the discovery of the body and his observations at the crime scene. He would not testify to hearing Michael Stohler confess to the crime.

So now that both attorneys had given their opening statements, Judge Connerly invited Stanley Murdoch to call his first witness. With a little trepidation that he hoped no one in the courtroom sensed, Murdoch announced, "The Commonwealth calls Officer Dan Radford to the stand."

Officer Radford slowly approached the stand, climbed up into his designated spot, and was sworn in to tell "the truth, the whole truth, and nothing but the truth." He then sat down and awaited Murdoch's questions.

Murdoch started him off with an easy question just to establish his qualifications.

"Officer Radford, how long have you been with the Garrowville police department?"

"Nearly eleven years." Radford nervously answered. He didn't seem very composed up there. Murdoch didn't have a good feeling about this. He'd better get to the point soon before Radford had a breakdown.

"Officer Radford, please tell me about the morning of Friday, December 11ᵗʰ, 2009."

"Well, um, Chief Lumpkin instructed me to check out the Stohler residence. He said that Jennifer Stohler hadn't reported to work that morning, and hadn't called out. She wasn't answering her phone and they were worried about her. So, I drove over there to see if she was ok."

"And what did you find when you got there?" Murdoch asked trying to move Radford along.

"I found that her car was on the driveway and there was a light on in the upstairs window, so it appeared that she was home. I parked, walked up to her front door, and noted that it was open a little bit. It seemed strange to me. I rang the doorbell but there was no answer. I then stepped inside and yelled out both Jennifer and Michael's names to see if either of them was home. There was still no answer."

"What did you do then?"

"I searched the house while still calling out their names. I started with the downstairs level but found no one. Then I went upstairs and that is when I found her."

"Who did you find Officer Radford?"

"I found Jennifer Stohler lying dead on her bedroom floor. She had a single gunshot wound in the middle of her forehead. She had been murdered."

"How did you make the determination that she had been murdered as opposed to a suicide?" Murdoch asked.

"There was no gun found at the scene. If she had shot herself like that in the head she would have died instantaneously and the gun would still be in her hand or nearby. No gun meant no suicide."

"What other observations had you made at the crime scene?"

"I had noted that there was no sign of forced entry, which seemed to indicate that the killer either had a key or was let in by Jennifer. Either way, she likely knew her killer."

"Did you check all other doors and windows? Were there any other ways that an intruder could have forced his way into the house that you wouldn't have noticed?"

"I phoned in the murder and the entire Garrowville police department was on the scene within a few minutes. We all searched the premises very carefully. Every square foot of that house was closely inspected. We found no evidence of any forced entry anywhere."

"What else did you notice at the crime scene?"

"I noticed that Jennifer's wedding ring was not on her finger and didn't appear to be anywhere in the vicinity."

"Has it been subsequently found? Maybe it was just in a drawer, or a locked compartment somewhere for safe keeping at night?

"No. We checked everywhere. I even visited the house again later on with the defendant. The ring is still missing."

"Was there anything else in the house known to be missing?"

"No."

"So, is it your belief, Officer Radford, that based upon your observations at the crime scene after your thorough examination of the premises, and your extensive experience as a law enforcement officer, that Jennifer Stohler was in fact murdered and that the killer most likely took her wedding ring?'

"Yes. That is my belief."

At this point in time, Murdoch would have liked to question Radford about who he believed killed Jennifer and how he came to such beliefs. But, he couldn't be sure of the answers he would get. And Murdoch knew that a good lawyer never asks a question for which he or she doesn't know the answer that will be received. Therefore, he made the strategic decision to end his questioning of this witness at this point. He had plenty of other witnesses to call to establish his case.

"No further questions your honor." Murdoch stated to Judge Connerly.

"Mr. Orensen, cross-examine?"

"Yes your honor." Orensen stood and faced Radford on the stand.

"Officer Radford. You mentioned that you and your colleagues thoroughly investigated the crime scene, is that correct?"

"Yes."

"And in your collective investigations, did any of you discover any evidence that directly linked the crime to Michael Stohler?"

"Well, like I said before, we noted no sign of forced entry. That would.."

Orensen interrupted him. "Officer Radford, isn't it possible that someone else besides Michael Stohler could have a key to the house?"

"Well, I suppose it is possible, but…"

"Isn't it possible that Jennifer might have let someone in; a friend for instance?"

"In the middle of the night? I don't think that is likely."

"I didn't ask what you thought was likely. I asked if it were possible. Jennifer had a lot of friends. She lived in the neighborhood her whole life. She knew everyone and everyone knew her. By all accounts, she was always willing to help anyone who needed help. You knew Jennifer for a long time Officer. Is my description of Jennifer correct?"

"Yes."

"Then if a friend or anyone she knew in the community knocked on her door in the middle of the night asking for help of some kind, wasn't it within her personality to have opened the door to try to help?"

"Yes."

"Such a scenario therefore would not have required a forced entry, isn't that correct Officer?"

"Yes."

"Isn't it possible that the Stohlers may have at some point in time, exchanged house keys with friends or neighbors in case of an emergency?"

"I suppose that is possible."

"So, isn't it possible that some of these people may still have a set of the Stohlers' keys?"

"I don't know. Maybe that's possible, but I…"

"If that were the case, and other people besides Michael Stohler had a set of house keys, if one of them were to be the killer, wouldn't he or she be able to enter the premises simply by using the keys?"

"I guess so."

"Going back to your extensive search of the crime scene, did you or any of your colleagues uncover any fingerprints, footprints, DNA, or anything other physical evidence which you were able to tie to Michael Stohler?"

"No."

"Were there any eyewitnesses to the murder?"

"No."

"So, it is fair to say that there is no one who can definitely say that they witnessed who killed Jennifer Stohler. Is that correct?"

Murdoch jumped up, "Objection your honor. Asked and answered."

"Sustained. Move on Mr. Orensen."

"No further questions your honor."

Orensen was pleased with his cross-examination. He hoped that his speech to the jury about reasonable doubt, coupled with the reasonable doubt he believed he portrayed in his questioning of Radford had scored some points. But there was still a long way to go.

Murdoch on the other hand was livid. Orensen had just punched holes in everything to which Radford had just testified and Murdoch couldn't ask Radford about the confession he overheard, nor could he risk asking anything in re-direct, so he figured it was time to just move on to the next witness.

At least Murdoch had established there had been a murder. But he knew he better have more success with his other witnesses if he stood any chance of winning this case.

Chapter 76

"The Commonwealth calls Ben Alford to the stand." Murdoch declared after Radford had departed.

Ben Alford was the lead CSI investigator on the scene and had thoroughly analyzed all evidence both at the scene and in the lab afterwards. Murdoch established his credentials and experience to qualify him as an expert witness. He then started his case specific questioning.

"Mr. Alford, please take us through your findings at the crime scene." Murdoch requested.

"A young woman, appearing to be in her 30s, later confirmed to be thirty-four years old, was found dead on her bedroom floor of a single gunshot wound to the head. We found the bullet's shell casing, and the actual bullet which had exited through the back of her head. These findings confirmed that the weapon used was a Beretta .22 caliber handgun. From our analysis of the trajectory of the bullet, the resulting blood splatter, and the position in which the victim fell, we were able to reasonably pinpoint the location of the shooter and derive certain facts about the shooter."

"Can you please elaborate as to those findings?"

"Yes. The trajectory of the bullet was slightly downward, yet still went through the middle of the victim's forehead. That would lead us to believe that a shooter, who in likelihood would be shooting at shoulder height or lower, had to be significantly taller than the victim. Even factoring in that the shooter was probably wearing shoes and victim was not, the height difference was likely to be at least one-half foot, maybe more. We know the victim was 5'6", which would put the shooter at a minimum of six foot, and I would guess even taller than that."

"What else could you deduce about the shooter?"

"The bedroom door was partially open and the victim was lying near the door with her feet closest to the door. It would appear that she may have just opened the door to her room just before being shot. Again, based on the trajectory of the bullet, we can deduce where the shooter was standing at the time of the shot. Placing the shooter helped us determine that the shooter most likely shot the victim using his left hand. He wouldn't have had a clear shot with his right hand with the partially opened door in the way. Based on this fact, and the precision of the shot, we believe that the shooter was most likely left-handed."

"So, in your expert opinion, we have a tall, left-handed killer. Is that correct?"

"Yes. I believe that to be correct." Alford answered.

"Mr. Alford, were you able to establish a time of death?"

"Yes. Based on the victim's body temperature, we estimated at the crime scene that she had been killed roughly between 2 a.m. and 4 a.m., which was six to eight hours prior to our examination. We later confirmed that estimate with further analysis back at the lab."

"Did you notice if there were any valuables in the room near the victim where she was shot?"

"Yes. There appeared to be various items of jewelry on the dresser near where she fell."

"Were they out in plain sight?"

"Yes."

"So it would appear that robbery was not the primary motive here, wouldn't you agree?"

"Objection!" Orensen shouted. "Speculative."

"Sustained." Judge Connerly ruled.

"No further questions your honor." Murdoch then stated.

Orensen then rose to commence his cross-examination.

"Mr. Alford. What would estimate is the present day population of the United States?" Orensen asked.

"Objection!" Murdoch emphatically stated. "Relevance."

"Mr. Orensen, I assume you will be going somewhere with this?" Judge Connerly asked.

"Yes your honor." Orensen answered.

"Ok. I'll allow it. Get to the point quickly. The objection is overruled. Mr. Alford, you may answer the question." Judge Connerly declared.

"I don't know. I'd say maybe around 300 million." Alford answered.

"That's a good guess. The latest estimates in this census year is that the census will come in at somewhere between 300 and 310 million. So, let's go with your estimate of 300 million. It is fairly accurate. Now, Mr. Alford, what percentage of that population would you estimate is at least six feet tall?"

"Objection." Murdoch cried out again.

"Overruled." Connerly ruled once again.

"I don't know." Alford answered.

"Well, would you be able to dispute that according to several sources, which I will submit collectively as Defense Exhibit A along with these other statistics I am presenting, the estimated percentage of the U.S. population that is at least 6 feet tall is roughly 3 to 4%. Do you have any knowledge or information that is contrary to that Mr. Alford?"

"No."

"Finally, Mr. Alford, one more of these statistics. What percentage of the U.S. population would you estimate is left-handed?"

"I don't know." Alford answered a little less patiently this time.

"So, I assume therefore, you wouldn't dispute these studies I am submitting that estimate the percentage of our nation's population that is left-handed is roughly 12%. Do you have any information to the contrary?

"No."

"Ok. Now let's do a little math. We have a population of roughly 300 million people in this nation. If we take 3%, which is the low end of the estimated range of those people who are at least six feet tall, it means we have about 9 million people who fit your height requirement. Then, if we say that about 12% of those 9 million people are left-handed, we have over 1 million people who fit both of your criteria. So, my question to you Mr. Alford is this; did you find any specific physical evidence that differentiated Michael Stohler from the other over one million people who also fit the two criteria you described?"

"Well, no, other than…"

"And, of course, these calculations are just for U.S. citizens. We don't even know for a fact that the killer is among the numbers we are citing. Now, let's further examine your height and left-handed criteria. They are, after all, educated guesses as opposed to known facts, is that correct?"

"We did a thorough analysis of the crime scene counselor." Alford answered defensively.

"I don't doubt that Mr. Alford. What I mean is that even after your careful investigation, there could theoretically still be other explanations. For example, couldn't a shooter have shot with his left hand, but still be right-handed? Is that completely impossible?"

"It is not likely."

"I didn't ask what was likely. I asked if it was possible that a right-handed shooter, for whatever reason, such as having another object in his right hand, or due to be startled by the encounter with the victim, thus wasn't completely ready for the shot, could have shot with his or her opposite hand?"

"The shot was pretty precise to think that it was done with someone's opposite hand." Alford stated.

"How do we know about precision? Maybe the shooter actually meant for it to be a warning shot over the victim's head. Or meant to hit the victim's arm to injure but not kill. Or maybe the shooter didn't mean to shoot at all but had less control of the weapon in his or her opposite hand. Is there anything specific that you found that would definitively rule out these possibilities?"

"No."

"Finally, Mr. Alford, in your very thorough investigation of the crime scene, did you or any of your CSI team find any physical evidence, such as fingerprints, footprints, or DNA that would tie this murder to Michael Stohler?"

"No."

"No further questions your honor." Orensen said toward the judge.

Murdoch then stood up and declared, "Re-direct your honor."

"Go ahead."

"Mr. Alford, Mr. Orensen asked you a question before regarding if there was anything from the crime scene that would differentiate Michael Stohler from anyone else who fit the height and left-handed criteria. You started to say something to answer that question, but were interrupted by his next question. What was going to be your answer to what differentiates Michael Stohler from the other million people Mr. Orensen quantified?"

"Just that the crime scene itself was in Michael Stohler's home and it was his wife who was shot. Neither of those facts can be attributed to any of the other million people." Alford responded.

"Thank you Mr. Alford. No further questions your honor." Murdoch smugly declared as he proudly marched back to his seat.

Chapter 77

It was mid-afternoon by the time Ben Alford's testimony had ended. Murdoch didn't want to call any of his key witnesses and get interrupted by the end of the day. So instead, Murdoch simply called a quick procession of several close friends of Jennifer Stohler. Each of their testimonies essentially said the same things; that Jennifer had confided in them about the Stohlers' marital problems and that Michael had been recently staying at his parents' residence instead of at home with her. Murdoch simply wanted to end the day by clearly establishing that times were rough in the Stohler marriage. It would set up nicely for the next day's witness list which would start with the divorce attorney Jennifer had visited.

Jeff Orensen's cross-examinations of Jennifer's friends were fairly quick, as they weren't key witnesses. With each one, Orensen got them to say on the record that they had no actual evidence that Michael Stohler had committed the crime, they hadn't known Michael to be violent toward Jennifer at any time during their twelve year marriage, and they had never seen or heard anything about Michael owning a gun or ever even having touched one.

It was the end of an exciting day in court in the Stohler case, during which time Mug was having an exciting day of his own.

On Tuesday morning, based on his discussion with Christine Dennison the night before, Mug located the Ace Pawn Shop in Southeast Washington, D.C. As expected, it was not in a nice part of town. Pawn shops generally aren't in the better areas of the community, but Mug noted that this neighborhood seemed particularly rough, even in comparison to the many "wrong side of the tracks" type areas Mug had grown up in and frequented as part of his unusual vocation.

It made him wonder how and why Willie Dennison had come here. There must have been closer options. Mug's best guess was that when Willie first had to go to a pawn shop for money, he hadn't told his wife and therefore, he had to go somewhere he wouldn't be recognized. Afterwards, because he was familiar with this one place, he simply returned there as needed.

These weren't the key points, however. The key to this morning's visit was to ascertain if Willie Dennison had pawned Jennifer Stohler's wedding ring here. So, after having spoken with Christine Dennison last night, Mug contacted George Stohler to get more information about the ring. George emailed Mug a photo of the ring and a copy of the latest appraisal which included the ring's specifications.

Mug walked in and asked to speak with the owner of the establishment.

"That would be Rocco" answered a burly and sour man behind the counter, who didn't seem to be overly concerned with the concept of "service with a smile."

"Well, is Rocco here at the moment?" Mug asked.

"Who wants to know?" Mr. Customer Service asked.

"I do." Mug sarcastically answered.

"And who the hell are you?"

Mug flashed is private investigator's badge. "I am an investigator. I need to speak with Rocco ASAP. Now go get him, otherwise, this place will be swarming with police before you know what hit you."

It was an empty threat, of course, but Mug figured places like these generally do not want the police snooping around. Who knew what was and wasn't on the 'up and up' here? Mug's bluff worked. The surly clerk glared menacingly at Mug, but ultimately did as instructed and retrieved Rocco.

"What do you want?" asked another large personable character while walking out from an office behind the register.

"Are you Rocco?"

"Yes."

"Let's go into your office so we can talk in private." Mug suggested.

As they walked into Rocco's office, Mug thought to himself how there can't be many conversations going on in the world right now involving two people known as 'Rocco' and 'Mug.'

Once inside Rocco's office, Mug took out the DMV photo he had of Willie Dennison and showed it to Rocco. "Has this guy been in your store?"

"Maybe. We get a lot of people in here."

Mug took out a hundred dollar bill. "Look Rocco. I'm investigating a murder. We can do this one of two ways. The easy way, in which you cooperate with me and I'll give you some money for your information, or the hard way, in which I contact the police who undoubtedly will come in here with a lot more intrusive questions and without paying you anything. Which way is it going to be?"

Rocco took the money and Mug made a mental note to add it to the Stohler tab.

"Yes. He's been in here." Rocco said. "Several times in fact. He's become my best customer. He must be in a pretty severe financial mess."

"Why do you say that?" Mug asked.

"Well, for starters, he doesn't really match the profile of my usual clientele; at least not the ones who come in often. He's more clean-cut looking than my regulars. He looks more like the one-time client who comes here when in a sudden, desperate financial mess. Some of those people even buy their stuff back later on. But your dude is different. He comes in every so often with new stuff to sell. And valuable stuff too. He's never interested in buying anything back. Just continues selling more stuff. That is why I assumed he must be in bad shape financially."

"What kind of valuable stuff has he sold to you?"

"Mostly jewelry. Diamond earrings, rings, etc. He even pawned his wife's wedding ring. If that doesn't represent a dire financial crisis, then what does?"

"Was his wife with him the time he sold you her wedding ring?"

"No. But she's been in here with him before. And, she came in once to buy some earrings back without him."

"So, how do you know it was her wedding ring?"

"I don't really. He just said it was. I didn't ask any follow-up questions. I was just focused on appraising it and negotiating a price."

Mug then took out the photograph of the ring. "Was this the ring?" he asked.

"It looks like it. A lot of rings could be similar in a photo though. I'd need to know the specifications of the ring in the photo to tell for sure; you know, the size, clarity, etc."

Mug then took out the information he'd received from George Stohler and showed Rocco.

"Yes. That's the ring." Rocco said.

"Do you still have it?" Mug asked as he tried to keep his excitement in check.

"You're not getting the ring unless you buy it or you have a search warrant. I paid a lot of money for that ring." Rocco defiantly stated.

"How much did you pay for it?" Mug asked.

"Well, what I paid for it and what it's worth are two separate matters. I appraised it at approximately $15,000. I paid $5,000 for it. That's how we operate in the pawn business."

"And how did you know that you weren't buying stolen goods?" Mug asked.

"I checked to see if the ring was on the local police's stolen item list. They often provide us with items to be on the lookout for. This item wasn't on any such list. Nevertheless, it is due to the risk that I could learn later on that an item is stolen, that I give low ball offers to the sellers of such items, as I did with this one. Not to mention that these sellers are desperate and will take any money I'm willing to throw at them."

Mug didn't want to buy the item from Rocco, because number one, he'd be knowingly purchasing stolen goods and number two, he then may have a harder time proving that he found the item at this pawn shop as opposed to finding it somewhere else, like in Michael Stohler's possession. Instead, he wanted to come back with a search warrant to retrieve the ring. But he needed to make sure Rocco didn't discard the ring first to avoid surrendering it to law enforcement. So, he came up with the best strategy he could think of in the moment.

"Here's the deal Rocco. Your effort to make sure that you weren't purchasing stolen property was pretty piss-poor. You're supposed to proactively contact law enforcement when you receive a valuable item such as a diamond wedding ring, which is a fairly high risk of being hot. You could be in trouble for this. Also, I am informing you that this ring is in fact stolen property. Additionally it is critical evidence in an ongoing murder case. Therefore, if you sell this item, or move it in any way from this point forward, you will be prosecuted for knowingly fencing stolen property and/or for obstruction of justice. I will be back shortly with a warrant for the ring at which time you will surrender it. If you cooperate, I will see to it that law enforcement looks the other way regarding your purchase of the ring and I will also make sure that you will get the $5,000 back you paid for the ring. If you don't cooperate, you will be prosecuted and your business will likely be shut down. I would think that getting your money back and staying in business is your best play here."

"Look man, I don't want to lose my business. It's all I got. No one item is worth risking everything for me. I'll cooperate."

Mug believed him. And most of what Mug had told him was true. Law enforcement wouldn't push the matter with him if he gives the ring back. Mug knew that this guy wasn't getting his $5,000 back, but he needed to say that to make sure that Rocco and the ring stayed where they were for a few more days. So, Mug rationalized that a little deception to a slimy pawn broker to save an innocent man from being wrongly convicted of murder was the right thing to do in the circumstances.

Chapter 78

Mug immediately started his drive back up north. He needed to meet with Orensen. It would be time to get law enforcement involved with the information he had uncovered but that he had to fill Orensen in first and discuss the best way to approach the situation.

In the meantime, he had a few follow-up questions for Christine Dennison, so he called her on her cell phone during his drive.

"Hi Christine. This is Mug. I just want to ask you a few more questions."

"Sure. No problem."

"Did you ever have a spare set of house keys to the Stohler residence?"

"Yes. We were next door neighbors. Jennifer and I were very close and wanted to each have keys to the other's home in case one of us got locked out, or in the event of an emergency. Why?"

Mug ignored the return question for now and quickly asked, "Did you return the keys to her when you moved out?"

"Yes. I believe so. We wouldn't have any use for them anymore from down here. Why are you asking?"

"Did you possess their keys or did Willie?"

"Neither of us specifically. It was kept in our jar of keys on a table near our front door. So, both of us had access to it."

"Do you know if Willie may have made a duplicate copy of the keys before you returned them?"

"He didn't mention doing so. I guess he could have. But why would he need to?"

"Did Willie ever go to the Garrowville Park that was near where you used to live?"

"Yes. He loved that park. He jogged there all the time. Why are you asking all these questions?"

Mug wanted to come clean. Christine Dennison had been very helpful and was not a high risk to sabotage the investigation as she was clearly on the outs with her husband. But he couldn't chance it. Not with the finish line so close. So he said, "Thank you Christine. I think I may be getting close to finding the gun. I'll be in touch soon, hopefully, with some answers for you. Have a great day." Mug then hung up.

Mug knew he had solved the murder. He left a message for Orensen that he needed to meet with him in Orensen's office after court today. He made sure to tell Orensen in his message that the meeting was urgent. He received a text message back from Orensen telling him to meet him at 6 p.m.

Mug arrived early and waited in Orensen's lobby while compiling notes for the upcoming meeting. Orensen arrived on time, warmly greeted Mug, briefly informed him as to how the trial had proceeded thus far, then asked Mug for an update.

"Well Boss. I think we've solved the murder. Your boy is innocent."

Mug then proceeded to tell Orensen everything he had learned in the past few days down in Virginia and in Washington, D.C. Orensen was shocked and was speechless at first. Then, he said, "Ok. Let's summarize exactly what we have on Willie Dennison, then we'll discuss what to do next."

"I'm a step ahead of you Boss. I've put together the following list of exactly why I believe Willie Dennison is the killer. Here it is:

- Laid off by Michael Stohler – goes to motive.
- Had access to the Stohlers' house keys – goes to opportunity.
- Locksmith says he came in shortly before moving away to make copies of keys.
- Tall and left-handed – fits CSI description of shooter.
- Army background – highly skilled shooter.
- Had access to Larry Dennis' gun, which was the same type used in the murder.
- Was left alone in Dennis' residence during exact timing of murder.
- Larry Dennis' gun goes missing during timeframe of the murder.
- Larry Dennis' gun is found several hundred miles from his residence. It is found in Garrowville Park very close to where Willie Dennison used to live.
- Willie Dennison ran in the park often so would be knowledgeable as to where he could hide a gun in the park.
- Willie Dennison had possession of and sold Jennifer Stohler's missing wedding ring.

Orensen pondered the information quietly for a few moments. Then he said, "Ben Alford testified today about finding the shell casing and bullet at the crime scene. I think we need to give him the gun to determine definitively that it was the weapon that fired the recovered bullet. Also, let's see if he can still lift any prints off the gun. It's a long shot on that front, but worth a try. I assume you've handled it carefully since you found it so as to not wipe any prints that may still be there?"

"Yes. I haven't touched it with my bare hands. But, if Alford is a witness for the prosecution will he cooperate?" Mug asked.

"Yes. He wasn't a witness for the prosecution per se. He was a witness called by the prosecution to testify objectively as to what he found in his investigation. He would do the same with updated information if we called him to the stand to testify on the latest information."

"What about discovery? Will you need to tell Murdoch about this?"

"Eventually yes. And of course we will be happy to if it all works out. But we need to run the tests first, get the results, then inform Murdoch."

"What are we going to do regarding the ring?" Mug asked.

"Let's get in touch with some of your law enforcement contacts, explain the situation to them, and have them in on the calls down to the D.C. police requesting them to get a search warrant for the pawn shop to retrieve the ring. We'll then also subpoena the owner to have him testify as to his identification of Willie Dennison as the seller of the ring."

Orensen went on, "If the gun tests come back in our favor and it's the right ring, we should be able to get an arrest warrant on Dennison. That would be enough to at least suspend this trial pending how the Dennison matter ultimately unfolds. In the meantime, we need to act fast on this to make sure we get the arrest of Dennison before Stohler is wrongly convicted of murder. If we hit any delays on the arrest front, I'll try to string the trial along as much as I can."

Orensen knew that it was now a race as to what happens first, Dennison's arrest or a verdict in Stohler's trial. It was a race that may come down to the wire.

Chapter 79

Shortly after his meeting with Orensen was concluded, Mug made some calls to his old law enforcement contacts and explained the situation to them. Will Porter, a close friend of his late father from back in the day in the Shelton, Ohio police department, was now the police chief in Columbus. Porter agreed to set up a conference call with the D.C. police to get them to request a warrant to search the pawn shop. Initially there was some hesitancy among the D.C. police without knowing the results of the gun test, but Porter noted to them that at minimum they have enough probable cause to suspect the theft and sale of stolen goods to justify the warrant. The D.C. police agreed to request a warrant the next morning and if they get the warrant, they would conduct the search immediately given the time sensitivity of the matter.

At the same time, Orensen called Ben Alford to explain that they had recovered a gun they believed may have been used in the murder and that he wanted Alford to determine if that was the case.

"Does Murdoch know about this?" Alford asked.

"Not yet." Orensen replied, then added, "If it turns out to be the correct gun, we will be happy to inform him. If it isn't the right gun, there is no relevance anyway."

"Where did you find it?"

"Garrowville Park. Near the Stohler residence."

"Ok. Bring it to my lab. I'll test it."

"Thank you. One other thing; do you think you can test it for fingerprints? How long do fingerprints last on a gun?" Orensen asked.

"Fingerprints can last for a long time depending on the environment in which it is kept. A gun in ideal circumstances can maintain fingerprints for months. However, if you found the gun outside in a park, it would have been subjected to the elements, which would greatly reduce the odds that fingerprints, if there were any to begin with, would be retained this long. But I'll try and I'll let you know."

Orensen thanked him again and informed him that his associate would bring the gun to him in the morning. Orensen left Mug a voicemail instructing him to do so first thing on Wednesday morning.

Despite all of these interesting developments, the trial proceeded as normal on Wednesday morning at which time Stanley Murdoch, who was unaware of the activities outside the courtroom, continued presenting the prosecution's case.

"The Commonwealth calls David Bergman to the stand" Murdoch announced.

Bergman was dressed sharply, and as a lawyer himself he had a lot of courtroom experience. Murdoch hoped that he would be come across as a polished, well-spoken witness who would make a positive impression on the jury.

Murdoch asked a few initial questions to establish who he was and his credentials, then shifted to the topic on hand.

"Mr. Bergman. Did Jennifer Stohler come in to see you as a potential client?"

"Yes."

"When was that?"

"She came in on Wednesday, December 9, 2009."

"That would be less than two days before she was killed. Is that correct?" Murdoch asked.

"Yes. That is correct."

"Was that her first appointment with you?"

"Yes."

"What was her frame of mind during that meeting?"

"She was distressed. She expressed to me that she was having marital problems that have been going on for a while and have been getting worse. She made it clear that she was seriously contemplating divorce and she wanted information from me as to the process should she decide to proceed with it."

"How did you respond?"

"First I told her that she should make sure she is certain about going ahead with the divorce before proceeding. I recommended that if she wasn't already doing so, she should see a marriage counselor, either individually or preferably with her husband. I told her that I could recommend one for her if she wanted. I then told her that if she did want to go forward with the divorce, I could certainly be an asset for her in the process in that I have extensive experience in this area."

"Was it your opinion that she would proceed with the divorce?"

"Objection. Speculative." Orensen yelled out.

"Sustained."

Murdoch asked a different question. "How did you leave it with her at the end of your meeting?"

"She took my card and said she would think about it some more. She said that if she decided to go through with it she would give me a call. She then called me the next morning to schedule another appointment for the following week."

"No further questions your honor." Murdoch stated as he sat down.

Orensen then started his cross-examination. "Mr. Bergman, did Jennifer Stohler give you any indication that her husband knew about her meeting with you?"

"No."

"Did she give you any indication that she had ever mentioned to her husband that she was considering divorcing him?"

"No."

"So is it fair to say that as far as you know, Michael Stohler didn't have any knowledge that his wife was thinking of divorce?"

"I don't know if he knew or not. It wasn't relevant to my conversation with her."

"Did Jennifer Stohler make any comments along the lines of any violence or threats of violence from her husband?"

"No."

"Was she fearful of him in any way?"

"Not that I can tell."

"You are an experienced divorce attorney. You've handled many couples' divorces. Did anything Jennifer tell you in your meeting make you believe that the issues her marriage faced were worse, or unique, to many other struggling marriages that do not end in murder?"

"No."

"You can't even be certain that Jennifer was going to go through with the divorce anyway. Isn't that true, Mr. Bergman?"

"That is correct."

"No further questions." Orensen informed Judge Connerly.

On re-direct, Murdoch simply had Bergman reiterate that Jennifer was visibly upset about her marriage and that she was serious about the possibility of divorce. Bergman was then excused and Murdoch called his next witness.

"The Commonwealth calls John Rollins."

"Mr. Rollins. Did Michael Stohler purchase a life insurance policy on his wife with you?"

"Yes."

"When did he purchase this life insurance policy on his wife?"

"In March 2009."

"That was less than a year before she was murdered. Is that correct?"

"Yes."

"How much was the policy for?"

"$250,000."

"Has the insurance company paid that sum to Michael yet?"

"No."

"How have sales of life insurance policies been recently? Have you sold a lot of them of that magnitude in recent years?"

"No. Times have been tough financially these days so people haven't been inclined to take on an additional expense for something they don't want to contemplate as a possibility."

"So, during difficult financial times when few people are buying life insurance policies, Michael Stohler, less than one year before his wife is murdered, purchased a policy from you in the amount of a quarter of a million dollars. Is that correct?"

"Yes."

"Thank you Mr. Rollins. No further questions."

It was Orensen's turn for his cross-examination.

"Mr. Rollins. When Michael Stohler purchased the policy from you, did you try to sell him a larger one?"

"Yes. I always try to up sell my clients; especially when business is slow."

"And what happened when you tried to up sell Michael Stohler?"

"He declined."

"Is it true that you then offered him a deal whereby he could double the policy to $500,000 for less than a proportionate increase in the premium?"

"Yes."

"And what happened?"

"He declined."

"So you fairly aggressively pedaled a larger policy to Michael Stohler, yet he was not interested. Is that correct?"

"Yes."

"No further questions." Orensen declared as he sat down.

After passing on re-direct, Murdoch then called Morton Engfield to the stand.

"Mr. Engfield, please describe what you saw in the early morning hours of Friday, December 11, 2009?"

"I saw a large 4-door vehicle with a right headlight out, speeding toward me as I was waiting to make a left turn onto my driveway."

"And where do you live Mr. Engfield?"

"673 Penley Lane."

"Where is that in relation to where the murder took place?"

"It is just a few blocks away."

"What time did you see the vehicle speed by you?"

"Approximately 2:45 a.m."

"And are you certain about the time?"

"Yes. I get off work at 2 a.m. sharp every night, and I get home each night between 2:30 a.m. and 2:40 a.m. On this particular night, I was delayed a few minutes because I had to stop for gas. So, my estimation of the time being 2:45 a.m. is fairly accurate."

"Were you able to decipher anything about the driver of the vehicle?"

"The driver was male and was driving too fast."

"No further questions your honor."

Orensen then rose and asked, "Mr. Engfield, it was very dark at 2:45 a.m. was it not?"

"Yes."

"Are there any street lamps on your block?"

"No."

"And the car was going very fast, as you testified. Correct?"

"Yes."

"So, based on the darkness and how fast the car must have gone by you, you must not have been able to see much inside the car. Correct?"

"I only saw that the driver was a male."

"Were you able to see anything else about the car itself? License plate, color, make, model?"

"No."

"So, it could have been any male driver, driving any large 4-door vehicle with a right headlight out. Is that correct?"

"Yes."

"No further questions your honor."

After Murdoch stated he had no re-direct, Judge Connerly announced that the court would recess for lunch. Orensen then raced out of the room to check on developments outside the courthouse.

Chapter 80

Orensen had voicemails waiting for him from both Alford and Mug. He called Mug first figuring that Mug would know the news on both the gun front and the Washington D.C. front.

"Good news and bad news Boss, on the gun." Mug said immediately upon answering the phone.

"What is it?"

"The good news is that it is definitely the murder weapon. Alford tested it and is 100% sure it is the gun that fired the bullet recovered at the scene."

"And the bad news?" Orensen asked.

"He couldn't extract any fingerprints. Either there were no prints on the gun to begin with, or, they were compromised by the elements it sat in for four months."

"I figured he'd have a hard time with the prints. But, it's great news on the match. Dennison is our guy. What's doing with the search warrant of the pawn shop."

"The request has been made. They're awaiting approval from the court down there."

"Ok. Keep on it and keep me updated." Orensen ordered.

"You got it Boss. Are you going to tell Murdoch what is going on?"

"I have to now. We have the murder weapon. Discovery laws would require it. I need to contact him now before Alford does and Murdoch accuses me of withholding evidence. I'll call you later. Leave me a voicemail with any news."

Orensen figured that he wouldn't get anywhere with Murdoch, but as he told Mug, he wanted to be on the record as having informed Murdoch of the situation, and maybe by some slim chance, he'd actually get a stoppage of the case. In order to be 'on the record' in his discussion with Murdoch, Orensen made some calls to arrange a meeting with Murdoch in Judge Connerly's chambers before court would resume in the afternoon.

A little while later, the two counselors and Judge Connerly were convened in Connerly's chambers. After some brief small talk, Judge Connerly called the meeting to order and declared that they were now on the record.

"Ok. What do you want Orensen?" Murdoch immediately snarled. He was clearly irritated by this surprise get together.

"I want to formally inform the Commonwealth and the Court that we have recovered the murder weapon. It was found in Garrowville Park. We've…"

"A ha!" Murdoch jubilantly interrupted. "The proverbial 'smoking gun.' How long have you known about this Orensen? Is your boy going to plead guilty now to avoid the death penalty? Is that what this is all about?"

"Not so fast Murdoch. We've also got a lead on the missing ring. We should hopefully have it recovered shortly. The gun and the ring have been traced to a person of interest in this case who will more than likely be arrested later today." Orensen then turned toward Judge Connerly. "For this reason, I am suggesting that we suspend the case until these events have played out. It may ultimately save the Commonwealth the time, cost, and embarrassment of continuing a fruitless prosecution."

"Hog wash!" Murdoch emphatically declared. "How dare you! You say you've recovered a gun, which you've probably had for a while, just minutes from your client's home. Then you concoct this fantasy about it tracing back to someone else without giving us so much as a name, or any evidence for that matter. And you have the nerve to ask to stop the case! Ridiculous! You'll need to prove all this before the Commonwealth stops prosecuting who I, and everyone else, firmly believe is the real killer!"

Judge Connerly put his arms in the air to maintain calm in the room. He then quietly said, "Mr. Orensen. Are you prepared to provide the prosecution with specifics as to your findings?"

"We will very shortly, your honor. A search warrant in another jurisdiction has currently been requested and we'll soon have more information. Possibly even an arrest. When this occurs we will of course disclose all pertinent information. Right now I just wanted to be on the record as informing Mr. Murdoch of the situation."

"Informing me! Ha! That's a laugh. What exactly have I been told? That you've concocted a story to explain why the murder weapon was practically in your client's back yard? Your honor; clearly this is an amateurish ploy to derail the momentum right in the middle of the presentation of the Commonwealth's case."

"Ok. Ok." Connerly tried to calm Murdoch down. "Mr. Murdoch; I presume that you wish to continue with the presentation of your case at this time?"

"Of course I do, your honor. This garbage is not going to stop the prosecution of a killer. The people of Pennsylvania wouldn't stand for such lunacy!"

"Very well, Murdoch. Don't say I didn't try to warn you." Orensen ominously stated.

Judge Connerly then stated, "We will proceed as scheduled. Mr. Orensen, if you wish to add any witnesses to the list you provided to the court and to Mr. Murdoch prior to the trial, you need to inform the court in advance and I will give Mr. Murdoch time to prepare for the added witness or witnesses. Is that understood?"

"Yes your honor." Orensen responded.

"Very well. Let's get back to court. Meeting adjourned."

Both lawyers filed out of the chambers and back into court. Orensen had figured that the meeting would unfold precisely as it had. He didn't expect to get a stoppage of the case. He merely wanted to be on record as having informed the court and Murdoch of what was going on, while revealing as little as possible. He believed he had accomplished those objectives.

Murdoch on the other hand, while acting with bravado outwardly, was apprehensive about this unusual development. Why would Orensen tell such tales if there was absolutely nothing to them? The only logical reason to do that would be to bluff his way to a plea bargain. But he hadn't expressed any desire to negotiate a plea. Murdoch knew that he'd have to get to the bottom of this, so he hurriedly barked some orders to various assistants in the courtroom with him and in his office to find out what was going on.

Murdoch also knew that he'd have to speed up the presentation of his case. Just in case Orensen had something in the works outside the courtroom, Murdoch was determined to make sure he got his conviction before any of Orensen's antics could seep reasonable doubt into the trial.

The race was still on, only now, both sides were aware of it.

Chapter 81

Court had resumed for the Wednesday afternoon session. Murdoch, now a little more antsy to get to the crux of his case, decided to forego the remaining few supporting, peripheral witnesses, and instead went right for the jugular.

"The Commonwealth calls Chief Carl Lumpkin to the stand."

Lumpkin excitedly marched toward the witness stand. He had been looking forward to testifying. He was proud of the job he did cracking this case and now was to be his moment in the spotlight to tell the world of this accomplishment.

Murdoch first asked about Lumpkin's experience to establish his credentials. Lumpkin enthusiastically told the jury of his many years in law enforcement and how he worked hard to ascend to the position of Chief of Police. He was clearly enjoying his "fifteen minutes of fame."

Murdoch then started his case specific line of questioning.

"Chief Lumpkin, please tell us about the morning of December 11, 2009."

"I had received a phone call from Principal Ronald Walker of the Garrowville Elementary School. He and I go way back. He called to inform me that Jennifer Stohler, one of his best teachers, had not showed up for work that morning, which was very strange for her, especially in light of the fact that it was the day of a school trip she had personally arranged. He was very concerned about her."

"What did you do?"

"I instructed one of my officers to check in on her at her residence to make sure that she was ok."

"That would be Officer Dan Radford. Is that correct?" Murdoch asked.

"Yes."

"And what did Officer Radford report back to you?"

"He called to inform me that he found Jennifer Stohler dead on the floor in her bedroom. Single gunshot wound to the head."

"What did you do next?"

"Of course, I immediately raced over there, called the rest of my officers in to do the same, and contacted the CSI unit."

"What did you and your team find at the crime scene?"

"We investigated the scene very carefully and repeatedly. We noted several important facts. First we noted that there was no forced entry anywhere around the premises. That most likely indicated that the killer had a key or was let in by the victim. Either way, it pointed toward someone that she knew. We noted that the murder weapon was not at the scene, which clinched the fact that it was a murder, rather than a suicide. We noted that there was jewelry in clear sight around the room in which the victim was found; which indicated to us that murder, not robbery, was the primary intent here."

"At what point in time did you start considering the possibility that Michael Stohler, the husband, was the killer?" Murdoch asked.

"Any time a wife is murdered, the husband is an initial suspect until he can be ruled out. There is too much statistical evidence that would indicate that more often than not the husband is somehow involved. For that reason, we considered Michael Stohler immediately as a suspect. We never reached a point where he could be ruled out, so he always remained a suspect. We were careful of course to still investigate other potential scenarios, but none came to our attention during the course of our work that ever seemed to be a plausible alternative explanation as to what happened. Additionally, in this particular case, there were several other reasons besides just being the husband that made Michael Stohler a prime suspect."

"And what were those reasons?"

"Well for starters, the location and timing of the murder. Like I said, when a wife is found murdered, the husband is often the killer. Add to it that the murder took place in her home and in the middle of the night, and the odds that it is the husband increase drastically. In addition to that, we learned from interviews of numerous people that the Stohlers had been having marital problems. That increases the odds even more significantly."

"What else did you learn about their marriage from your investigation?"

"While searching the house we discovered the victim's calendar, on which she had indicated that she had visited a divorce attorney just two days earlier."

"Did Michael Stohler know about that visit?"

"Well, we can't say for sure, but upon our examination of his phone records, we learned that he had spoken to Jennifer on the phone the night of her appointment, very shortly after she had that meeting. Also, in my various interrogations of the defendant, he had repeatedly claimed that he and his wife were 'working things out' as he put it. Clearly, that wasn't the case."

Orensen jumped up, "Objection your honor. The last comment is the witness' opinion, not a statement of fact."

"Sustained. Please strike that last sentence from the record. The jury is hereby instructed to disregard it."

Murdoch continued, "What else did you learn from your interrogations of Michael Stohler?"

"I learned that he had a $250,000 life insurance policy on his wife."

"Did you determine when he had purchased that policy?"

"Yes. It was earlier in the same year. So it was less than one year before his wife was murdered."

"Going back to your examination of his phone records, did you find anything unusual?"

"Yes. We found that his cell phone was turned off throughout the entire time frame during which the murder occurred. This fact prevented the cell phone's signal from indicating location during the time it was off."

"Was it typical of him to have had his phone turned off?"

"We looked at several weeks of phone records and it was the only time period in which his phone was off, so I would say it was highly unusual. It seemed like too much of a coincidence that this one time occurrence would happen at the same time his wife was murdered."

"How do you know when Jennifer Stohler was murdered?" Murdoch asked.

"The CSI unit who responded to the scene initially estimated a time of death between 2 a.m. and 4 a.m. that same morning. Later examinations back at the lab confirmed that timing."

"And is there any significance to that specific timing?"

"Yes. Per my interrogations with the defendant, and per my follow-up investigations, I learned that Michael Stohler's alibi ended at 2 a.m. He had no alibi for his whereabouts after 2 a.m. until showing up late for work the next morning."

"Was it typical that Michael Stohler would be late for work?"

"No. Quite the contrary. We questioned many people at his company throughout our investigation, and we were informed that he was almost never late for work. In fact, he was usually an 'early bird.'"

"What was his timeline of activity that evening and early morning?" Murdoch asked.

"He was at O'Leary's Pub earlier in the evening, then went to his parents' home where he arrived at approximately midnight. He reported that he stayed up talking with his father until about 2 a.m. at which time he claims to have gone to sleep. No one can corroborate his whereabouts after 2 a.m."

"And how far away is his parents' house from his own home with Jennifer?"

"Just a few miles. No more than a ten minute drive. Very easy to go to his own home and get back to his parents' place quickly without anyone knowing he was gone. He had ample time after 2 a.m. to do that within CSI's timeframe of the murder."

"Is there any other relevance of the estimated time frame of the murder?"

"Yes. We received a tip on a hotline we had set up for the investigation. The tipster informed us that he had seen a large 4-door vehicle speed by him just in front of his residence at approximately 2:45 a.m. on the night of the murder."

"What did you learn upon following up on this tip?"

"We learned that the person's residence was just a few blocks from the crime scene and was en route between the crime scene and the defendant's parents' home."

"Did the tipster note any other distinctive features of the vehicle?"

"Yes. He noted that the right headlight was out."

"Was the same true of the defendant's vehicle?"

"No. But we subsequently noted that his parents' car also had a right headlight out. Their vehicle is also a large 4-door. So, it would appear that the defendant had driven his parents' car to and from the crime scene that night."

"Objection. Speculative." Orensen protested.

"Sustained" Judge Connerly ruled. The last sentence will be stricken from the record and the jury is instructed to disregard it.

Murdoch then switched subjects. "What else did you learn from the CSI unit?"

"We learned that the shooter was at least six feet tall and was most likely left-handed. Both of these descriptions match the defendant."

"I can see the height, but how did you ascertain that Michael Stohler is left-handed?"

"It is common knowledge actually. He had been a quarterback at Garrowville High School and everyone in the community remembers him as being a left-handed quarterback. There are many photos and film of him in his playing days."

"Chief Lumpkin, did you and/or your officers notice any items missing from the Stohler residence?"

"Yes. We noted that the victim's wedding ring was missing."

"What about any other jewelry or other valuables?"

"No. Nothing else seemed to be out of place."

"You testified before that there were other pieces of jewelry in plain sight. But now you are saying that it was only the wedding ring that was missing. As an experienced investigator, what did this fact pattern seem to indicate to you?"

"It indicated that robbery wasn't the primary motive here."

"How then does the missing wedding ring fit your theory that robbery wasn't the primary motive?"

"It fits in three ways. Number one, the taking of the wedding ring was likely an attempt to throw us off into thinking that perhaps it was simply a robbery gone wrong. In fact, in numerous discussions with me and my staff, the defendant seemed anxious to relay to us his theory that this was just a random robbery. Number two, he took the most valuable piece of jewelry, for which he'd be able to get a decent amount of money selling it somewhere. That fits with the financially driven motive in this case. And number three, he took the only item for which we subsequently learned he had an insurance policy. So, in addition to the money he'd get from selling a valuable piece of jewelry, he can double up by submitting a claim to the insurance company for the missing ring."

"Thank you Chief Lumpkin" Murdoch gratefully stated in the most heartfelt manner he could muster for the benefit of the jury. "You've done a great job investigating this case."

He then turned to Judge Connerly and said, "No further questions your honor."

Judge Connerly announced that it was a good time for a short recess before the defense starts their cross-examination.

It was also a good time for Orensen to check in with Mug.

Chapter 82

"Mug, what's the latest on the warrant?" Orensen hurriedly asked. Time was short before he had to get back into court and he was anxious for any information Mug may have for him.

"Hey Boss. The search warrant just came in. They're heading over to the pawn shop right now."

"Ok. Thanks. I'll call you after court."

Orensen hung up, then spent a few minutes reviewing his notes for his upcoming cross-examination of Chief Lumpkin. Just in case the investigation fell apart in D.C. and the trial reached a conclusion, Orensen knew that his cross-examination of Lumpkin would be a key factor in whether he won or lost the case.

Court was called back to order at 3 p.m. Judge Connerly looked toward Orensen and said, "Counselor, your cross-examination."

"Yes. Thank you your honor."

Orensen spent the first few minutes asking an array of repetitive questions regarding the absence of any physical evidence pointing directly to Michael Stohler. Chief Lumpkin was forced to answer "no" to question after question such as, "Did you find any fingerprints? Footprints? DNA? Bloody clothes? Eyewitnesses?" Orensen made sure to hammer home the point that Lumpkin had found nothing to definitively prove Michael Stohler was the killer.

Then, after he was satisfied that he sufficiently made his point, Orensen asked, "Chief Lumpkin. We've clearly established that you had no direct evidence against Michael Stohler and you testified earlier that you had also investigated other possible scenarios. Can you please tell us what other possible scenarios you investigated and how you managed to rule them out while not ruling out Michael Stohler?"

"Well, we searched the perimeter of the house to see if anyone could have gotten in without force through an open window or unlocked door, but found nothing. We thought about who else might have had motive, but found no one. The bottom line was, there was only one suspect who made sense."

"That doesn't sound like a very thorough investigation, Chief."

"Objection." Murdoch shouted. "That was a statement; not a question."

"Sustained." Judge Connerly ruled. "Please strike it from the record. The jury is instructed to disregard that last comment."

"Let's talk about the supposed motive, Chief. Do you have any direct evidence that Michael Stohler knew that his wife was contemplating divorce or that she had visited with a divorce attorney?"

"For starters, he called her right after her appointment with the divorce attorney. It timing would seem pretty coincidental if the subject of the appointment didn't come up."

"Chief, did you listen in on that conversation? Or subsequently hear a tape of it?"

"No."

"So, it is fair to say that you don't have any direct knowledge as to what was or wasn't discussed in that phone conversation. Is that correct?"

"Yes."

"Chief, you saw Michael's phone records. Weren't there a lot of calls to his wife?"

"Yes."

"Most nights, wouldn't you say?"

"Yes."

"So, is it so unreasonable to think that he may have just been calling her to say hello, or to talk about anything; just as he had been doing almost every night?"

"I gathered from my extensive interrogations of him that he was being misleading as to the current status of his relationship with his wife."

"Did he ever specifically state anything to you that he knew about the appointment or that his wife wanted a divorce?"

"No."

"Now let's talk about the cell phone. You testified that it was off during the timeframe of the murder. Is that correct?"

"Yes."

"Are you able to distinguish between a cell phone that is turned off intentionally as opposed to a cell phone whose battery had died?"

"No."

"So, isn't it possible that Michael Stohler's phone battery had simply died rather than him intentionally turning it off as you assumed to be a fact?"

"Again, it would be very coincidental for that to happen right around the time of the murder when it hadn't any time in the previous few weeks. I didn't get to be Chief of Police without being highly skeptical of too many coincidences."

"But, you have no direct evidence that Michael Stohler intentionally turned off his phone. Is that correct?"

"Yes."

"You also testified that he had been out at a pub during the evening, then was up late at night afterwards at his parents' house. Is that correct?"

"Yes."

"Isn't it possible then that his being out that evening, and up late, that he either didn't have an opportunity and/or forgot to charge his phone? Is that an unreasonable scenario, especially in light of the fact that he had been drinking? Couldn't he have simply forgotten to charge it when he was tired and somewhat intoxicated?"

"Again, too coincidental." Lumpkin stubbornly responded.

"Let's talk about the supposed lack of an alibi, Chief. You testified that Michael Stohler's activities ended at approximately 2 a.m. and that the murder took place between 2 a.m. and 4 a.m. Is that correct?"

"Yes."

"Where did Michael Stohler claim to be after 2 a.m.?"

"He said that he went to sleep."

"Did anyone specifically report otherwise to you?"

"No."

"So, no one saw Michael Stohler anywhere other than where he claimed to be during the time of the murder is that correct?"

"It was the middle of the night. There weren't many people out."

"Your honor. Please request that the witness answer my questions." Orensen requested to Judge Connerly.

"Chief, please be sure to directly answer the counselor's questions."

"Yes your honor." Lumpkin obediently replied.

"I'll ask the question again." Orensen said. "Is it correct to say that no one saw Michael Stohler anywhere other than where he claimed to be during the time of the murder?"

"Yes."

"Do you find it unusual that someone who has to be up for work in the morning would claim to be asleep at 2 a.m.?"

"No."

"You also testified that he was late to work the next morning. But you knew he had a late night even without contemplating his involvement or non-involvement with the murder. Isn't it feasible he simply overslept after having been up late and drinking? Is that an unreasonable scenario?"

"He was rarely late. Too many coincidences." Lumpkin answered.

"You seem to fall back to the 'too many coincidences' response, Chief. Does it seem to you that your entire case is based on a lot of assumptions, statistics, and a general opposition to coincidences?"

"No. In aggregate, there is a lot of evidence, as I've already testified."

"Tell me which piece or pieces of this abundance of evidence definitively points to Michael Stohler as the killer to the exclusion of any other reasonable possibilities."

"As I said, in aggregate, it all points to him." Lumpkin defiantly responded.

"You testified that the missing wedding ring was an attempt by Michael Stohler to throw off the investigation by making it seem like a robbery gone wrong. Is that your belief?"

"Yes."

"Yet there was a lot of other jewelry all around the room where Jennifer Stohler was found. Is that correct?"

"Yes."

"Doesn't it seem strange to you that someone who you claim planned and executed this murder would take the time to take just one piece of jewelry to the exclusion of all others when he was allegedly trying to make it seem like a robbery?"

"No. As I stated earlier, it was to throw us off and for what he could get hocking it later."

"Granted, I am not an investigator. But I would think that the act of taking just one piece of jewelry when there are other items of jewelry all around, would more logically seem to me to be the act of a person who was in a panic to get out after unexpectedly encountering and shooting someone. Is that an unreasonable scenario?"

"Such a hypothetical person doesn't have all the other motives we discussed like the defendant has." Lumpkin answered.

"Yet you have no specific evidence to rule out a simply robbery gone wrong, do you?"

"There was no forced entry. That is our evidence."

"Is it possible that Jennifer Stohler simply forgot to lock her door? Or someone rang the doorbell claiming to be in need somehow, such as a broken down car? Or someone else had a key to the house? Aren't these all feasible scenarios that would involve no forced entry?"

"Doesn't seem logical. Who was she opening the door to in the middle of the night? Or who else would have the keys? Common sense points to Michael Stohler."

"Did you investigate who else had keys to the house?"

"It was just the two of them who lived there and no one else left on the block."

"So, I am assuming that is a 'no' you didn't investigate who else may have keys. Is that correct?"

"There was no need to in light of all other evidence in the case."

"Do you solve all your cases so quickly based on circumstantial evidence and assumptions?"

"Objection!" Murdoch shouted.

Before he could say anything else, Orensen said, "Withdrawn." He'd made his point.

Orensen then asked, "Chief Lumpkin, let's talk about the tip you received on the car with the right headlight out. You testified that this car was spotted at approximately 2:45 a.m. on Friday, December 11th. Is that correct?"

"Yes."

"You then testified that the defendant's parents' car also had a right headlight out. Is that correct?"

"Yes."

"When did you discover that the defendant's parents' car had a right headlight out?"

"On Christmas Day. One of our officers pulled the defendant over and issued him a ticket for the missing headlight. He was driving his parents' vehicle."

"So, it was two weeks later. Is that correct?"

"Yes."

"Isn't it true, Chief Lumpkin, that your officers had been tailing the defendant for essentially all of that two week period?"

"Yes."

"And isn't it true that throughout that timeframe, the defendant had been driving his parents' car due to the fact that his own car had been confiscated by the police?"

"Yes."

"Yet, during that two week timeframe, no one noted that the right headlight was out? Is that correct?"

"He drove only to and from work during daylight hours so there wouldn't have been an opportunity to see the headlights on."

"Therefore, Chief, the answer to my question, is that none of your officers, despite around-the-clock surveillance, noted the right headlight out during the full two week period between December 11 and December 25. Is that correct?"

"Yes."

"Isn't it possible then, that the right headlight of the defendant's parents' vehicle went out sometime after December 11? Would you have any information or evidence to refute that possibility?"

"Again, too many coincidences." Lumpkin stubbornly responded.

"And again, Chief Lumpkin, too many holes in your investigation. No further questions, your honor."

After a brief re-direct by Murdoch which didn't uncover anything new, Chief Lumpkin was excused. It was precisely 5 p.m., so Judge Connerly announced that court would be adjourned until 9 a.m. the following morning.

Chapter 83

As was his routine now at every stoppage in the trial, Orensen immediately contacted Mug for an update on events unfolding in the Washington, D.C. area. "The D.C. police sent a few officers to the pawn shop with the warrant. The guy there was very cooperative. He gave up the ring immediately so that they wouldn't trash his place looking for it. He also told them everything he told me regarding who sold him the ring." Mug stated.

"Did you give them the documentation so that they can prove that the ring was Jennifer Stohler's?" Orensen asked.

"Yes. I scanned a photo of the ring and the latest appraisal, both of which I got from Michael's dad. The guy from the pawn shop admitted it was the same ring. He knew all the specifications. He needs to be able to appraise merchandise in his business, so he knew the size, clarity, and whatever other criteria there are." Mug said.

"So, are they arresting Dennison?" Orensen excitedly asked.

"Well, here's the thing, Boss. Yes, they are going to arrest him any minute now, but they could only do so for selling a stolen item. All they know is he pawned a stolen ring."

Orensen was frustrated. "What about the gun? Isn't that how we got to him in the first place? We know it was used to kill Jennifer and it was traced back to the house he was living in?"

"I mentioned that, but there were four people in that house. Could have been any of them, or anyone else who knew the gun was there."

"The other three people in the house were out of town and he's the one with the motive, is the correct height, and is left-handed. We both know it was him."

"Yes, Boss. I understand. But they aren't a bunch of Chief Lumpkins down there. They want more evidence. Not just circumstantial evidence. Anyway, he's getting arrested very soon; may even be happening now. They are going to charge him with the sale of stolen property but they will spend most of their time interrogating him about the murder. Maybe he'll slip or confess."

"We need that to happen very soon. Murdoch is just about done with his case. I don't have a lot of witnesses to call. The trial probably only has a few days left.

"Yes, Boss. I'll make sure they know to push hard in their questioning. I've given them all the information I have on the case, so they know everything down there. They agree he's probably the killer so they'll go after him hard. They just won't charge him with the murder yet, without more evidence or a confession."

"Ok. Talk to the wife again. Then tell her everything. Maybe she'll have new information now that she'll know you're investigating the murder rather than just thinking you were looking for a missing gun."

"Ok. No problem, Boss. She hates him. She'll be happy he's getting arrested and if she knows anything, she'll tell me. I'll call her now." Mug stated.

After they hung up, Mug immediately dialed Christine Dennison.

"Hi Christine. It's Mug. I have some news for you."

"Hi Mug. What is it?"

"I wanted to inform you that your husband is about to be arrested."

"Why? What happened?"

"Well, he's currently being arrested for selling stolen property; specifically, Jennifer Stohler's wedding ring. We also found your brother's missing gun. It was used in the murder of Jennifer. We believe that your husband killed Jennifer Stohler, stole her ring, then pawned it at the pawn shop you told me about."

Christine Dennison was speechless. Mug heard a few gasps from Christine during his little speech, and some "Oh No's!" Mug sensed that Christine's mind was racing a thousand miles an hour and he didn't know what she was going to say next.

Mug let her think for a moment, then started asking his questions.

"Christine. I'm sorry to have to break this horrible news for you, but I do need to ask you a few questions."

"Ok." Christine Dennison asked nervously.

"Jennifer Stohler was killed in the early morning hours of Friday, December 11, 2009. We know that you, your brother, and his wife were all in Miami at that time and that Willie didn't go on that trip. Therefore, it is our belief that Willie drove up to Garrowville sometime just after you left for Miami on Thursday, December 10th, and likely returned just after killing Jennifer on the morning of December 11th. Do you remember anything out of the ordinary about Willie just before your trip, after you got home, or during any correspondences with him while you were away? Anything he said, or did, that seemed different to you?"

"That was what I was just thinking of." Christine answered. "I am putting two-and-two together in my head."

"What do you mean? What are you piecing together?" Mug anxiously asked.

"I was the one who paid the bills when we received them. I remember seeing a credit card statement in January that had an unusual charge on it for a towing company in December during the weekend we were out of town. I asked Willie about it and he said he had gone out for a drive and the car broke down. I thought it was strange because I recognized the towing company as being located in Pennsylvania, so, I knew he didn't just go for a quick drive. When I asked again where he went, he wouldn't say. He just cursed at me about always interrogating him. It was a strange response. I left him alone on it after that."

"What was the name of the towing company?" Mug asked.

"Kurlin Towing Company."

"Do you still have a copy of the credit card bill?"

"Yes."

"Great. I'm going to have a police officer stop by to see you and ask you some more questions. Can you please give him the credit card statement?"

"Ok. No problem."

"Christine, is there anything else that you can think of that may be related to the Stohlers, or that weekend?"

"Not that I can think of right now."

"Ok. If you think of anything else, please call me as soon as possible. Thanks Christine."

After they hung up, Mug phoned the D.C. police with the latest news. He was told that an officer would be over to see Christine Dennison immediately and that they'd ask her to come in to answer some questions. Mug assured them she would be very helpful and that she is not a spouse they'd have to worry about trying to cover up for her husband.

Mug was then informed that the arrest of Willie Dennison for fencing stolen property had just been made. Dennison was on his way to the Southeast D.C. police precinct where a long, grueling interrogation would commence.

Chapter 84

Willie Dennison arrived at the police precinct at 6 p.m. on Wednesday night, at which time he was taken through the usual booking process. Afterwards, he was escorted to the interrogation room where he was kept waiting for over an hour, while being observed through a one-way window in a room wired for the officers on the other side of the window to listen in. Dennison had been read his rights upon being arrested, so anything he said from here on out could be used against him. The officers watched and listened, hoping Dennison would mumble something of interest to himself, thinking no one was around to hear. At minimum, even if he just sat quietly, keeping him waiting was a bit of psychological gamesmanship designed to start the process of ultimately cracking the suspect in the interrogation to follow.

Dennison just sat quietly, awaiting whatever was to follow. He said and did nothing of interest to the observing officers. At 7:30 p.m., Ralph Norwood, a big, burly officer finally entered the room, pulled out the chair opposite Dennison, but didn't sit down. Instead he stood opposite Dennison and stared down the suspect for several long and awkward minutes.

Norwood had a lot of experience interrogating suspects during his fifteen years on the squad. He looked and acted tough, often using intimidation as his primary tactic, as well as any other trick he and his colleagues could formulate to achieve the goal of getting a confession before a suspect requests an attorney. It took a special skill to accomplish this, pushing just hard enough without going too far. In this regard, Norwood had an impressive track record.

He finally broke the silence by asking, "Do you understand why you are here Dennison?"

"They say I sold a stolen ring. But I didn't do it." Dennison defiantly responded.

"So how did the stolen ring wind up in a pawn shop with a guy who says you sold it to him?"

"He's lying."

"Do you know who the ring was stolen from?"

"No."

"It belonged to a woman by the name of Jennifer Stohler. Do you happen to know anyone by that name?"

"Yes. She used to be my next door neighbor."

"That's right Dennison. Now we're getting somewhere. Do you know what happened to her?"

"Yes. I heard her husband killed her."

"So, here's a question for you Dennison. How did the wedding ring of a woman who was killed up in Pennsylvania, who you happened to have lived next door to, wind up in a pawn shop in D.C. that you frequent?"

"I don't know. Maybe her husband sold it to him."

"Isn't that a bit coincidental? That he would go that far away and find the very pawn shop that you happen to go to also?"

"Maybe he knew I went there. He and the pawn shop guy are framing me."

"How would the dead woman's husband know which pawn shop you go to so that he can frame you there?"

"I don't know. Maybe he followed me there."

"Come on Dennison. You're making no sense."

"Well, I don't know what happened. I just know that I didn't steal any jewelry."

At that time, Ned Granger, another D.C. police officer, entered the room and handed a piece of paper to Norwood. Norwood pretended to read the sheet of paper carefully, though he already knew what was on it. This had been a pre-arranged ruse to make it look like there was some "breaking news" to report.

Norwood just shook his head slowly a few times, before saying anything. He wanted to add to the suspense for Dennison as he waited to find out what Norwood was reading. It was another psychological ploy.

"Well, well, well. Seems we've gotten some interesting news here Dennison. They just ran some ballistics on the weapon used to kill Jennifer Stohler and they were able to trace the gun to a guy named Larry Dennis. Do you know him?"

"Yes."

"Who is he?"

"My brother-in-law."

"Interesting, don't you think? A woman who had previously been your next door neighbor in Garrowville, Pennsylvania, is murdered. Her wedding ring is missing from the crime scene and turns up at a pawn shop that you frequent. The pawn shop owner states that you sold him the ring. And now, the gun used in the murder belongs to your brother-in-law, who I understand you were living with at the time of the murder. What do you make of all that Dennison?"

"I don't know. Maybe Larry killed her. It was his gun."

Norwood turned to his partner Granger and said, "Do you believe this guy? He'll throw anyone under the bus. He says the husband kills her and that the husband and the pawn shop guy are framing him. Now he's pinning the murder on his brother-in-law."

Granger just laughed while shaking his head as he looked mockingly at Dennison. They were making it clear they weren't buying it. They waited in an intentionally awkward silence designed to illicit comment from the suspect. Most suspects won't just sit silently when they know their story isn't believed. The suspect will usually force the matter, which is often when they slip.

Soon Dennison said, "Look guys. I don't know what happened up there. I just sold some jewelry to the pawn shop because I needed money. Maybe Larry killed her and stole the ring and I found it among my wife's jewelry and took it by accident. I don't know. I just know that I didn't steal anything and I didn't knowingly sell stolen property."

"Why would Larry Dennis kill Jennifer Stohler? Did he even know her?"

"They've met before."

"Oh. They've met. Well, that changes everything!" Norwood mocked.

"How do we even know it is the same ring? Don't a lot of rings look alike?" Dennison asked, attempting to turn the tables.

"We've got the stolen ring's specifications, and it matches the ring we secured in our search of the pawn shop. You know, Dennison, the 4 'C's' – cut, color, clarity, carat. They all match."

Norwood emphatically slammed down the two documents in front of Dennison to show him the two analysis of the ring, proving they were from the same ring.

Granger then mockingly joked to his partner, "I don't think he knows the 4 'C's'. He doesn't seem like much of a diamond connoisseur. He's probably never purchased any jewelry. It's much easier just to steal it." The two officers had a good laugh over that one.

"Like I said guys, I don't know what happened. I didn't do anything wrong." Dennison meekly stated.

Norwood then turned toward Granger and said, "Let's check out a few things about that gun." As they walked toward the door, Norwood turned back to Dennison and ominously said, "We will be back!"

Again, they made Dennison wait. This time the wait was for over two hours; more mental anguish for the suspect. It was even worse than the previous wait as this one was longer, and Dennison now had more than just a stolen property issue to worry about. It was becoming clear to Dennison that he may be a suspect in the murder.

As a result, Dennison's actions as he waited were more emotional this time. He put his head down on the table and pounded the table a few times. He seemed to be much more worked up now than during his first waiting period.

Eventually, Norwood returned to the interrogation room. He was by himself for the time being. "My partner is still looking into a few things. He'll be in soon with an update." Norwood stated as if to warn that more bad news is on the way. He was great with the mind games.

Norwood then went on with the interrogation. "Let's talk some more about the gun. You know what I just learned out there a few minutes ago? I learned that the murder weapon was found in Garrowville Park. How about that Dennison?"

"So?" Dennison said, more as a defiant statement than as a question.

"So, Dennison, I find it interesting that you had lived so close to that park. You must have been there many times. You probably knew it inside and out. Who better than you to know where in that park to hide a gun?"

"Anyone who killed her could have gone there to hide the gun. It is right near where the murder took place."

"True Dennison. But you knew that park. You lived right there. An outsider, like Larry Dennis for instance, may not know about the park or where in the park to hide a gun so that it wouldn't be found for several months."

"Maybe he does. He'd visited us up there before."

Just then Granger returned with more paperwork. The two officers again went through their ruse of looking over the documents and shaking their heads. They weren't too concerned about redundancy in their routine. They knew that these routines and redundancies served their purpose many times in the past. And they knew that they were getting closer to their objective again in this case. It was only a matter of time.

Chapter 85

"We've got some background information on you, Dennison. You know what we've learned?" Norwood asked.

No response from the increasingly despondent suspect.

Norwood proceeded anyway. "We learned that you had worked for Michael Stohler and were laid off by him. Is that true, Dennison?"

"Yeah, so?"

"So, Dennison, it seems you had a revenge motive here. Didn't you?"

Again no response from the suspect.

"Tell me Dennison, what happened after you got laid off? Why did you move out of the area?" Norwood asked, even though he already knew the answer.

"My wife wanted to move to Virginia, that's why."

"I suppose your wife wanting to move to Virginia had nothing to do with your house in Pennsylvania getting foreclosed." Norwood sarcastically replied.

"What's all this got to do with the charge against me?" Dennison asked. "I thought I'm being charged with selling stolen property. Why am I being asked all these other questions?"

Norwood ignored the questions and simply proceeded with the interrogation.

"You were fired by Michael Stohler, and you lost your house shortly afterwards. And, you've been pawning jewelry, stolen or otherwise, to stay afloat financially. Meanwhile, the Stohlers still have their house, right next door to where you used to live. No jealousy there, Dennison? No temptation for revenge? You know, take something from someone who took so much from you?"

"No. You guys are way off. I just accidentally sold a ring stolen by someone else. That is all. How much longer is this going on? I'm getting tired."

"Let me see what my partner is up to. Maybe he has more information. I'll be back Dennison. We'll get to the bottom of this." Norwood stated, more as a warning than anything else. He then left the room once again.

It was now approaching midnight, but the party had just begun. They were cracking a tiring suspect, who hadn't asked for a lawyer yet, so they still had the green light to work him toward a confession.

They let him sweat in there for nearly three hours. Dennison even briefly fell asleep with his head down on the table at which he sat. The officers let him snooze for a few minutes; just long enough so that he'd be a little groggy when awoken. Then they loudly re-entered the room, startling the dazed suspect.

"Dennison, do you have any recollection where you were on Thursday December 10, 2009 and Friday December 11, 2009?" Norwood asked.

"No. Why would I? I assume I was in Virginia, doing nothing; like usual."

"Do you specifically remember those dates?"

"No."

"Well, let us remind you." Norwood stated as he reached for a file handed to him by Granger.

For effect, Norwood took his time perusing the file before finally saying, "It seems that on Thursday, December 10th, your wife and her sister-in-law flew to Miami to join Larry Dennis who was there on business. You didn't join them. Why not?"

"Didn't want to. Is that a crime? Wanting to stay at home and away from my nagging wife?"

"No. But you know what else happened then, Willie?" Norwood asked. He had intentionally switched to the suspect's first name; like he was talking down to a naughty child.

"No."

"That was the time frame in which Jennifer Stohler was murdered. You know, the same Jennifer Stohler whose wedding ring wound up in the pawn shop you frequent. You know, the same ring the shop owner says you sold him. And she was murdered with a gun owned by your housemate, who happened to be in Miami at the time. What do you make of all this, Willie?"

"I don't know. Obviously I'm being framed here. Can't you idiots see that?" Dennison angrily asked.

"Where were you during the night of Thursday, December 10th to Friday, December 11th, Willie?"

"Where do you think I was? I was asleep in my brother-in-law's house. Where else would I be?"

"Anyone who can vouch for that?" Norwood asked.

"Who can vouch for that?" Dennison asked. "You just said yourself everyone else was in Miami. I was alone in the house. How can I prove that?"

"Well, did you make any calls from the house during the night? Use your cell phone during that timeframe? I'll tell you what Dennison, we'll have you sign a form giving us permission to examine your phone records, and maybe we can prove you were home that night."

It was another ruse. They had already secured a warrant to obtain those records. But they wanted to watch him sign the form to verify that he was left-handed. Mug had fed them all the information on the Stohler case, and they knew that the CSI unit was fairly certain that the shooter was a lefty. This little trick was simply to add another reason to an increasingly growing list they had to believe Dennison was the killer.

"Give me the damn form!" Dennison demanded. "If this will get you idiots off my back, then knock yourselves out!" Dennison grabbed the form, slammed it down on the table, and signed it. He signed it with his left hand.

It was nearing dawn. Norwood took the signed form from Dennison and said, "We'll look into this right now, Willie. We'll be back soon."

Again Dennison was left alone in the interrogation room. It would be mid-morning before the officers came back with another round of exciting developments for him.

Chapter 86

Meanwhile, up in western Pennsylvania on Thursday morning, Jeff Orensen decided it was time to tell his client what was going on in D.C. For the past couple of days, he had been tempted to do so, but didn't want to give Michael Stohler false hope, only to be subsequently let down. However, now that Willie Dennison had been arrested, Orensen decided it was time to bring Stohler up to speed. Stohler had the right to know what was going on, but Orensen also wanted to be sure not to express with any certainty what will result from this development. After all, at this stage, Michael was still the only person charged with the murder of his wife.

"Good morning Michael." Orensen warmly greeted his client in a conference room inside the courthouse. "I have some interesting news for you."

Michael was intrigued. "What is it?" he asked excitedly.

"Do you remember a guy named Willie Dennison?"

"Yes."

"Well, he was arrested last night down in Virginia. It seems he had sold your wife's ring to a pawn dealer in Washington, D.C."

"What? How is that possible? How did this get discovered?"

"It was all Mug. He uncovered this and he is feeding the police down there all the information he has on Dennison." Orensen then filled him in on all the details. Needless to say, Michael Stohler was stunned. He was also filled with optimism and hope for the first time since his wife's murder.

Orensen sensed the increasing level of excitement, so he needed to caution Michael that this development didn't guarantee anything yet. "Listen Michael. I know this is exciting news, but please understand that we are not out of the woods yet. Right now, Dennison has only been charged with possession of and selling stolen property. He is being interrogated as we speak and the police down there, with Mug's help, are trying to piece together a case that he is the murderer. But there has been no such charge as of yet."

"What does all this mean for my trial?" Michael asked.

"Well, I'm about to go into a meeting in the judge's chambers with Murdoch and Judge Connerly to discuss these developments. I am going to request a stoppage of the trial while the events in D.C. unfold. I'm fairly certain that Murdoch will be against stopping the trial and he'll argue that no one else has been charged besides you. It will then be up to Judge Connerly."

"Ok. Thanks for telling me." Stohler replied.

Orensen then excused himself to attend the meeting in chambers. When both lawyers were present in front of the judge's desk, Judge Connerly stated they were now on the record and then requested that Orensen update them on the events down south.

"Thank you your honor. As you will both recall, I informed you yesterday that there was a suspect in Virginia to whom we had traced the murder weapon. Subsequently, we also traced the missing wedding ring to a pawn shop owner who has identified the same suspect as the person who sold it to him. Well, that individual has been arrested last night and is currently in custody in Washington, D.C. With this in mind, it is my suggestion that we discontinue the trial pending the developments down in D.C. Why continue to waste time and the taxpayers' money if ultimately someone else will be charged with the murder?"

Unlike the previous meeting on this subject, this time, Murdoch was prepared. He and his staff had been keeping tabs on the events in D.C. and knew everything going on. So, he was practically jumping out of his skin when he angrily responded, "Your honor. This individual has not yet been charged with anything other than possession of and selling stolen goods."

"The stolen goods include Jennifer Stohler's wedding ring!" Orensen stated, interrupting Murdoch.

Murdoch was not derailed. "And there is no evidence as to how he came into possession of it. Maybe Michael Stohler planted it on him. Or maybe the two of them were in cahoots. This does not exonerate Stohler and as of now, Stohler still remains the only person charged with the murder." Murdoch emphatically countered.

Judge Connerly thought carefully for a few moments, then ruled, "Ok. For now the trial should proceed as no one else has been charged with the crime other than the defendant. However, we will continue to monitor the investigation down there and will reconsider as new information comes in. Now, let's get into court and get started today. Meeting adjourned."

The trial was still on. At least for now. Would it reach its conclusion? And if so, what would that conclusion be? Or, would Mug and the Washington, D.C. police get everything figured out down there in time to save Michael Stohler from a possible conviction? The race was definitely down to the homestretch and all parties knew it.

Chapter 87

Stanley Murdoch was sensing that his dream conviction and all the accolades that would come with it were starting to slip away. He needed to get this trial over with as quickly as possible and get his conviction before anything down in D.C. could strip him of that glory.

"The Commonwealth calls Ronald Johnson to the stand." Murdoch announced immediately after court reconvened. Johnson was sworn in and Murdoch began his questioning.

"Mr. Johnson, you are a former employee of the defendant's company, Stohler Steel, is that correct?"

"Yes."

"And you were still employed there in December 2009 after the defendant's wife had been murdered. Is that correct?"

"Yes."

Eager to get to the point and move the trial along, Murdoch then asked, "In that time frame, did you overhear the defendant say anything relevant to his involvement in the murder of his wife?"

"Yes."

"What did you hear him say?"

"I overheard him saying that 'I killed my wife.'"

"No further questions, your honor." Murdoch stated.

Orensen had sensed that Murdoch would try to speed things up after this morning's meeting in chambers, but he was surprised with the haste in which Murdoch had completed his direct questioning of this witness. Orensen would be sure to take as much time as possible. The more time the trial took, the more time they had down in D.C. to charge Dennison with the murder.

"Mr. Orensen. Did you want to cross-examine this witness?" Judge Connerly asked when Orensen didn't make an immediate move to do so.

"Yes. Your Honor. Thank you."

Orensen slowly rose, walked toward the podium, gathered his notes, then finally asked his first question.

"Mr. Johnson. Where was Michael Stohler when you allegedly overheard him say what you claim he said?"

"He was in his office."

"Were you inside his office when you heard his supposed confession?"

"No."

"Where were you?"

"Outside his office." Johnson responded. There was light laughter from the courtroom audience.

"Was the door to Michael Stohler's office open when you heard his supposed confession?" Orensen kept repeated terms like "supposed" and "alleged" to make it clear to the jury that he was very skeptical of this testimony.

"No."

"So, you heard this supposed confession through a closed door. Correct?"

"Yes."

"Was he talking to you through the closed door?"

"No."

"Who was he talking to?"

"His secretary."

"That would be a woman named Brenda Challey, is that correct?"

"Yes."

"Did she ever state to you that Michael Stohler had confessed to her?"

"No."

"How long were you eavesdropping outside the closed door to Michael Stohler's office while he was talking to someone else inside?"

"I wasn't eavesdropping."

"Then what were you doing outside the closed office door that enabled you to hear the conversation inside so clearly?"

"I had come to see Michael on a business matter. His door was closed. I went to knock on it. Just before I had a chance to knock I heard him say the words, 'I killed my wife.' At that point, I didn't knock because I was afraid. I just went away from his office as quickly as possible." Johnson stated.

"So, Mr. Johnson, based on your testimony, you must have just been at that office door very briefly. You walked up, were about to knock, heard a few words inside, then scurried away. Is that correct?"

"Yes."

"Because you were there so briefly, is it possible that you may have heard the words out of context?"

"What do you mean?"

"I mean, could he have said something like, 'I can't believe everyone thinks I killed my wife' or 'Do you think I killed my wife?' or "The police are convinced that I killed my wife.' I think you get my point, Mr. Johnson. There are a lot of sentences that contain the words you allegedly heard. In light of how briefly you were at the office door, and in your haste to move away from the office door, isn't it at least possible that you only heard a portion of the full statement?"

"I don't know. I know he said 'I killed my wife.' I don't know what else he might have said."

"No further questions your honor." Orensen informed the judge.

Murdoch didn't want to waste time with a re-direct that wouldn't get him any new information. He was anxious to call his next witness, who would testify more directly to a confession. It would also be his last witness.

Chapter 88

"The Commonwealth calls Greg Luckman to the stand." Murdoch emphatically declared. Again, Murdoch was not going to waste any time.

"Mr. Luckman. Please tell the court how you know the defendant."

"I was his cellmate in prison."

"When was that?"

"Just after he arrived."

"And did the two of you converse much?"

"Yes. All the time. Michael was a chatterbox."

"What did you talk about?"

"A lot of things, but mostly about him, his wife, and how he killed her."

"He just came out and said this to you?"

"Well, not at first. It took a little time for him to confess. But, you know how it is. You can't keep something like that bottled up. Everyone needs to confess to someone. I was that someone for him."

"And just for the record Mr. Luckman, what exactly did he say?"

"He said he killed her. He shot her in the head. He did it for the life insurance money. He said he wasn't going to let her divorce him and get the last laugh on him."

"And he said all this directly to you? It wasn't something you had overheard from afar?"

"That's right, man. He said it directly to me. Many times."

"And have you been specifically promised anything in exchange for your testimony here today?"

"No."

"No further questions your honor." Murdoch said as he sat down.

Orensen then rose and started his cross-examination.

"Mr. Luckman, how is it that you found yourself incarcerated in the first place?"

"I was wrongly convicted of a crime."

"And what crime might that be?"

"Embezzlement."

"You also had previous convictions as well. Is that correct?"

"Yes."

"Is it also correct that your previous convictions were for various types of financial fraud?"

"Yes."

"All of those were wrongful convictions too, I suppose?" Orensen asked with a chuckle.

"They were trumped up charges."

"Let's see, your first felony conviction involved running a scheme to trick elderly persons into giving you their bank account information so that you can wire money from their account into yours. Is that correct?"

"That is what the prosecution claimed."

"So you lied to these elderly people for your own financial gain. Is that correct?"

"Again, that is what the prosecution claimed."

"You were convicted, right? So, the jury must have believed the evidence against you."

"Whatever you say, man. Has nothing to do with what I heard your boy say."

Orensen ignored that comment, and instead asked, "A few years later, you were convicted of setting up a fake 501(c)(3) charitable organization to elicit donations, which you then pocketed for yourself. Is that correct?"

"Objection your honor." Murdoch shouted. "Relevance and prejudicial."

"It goes to the witness's credibility, your honor." Orensen countered.

"Overruled. I'll allow it." Judge Connerly ruled.

"I'll repeat the question. Isn't it true you were convicted of setting up a fake charity to gather donations which you then kept for yourself?"

"Whatever you say, man."

"So, essentially, in both of these matters, you were convicted of an offense in which you lied to many people. Is that correct?"

"I didn't do what they said I did."

"So, with your history of deceit, how do we know that you are telling the truth now?"

"I was sworn in."

"Yes, I am sure that is very meaningful to a person like yourself who values the truth so much." Orensen mockingly stated.

"Objection!" Murdoch cried out.

"Withdrawn." Orensen said. He had made his point anyway.

"Make sure to ask questions, not make statements, Mr. Orensen." Judge Connerly advised.

"Yes, your honor." Orensen replied, then turned back toward the witness and asked his next question.

"You testified that you weren't promised anything in exchange for your testimony, is that correct?"

"Yes."

"Isn't it true however, that very soon after you were cellmates with Michael Stohler, you were transferred to a lower security prison?"

"Yes. To keep me away from that nut job" Luckman responded while pointing to Stohler.

"Did Michael Stohler ever threaten you or cause you physical harm?"

"No."

"Then why the need for the transfer?"

"Because if he caught wind of the fact that I had snitched about his confession, he may have caused me physical harm."

"You could have been put in protective custody in that same prison, or put in a different prison of equal security, but instead, you were transferred to a much cushier institution, is that correct?"

"The new place is nicer, yes."

"And the new place is closer to your family, is that correct?"

"Yes."

"And this transfer occurred immediately after you reported the alleged confession, is that correct?"

"Yes."

"So, just to be clear about the fact pattern here; you are testifying that Michael Stohler, who has emphatically maintained his innocence throughout this ordeal, happens to repeatedly confess his guilt to you, a person he hardly knew. Then, despite the fact that you weren't promised anything in exchange for your testimony, you found yourself in a much cushier institution immediately after the alleged confession. And finally, despite your long, well-documented history of deception, we are all to believe that you are being truthful this one time simply because you were sworn in. Is that correct?"

"You got it, man."

"No further questions your honor."

Murdoch did a quick re-direct to re-emphasize that Stohler had confessed multiple times and that Luckman wasn't promised anything in advance of his reporting these confessions. Murdoch also had Luckman testify that he didn't know where he would be transferred at the point in time in which he informed the warden of Stohler's confessions.

Luckman was then excused, and with great flamboyance and showmanship, Murdoch then announced very loudly and proudly, "Your Honor, the Commonwealth rests!"

Court was adjourned for lunch.

Chapter 89

Willie Dennison had been given a bathroom break after which he was given a bagel for breakfast as he waited for the next round of the interrogation to begin. So far, this had been going on for more than twelve hours since he had been booked. He had been taken to the restroom a couple of times during his waiting periods of the interrogation and had been given water. Despite these little acts of humanity, the process had been torturous for Dennison. When will it end? He was getting very tired and obviously hadn't had a chance to get much sleep.

He dozed on and off while lying on the floor of the interrogation room, all the while, watched by officers on the other side of the one way mirror. Finally, at 9 a.m., Norwood, who was pulling an all-nighter himself, returned with another thick pile of papers. He slammed the door shut very loudly to wake Dennison up. Dennison sat up groggily and slowly rose to sit back in the chair at the interrogation room table. He was getting very tired and frustrated with the length of the interrogation. Hopefully, the cops will give up their wild goose chase and realize they had nothing on him.

"Alright Willie. This has dragged for way too long. Enough is enough. Let's get to the bottom of this. Do you know with whom I've been speaking for the past couple of hours?" Norwood asked.

Dennison was too tired and irritable to bother to respond. He just grunted.

"I've been having a nice chat with your wife." Norwood stated, answering his own question.

That got a rise out of the suspect. Dennison suddenly sat up straight and glared menacingly at Norwood. Obviously Norwood had hit a nerve, so he pressed on.

"She had a lot to say about you Willie. Nothing good. Seems she is not too high on you anymore Willie."

"Don't listen to what she says!" Dennison angrily snarled. "She's got it in for me."

Norwood pushed on, "She told us all about how much you hated the Stohlers. Michael Stohler fired you. He still had his job, you didn't. The Stohlers still had their house, you lost yours. They had money. You didn't. She told us everything Willie. It's over."

"No! No! No!" Dennison screamed, while pounding his fist on the table. He was losing it. The stress of being arrested, followed by an all-night interrogation, and now the anger of having his wife turn against him, were all accumulating into a furious eruption. He stood up and tried to get to the door. "I'll kill her! Where is she?"

Norwood simply watched Dennison struggle with the door which was locked from the inside. Dennison realized he was trapped inside, which infuriated him even more. A couple of officers waited on the other side of the door just in case they had to charge in if Dennison attacked Norwood. But for now, Dennison was just taking his frustration out on the door itself, pounding both fists into it while screaming obscenities about his wife.

Norwood then said, "Come on Willie. Make this easy on yourself. Tell us what happened that night. I'm sure you didn't really intend for what happened."

Dennison angrily screamed at Norwood, "Listen man! I was in Virginia; hundreds of miles away from the Stohlers. Don't you get it? I've been telling you this all night! You cops are idiots! I even tried to help you. I gave you permission to check my phone records. Check anything you want. You'll see, I was in Virginia; hundreds of miles away from the Stohlers." Dennison just kept shaking his head with frustration at the apparent ineptitude of the police.

"Well, Willie, these documents here seem to say otherwise. Any ideas what they might be?"

"If it's anything from my wife I wouldn't believe a word of it. She's a back-stabber!"

"It's not from your wife, Willie." Norwood taunted. "It's from a towing company. Ever hear of Kurlin Towing Company, Willie?"

"No."

"I think you have. See, it shows here that Kurlin Towing Company towed your vehicle at about 3:30 a.m. on the morning of December 11, 2009 in Pennsylvania. Less than an hour away from the Stohler residence."

No response from an enraged Willie Dennison.

"I also have your credit card statement, Willie. It shows that you paid Kurlin Towing. I even have the credit card receipt you signed, Willie. The signature matches the form you signed for me earlier this morning."

Still no response from an increasingly enraged Dennison.

"I have a positive identification of you from the guy who did the towing. Seems he remembers you quite well. I emailed him a picture of you and he had no trouble remembering you. You made quite an impression on him. He said you were angry, impatient, and obnoxious. His words exactly. I guess I can't blame you for feeling that way when your speedy escape was derailed by a flat tire."

Dennison started making some strange angry growls, mumbling to himself incoherently and banging his fist against his forehead.

"We also have here on the same credit card statement that a few days later, you had some auto repairs done on your vehicle. Do you remember what that was?"

Dennison didn't respond. He just kept banging his fists on the table and his head.

"You had a right headlight repaired; which is very interesting in light of eyewitness testimony up in Garrowville, just a few blocks away from the Stohler residence, that a vehicle with a right headlight out sped by the witness around the time of the murder."

Norwood continued pressing. "We know you killed Jennifer Stohler, Willie. It's over. We have all the information. Even your wife says you did it."

Dennison let out a primal scream. He couldn't take another mention of his wife. He had finally lost it. Stress, sleep deprivation, and the mounting evidence against him had all taken its toll. Now the repeated mentions of his hated wife had driven him over the edge.

"Alright! Alright! I did it! I killed her! Are you happy now! Now get me out of here!" Dennison shouted as he pounded on the door.

Chapter 90

Dennison crumbled down onto the floor by the door and started crying. "I killed her. I killed her. I'm sorry. Now can I get out of here?" he kept repeating as he cried on the floor.

Clearly he wasn't getting out of there. Norwood helped him off the floor and sat him back down at the table. He offered Dennison a drink, and signaled through the one-way mirror for one of his colleagues to bring the drink in. Norwood then said, "We'll get you some food and some sleep real soon. Just tell us everything that happened and we'll get you out of this room in no time.

Dennison breathed in deeply to calm himself down a bit, wiped his tears, took a few sips of the coffee that was brought to him, and started his story.

"You know a lot of it already. I lost my job at Stohler Steel. Michael fired me. After years of hard work and loyalty he fires his friend and next door neighbor. He knew we were hurting for money but he fired me anyway. We couldn't afford our house anymore and it was foreclosed.

"We had to leave town. A town I had loved. We moved in with my brother-in-law and his wife in Virginia. I never liked them and I was miserable there. We had no money and couldn't find any decent work. I had to pawn a lot of stuff.

"We were fighting often and my marriage was falling apart. It wasn't just my marriage, but my whole life was falling apart. And it had all started when Michael Stohler fired me. It was his fault. He caused all this misery.

"Even after pawning a lot of stuff, we were still desperate for money. On Thanksgiving, my brother-in-law showed off a gun that he kept in the house. I had known previously that it was there, but now, seeing it again, made a previous idea of mine resurface. I had always wanted to steal from the Stohlers; to take something from them after they had taken so much from me.

"Now, after seeing the gun again at Thanksgiving, and given our hopeless financial situation, I started thinking again about robbing them. I had retained a duplicate copy of their house keys. We were given a copy of their keys, in case of an emergency, when we were neighbors. I always made duplicate copies of all keys as a habit; just in case a set got lost. We returned the original set to Jennifer Stohler. I held onto the duplicate set in case one day I wanted to carry through my dreams of robbing them. No one knew I had an extra set.

"I still didn't think I'd actually go through with it. I'd never committed a crime before in my life. But in the next week after Thanksgiving, we were fighting a lot about money and we were just so miserable. Then, an opportunity presented itself. My wife and her sister-in-law decided last minute that they would join my brother-in-law on a business trip in Miami for a brief getaway. I didn't want to go for two reasons. Number one, we needed the time apart, and number two, I wanted to be alone to carry out my plans.

"They left on Thursday, December 10th during the day. I left for Garrowville later that day. After deciding that I was doing this, I then debated two other things; whether to do the robbery during the day or at night, and whether or not to bring the gun.

"I chose to do it at night because I was concerned about being seen coming or going in broad daylight. Even though I figured that the Stohlers would be home at night, and may not be home during the day, I figured that I could use the keys in the middle of the night, sneak in and out and not be seen by anyone. Choosing to go at night though meant I needed to have the gun with me just in case I do encounter one or both of them. What if they had a gun? I needed to protect myself. Also, I would need to have a way to make them do what I ordered and to prevent them from calling the police.

"I had no intention of ever using the gun. It was supposed to be just for protection. That's all. I wore a ski mask so I wouldn't be recognized. I didn't want to have to kill anyone because they could identify me. I got into the house and snuck upstairs. I went to the wrong bedroom first. I had never been upstairs in their house before, so I wasn't sure which room was theirs. I then turned around and went across the hallway toward the other bedroom.

"Just as I was starting to reach for the doorknob, the door swung open and the light from the room shined in my face. I was startled by this and just then she let out a loud scream. The scream scared me and I accidentally pulled the trigger. I never meant to; I was just taken by surprise by the encounter and her scream. I only shot once.

"I knew the shot got her because she fell backwards. I was so upset. I didn't mean to shoot her. I was praying she was ok, but I could tell she wasn't. I was scared and I was upset. I liked Jennifer. She was always very nice to me. I never meant to hurt her.

"I needed to get out of there. I didn't know where Michael was or if he'd be coming in soon. I started to step back to leave, but realized that I couldn't have come all this way and leave empty-handed. So, I just grabbed the largest and closest piece of jewelry I could see in plain sight and bolted as quickly as possible. I couldn't take time to look around for more stuff. My main thought was get out of there.

"As I drove off, I realized that I had to ditch the gun. I didn't want the murder weapon to be back in the house where I was living. I knew about a park nearby, so I went there and hid the gun. I dug a hole in the dirt behind some bushes in a quiet part of the park, and put a large stone over the hole.

"Then I drove home, but the car broke down on the way back. That is why I got towed. When I finally got home, I quickly pawned the ring. I needed the money and I didn't want the stolen ring to be found in the house when everyone else came back from Miami.

"That's all. So you see, I am guilty of stealing the ring, but shooting her was an accident. I swear. I never meant to kill her." Dennison starting crying again.

Norwood had only one follow-up question for Dennison. It was to inquire as to whether or not anyone else had any involvement with his crime. Norwood didn't mention Michael Stohler by name because he feared that Dennison might still be seeking revenge against Stohler, but the point of his question was to hopefully have Dennison admit that he had acted entirely on his own. Dennison confirmed that was the case. No one else was involved in the murder.

Norwood had some documents brought in for Dennison to sign. It contained his official statement confessing to the crime. It outlined all the relevant facts of the story Dennison had just told, including wording stating that only he was involved in the crime in any way. Norwood told him that some hot food was on its way. They just needed for Dennison to sign the statement. They would then be done with him and would bring him the food, then let him get some sleep.

Dennison didn't hesitate. He immediately signed his confession statement. Just in time for lunch. All he could think about was food and sleep.

Chapter 91

The flurry of phone calls from Washington, D.C. to western Pennsylvania started almost immediately. Within minutes, both lawyers, Judge Connerly, and all of the media knew about the Dennison confession. Jeff Orensen received the news from an elated Mug who had gotten the news himself from Will Parker. Parker had been called directly by Norwood. It was an adult version of the game "Telephone" played at lightning speed.

Orensen had the joyful task of informing Michael Stohler of the news. Michael was in his holding cell during the lunch recess. Orensen entered the cell and said, "Michael, I have some wonderful news for you. Willie Dennison has confessed to the murder. He signed a confession just a little while ago."

Michael was shocked and speechless. Even though he had been updated as to Dennison's arrest and the ongoing interrogation, he never imagined that it would all work out for him. Everything had gone so horribly wrong over the course of the past few months that Michael was incapable of feeling any sense of optimism. Now, even having been given this news, he still couldn't believe it.

Finally he said, "So, what happens now? Am I free to go?"

"I'm about to go into another meeting in chambers with Judge Connerly and Murdoch. I will move to have the case dismissed, which I believe will happen. Murdoch may try to make some feeble argument about how you could have been in cahoots with Dennison, but I already have a faxed copy of the confession. Dennison states in it that he acted alone. Murdoch can have no argument to that. The case will be dismissed right after lunch."

Michael started crying. It was the first time in this whole ordeal that the tears were derived from elation rather than misery. Orensen sat next to him and put his arm around him. Through the tears, Michael repeatedly thanked Orensen for everything he had done.

"It is really Mug we both need to thank." Orensen replied. "He's the one who cracked the case and pushed everything along down there."

They sat together for a few minutes before Orensen said, "Listen Michael. I have to go into that meeting in chambers. Hang tight for just a little while longer. This will all be over very soon."

Orensen left the cell and headed for Judge Connerly's chambers. Murdoch was already in there when Orensen walked in. Orensen heard Murdoch arguing exactly what Orensen had predicted.

"Stohler could have been working with Dennison. He may have even paid Dennison to do it." Murdoch argued to the judge.

"Murdoch, I have the signed confession right here." Orensen said, holding up the faxed copy he had received. "Dennison's confession says as clear as day that he worked alone. No one else was involved in the crime." Orensen handed a copy to both Judge Connerly and to Murdoch.

After giving a moment for each of them to read the confession, Orensen stated, "Your honor, in light of this latest development, I would like to move to have the case against my client dismissed."

Murdoch started to argue, but Judge Connerly cut him off by saying, "That's enough, Mr. Murdoch. It is clear that the trial against Michael Stohler cannot go on with a signed confession by someone else who also states he worked alone. And truthfully, the case against Michael Stohler was somewhat weak to begin with anyway. I am going to dismiss the case. If you like, I will give you the courtesy of announcing the news of the confession and that the Commonwealth will drop the charges, as opposed to me doing so and it appearing that I have forced the matter upon you."

"Thank you your honor." Murdoch meekly responded.

"Thank you your honor." Orensen also said, but more enthusiastically.

The meeting was adjourned and soon afterwards court resumed for an afternoon session that was bound to be very brief.

Chapter 92

Judge Connerly entered the courtroom, sat down, looked toward Stanley Murdoch and stated, "Mr. Murdoch, I understand that you have an announcement that you would like to make to the court."

Stanley Murdoch rose, and despite it being the last thing in the world he would have wanted to do, he made the following statement with as much flamboyance, confidence, and enthusiasm as he could.

"Yes. Thank you your honor. Due in large part to the hard work and professionalism of the law enforcement community, we have uncovered another suspect in this case who has just recently confessed to the murder. The suspect's signed confession states that he acted alone in committing his heinous act. Based on this latest information, the Commonwealth is happy to drop the charge of first degree murder against the defendant, Michael Stohler. As always, it is Commonwealth's first and foremost objective in any criminal case to assure that justice is served and we are pleased that justice will be served by the confession and incarceration of Willie Dennison for this crime."

"Thank you Counselor." Judge Connerly replied. He then turned toward Michael Stohler and declared, "I hereby rule that the case against the defendant Michael Stohler is dismissed. Thank you to the jury for your time and service. Mr. Stohler, you are free to go." Connerly pounded his gavel, got up, and exited the courtroom.

A jubilant and tearful Michael Stohler embraced his lawyer and then his parents, who were seated behind him in the front row. The bailiffs came over to him to help escort him out. But this time, they were escorting him toward the front of the courthouse and out toward freedom, rather than through the dark hallways toward the back holding cells.

Michael Stohler was once again a free man. Free to live the rest of his life as he chose. It was a very happy day for him. But, while being set free was certainly a much better fate than what the alternative could have been, Michael Stohler couldn't help but think as he walked out of the courthouse into the midday sunshine, how the events of the past few months guaranteed that he could never truly return to the life as he had known it before "The Murder."

Five Years Later

It's April 2015; five years after my case was dismissed and I regained my freedom. I'm now living in Tempe, Arizona, which is over 2,000 miles away from my former life in Garrowville, Pennsylvania. But more on that later. As today is the 5th anniversary of my release, it is a good time to update you on my life since that day.

I remember walking out of that courtroom like it was yesterday. I was feeling every imaginable emotion, ranging from the elation of being free once again, to the sadness of realizing that I couldn't simply return to my life as I had previously known it before these tragic events unfolded.

My wife was still gone. I had never experienced any happy moments in my adult life without sharing it with her. How could I truly be happy, even on that day, without sharing the joy with Jennifer?

As I exited the courtroom, I was bombarded by the frenzy of media I had grown accustomed to seeing. But this time, I stopped briefly to say a few words. I resisted the temptation of saying "I told you I didn't do it" to all the people who had been so blindly convinced that I had killed my wife. Instead I simply thanked my lawyer, Jeff Orensen and his incredible investigator, Mug, for all their hard work. I made sure to emphasize how brilliant they both were so that they would get the accolades they so deserved. Mug has become somewhat of a celebrity as a result of the publicity from my case, and of course, from his unique name and characteristics. I also thanked my parents for their unwavering faith in me throughout this ordeal. I went on to say that it is a bittersweet moment for me because I didn't have Jennifer with whom to share it. I then walked away, ignoring the frantic questions being shouted back at me.

In addition to no longer having Jennifer, I also no longer had my own home. It had been foreclosed while I was incarcerated. So, I temporarily returned to my parents' home to figure out what to do next with my life.

Of course, I also no longer had my business, and as you can imagine, I had soured on my lifelong home town of Garrowville. A home town is supposed to be more than just a location on a map. It is supposed to be a place where you feel at home; a place where you are surrounded by friends and neighbors, who are like family to you and who you trust and they trust you. It's supposed to be a place where you can count on those friends and neighbors for support in times of need. Clearly, Garrowville was no longer such a place for me.

I no longer had my wife; no longer had my home; no longer had my business; and no longer had many friends in the area. It's amazing how much had been taken from me for a crime that I didn't commit.

Eventually, one thing I did have was the $250,000 life insurance money that was paid to me shortly after my release. However, as a result of the depressed real estate market and the fact that my house had been the scene of a murder and was continually getting vandalized, the bank wasn't able to recoup much from the foreclosure of my home. As a result, I still owed them a substantial sum for the difference. I paid that debt off with part of the proceeds of the life insurance money.

I also paid off the remaining amounts owed to Jeff Orensen and to Mug, which also was a substantial figure, though very worth it. I repaid my parents for some of the money they had laid out for my defense while I was incarcerated. And finally, I even drove down to Washington, D.C., and reimbursed Rocco, the pawn shop owner, the $5,000 he had laid out for Jennifer's ring.

I know I didn't have to do that, but as Mug had explained to me, Rocco could have stashed the ring somewhere in the time frame between when Mug left him and when the police came back with their warrant. But he didn't. He cooperated instead and it was a very significant piece of evidence that helped the police finally apprehend the right guy for the crime.

Also, I figured that the pawn shop was in a high crime area just a few hours away from western Pennsylvania, so you never knew when Mug may find himself in that vicinity on a case in the future. Now, as a result of my reimbursement to Rocco, Mug, who had promised Rocco he'd get his money back, would have credibility with him. Rocco probably knew every slimy character in the Southeast D.C. It was the least I could do for Mug who had done so much for me.

So, after all those expenditures, I wasn't left with a whole lot of the life insurance money. I had just enough to pack up my stuff and move somewhere far away. Tempe, Arizona seemed like as good a place as any; nice area, warm weather, and significant distance. I rented a two bedroom apartment in downtown Tempe and after a couple of months, found a job working in a plastics manufacturing plant. It was somewhat of an adjustment for me working as one of the many employees of a plant rather than as the boss and owner, but I'm thankful to have a job and to be getting back on my feet again.

A few months later, my parents moved down here as well. They sold their home in Garrowville, and as they no longer had their condo in Florida (another casualty of the wrongful prosecution of me), they decided to join me in Arizona. They too had no desire to remain in Garrowville, a town where they had lived their whole lives.

Now, to update you on the lives of some of the other people you've gotten to know throughout my ordeal. First, and most significantly, after confessing to the murder of my wife, Willie Dennison was provided a court-appointed attorney. The attorney immediately got to work trying to have the confession thrown out. He initially argued that Dennison had not been read his rights. That argument was false and was proven as such by audio and videotape of the arrest. He then argued that Dennison had repeatedly requested, and been denied, an attorney during the interrogation. That argument was also false. Fortunately, the D.C. police had videotaped everything, from the initial arrest throughout the interrogation.

Dennison's attorney then argued that the interrogation constituted "cruel and unusual" punishment due to its length, and that Dennison hadn't been given sufficient food, drink, sleep, and bathroom privileges. This argument had a little more merit and there was a hearing on it. Ultimately, due to the fact that breaks had been taken, Dennison was provided with access to a bathroom, and was given food and water, the motion to have the confession dismissed was denied.

After a few other failed attempts to have the confession tossed, Dennison eventually resigned to the fact that he couldn't win a trial with the confession and the evidence against him. He was offered a deal whereby if he pled guilty, thus avoiding a long, drawn out trial at the taxpayers' expense, he would be spared the death penalty. Dennison agreed and he was given a sentence of twenty-five years to life. Theoretically, he could be released when he is somewhere around 60 years old.

I find it to be somewhat ironic that because I had the nerve to plead 'not guilty' and to exercise my constitutional right to a trial, I faced the prospect of a death sentence. But one who pled guilty, and who actually did commit the crime, gets to avoid the death penalty and may even be released early enough to still have a few good years of freedom left.

Another bit of irony pertained to Officer Dan Radford. As you may recall, Mug observed him transacting with drug dealers in Garrowville Park; an event that apparently took place on a monthly basis going back for a long period of time. Here was a guy whose chosen profession was to uphold the law and to protect his community from shady characters such as drug dealers. Yet, he regularly dealt with them in his hometown's park.

Mug and Orensen had briefly contemplated informing the District Attorney's office of this ritual, but ultimately decided against it. For starters, as it turned out, Radford had nothing to do with my wife's murder. Radford had also abided by Mug's "request" that he not testify to the bogus confession he claimed to have overheard.

Additionally, Mug didn't want to risk losing his street cred with Rome, one of his key informants. It was Rome who had tipped Mug off to the monthly meetings at the park. Mug believed that Radford, who was merely a harmless loser with a drug addiction, wasn't worth hurting this crucial contact who had helped Mug in many cases, including mine. Also, no one felt like spoon-feeding what would be another high-profile prosecution to Stanley Murdoch. So, the irony here is that I had done nothing wrong and had my life destroyed, but Radford, one of my arresting officers, continues to get away with his criminal activity.

Speaking of people who got away with criminal activity; do you remember my chatty cellmate, Greg Luckman? Well, after blatantly committing perjury on the stand during my trial, he continued to serve his time in a cushy minimum security prison before being released a few months ago. He served roughly half of his sentence and was never prosecuted for his perjury.

In fact, no one has been prosecuted for anything associated with my wrongful arrest. Chief Lumpkin is still the police chief of Garrowville and has never been so much as questioned as to his investigative tactics in my case. His reputation in the community remains completely unscathed by the whole episode.

Do you want some more irony? How about the subsequent story of District Attorney Stanley Murdoch? Apparently the minor detail of very publicly and flamboyantly prosecuting the wrong person in a high profile murder trial did not harm his public reputation. Like a true politician, he was able to spin the situation positively for himself.

Right after my case was dismissed, Murdoch held a press conference in which he praised all of the officers involved in the apprehension of Willie Dennison. He also spoke at great lengths about how the sole objective of his position as district attorney was to assure that justice is served. He practically made it sound as if the justice that ultimately prevailed in my case was his doing. Every newscast ran his sound bites that evening. He had become a household name as a result of my trial and despite the negative outcome in that trial for him, he managed to come away from it with an improved public opinion rating. Amazing!

So, naturally, in November of that same year; just seven months after my release, Stanley Murdoch was elected to the U.S. House of Representatives. I can't help but think what kind of shape our nation must be in if we have people like Stanley Murdoch representing us in Congress.

But the biggest irony of all pertains to what had happened to me. Despite the fact that I was never convicted of anything in any criminal court, my life was destroyed. I learned a lot of lessons throughout this dreadful ordeal, but the most

THE COURTS OF GARROWVILLE

important lesson I learned was that a whole other court runs concurrently to the criminal court system, and it runs by a very different set of rules.

On one hand, our criminal justice system is governed by a multitude of rules and guidelines pertaining to evidence, procedures, and required standards of proof. Perhaps the most important aspect of our criminal justice system is the concept that we are presumed to be innocent until proven guilty beyond all reasonable doubt. While of course no system can ever be perfect, these guidelines and parameters make sense as it serves to significantly reduce the possibility of convicting an innocent person and as a result, unjustly ruining that person's life.

But as I learned the hard way, there is also a whole other "court" operating at the same time. This court, known as the "court of public opinion" does not have the same rules of evidence or a minimum burden of proof for conviction. The court of public opinion is free to run rampant as people can jump to whatever conclusions they want, as soon as they want, and freely express them wherever they want. As a result, the court of public opinion is equally as powerful to destroy lives, as clearly illustrated in my own case.

Wouldn't it be nice if the public at large; the very people who comprise the court of public opinion, applied a similar "innocent until proven guilty" approach upon learning that someone within the community was accused of some type of wrongdoing? Or, at very least, wouldn't it be nice if we all simply took a "wait and see what the evidence ultimately says" approach and thereby reserved judgment for a later time? Don't you think that these courses of action would be more appropriate than the actions of my friends and neighbors in Garrowville? There is plenty of time later on to rail against an accused person if he or she is ultimately proven to be guilty. Why do we need to do it prematurely and run the risk of ruining the life of a potentially innocent person?

Thank you for reading my story. I hope that if you take one lesson from my unfortunate tale, it is that we should all reserve judgment on our fellow human beings when one is accused of any type of offense until all relevant information has been accumulated. Jumping to immediate conclusions increases the likelihood of causing irreparable damage to someone who may turn out to be innocent.

Author's Notes

While the story and the characters depicted are works of fiction, the basic premise behind the storyline is realistic. In an era of massive social media and around-the-clock news coverage, we are always bombarded with stories of gossip, allegations, and arrests. We can turn on our televisions, computers, and cell phones and see an accused person's perp walk and mug shot practically in real time. We can then instantly communicate the photos, captions, and our thoughts to everyone we know via email, Facebook, Twitter, and many other social media tools.

These realities make the court of public opinion all the more powerful as the population can be swayed by such images, jump to immediate conclusions of guilt, and spread the word of such viewpoints much faster and more effectively than ever before. Innocent lives can easily be ruined in as little time as it takes to click a mouse.

I wrote this book with the primary objective of portraying this risk in what I hope you found to be an entertaining way. As such, some facets of the book were carefully chosen. For instance, the title the book, "The Courts of Garrowville" had special meaning. I made the word 'Courts' plural in the title to represent the fact that there is more than one court at work in determining the fate of the accused. There is the official criminal court system, and, as illustrated by the story of Michael Stohler, there is also the court of public opinion. Both courts have substantial power to destroy lives.

I also had a special reason for choosing 'Garrowville' as the name of the fictional town in the story. I named the town after Sir William Garrow, an English lawyer who is credited with coining the phrase, "innocent until proven guilty."

I then needed to choose a part of the United States to place the fictional town of Garrowville. Other than the fact that some states do not have the death penalty, events similar to those in the story could occur in any part of our country; therefore, I had a lot of options as to where to place Garrowville. After careful consideration, I wanted to portray a close-knit, blue collar type of community where families may have roots for generations and the people of the town have likely known each other their whole lives. Watching a Pittsburgh Steeler home game one night on television gave me the idea that the blue collar, steel factory environment of western Pennsylvania may be a good venue for my story. It also led to my decision to make my main character the owner of a steel factory, where many people in the town worked.

I chose the names 'Michael' and 'Jennifer' for my main characters simply because I wanted to make them an everyday, normal, married couple. I wanted basic, common names, because these were ordinary people. The events portrayed in this story are not reserved for any specific, unusual type of person, but rather, can happen to any one of us. The common names of these characters were chosen to represent that fact.

It is difficult to write a book about a falsely arrested and prosecuted person without portraying the specific law enforcement personnel in the story in a negative light. I would like to take this opportunity to say that I did not intend this work of fiction to be interpreted as an anti-law enforcement campaign. The overwhelming majority of police personnel all around our nation are very hard-working, decent, honest people who risk their lives every day to protect us. While there are always a few rotten apples in every batch, the small minority of such rotten apples should not dictate our views of a noble profession and the many great people in that profession. I intended the police and the prosecutor in this book to be looked upon as being among the few rotten apples rather than as being representative of all law enforcement.

I would like to thank my wife Heather for her proofreading assistance with the book, for being patient and understanding of the many late nights that went into my writing this book, and of course for being the best wife any guy can ever have. I would also like to thank my brother Dave and his wife Stephanie for taking the time to proofread the book as well. Dave is a very funny stand-up comedian. If you enjoy comedy, I encourage you to check his schedule at davesiegel.com and to go to one of his performances when he is in your area. Stephanie is a very talented journalist in New York and is the founder of Reel Media Group. If you are an aspiring television reporter, I encourage you to connect with Stephanie Siegel.

Finally, I would like to thank everyone who took the time to read my first book. I hope that you enjoyed reading it as much as I enjoyed writing it.

About the Author

"The Courts of Garrowville" is Ken Siegel's first published novel. He also writes for the sports section of the magazine, "Nostalgic America" which can be accessed at www.nostalgicamericamagazine.com. Ken Siegel is originally from New York, and currently resides in Florida with his wife, Heather. He invites you to visit his website at www.garrowville.com where you can find more about the author and contact information.

CPSIA information can be obtained
at www.ICGtesting.com
Printed in the USA
BVHW01s0936261217
503650BV00029B/1970/P